A NOVEL
BOOK TWO

NORMAN WOOD

2950 Newmarket St., Suite 101-358 | Bellingham, WA 98226
Ph: 206.226.3588 | www.bookhouserules.com

Thorn: Book 2 and prequel, *Red Sword: Book 1*, are fictional accounts based on actual events related to the planned coup and assassination of Soviet General Secretary Mikhail Gorbachev.

10 9 8 7 6 5 4 3 2 1

Printed in the United States of America

Library of Congress Control Number: 2022900365

ISBN: 978-1-952483-37-0 (Paperback)
ISBN: 978-1-952483-38-7 (eBook)
ISBN: 978-1-952483-39-4 (Audiobook)

Editor: Julie Scandora
Cover design: Scott Book
Book design: Melissa Vail Coffman

For more information visit NormanWoodBooks.com

This book is dedicated to Special Agent Ray Tipton, US Coast Guard. Without his help and friendship, and that of other members of the US Coast Guard and the US Customs Service, the successful conclusion of this case would not have been possible. I would also like to sincerely thank the great personnel of the IRS, DEA, JTF-5, PacArea-Intel, OCDETF San Francisco, US Attorney's Office, and the intelligence community. And finally, to IK. No mother loved a son more. May you and your son rest in peace.

CONTENTS

PROLOGUE

7:00 p.m., May 23, 1988, San Francisco

"SHIT!" US COAST GUARD SPECIAL AGENT Ray Taylor yelled after calling his headquarters.

"What?" US Customs Special Agent Tony Davis shouted across his office at 1700 Montgomery Street.

"The *Valiant Venture* is ahead of schedule. The *Cape Romain* must leave now if it's going to intercept it at the gate!" Taylor yelled back.

"Tell Commander Goodman he can't leave the dock until we get there. If he does, I lose my nexus and we'll not be able to cut open that barge. We leave now!" Davis yelled, running for the door and then to the parking garage across the street.

Taylor yelled into the receiver, "You do not leave. I'm on my way!" slammed it down, and ran for the door behind Davis.

Nearing the garage, Davis yelled to Taylor, "We don't stop for anything or anyone. Stay on my six."

"Roger that," Taylor yelled back.

Both men jumped into their undercover cars and sped out of the parking garage, Davis in his Mustang and Taylor in his white Diplomat.

Normal driving would take forty-five minutes to get through San Francisco traffic and halfway across the Oakland Bay Bridge to Yerba

Buena Island where the US Coast Guard facility is located. When you're racing seventy miles per hour down the Embarcadero, running red lights and stop signs, it doesn't take near that long.

"Stay with me, Ray," Davis yelled as he could hear a siren and see in his rearview mirror a San Francisco Police cruiser with its lights flashing right on Taylor's bumper.

Seeing another San Francisco Police cruiser coming from a side street, trying to cut the pair off, Davis swerved into the outside lane and punched the accelerator of the Mustang with Taylor staying right behind him.

"We're not stopping, Ray!" Davis yelled. He could see Taylor trying to hold his badge up so the SFPD officers could see that he was cop. But the cars were going so fast and darting in and out of traffic, it would be impossible to see what Taylor was holding. By the time the Mustang and Diplomat jumped up on Interstate 80 and were flying across the Oakland Bay Bridge, there were three San Francisco Police cruisers chasing them. Seeing the SFPD cars stop at the city limits, Davis and Taylor raced across the bridge and got off at the Coast Guard facility halfway to Oakland.

Sliding their cars to a stop, they ran for the vessels and could see the USCG Cutter *Cape Romain* was away from the dock but standing by. The Coast Guard Patrol Vessel *41403*, with an armed boarding party, was still being held at the dock, waiting for the special agents. Jumping on board, Taylor yelled at Commander Steve Moher, "Let's go!"

Taylor looked at Davis and said, "I can't believe we made it!"

"You did good. I could see you holding up your badge," Davis said with a laugh.

"Yeah," Taylor laughed. "This is like a damn movie."

Holding onto the railing of the speeding craft, the agents watched the vessels race towards the Golden Gate Bridge.

"Yes, just like a damn movie," Davis said, thinking how far he'd come in barely eighteen months.

CHAPTER 1

A New Year

January 1987

The Soviet Central Committee consolidated and approved many of General Secretary Mikhail Gorbachev's political reforms, including multi-candidate elections and the appointment of non-party members to government positions. Gorbachev couldn't have been more pleased. He even began working on a book that would be released later that summer, *Perestroika: New Thinking for Our Country and the World.*

For General Vadim Vanerev, Soviet Commander of Russian Forces in Afghanistan and KGB Agent Vladimir Yukorov, things were finally falling into place for members of Red Sword, the top-secret group that was planning to remove General Secretary Gorbachev. They needed one hundred million dollars to have a successful coup d'état. Towards that end, they devised an ingenious plan to sell one hundred tons of hashish to the Americans to make their money.

"General, I've been told there has been an excellent harvest of hashish this past year," Yukorov said. "We'll be able to get forty-five tons to ship to the American by August. If that operation goes without a problem, the drug lord said we can ship another load in November."

"Will that make us our money?" General Vanerev asked.

"Yes, sir," Yukorov said. "If we are able to ship forty-five tons and then another forty-five tons later, we'll make 1.1 million dollars per ton. That'll give us ninety-nine million dollars. Even after we pay the drug lord and the American, we will still have eighty-nine million dollars, General."

"That'll have to do," the General said. "I can then order the removal of our forces from Afghanistan over the winter and be in place by spring. We can't wait any longer. Gorbachev has not come to his senses, and he's continuing to press his liberal agenda. He and his progressives must be stopped. We must take over the government next year, or our country will cease to exist."

"Yes, General, I agree he must be stopped," Yukorov said. "As soon as the snow melts, we can start, General."

CIA SPECIAL AGENT TONY DAVIS WAS enjoying the California spring. He was amazed at how early everything bloomed there with the bright yellow fields of wild mustard simply beautiful in January. Still not being an official member of the Customs Service, he used that time to continuously drive around the Bay Area and familiarize himself with the different small communities and roads. Northern California Wine Country from Santa Rosa to Napa was absolutely amazing, and he learned every inch of it.

Driving the CJ through the backcountry of the Northern Bay Area, he ran upon Jack London State Park near Glen Ellen. He remembered reading all London's books as a young man. *Call of the Wild* and *White Fang* were two of his favorites. Davis walked among the remains of *Wolf House*, the stone mansion London had been building. It would have been a magnificent structure, except for it burning to the ground two weeks before London was to move in. Driving the back roads, Davis especially liked Trinity Road that went from Route 12 on the Sonoma Valley side, ran up over the mountain, and came out in Napa Valley at Oakville. You could see the Wine Country for miles, what splendor, and the drive across the mountain reminded him of home. He could see how his mother had adapted so easily to the area, and he welcomed the chance to see her and Bud while he was stationed in the area. He'd told them he couldn't talk about his work, but he never let on that he was working under an alias. To them, he was still Nathan West.

Helping his mother and stepfather in delivering furniture to different homes, Davis began to understand why his mother loved Bud so much. He was truly a wonderful, genuine, caring man. When Davis's mother asked him if he could help with a furniture sale one evening at the store in Sonoma, he couldn't turn her down. If he'd known what he was getting himself into, he would've run.

When the auctioneer, Mr. Trevy, came to the next item for sale, West would read the tag and state what company manufactured the piece of furniture, the retail price, and then the sale price. West felt like Vanna White and was glad when the sale had concluded. Still, he found it worth the effort when his mother said, "You did a fine job, Nathan." The entire time she and Bud had hidden in the office, giggling at what West was doing.

But West did accomplish some important matters during that spring. He learned the California coast from Monterey Bay to Mendocino County, quickly eliminating most of the coastline for any substantial drug offloading. It was just too rough and very few places to hide to remove one hundred tons of drugs. Even an inlet like Bodega Bay was too populated and exposed. Moving his search inland, he found what he was looking for. Thousands of miles of waterways in the Sacramento–San Joaquin Delta. Once you got east of Vallejo, the possible hiding locations were too numerous to count. There were multiple small harbors, docking facilities, and small waterways called sloughs, where you could hide a thousand boats. He knew in his bones; this was where he needed to be concentrating his search. It was a drug smuggler's paradise.

Carlin Rogers, Billy Little, and Terrence George Valley thought the same thing.

"When we get the *California Rose* ready to sail in May, we'll take her to McAvoy Harbor near Pittsburg," Carlin said as they were enjoying a cold beer at Valley's home.

"Why do you like McAvoy?" Valley asked.

"It's close. I can be there in under an hour. And the docking area is big enough for the tug and a barge. It's also behind a locked gate. I'm going to bring Howe back down from Oregon, and he'll run the *Rose* up with Willard."

"Good. I should be hearing from the Russian soon," Valley said. "I think what I proposed will be approved, and we'll be in business by April or May."

"About time," Carlin said. "Bill and I found an old navy barge in Concord that I can lease. It's rough and will need some work, but it's a fifty-ton barge and will do the job."

"Who has it?" Valley asked.

"Sacramento Tug, Chuck Stevens," Little said. He's the same guy we bought the *California Rose* from. He wanted to know what we were using it for. I first told him we may have to move some gravel. But he didn't like that idea, said it would weigh too much. So I told him we'd only use it to haul a couple containers and machine parts. He agreed to that use, reminding me the barge was old and he wasn't responsible for uses he didn't approve."

"As long as it floats and we can get it from here to there and back," Valley said.

"Where's there?" Rogers asked.

"It'll be somewhere north of Hawaii," Valley said. "There's no need to be elsewhere. It'll be safer to keep the drugs on the larger vessel as long as possible. If a bad storm comes up, I don't want to be on an overloaded small craft out in the middle of the Pacific. How do you pull a barge, or do you push it?"

"You pull it with the winch cable on the tug," Rogers said. "On the river, you'll see tugboats pushing a barge. But on the open water, you pull it."

"What happens if the barge sinks? Does it pull you down with it?" Valley asked.

"If you can't cut the cable on the winch, it sure as hell will," Little said.

"Fuck that," Valley said. "I'll meet up with you guys on land."

Colonel Dimitri Petroff had been staying at Sinesha Orlov's apartment a few nights a week. He refused to take her to his place, feeling that was a horrible thing to do. But his loneliness and misery were allowing him to be with the woman, if not for the company, then for the sex. He never pried into her life and came and went as he pleased. She kept him supplied with the vodka he now drank regularly and would straighten his uniform before he left the house, something that hadn't been done for him in many years. He suspected her of being a high-priced prostitute for the rich men of the city, but he didn't care. And it never entered his mind that she was a KGB assassin there to kill him if ordered by Yukorov.

Senior Special Agent Buddy Hayden, CIA Federal Law Enforcement Training Center (FLETC) Division Chief, was having sex with CIA psychiatrist Melinda Hicks as often as he could. That was the only way he found not to worry about CIA Special Agents Reynolds and Davis, at least for as much time it took to complete the act. On more than one occasions, he would stop in the middle and say, "I can't. I'm sorry. I have to go to the office," where he would reread all the files again. He would glance at his pager repeatedly and continued to make sure the STU had a dial tone. But still no word from the colonel.

CIA Director William Casto was fighting his personal battle with a brain tumor. Still, being able to do his duties was important to him, but he wasn't sure just how much time he had left. In anticipation of the inevitable, Director William Weatherby of the FBI was being prepared to take over the CIA. Casto and Weatherby met often, and Weatherby was made fully aware of Red Sword and Thorn, the codename for the CIA's operation to stop it.

One thing Casto made Weatherby do was make a promise. "After I'm gone, you let those men do their jobs. Don't start any new teams in Thorn."

"I promise," Weatherby said shaking hands with the dying director of the CIA.

CHAPTER 2

It's Official

Thursday, February 19, 1987

DAVIS WAS LEAVING SACRAMENTO, HEADING SOUTH on Interstate 5, when his bag phone rang. "Hello," he said, quickly pulling the CJ over onto the berm so he could hear.

"I got your paperwork back this morning," US Customs Service SAC Robert Klass said. It's official; you're now a Customs Service Special Agent. I'll drop by your place tonight eight p.m. and bring you your temporary credentials. Do you have a suit?"

"Yes."

"Have it on tonight. I'll need to take a picture for your permanent ID. But you'll be fine until I get that back."

"Roger that," Davis said as Klass hung up.

Davis had filled out and sent the paperwork back to Klass in October. It had taken the government four months to process his direct hire. Klass had said it normally takes six months, so Davis figured that was somewhat of a blessing. Driving back to Hayward, he thought it would be good to finally have official credentials. He needed to start doing serious work, and nothing opens up doors like a badge.

At 8:00 p.m., Klass arrived at Newport Street in his silver Taurus. Davis, wearing a suit, held the door open as Klass entered the house.

He continued to the kitchen table where he sat down with his briefcase and opened it. Handing Davis a folder, Klass said, "All your temporary creds are there. You have your ID, government credit card, access cards for 1700, the parking garage, and password. You use that credit card for gas or anything else whenever you're in your G-Ride. Is it in the garage?" Klass asked.

"Yes, I've been running my Jeep, traveling the back roads and waterways."

"Good, keep using the Jeep as much as you can in the back country. No one would think it was law enforcement, especially with the headers," Klass said having glanced at them on his way into the house. "They'll think you're just another local." Taking a camera out of the briefcase, Klass said, "Stand up against that wall."

Davis stood up and moved over against the white wall in the kitchen. "How do I look?"

"Like somebody getting ready to get his ass shot off."

Davis didn't smile, and Klass took the picture, "Perfect," he said. "I like the look. I'll get this on your permanent ID with a real badge by the time you start the task force." Putting the camera back into the briefcase, Klass sat back down, took out a document, and handed it to Davis. "Sign that," he said.

Davis glanced at the heading, Firearms Certification, while writing his signature and handed the document back.

Then Klass signed it and said, "I hope you can shoot because I just certified that I watched you qualify."

"I can shoot."

"Okay, that's it for the paperwork. What have you found out? I do know there's been no additional information from the source."

"None," Davis said. "I've been learning all the waterways. I think we can forget about the coast. It's too rough and populated for this big of an operation. If someone was throwing out a few hundred pounds of cocaine or weed, sure, but not one hundred tons."

"I agree."

"I'm going to concentrate my surveillance east of Vallejo. That's where I'd be. Some of those areas are remote, and there's nothing out there—a occasional building or store—but that's where I'd be hiding out."

"How you going to do that?" Klass asked. "We consider it wasteland, and you're right, there's nothing out there. You'll absolutely be on your own, and if shit goes south, there'll be no calvary coming for your ass anytime soon."

"Yes, I know. I'm going to get myself a boat and go fishing. That way, I can go anyplace where there's water, and I won't have to worry about trying to find a road where there may not be one. The CJ won't be as exposed, and no one will give a shit about a local fisherman. I'll need a side job for my cover. I've been thinking about that too. I'll try to find work at one of the vineyards."

"Can you speak Spanish?" Klass asked. "If not, you may find it difficult. All those vineyard workers are beaners. Not easy for a gringo to find work in the fields."

"No, I can't speak Spanish. But I can run equipment, tractors, dozers, and I'm a halfway good mechanic. So I'll see what happens."

"Okay, now for what I need out of you. All my new people have to spend the first two weeks at the airport. I don't even want to see you at Montgomery Street. At SFO, I have a couple of agents, and there are also Customs inspectors. You don't need to do anything. Just hang out there with the other agents. Get to know everyone and how things work."

"I've reviewed the files on Landers and Wallace," Davis said.

"Good, both fine people. Hang out with them. Let them take care of any legal issues with passengers. You may get to see some heroin swallowers or other contraband trying to come in. Landers and Wallace are both are very sharp. You just stand back, watch, and learn," Klass said.

"I can do that. How long during the day do I need to stay there?"

"Most of the day. Monday through Friday. Eight to five, unless you have something pressing. Do that for two weeks straight. After that, you can come and go as you see fit. But for the first two weeks, be at SFO as much as possible."

"Roger that."

"In two weeks, I'll assign you to the Organized Crime Drug Enforcement Task Force, OCDETF. The only agent I have there now is Senior Special Agent Harvey Waskovic. Good man, you'll like him. I'm sure to get flak over putting you there. The only people that go to the task force are the best and most experienced agents of any agency. You haven't even been to one of our schools, and no federal arrest yet. It's going to be a hard sell to my senior staff, but I'll take care of that."

"Sorry to put you in a rough place. I certainly don't what to make you look bad." Davis knew his mistake before he made the *d* sound in *bad*. But it was too late to take it back.

Klass pointed at his face where the .45 caliber slug tore through the side of his head and said, "You see these scars? I don't give a fuck about looking bad. You just make sure you don't screw up on my watch. And if you do, you better disappear. If my people learn I've allowed an outside agent within our family without letting them know, I'll lose all their trust. If that happens, the service will not try to transfer twenty-five agents out of a bad situation. I'll have to take one for the team, knowing full well that my early retirement is my own created sham. And if I have to do that, you better damn well be invisible."

"I understand," Davis said.

"Okay, you be at SFO on Monday," Klass said. "Meet the team there, and let's get this investigation moving forward. Buddy filled me in on what this is about. Make no shit, this is important. So get your ass in gear, and let's do something about it. Like I told Buddy, every once in a while, there's something of such historical importance that you hope God would intervene. Let's hope he's paying attention." As he got up to leave, Klass said, "Walk out with me. I have something I need to give you."

Reaching his car, Klass opened the door and picked up a small police red light off the seat. "Keep that hidden in your glove box. Whenever you're at the airport or downtown, you can put it on your dash and not get ticketed."

"Thanks, Bob," Davis said, taking the small light and shaking hands with the SAC.

"No fuckups," he said, getting in his car and pulling out.

Davis walked back into the house, locked the door, and went to the table. Laying the light down, he looked at his ID with the name of Tony L. Davis. It showed a badge number of 27141. The number appeared strange to him, but he couldn't figure out why. One thing he was sure of; Robert Klass was a man not to be fucked with.

CHAPTER 3

They Call Me Kit

8:00 a.m., Monday, February 23, 1987

Davis parked the tan Mustang along the curb at SFO. Taking the red light out of the glove box, he placed it on the dash. He entered the door that had a large US Department of the Treasury seal on it with US Customs Service above it. Davis approached the counter and showed his identification to the lady who spoke in a friendly voice, asking if she could help him.

"Yes, ma'am, I'm looking for Dan Landers."

"I believe you'll find him in the cafeteria. He's now having breakfast. It's that way," she said, pointing down the hall.

"Thank you," Davis said walking towards the direction she had pointed. In the cafeteria, Davis spotted a man sitting against a wall, eating by himself. Davis walked up to him and asked, "Are you Dan Landers?"

The man looked up and said, "Yes, I am."

Davis extended his hand and said, "Hi, I'm Tony Davis, and I was told by Mr. Klass to look you up."

"Hello, nice to meet you. Would you care to join me?" Landers asked as they shook hands.

"Yes, thank you," Davis said as he sat down.

"Klass told me a new agent was coming today."

"Yes, I just arrived from back East."

"Well, welcome aboard," Landers said with a smile. "Did you transfer in from another agency, or how did you come to be here in San Francisco?"

"No, I just left FLETC. I wanted to see what the West Coast was like."

"I see," Landers said. "What did you do before joining the Customs Service?"

"I was a West Virginia State Trooper for eight years."

"Good. I like former law enforcement personnel. I was in the Department of Corrections in Marysville, California, before joining the service."

"That's cool," Davis said.

The two men made small talk as Davis studied Landers. Davis thought, I know this guy from somewhere. Then it came to him. Twenty years ago, Landers could have played Ralphie in the movie *Christmas Story*. He was short with straight blond hair, blue eyes, round wire-rim glasses on a somewhat oval shaped head that he canted and slightly bobbed when he spoke.

Not being sure of what to talk about with Landers, Davis asked "What are your hobbies?" Thinking he would respond with chess or reading. Davis was greatly surprised when Landers smiled and said, "Bowhunting."

Having that same passion when he was growing up in West Virginia, Davis said, "No shit."

Landers said, "That's correct," and added that he liked to hunt in northern California when he got the chance.

Davis asked Landers, "What's it like up there where you hunt?"

Landers made a response that both amused and awed Davis. "Igneous rock formations, mainly coniferous forest with a scattering of deciduous flora."

Davis looked at Landers for a moment, chuckled, and said, "You mean a lot of rocks, pine trees, and not much seasonal change."

"Well, that's correct," Landers said nodding as he spoke and tilting his head slightly to the left.

Davis felt immediate friendship to this man with a vocabulary like Webster.

After breakfast, Landers showed Davis a desk he could use.

Davis sat down and was leaning back in his chair to think when he heard, "They call me Kit," from across the divider.

Getting up, Davis peered into the next cubicle.

His first thought was Jesus! But he was able to extend his hand and squeak out, "Tony, Tony Davis," as he shook hands with Special Agent Katherine Wallace.

Kit was a soft-spoken, beautiful, voluptuous brunette with hazel eyes. Davis immediately knew that he'd be having some serious professional conduct problems if he worked around her very long. You try not to get that close to your partners, but it does happen. And Kit was a hottie. Just the way she sat there was sensuous.

Davis surprised himself. He hadn't felt anything like that for a long time. Keep your head on straight, he thought. Need to concentrate on the job. Maybe after this case is over, he'd feel safe in getting to know her better. He sat back down and asked Kit through the divider, "Where can I get a newspaper? There's something I need to look up."

"Go back out to the counter. They'll probably have today's *Chronicle*."

"Thanks," Davis said. Walking back out to the counter at the door, he asked the lady, "Do you have today's paper?"

"Yes, I do," the receptionist said, handing Davis the *San Francisco Chronicle*.

"Ma'am, may I ask your name?"

"Carol," she said.

"Hi, I'm Tony," Davis said, shaking hands with the lady. "Thank you, Carol."

"You're welcome."

Davis walked back to his desk and sat down.

"She have one?" Wallace asked.

"Yes, thank you."

"What are you looking for?"

"I need a boat. Do you know someone that has one for sale?"

"No, I don't. What are you going to do with it?"

"I like to fish. I'll be staying with my mother in Napa until I find a place of my own. So I'm going to try the area lakes and rivers."

"Oh, you'll like Napa. I love it up there. You need to go on a wine-tasting tour."

"That sounds fun. Perhaps you can show me someday," Davis said listening intently to her reply.

"Nope, won't happen. I'm engaged to a San Fran doc. Sorry."

Davis chuckled and said, "That's okay. I don't drink much wine anyway."

Wallace laughed with him.

Finding the classified section, Davis began looking through the pages until he found a section for watercraft. Looking down through the listing, he found a possibility: "12-foot V-hull, 35 HP Johnson motor with trailer, needs paint. Madrone Vineyard, 776 Madrone Road, Glen Ellen. Talk to Clarence," and it gave the phone number. Davis picked up the phone and called the number listed.

"Hello," a lady said.

"May I speak to Clarence?"

"He's out in the garage. This is Becky, his wife. What can I help you with?" she said, speaking quickly as if she was in a hurry.

"I'm calling about the boat. Does he still have it?"

"Yes, come and get the damn thing. I'm getting tired of seeing it in the yard. It hasn't been used in a couple of years, but I think it'll still float."

"Will Clarence be home tonight around seven or eight?"

"Yes, if I don't kill him."

"Ma'am, may I ask you last name?"

"Becky, Becky and Clarence Jacobs. You coming to get that damn thing or not?" Mrs. Jacobs asked in an aggravated voice.

"Well, I'll certainly be up to look at it tonight," Davis said

"Okay, I'll make sure Clarence is here. Even if he's dead, you can pay me."

"Sounds good," Davis said with a laugh, hearing Mrs. Jacobs yelling "Clarence!" and then the phone went dead.

Davis was still laughing when he asked, "You still over there, Kit?"

"Yes," she said.

"How long would it take to get from here to Glen Ellen? Three hours?"

"With the traffic, you'd better give yourself a good three, if not longer. You need to get out of here by three p.m. if you're wanting to get there by seven. Do you know where it is?"

"Yes, I've been to Jack London State Park. Pretty up there."

"Yes, it is. I can never get Thomas to go up there with me. He's such a stick-in-the-mud. He likes his research and doesn't have time for anything else, except looking through a microscope."

"Sounds like a smart guy. That's no easy task. Takes a lot of hard work and dedication."

"You sound like you know something about that," Wallace said.

"Well, I know a few docs," Davis said. But then he thought, If he likes research, he's probably a strange bird; most people like that are smart as hell but a little weird.

CHAPTER 4

Hired Hand

7:00 p.m., Monday, February 23, 1987

DAVIS LEFT SFO AT THREE AFTER saying goodbye to Dan and Kit. He would see them in the morning. Heading north on Highway 101 towards San Francisco, Davis wasn't sure how long it would take him. He thought he was at least an hour ahead of rush hour but was at its afternoon start for San Francisco. Finally getting across the Golden Gate Bridge, he didn't feel all that comfortable driving sixty miles per hour and being literally on someone's bumper. But whenever he would drift back even a car length, someone would sure as hell slide into the space from the other lane. Accepting it for what it was, he began to drive as crazy as everyone else. Well, he thought, if it happens, there'll be forty cars up my ass.

Finally getting to Glen Ellen and Madrone Road, he looked for 776, found it on a mailbox, and pulled into the property, There was a large old home in the front, and as the road made a circle around the property, there was a newer home in the back. Driving to the new home, Davis saw an old white-and-blue boat sitting to the left in some high weeds on a trailer. As he pulled up, he could see a man with reddish hair under a big floppy hat, wearing dirty overalls. Big barrel-chested with broad shoulders, the man was looking at the engine of a D2 Caterpillar crawler.

The man glanced at Davis as he got out of the Mustang but didn't say a word. Walking up to the machine, Davis asked, "Not running well?"

"Won't start," the man said.

"Fuel filters good?" Davis asked.

The man turned, looked at Davis standing there in a suit, and said in a skeptical voice, "You ever worked on one of these?"

"Nope, never owned a Cat. But have a 350 JD back home, and the rust in the tank always clogged the fuel filters."

"Who are you, and what do you want?" the man asked, somewhat perturbed.

"I called earlier and talked to Becky about the boat you have for sale."

"Oh, yeah. She told me. Come with me," he said and then walked back up the road to the boat Davis saw when he drove in.

"This is it," the man said. "Two hundred bucks and it's yours, trailer and motor included."

Davis looked at the old fiberglass boat with a small plywood bow cover that needed replacing. "Does the engine run?" Davis asked looking at the old 35 horsepower Johnson motor.

"It did when my nephew parked it here two years ago."

"How about if I pay you two hundred fifty dollars?"

"Now, why would you want to do that?"

"So you'll let me work on it here and use some of your tools," Davis said.

"You sure have a funny way of dickering," the man said. "But I have one condition. You take it out of here in thirty days, one way or the other. Deal?"

"Deal. I'm Tony," he said extending his hand.

"Clarence," the man said, taking Davis's hand and shaking it.

Davis could tell this man did serious work. His hand felt like a farrier's rasp, it was so calloused and hard.

Clarence Jacobs was also assessing the other's hand but not in the same terms. He thought, *This man's hand is as soft as a woman's.*

After paying Clarence two hundred fifty dollars, Davis asked, "Can I borrow a sander, wire brush, circular saw, drill, screwdriver, Philips and flathead, and a hammer?"

"Come with me," Clarence said.

Davis followed the man to a shop next to the house. Clarence opened the door, and Davis could see it was full of various hand and electric tools.

"Use whatever you need. Just make sure you put them back where you found them."

Davis looked at the various tools and thought of his own garage full of tools back on Fish Creek. "Thank you."

"You're not from here. Where you from?"

"West Virginia."

"What brings you out this way?"

"I've never seen the West Coast before and wanted to explore a little bit before I got too damn old to do it."

"What are you doing in a suit? You working somewhere?" Clarence asked.

"No, but I had an interview at a furniture store in Sonoma, Yoder's. May be working there part-time."

"Can you run a cat?"

"Sure, dozers, crawlers, highlift, backhoe, tractors; can weld, stick and MIG," Davis said. "Grew up on a farm."

"Come with me," Clarence said walking towards the rows of grape trellises. "See all these rows of grapes? All these need to be pruned and now. After that, we'll have to disc between each row to cut out the weeds. It's hard dirty work. You interested?"

"I can't speak Spanish."

"You only need to be able to speak to me. You interested?"

"Yes. I'll be limited the next couple of weeks. But after that, I'll be able to give more time. Until then I can come on the weekends, as long as you give me time to work on the boat."

"That'll work. I'll see you Saturday. You going to ask me how much I'll pay you?" Clarence asked.

"No, I'll see you Saturday," Davis said. Walking back to his car, he thought he liked Clarence and that boat would be perfect.

"He's an odd fuck," Clarence Jacobs whispered, smiling as he watched Davis drive away. Then he shook his head when he heard "Clarence!" coming from the house.

CHAPTER 5

Task Force

Monday, March 9, 1987

For the past two weeks, Davis was at SFO daily with Landers and Wallace. Having been shown several incidents of seized contraband, Davis was starting to understand the world of a US Customs Agent and that of the inspectors. A tough job, Davis thought, looking for a needle in a haystack every day as thousands of people pass through SFO. And although profiling may be helpful, Davis quickly learned that everyone was suspect after seeing an eighty-one-year-old grandmother trying to smuggle in Mexican brown heroin for her grandson.

One thing he knew for certain, he really liked Dan Landers, super smart and funny as hell. Davis loved to listen to him speak and asked if he'd always spoken that way. Landers said that he had always enjoyed speaking in front of others and was on his high school debating team. But he shared that his speaking style did at times cause problems with others. One time he and his friend Chris had been bowhunting in northern California when they had gotten somewhat lost. Finding a road and then a small country store, the pair entered the establishment. Dan asked the two older men who were sitting there in rocking chairs where they were.

Not quite understanding Landers's speech and mannerisms, the two old farts thought Dan was making fun of them and told him and Chris to get the hell out of their store, refusing to even sell them something to eat or drink. Davis laughed until he cried when Landers told him that story, understanding exactly why the old men would respond that way. Dan Landers was a gem of a man.

Kit Wallace was a different story. Davis found himself wanting to get to the airport each morning just to see her. What a sensuous woman, Davis thought as he watched her walk around SFO. Beautiful face and a hell of a body, Kit was an amazing lady in all aspects. She picked up on Davis's interest when she saw him looking at her, and she seemed to be more friendly but only up to a point. She still had stick-in-the-mud Thomas at home, at least for the time being. Not ever letting on, Kit Wallace was about to dump Thomas in the mud and be done with his lack of attention. She deserved better, and she knew it. And the one thing she really resented about Thomas was he could never understand why she slept with a pistol under her pillow. Pussy, she'd thought. Kit Wallace was the real deal.

Sunday, March 8, 1987

KLASS ONCE AGAIN VISITED THE HAYWARD safe house. Giving Davis his official credentials with a real badge numbered 27141 and his photo. Davis again looked at the number and then smiled, finally getting the significance.

"What's so funny?" Klass asked.

"It's nothing, just the number."

"What about the number?"

"It's fifty-six."

"What?" Klass asked knowing the number was not fifty-six.

"Seven minus two is five, and one plus four plus one is six," Davis said. "Fifty-six."

Looking at Davis, Klass said, "Right now is a particularly good time for a little more explanation before I call Buddy and tell him you're a whack job, to pull your ass off of this assignment, and to get someone who can do the job."

Smiling Davis explained, "I grew up on a farm with fifty-six acres. My first unit number in the state police was five-six-one. My second unit number was four-five-six. And my final unit number was four-seventeen. So, it appears that the number fifty-six keeps coming up in my life. I'm either going to have an exceptionally good year when I'm fifty-six years old or a very bad one."

"That may be interesting to you, but that doesn't mean shit to me. Let's keep our head in the current situation and get some things accomplished. Listen up. Tomorrow, you're officially on OCDETF. I need you to come to the office at one p.m. and meet ASAC Sherman, Senior Special Agent Harvey Waskovic, and some of the other agents. Have your hair high and tight; then you can grow it long for your UC work."

"Got it."

"These guys are going to ask you some pointed questions. Bring up your state police experiences. I want you looking like a trooper. That's all we have to offer for your cover and my appointing you to the task force."

"I can do that. And I actually do have an extensive criminal investigative experience."

"All right. That's the plan. We'll have to play it by ear as we progress," Klass said.

"I'll get my hair cut in the morning and will be there by one p.m.," Davis said. "I'll wear my suit and have on a hat and dark glasses. I want my countersurveillance dossier being someone they'll never see in the Delta."

"You make sure of that. Okay, see you tomorrow." Klass shook hands and then left Newport Street.

The next morning, Davis found a barber shop off Hesperian Boulevard. Walking in, he asked the barber, "Can you do high and tight?"

"Absolutely. Have a seat," the barber said. "How high and tight do you want it?

"Quarter inch on the sides and one inch on top."

"Neck shaved?" asked the barber.

"Yes, please," Davis said.

"You look a little old to be joining the military."

"Not joining. Just a special event, and I need to look the part."

"Well, I can certainly make you look that. Walter's the name. What's yours?" the barber asked.

"Tony. Nice to meet you, Walter," Davis said. "Hey, Walter, do you know where a guy could get a nice fedora or wool cap?"

"Yes, around the block. There's a gift shop, and I know they carry some hats."

"Thanks."

Thirty minutes later, Davis was in the gift shop trying on different hats and sunglasses. My state police hat size was 7⅛, he thought. Finding a nice grey fedora with a black silk band, he liked how it felt on his recently trimmed head. He also found a large pair of aviator sunglasses and purchased both. Back at Newport Street. he put on his suit and pulled the Mustang out of the garage, having laid the fedora on the seat beside him. Closing the door with the remote, Davis headed north into the city and to Montgomery Street. When he got off on the Embarcadero, he put his fedora and dark glasses on. With both, he would be difficult to recognize, especially with a limp, he thought.

At 12:30 p.m., Davis used his parking garage key and pulled into the parking garage across from 1700. Getting out of the car, he walked down the stairs and then limped across the street to the entrance. At the elevator, he used his access key for the elevator to take him to the fourth floor where there was a bulletproof glass entry with a receptionist.

"Good morning. I'm here to see the SAC," Davis said sliding his ID through the slot to the receptionist.

"Good morning, Agent Davis. I was told you were coming," the lady said sliding the ID back to him.

Hearing the electronic door lock disengage, he opened the door and was told, "Last room at the end of the hall."

"Thank you, ma'am," Davis said and started down the hall without the Buddy Hayden left-hip limp and removing his hat and glasses. He knocked on the door at the end of the hall with the name plaque of SAC Robert Klass.

"Come in."

Opening the door, Davis saw Klass standing with two men at a table to the left who Davis recognized from their file photos as ASAC Sherman, and SA Waskovic.

"Afternoon," Davis said.

"Tony," Klass said, "this is ASAC Paul Sherman and Senior Special Agent Harvey Waskovic."

Davis shook hands with both men.

"Have a seat, gentlemen," Klass said. "I've been filling in Paul and Harvey on your history, Tony. Can you go ahead and tell us about yourself?"

For the next several minutes, Davis gave his life history and his accomplishments while a West Virginia State Trooper, including being the honor graduate of the thirty-first Cadet Class and assigned to the Pistol Team, the original SWAT Team, and later as the Company A Team Leader. He described the numerous investigations he'd been in charge of or took part in, including murders, rapes, robberies, burglaries, drug cases, and assaults. One he detailed was tracking George Martin in the mountains for two days and how Martin stiffened up when Davis put the barrel of his CAR-15 at the base of his skull and clicked the safety on. They laughed at that story. He also explained how he'd been recruited by Buddy Hayden as an intern and had been assigned as a driving instructor at FLETC.

Waskovic was the first to ask a question. "What made you want to come to California from West Virginia?"

"My mother's remarried and lives in Napa. I wanted to come out and spend some time with her," Davis said. "I like it here. It's a nice place."

"What makes you think you deserve to be on the task force?" Sherman asked point-blank as Waskovic and Klass listened intently.

"I think that's Mr. Klass's decision," Davis said. "But in his defense, I think it would be safe to say that I have more felony arrests than all the agents in this building combined. And some of those arrests were killers and rapists. Unless you have a former state trooper or big city detective among your ranks, I'd bet that's a true statement."

Klass liked Davis's smooth, cool, and excellent reply under some pressure. Waskovic liked it too, while Sherman thought Davis was a cocky rookie with the fedora he was carrying.

"Anything else you men what thrown back in your face?" Klass asked. With no reply, he said, "All right, let's introduce Tony to the crew."

Getting up, Klass led the group into the next room down the hall on the left. The large meeting room was filled with people. He immediately saw Kit standing next to Dan, and both were waving. Davis waved back, looking at Kit.

"Ladies and gentlemen, this is Special Agent Tony Davis," Klass said. "He's a new assignment from FLETC and will be working with Harvey at the task force."

Several people, including Kit and Dan, clapped, and some did not. Still, Davis said, "Thank you."

After Klass asked everyone to state their names, the men and women of the US Customs Service Office of Enforcement, San Francisco, took turns and said who they were. One agent, a tall slender man with blond hair and a big smile, introduced himself as Aleo Bigettie and then asked Davis where he was from.

"West Virginia," Davis said.

"Western Virginia, isn't that were the hillbillies are from?"

"No, that's Virginia. I'm from West Virginia. We are mountaineers," Davis said and laughed at the common misconception of some people. Everyone laughed, at least most of them did.

"All right, does anyone else have any more questions where it shows how ignorant we are on the West Coast?" Klass asked. Everyone did laugh at that. No one had any more questions, and Klass said, "Tony, come with me, please."

Glancing at Kit's smile, Davis followed Klass to his office, shut the door behind him, and sat down in a chair next to Klass's desk.

"I don't want to see you here anymore than you absolutely have to be. I can personally vouch for all my people. But this place has eyes, and you can't be seen. Understand?" Klass said.

"Yes, I won't be here unless I absolutely need to. And if then, I'll be wearing my hat and glasses. I've developed a limp while outside these walls."

"Does that limp imitate anyone we know?" Klass asked.

"Yes, it does. Where do you keep your STU, in case I need it?"

"Right here," Klass said as he turned and opened the bookcase shelf behind him. "Have you read *The Hunt for Red October*?"

"No."

"Well, if you need to use the STU, you'll need to," Klass said as he pulled the book from the shelf and opened it to the center where Davis could see a key.

"Got it," Davis said.

"You need anything right now?"

"No, sir." Getting up out of the seat, Davis shook hands with Klass and said, "I'll keep you informed."

"You do that. And if you need anything, let me or Jack know."

"Will do," Davis said as he started walking down the hall towards the exit. Halfway, Davis passed SA Aleo Bigettie's office, which he shared with SA Paul Defano

"Hey, do hillbillies wear shoes?" Bigettie asked.

Davis stopped and backed up to the doorway. Smiling, he said, "Only when they're stomping someone's ass is what I've heard. As for mountaineers, we can stomp ass with or without shoes."

Bigettie and Defano laughed, as Davis, smiling, walked towards the door and put his fedora and glasses back on.

Klass overheard the comments and thought, Boys you best leave Davis alone. I think he can back it up.

Leaving the building, Davis limped to the parking garage and was surprised to see Kit standing next to his Mustang. "Hi," he said.

"Why you limping? You hurt your leg?" Kit asked.

"Yes, ran into the corner of the kitchen counter. It's just a bruise," Davis said.

"I was thinking about maybe taking you up on the offer of a wine tasting tour someday," she said.

"That'd be fun, but what about Thomas?"

"Well, things aren't going so great. They haven't been for some time. I can't make him go and do anything without a struggle. Then it's not any fun when you have to constantly push someone."

"I'm sorry. You have a pen and paper?" he asked.

"Yes," Kit said digging in her purse next to the 9mm she kept there.

After getting the paper and pen, Davis gave Kit his pager and bag phone numbers. "Call me anytime," he said.

"Are you coming back to the airport anytime soon?" Kit asked.

"Probably not. I'll be floating around, seeing if I can get into something," Davis said, belatedly realizing that was not a good choice of words.

Kit smiled and said, "Well, use protection if you do."

Davis felt immediately aroused and said, "I need to get out of here before I say something best left unsaid."

Kit laughed and said, "Okay, be talking to you later, Tony."

"See you, Kit," Davis said as he got in the Mustang, started out of the garage, and watched Kit drive away in a grey BMW 323i.

CHAPTER 6

Thai

9:00 a.m., Thursday, March 12, 1987

Terrence George Valley was watching CNN when his pager buzzed on the table. Picking it up, he recognized the number for Bergford Money Exchange, turned off the TV, and dialed the number displayed.

"Bergford Money Exchange. How may I direct your call?" the receptionist said.

"This is George Hannah. I was just paged," Valley said.

"Yes, just a moment, Mr. Hannah. Mr. Petrov would like to speak to you," she said as the Muzak began to play.

"Good morning, George. Hope I didn't page you too early," Steve Petrov said.

"No, not at all. I was watching a little news and enjoying my coffee."

"George, are you still interested in the Thai?"

"Yes, I am."

"I can provide the product for three hundred thousand per ton," Petrov said.

"Little higher than what I was thinking, Steve. Any reason for that?"

"Yes, George. The weather in that area of the world has not been as cooperative, and my costs have gone up," Petrov said. "And if we use the same terms as before, I'm still being generous."

Figuring in his head, Valley knew he would still make $550,000 per ton, even after he paid Yukorov his fifty thousand.

"It'll still work, Steve. Ten tons for the first load, and I may need to make another run later in the year or in '88 of another ten tons. You able to swing that?"

"Yes, George. I can make that work if you're going to run two or more shipments."

"Same terms as before? I pay you after I deliver the shipment, and I receive my money," Valley said.

"Agreed."

"Okay, deal, Steve. I'll let you know more soon. There doesn't seem to be any problem for my vessel to take on the shipment off the coast of Thailand in late July or August. You'll have to bring the Thai to my vessel off the coast," Valley said.

"Yes, I understand that. There'll not be any problems on my end either. We'll be able to rendezvous whenever you need to," Petrov said. "Write this down, George. The Thai vessel's name is *Mala* with Captain Saelao. They'll be operating on frequency 136.2."

"Got it," Valley said writing the information down. "Very good, Steve. I'll be in touch. Thank you, and have a nice day."

"You too, George. Have a nice day as well," Petrov said as he hung up the phone.

Valley sat on his couch and quickly figured in his head how much money he should have by the end of the year. Close to fifteen million, including the Thai money, and even if half of the hashish can be shipped, he thought. "Wow," he said. "I've never had that kind of money."

Hearing a truck coming down Little Bluff Road, he looked out the kitchen window and saw a dark-blue crew cab pickup truck traveling quickly south. He gave it little thought and turned the TV back on to CNN.

THIS WAS THE FOURTH TIME JACK REYNOLDS DROVE by Valley's property, first time during the day. He was being careful since Little

Bluff Road was a dead end. He could never do this again during the daylight. Still Reynolds couldn't see any activity or vehicles. He must keep his vehicles in the garage, he thought. Pulling over a mile past 6620, he turned around in the road and headed back north past Valley's property again and back towards Placerville.

Again, Valley watched the vehicle go by and gave it little thought.

Back at the safe house in Vacaville at 10:30 a.m., Reynolds pulled the truck into the garage and closed the door. Walking up the stairs and into the living room, he opened the safe behind the picture of Mt. Shasta, pushed the safe wall button, and heard the bookshelf unlock as he picked up the STU key. Rolling open the bookshelf, he walked into the hidden room. After picking up the receiver of the STU, he called Hayden's pager. When prompted, he entered 1021707, police ten code where 10-21 meant to call the 707 area code, Vacaville. Reynolds pulled the Beretta out of his waistband, laying it on the metal desk. He sat down in the chair and waited for Hayden to call.

After leaving Hick's place for lunch, Hayden had just pulled into his office at the DOD building at FLETC when his pager went off, showing 1021707. He walked into his office, closed the door, and got his STU out. After calling the Vacaville safe house and giving the customary three-two-one countdown, the secure call was initiated.

"What have you found out?" Hayden asked.

"Been by Valley's this morning during daylight. Still nothing. No sign of any activity or vehicles," Reynolds said.

"Would there be any at your place if you lived there?" Hayden asked.

"No, none. So we still don't know anything on Valley."

"Okay. I've still not heard anything from my source. I don't like that. It's going on seven months, and I don't even know if he's still alive."

"Well, we both know how these things go," Reynolds said. "Over the winter they don't move anything out of the high country in Afghanistan. Those people are all snowed in. And it's just now opening back up to travel. So if he's still alive and if this assassination attempt is still operational, I would think we should be hearing from him soon. That's if he's not dead."

"Yes, if he's not dead," Hayden said.

CHAPTER 7

Lost and Found

Saturday, April 4, 1987

Colonel Dimitri Petroff had become a drunk in his grief. Sometimes a man becomes lost, and the colonel certainly had. His grief over losing his wife had destroyed his once proud core, upending his life to where nothing seemed important enough to give even the slightest of effort. Even Luba, his secretary at the Kremlin, stopped trying to cheer him up. He was now usually still drunk when he came to work. Everyone just stayed out of his way, everyone but Sinesha.

Petroff had not stayed overnight at his own home now for a few months. He enjoyed Sinesha's company, and her sexiness, and she was always sexy. Having something light usually made for dinner, she continually had an extra bottle of Stoli when the bottle they were drinking became empty. He realized he was once again gaining weight. But it was all in his gut from the alcohol, and he didn't care. And it didn't seem like she did either.

The colonel hadn't spoken to Yukorov for weeks, and he really didn't mind the thought of Gorbachev now being removed. At least the vodka would be cheaper if it went back to the old price. His whole life and perspective had changed in just a few months.

Leaving the Kremlin early, he needed a drink and bad. His hands were shaking, and he felt horrible. Not wanting to drive, he called a taxi to come and get him. Ten minutes later, he climbed into the cab and asked the driver if he had anything to drink with him. "No," the cabbie said as he looked in his rearview mirror at the shaking and sweating Russian officer.

"Take me to the nearest bar," Petroff said feeling worse by the minute.

"The Gentleman's Club is nearby. You can get a drink there," the driver said.

"*Da,* make it quick please," Petroff said.

The cab was pulling into the parking lot of the bar where he had met Sinesha when he saw her car parked next to Yukorov's Volvo.

"Not here!" he yelled. "Pull out!" And he slid down onto the seat so as not to be seen. "Pull out!" he repeated.

"Okay, okay!" the driver said, pulling back onto the street.

"Take me back to the Kremlin."

"Are you sure? There are many bars nearby," the cabbie said.

"Yes, I'm sure. Take me back to the Kremlin and hurry."

Arriving at the Kremlin, he paid the cab driver and got out next to his own car. With shaking hands, he opened the back door and got in. Petroff lay down on the back seat and immediately threw up on the seat and floorboard. He shut the door, and then using his overcoat that was lying on the seat, he tried to cover up and sweat out the shakes. But he began to convulse with delirium tremens, and soon, Colonel Dimitri Petroff was gagging on his own vomit. By 3:00 p.m., the colonel was unconscious.

When he woke up, he didn't understand where he was. Someone or something was shining a bright light in one eye and then the other. He couldn't move his arms and was finally able to focus on his hands. One had a plastic tube coming out of it. His arms had been fastened down to the bedrails by straps.

"Colonel, can you hear me?" the doctor asked, who was looking into his eyes with the light.

"Where am I?" Petroff asked.

"Kremlin Hospital," the doctor said.

"How did I get here?"

"Ambulance. Someone found you on the backseat of a car. You went into DTs, and became unconscious. You could have died if they'd not found you."

"When can I leave?" the colonel asked in a weakened voice.

"I'll keep you tonight and get you on some medicine and fluids. In the morning, I'll see how you're doing. I should be able to let you leave tomorrow," the doctor said. "I'm going to give you some more medicine to help you sleep. I'll be here when you wake up."

As the doctor nodded to a nurse, the colonel watched her push a syringe into the tubing and inject a clear liquid. He glanced at a man standing in the doorway, but he lost consciousness fast and was out before she withdrew the needle and before recognizing Yukorov.

As the doctor was leaving the room, Yukorov flashed his KGB ID and asked the doctor if the colonel had been talking about anything.

"No," the doctor said. "He only answered my questions."

"No crazy talk or anything, Doctor?" Yukorov asked again.

"I'm not sure what you mean by crazy talk, but no. He's not spoken at all until just now when he woke up. Some alcoholics do hallucinate and talk, but he didn't."

Yukorov nodded as he moved out of the way, so the doctor could leave the room, and felt relieved the colonel had not talked about killing General Secretary Gorbachev. It could have been seen only as an alcoholic's hallucinations, but Yukorov wasn't willing to take that chance. He was there to kill the colonel if there'd been any mention of anything. Being satisfied he didn't have to do that, the KGB assassin left the hospital and got in his Volvo, joining another KGB assassin waiting there.

"You kill him?" Sinesha asked coldly.

"No," Yukorov said as he drove back towards the middle of town where they'd left her car.

CHAPTER 8

McAvoy Harbor

8:00 p.m., Wednesday, May 13, 1987

Carlin Rogers had been checking out the Pittsburg, California, area extensively. He was staying in the Motel 6 on Loveridge Road. That way, he didn't have to drive back and forth from Napa each day. He ate in the restaurant at McAvoy Harbor several days in a row, and the local people were beginning to look at him as just another businessman with Supply Masters, Inc. He felt comfortable there. Back in his room at Motel 6, he called Stanley Howe in Coos Bay.

"I've got a job for you," Carlin said when he got Howe on the phone.

"What is it?" Howe asked.

"Can you pilot the *California Rose* from Newport to San Fran for me? I want to bring her up to McAvoy Harbor near Pittsburg."

"How soon do you need it done?"

"As soon as you can. You free this weekend?"

"What's the weather supposed to be like down there?"

"Clear and smooth. We had a storm recently go through. But I checked ten minutes ago, and the west coast of California is good until the middle of next week," Carlin said.

"I can fly down to LAX on Saturday. Who's there now?" Howe asked.

"Willard and my brother's son, Jim. They can assist in whatever you need."

"How much you paying?"

"Thousand a day plus expenses. Should take you two and a half days once you get under way."

"Okay. I'll fly down Saturday. We'll start back that night. Tell Willard to have it completely fueled and ready to go when I get there," Howe said.

"That's no problem."

"Where's Dude?

"He's out of pocket right now, and I can't wait," Carlin said, knowing that Bill Smart, known as Dude, was serving a short stint in jail for being caught with some pot.

"All right. Tell Willard, I'll be down, and be ready to shove off when I get there. I'll keep in touch with you through the KMI operator once I get underway," Howe said.

"Great. I'll talk with you once you get on the water, and thanks," Carlin said as he hung up.

Carlin next called Willard's room at the Holiday Inn Express in Newport Beach. There was no answer, so Carlin left a message for him to call as soon as he got back to the room.

Thirty minutes later, Carlin's phone rang. "Hello."

"Yes, what's going on?" Willard asked.

"Howe is flying down from Coos Bay Saturday. When he gets there, you guys are immediately leaving for McAvoy. You be ready. Be completely fueled and have some food on board. This'll take almost three days," Carlin said.

"We're ready now. She's fueled up, and we have plenty of food on board for a week."

"Okay. Tell Jim, I'll let his dad know you guys are starting up this weekend. Be careful and do exactly what Howe tells you to do."

"No worries. We'll call you when we get underway."

"Okay. Talk to you later," Carlin said and hung up. That's good, he thought as he called Valley's El Dorado number.

"Hello," Valley said, answering his phone.

"*California Rose* will be on her way Saturday and should be in Pittsburg by Monday afternoon or evening."

"That's great. When are you getting the barge?" Valley asked.

"Few weeks. I need to finish painting the tug, and there's a little engine work that needs to be completed. And as soon as Dude gets out of jail, I'm having him put in a new radio and radar. I'm not trusting those old electronics when it's my ass out at sea."

"Who's bringing it up? Willard?" Valley asked.

"No, I called Howe. He's flying down Saturday from Oregon. He'll be the pilot," Carlin said.

"Good. Willard's not experienced enough."

"No, he's not. He's a good kid but a little young yet," Carlin said. And besides, his mother would make my life a living hell if anything ever happened to him. Okay, I'll keep you informed."

"Good. Talk later," Valley said, and both men hung up.

Bringing the *California Rose* up from Los Angeles was uneventful, and the vessel pulled into McAvoy Harbor at 4:00 p.m., on Monday, May 18. Carlin and Valley were both there when the vessel arrived. They assisted in tying the lines to the dock on the west side of McAvoy Harbor.

"Have any trouble?" Carlin asked Howe as the men shook his hands.

"None. The engine still needs a little tuning. But other than that, everything went well."

Handing Howe three thousand dollars in cash, Carlin asked, "We good?"

"Yes, that'll cover everything. Thanks."

"I'll have Willard put you up at the Motel 6 for tonight. Tomorrow, he'll take you to the airport and get you headed home."

"That'll work," Howe said, carrying his bag towards Willard's old pickup.

CHAPTER 9

California Rose

Noon, Saturday, May 23, 1987

Davis had been working at Madrone Vineyards for Becky and Clarence for almost two months and was learning a lot about grapes. He and the dozen Hispanic laborers he worked with daily finished all the pruning over the eighty acres of grape trellises. During the first couple of weeks, Davis's hands became so swollen from using the pruning shears that it was difficult to close them into a fist. But the swelling eventually went away as his hands became stronger and his forearms pumped up.

Clarence had even joked with him over his hands swelling, "That's very common when some pussy tries to keep up with the beaners."

Next was the dirty job of discing. Pulling the four-axled disc with the Cat crawler created an enormous amount of dust. And even though Davis wore a dust mask and goggles and put his head inside a T-shirt with only his goggles looking out the neck hole, he still choked.

Seeing Davis working hard, Clarence agreed to allow him to keep the boat there past the agreed-upon one month. Davis explained he only had a small place near Oakland and was afraid someone would steal it.

"That's what happens if you live near too many people," Clarence said.

"Yes, it is," Davis replied. Finally finishing up the boat and replacing the wood cover, he painted it white with a blue bow.

On the weekends, Davis began flying lessons at Angwin Airport near Calistoga. He enjoyed that very much, and Rinehart, the instructor, was a gentleman and a professional. Davis began solo flying after seven hours of beginner instructions. Flying over Northern California, he enjoyed looking upon the scenic beauty and especially the remoteness of some of the areas.

Davis also was using the Sacramento Delta Waterways map Klass had given him to explore the area. He traveled the waterways and rivers east of Vallejo with the blue-and-white boat, staying on the north side of Grizzly and Honker Bays. But he still hadn't found any vessels that appeared out of place to him. He wasn't sure if he would recognize one, even if it was. This weekend, he was going to try on the south side of the delta near Pittsburg and Port Chicago.

Davis was at Madrone Road early Saturday, hooking the boat trailer to the Jeep, when Clarence came out with two cups of coffee, handing one to Davis.

"Thank you," Davis said.

"Where you going today?"

"Going to try my luck near Pittsburg on the San Joaquin."

"What bait are you using?"

"I'm going to troll with Rapalas today and see if I can catch any of those big stripers. I'm sure they're in the river. But I've caught only some small bass so far."

"I have to go with Becky today over to Napa. Her sister Cindy is having a birthday party for one of the kids."

"Well, that should be fun." Davis said.

"I'd rather be run over by the crawler," Clarence said with a laugh.

"Thanks for the coffee," Davis said handing back the cup and was soon on his way.

Staying on Highway 12 from Sonoma, through Napa, and past Rio Vista, Davis crossed over the Sacramento River and turned south on Route 160 towards Antioch and Pittsburg. While crossing over the Antioch Bridge, Davis saw a large marina on the south side. Pulling off the highway and into the parking area of Driftwood Marina, Davis backed the boat and trailer into a large parking slot and unhooked it from the Jeep.

"I think I'll do some driving around without pulling this thing behind me," he said.

Davis saw several larger vessels tied up but very few over forty feet, and the ones that were, yachts and such, just didn't seem to be what he was looking for. After driving all the waterways in Antioch, he then drove all of Pittsburg's too, still not seeing anything that just looked different. Leaving Pittsburg, Davis hugged the shore roads as much as possible, heading west. Coming into McAvoy Harbor near Shore Acres, he stayed to the right past the café and was able to see two large boathouses.

There were many yachts tied up there, but nothing that could hold multiple tons of hashish. Driving on around towards a loop, Davis looked over across the harbor and could see a black-and-white tugboat tied up to a dock on the other side. He parked the Jeep next to three smaller boathouses extending out towards the tug. Walking out through the boathouse on the left, Davis wanted to get a closer look. Once at the end of the house, about fifty yards from the vessel, he could see the name on the gunwale, *California Rose*.

"Hmm," Davis said. "That just doesn't sit well with me." Looking around, Davis couldn't see anything that would need a sixty-plus-foot tugboat to push. That's kind of unusual, he thought. He had seen smaller tugboats in the area that made sense, but one that large just didn't fit. That boat is big enough to go to sea, he thought. Feeling the hair start to stand up on the back of his neck, Davis got a very uneasy feeling standing there and walked back towards the CJ.

Looking across the harbor, Davis could see that the outside wall around McAvoy was made of twelve-foot-high solid sheets of metal that prevented anyone from looking in. There was also a twelve-foot-high chain-link fence and gate across the road before you got back to where the *California Rose* was tied up. Davis climbed in the Jeep and left McAvoy without seeing or talking to anyone. Arriving back at Antioch Marina, he hooked up his boat and trailer. Heading back to Madrone Road in Glen Ellen, Davis thought, I need to call Jack.

CHAPTER 10

You're Drinking Crown Tonight

7:30 p.m., Saturday, May 23, 1987

PULLING INTO THE RANCH AND NOT SEEING ANYONE, Davis dropped the boat and trailer off where Clarence told him to keep it. He shoved the waterways map into his backpack, where his camera, bag phone, and pistol were kept, and headed south towards Oakland and Hayward. Two hours later, he arrived at the safehouse on Newport Street.

After taking a hot shower to wash the delta sweat off him, Davis sat down at the kitchen table and started writing in the notebook he had been keeping notes in for the previous six months. Starting a new page, he wrote:

5-23-87, 1200, *California Rose*
Black and white tug, approx. 60 feet length
McAvoy Harbor
Pitts, CA
No one on board or seen

Satisfied and not thinking of anything else, he opened the backpack, laid the 9mm on the table, and picked up the bag phone. Calling

Reynolds's pager, he entered, 1021510 and waited for Reynolds to call. Five minutes later, Davis's bag phone rang. "Hello," he said, not having any type of caller ID.

"Tony, it's Jack. What's going on?" Reynolds asked.

"We need to meet, Jack," Davis said.

Reynolds went quiet for a few moments and then said, "I'll come to you." At least for now, it'd be best if Davis stayed away from Barbera Court. "I'll be there in a couple of hours."

The two hung up, and Davis looked at his watch, 5:15 p.m. Being hungry as hell, he called the Chinese takeout and delivery on Hesperian Boulevard and ordered two large shrimp lo meins, four egg rolls, and two won ton soups. Taking the bag of Crown Royal he had purchased earlier off the top of the refrigerator, he set it on the counter with two glasses. As he sat at the kitchen table, he went over in his mind every picture he could see in his head. What he looked at in his mind still just didn't fit, and it made his heart pound.

Twenty minutes later, the doorbell rang. Davis stood, placed the 9mm in the back of his pants, and walked to the door. He looked through the door security peephole and saw an Asian man carrying a white plastic bag. Unlocking and opening the door, Davis asked the man, "How much?"

"Thirty-two dollas," the man politely said with a thick accent.

Taking two twenties out of his pocket, Davis gave them to the man and said, "Thank you. Keep the change."

The Asian man nodded back and said, "Thank you," as he turned and started walking back down the sidewalk.

Davis locked the door and took the food back to the table. Reaching in the bag, he took out one small bag of egg rolls and bit off half of one. "Damn, these things are good," he said. Pulling the rest of the contents out of the bag, he set them down on the far end of the table and put two forks and two spoons next to the containers. From his pack, he took out the waterways map, opened it up, and laid it on the other half of the table. Opening up one container of shrimp lo mein, he began to eat as he sat back down and studied the map.

Lost in his thoughts again, Davis heard a large engine vehicle pull into the driveway next to the Jeep. Getting up, he glanced out the door security peephole once more and could see Reynolds walking up the sidewalk.

Davis unlocked and opened the door and said, "Come in, Jack. How have you been?"

"Good, Tony. What's going on?" Reynolds asked.

"Come over here. Jack, help yourself to the Chinese."

Reynolds picked up a fork and immediately started eating the other container of shrimp lo mein. "Good shit."

"Yes, delicious. Okay, listen up," Davis said, not knowing he had made Reynolds smile with the command. Pointing at the waterways map, he said, "I've covered this area west of Vallejo by vehicle. All the way to the coast and from Monterey here in the south to Mendocino County here to the north," moving his finger along the map as he spoke. "Easy to cover by car and you can see everything." Glancing at Reynolds, he continued, "The problem is east of Vallejo. It's remote. There are hundreds, if not thousands, of miles of waterways that you may or may not be able to access by car. For the past few weeks, I've been covering these waterways on the Sacramento River side up near Rio Vista by boat."

"What boat?" Reynolds asked.

"Small fishing boat. I bought it from Clarence."

"Who the hell is Clarence?" Reynolds asked with his mouth full of lo mein.

"The guy I work for. Becky's husband."

Reynolds was trying to say something when Davis cut him off, "Would you just shut the fuck up for a minute. I'm trying to get to something important."

"All right. Go!" Reynolds said.

"So I've been covering this area of the Sacramento River near Rio Vista by boat," Davis repeated, pointing at the map. "And there's not much there, at least not any place where you would want to try to hide a drug-smuggling operation of this magnitude. I mean, it's remote in some places, but nothing that really knocks your socks off. So this morning, I decide to try over around Pittsburg on the south side," Davis said as he traced the map with his finger. "I was going to use the boat and fish again. But I haven't been catching shit, and I haven't found anything," Davis said now looking at Reynolds.

"I swear to God, if this is what you brought me down here for, to tell me you haven't been catching any damn fish, I'm going to beat you off every wall in this house," Reynolds said as he stopped eating and looking at Davis.

Davis looked at Reynolds and continued saying, "Jack, do you realize the impossible task that we've undertaken? There are thousands of miles of water and roads. And we don't have a goddamn clue who or what we're looking for. I've been breaking my fucking back, Jack, trying to find anything that I thought was even remotely suspicious. I have pruned more goddamn grapes in the last month than ten people will see in a lifetime. My hands were so swollen that I couldn't even close them for days. And then I ate enough goddamn Sonoma Creek dust driving a Caterpillar crawler discing between those damn grapes vines to plant a large maple tree."

"Tony, I swear to God if this is all you got, I'll kill you. How do you want it, knife or gun?" Reynolds asked in a serious tone.

Davis resumed, tapping his finger back on the map at McAvoy Harbor. "But," he said and then repeated, "but I just happened to drive into this little harbor. And what do you think I saw, Jack?"

"I'm warning you. The next bit of information coming out of your mouth better be something important."

Davis turned to the sink and picked up the bottle of Crown and the two glasses. Turning to the table he set both glasses down and poured a shot into them and said, "You're drinking Crown tonight." Pointing back at the map, Davis said, "This may be a wild-goose chase. But at noon today, right here," taping his finger on the map, "I found a sixty-foot oceangoing tugboat named the *California Rose*. Now why would someone have a tugboat this large, mainly used in waterways in the opposite direction, tied up in a little harbor? I've got a good feeling about this tugboat, Jack. It's not remote; it's kind of hiding in plain sight, but it made the hair on the back of my neck stand up."

Reynolds stood there for a few seconds not saying a word, stared at Davis, and then looked at McAvoy Harbor where Davis had been pointing on the map. Picking up one of the glasses at the same time Davis did, Reynolds said, "Goddamn!" and clicked Davis's glass as both men threw the shots of Crown into the back of their mouths.

"This tugboat was out of place to you?" Reynolds asked.

"Yes, I've been doing this now for seven months. I've been over a lot of territory, a lot of water, and I've looked at a shitload of vessels, and that tugboat did not fit. Somebody is trying to make it fit. But it's wrong, Jack. I don't know why, but it's wrong."

"Okay, what're you doing next?" Reynolds asked as he picked up the bottle of Crown and poured both another shot.

"I'm going to meet the agents of the United States Coast Guard next week," Davis said. "I need someone to run the background on that vessel."

"That's good," Reynolds said holding up his glass. "Cheers, you crazy hillbilly son of a bitch, only the best."

"Cheers, you butterfly knife asshole, only the best," Davis said, as both men clicked glasses and drank the Crown.

CHAPTER 11

USCG

Sunday, May 24, 1987

THE NEXT MORNING, AFTER SPENDING THE NIGHT, Reynolds was preparing to leave Newport Street and head back to Vacaville. "That's some good work, Tony. Keep at it and I'll let Buddy know what you've found."

"Will do and thanks, Jack," Davis said as Reynolds pulled away.

Feeling hungry, Davis got in the CJ and drove to McDonalds, got an Egg McMuffin and large orange juice, and returned to the safe house where he spent most of the day going over all the USCG personnel's files. Having the agents' contact information, he called the Coast Guard Headquarters on Yerba Buena Island.

"Good afternoon, United States Coast Guard, Yerba Buena Island, San Francisco. Lieutenant Nelson speaking. How may I help you?"

"Lieutenant, I need to speak with RAC Dale Case. He wouldn't happen to be in on Sunday, would he?" Davis asked.

"Yes, sir, he is. Who's calling, please?"

"Special Agent Tony Davis, Customs Service on the task force."

"Hold on, sir. I'll get him," the lieutenant said and put Davis on hold.

"Case," a voice said as the phone was picked up.

"Is this RAC Dale Case?" Davis asked.

"Yes, it is. How can I help you, Agent Davis?"

"I'm new to the area, and on OCDETF. I'd like to come over and meet you guys when it's convenient."

"How's tomorrow?" Case asked. "Agents Taylor, Robins, Amos, Royal, and I'll be here."

"That works, say ten a.m.?" Davis asked.

"Yes, that's good. Get on Oakland Bay Bridge and get off at Yerba Buena Island. Follow Treasure Island Road and turn right on Macalla. That will wind around to Northgate and then to Healy. Watch for the Coast Guard Sector Building; it'll be on your left. I'll tell security you're coming. Once here, I'll send someone down to get you."

"Great. I'll see you tomorrow. Thank you, sir," Davis said.

"Very good. See you tomorrow. Goodbye," Case said as he hung up.

Getting off the phone, Resident Agent in Charge, Dale Case, US Coast Guard, thought how he and his crew liked working with the agents assigned to OCDETF.

The next morning at 9:50 a.m., Davis, wearing his fedora and sunglasses and following Case's directions, came to the Coast Guard Security post. Handing the guard his ID, Davis said, "I'm here to see Special Agent Case."

"Yes, sir. Just a minute please," the guard said as he picked up the telephone and dialed a number. Waiting a moment, he said, "Special Agent Davis is here, sir. . . . Yes, sir, will do," he said, hanging up. "Sir, you can drive straight ahead and park in that lot over there," he said, pointing for Davis. "From there, walk to that curved building on the left, and someone will meet you. Have a nice day, sir."

"Thank you. You too," Davis said. He drove and then parked the Mustang where indicated, laid his hat and glasses on the seat, and got out. Walking towards the building, Davis saw a man with a full head of dark hair and sideburns come out of the building.

"You Davis?" the man asked.

"Yes, you Case?" Davis said.

"No, Ray Taylor," the man said, smiling and extending his hand.

"Tony Davis," Davis said, shaking hands with Taylor.

"Come with me, please. I'll show you around and then take you upstairs to RAC Case's office."

"Thank you, Ray. How long have you been with the Coast Guard?"

"Twelve years and love every day of it."

"Excuse me for being ignorant, but I've never been around any Coast Guard personnel. I'm from West Virginia, and we don't have any oceans. What do you guys do mostly?"

"Patrol the waterways. That's any ocean or river that has a nexus or connection to any of the borders of the United States. If we have a nexus, we have the authority to be there. We keep track of all the vessels that operate in our jurisdiction and do safety checks when we feel they're needed. But our big job is search and rescue for vessels that are having problems; it's called SAR. It might be something simple like an engine failure and the vessel is adrift. But sometimes, it's a real life-and-death situation, and we live and breathe for those calls. We also enforce federal law that has to do with smuggling, any type of contraband, or environmental dangers. And we do go up into your neck of the woods. We actually patrol the Ohio River."

"Wow, I didn't know that. The Ohio River?"

"Yes, and if I'm not mistaken, there's a Coast Guard facility in your eastern panhandle near Shepherdstown on the Potomac River. I was back that way years ago," Taylor said.

"I never knew that, and I was a state trooper. But I was never stationed along the big waterways."

Davis walked with Taylor around the large, angled building to an open area facing the water. "This is the Quad."

"Beautiful view," Davis said.

"Yes, it is, and I love the smell of the water," Taylor said.

"Yes, it's unique, isn't it?"

Following the sidewalk behind the building, the pair walked over to the water where Davis could see some docks and vessels.

"This is our small boat pier with the forty-one footers. These are our fast response patrol vessels. Now over there," Taylor said, pointing past the patrol vessels, "that's our large pier for the *Cape Romain*. That's our big dog, skippered by Captain Gary Goodman, great guy."

"Nice looking boats. I like the Coast Guard colors," Davis said. "That *Cape Romain*, that's a pretty good size vessel."

"Yes, ninety-five feet with two .50 caliber machine guns and capable of dropping depth charges."

"Depth charges?" Davis said.

"Sure as shit. That class of vessel can hunt submarines if it has to," Taylor said.

"Damn, that's very cool," Davis said, thinking these surface assets of the US Coast Guard just might come in handy. And beyond that, Davis really liked Ray Taylor.

"Okay, let's go upstairs, and you can meet the RAC," Taylor said. Returning to the angled building and going in one of the back doors, they went up the stairs where Davis could see a group of men talking in the hall.

"Fellows, this is Agent Tony Davis of Customs," Taylor said and went on introducing the men. "This is our RAC Dale Case and Agents Dennis Robins, Bruce Royal, and Wayne Amos."

"A very nice facility in a beautiful location," Davis said, shaking hands with each of the men.

"Yes, it is," Case said. "How long have you been with the Customs Service?"

"Very short time, few weeks. I was at FLETC as an instructor and then wanted to come out here to see the West Coast."

"Big change," Case said.

"Yes, it is. But I have family out here. My mother and stepfather live in Napa, so that makes it easier."

"Well, you make sure you let me or one of these fellows know if you need anything. One of our major objectives here is to support any way we can," Case said.

"Thank you. I'm sure I'll need something sooner than later. By the way, can you run a vessel's name and get owner and that kind of information?" Davis asked.

"Sure can," Case said. "Taylor, take his information and then run it."

"Come with me, Agent Davis, and I can take the information," Taylor said.

In his office, Taylor asked, "What's the vessel's name and type?"

"*California Rose*," Davis said. "Tugboat."

Taylor wrote down the information and said, "I'll run this through the database and see what we can find. Where'd you see the vessel?"

"Over near Pittsburg. I don't know squat about tugboats and was curious. To tell you the truth, Ray, I don't know squat about any boat. I was wondering what information is available if you query it."

"Quite a bit actually. We can tell not only who owns it but also where it's from, if it's been renamed, and if there have ever been any encounters with the Coast Guard, as far as safety inspections, violations, things of that sort."

"Great," Davis said. "Hey, you don't mind exchanging contact information, do you?" Would be great to have a contact in the Coast Guard who I know personally and can bounce things off of."

"Absolutely," Taylor said, giving Davis his phone numbers at his office, the duty officer's number, and his pager number.

Davis gave his contact information as well. "Cool," he said. "And if you ever need anything from my end, all you have to do is ask."

"That'll work," Taylor said, shaking hands with Davis.

"Well, thank you for the tour, and nice meeting all you guys. I need to run, but before I go, I have one question," Davis said.

"What's that?" Taylor asked.

"Do you guys ever sit around, look at each other, and say, 'They actually pay us to live here'?"

"All the time, all the damn time!" Taylor said with a laugh.

CHAPTER 12

Leave of Absence

Monday, May 25, 1987

Colonel Dimitri Petroff took two months leave of absence after being let out of the hospital. He stopped at Sinesha's place and got what clothes he had there, telling her, "I need to get my life under control. I've become a drunk. I'm moving back into my place until I sober up."

There was nothing she could say or do to stop him, short of putting a bullet in his brain, and for the time being, Yukorov said no.

The past two months were the hardest Petroff had ever been through in his life. Even taking the sedative twice a day and the vitamins that were prescribed by the doctor, he still shook and felt like his skin was crawling, all the while still crying for his wife. Finally, during the last couple of weeks, he was beginning to pull out of it. And this was his first day back at the Kremlin. He started by apologizing to Luba for his rudeness.

She gave him a big hug and said, "It's all right. You're back with us once again."

Getting into his office, he began to feel the passion for his country's service slowly returning. Thinking of Red Sword, the colonel needed to speak to Yukorov. Picking up his phone, he called the KGB agent's office and asked if he was in.

Recognizing the colonel's voice, the secretary said, "Yes, sir. He's in. May I tell him you're coming down?"

"Yes. I'll be down shortly."

Getting up from his desk, Petroff walked the two flights of stairs down to the second floor, thinking how weak his legs felt. He opened the door and was saluted by the two guards stationed there. Saluting back, he was glad to be in the Kremlin and sober.

As Petroff walked into Yukorov's office, the secretary immediately got up and opened the inner door, saying, "He'll see you now, Colonel. It's nice to see you back."

He smiled, and nodded as he walked into the long office, seeing the KGB officer sitting at his desk.

"Come in, Colonel," Yukorov said, getting up from his desk and extending his hand across the table.

Shaking hands, Petroff said, "It's good to be back, Vlad. I was in a very dark place."

"I understand, Colonel. You've been through a great deal, and to tell you the truth, you've been missed here."

"There are some empty spots in my memory. Can you tell me how I got to the hospital?"

"One of the secretaries was leaving and saw your overcoat sticking out the back door of your car. She was going to open your door and push the coat back inside when she found you and thought you were dead. Immediately, she got security, and they called the ambulance. The ambulance was leaving the parking area when I pulled in. I didn't know you were the one in the ambulance until I got inside and was told by security. I immediately went to the hospital to make sure you were all right."

"Thank you, Vlad. I think I vaguely remember seeing you at the hospital. But I can't be sure. I feel like a damn fool. Been living with a prostitute and drinking a fifth of vodka almost every night. I damn near killed myself." He watched Yukorov as he described Sinesha.

Yukorov didn't let on one bit.

"You're getting back to your old self now, Colonel, and that makes me happy. We have much work to do. Things are starting to fall into place. It's good to have you back, and now I don't have to worry about you being killed."

The colonel thought there were two meanings to that statement. "I'm not 100 percent. But I'm much better than I was. I'll not touch another drop of alcohol for the rest of my life. I'm done."

"Okay," Yukorov said. "I'm going to give you another week or two to really get your feet back on the ground. Then, I'll bring you up to speed. But let's give you a little more time because you're still pretty rough around the edges. You need a good healthy diet, and I've taken the liberty of contacting your former maid, Tanya. I asked her to come back to your place five days a week and cook for you. She has agreed and will be there tonight when you get home. She said she still has a key to your house and will have a good meal for you. We need to get you healthy again."

"Thank you, Vlad. I was actually thinking the same thing," Petroff said, lying. He had always suspected Tanya was a KGB plant. Now he felt certain since Sinesha was not sleeping in his bed. Yukorov was going to continue surveillance any way he could. "Yes. In a couple more weeks, I'll be even better."

That evening when Petroff got home, he could see Tanya's small grey car parked on the street. Walking into the house, he smelled the evening meal of potatoes, fresh bread, and meatloaf, and it smelled great. He hung his hat and coat on the rack by the door and walked into the dining room where Tanya was standing.

The two gave each other hugs.

Then looking at the prepared food, the colonel said, "Thank you."

"You're welcome, sir. Please sit and enjoy your meal."

Seeing her pick up her jacket to leave, the colonel said, "No, please stay. Eat with me, please."

Tanya laid her jacket back down, walked into the kitchen, and retrieved another plate and silverware. Sitting down at the table she said, "Thank you. I'll leave whenever you would like to be alone."

"Well, let's eat. It's good to have someone to talk to," he said.

CHAPTER 13

FINAL PLANS

Wednesday, May 27, 1987

GENERAL VADIM VANEREV FLEW TO TSELINOGRAD, Kazakhstan, two thousand miles north of Kabul. Meeting in the luxury suit of the Ishim Hotel, the assembled group seated at the large table was solemn but determined. They all felt the fate of their country depended on them to be strong. In their hearts, they all believed they were true patriots, and they were not going to let their country continue its ruinous slide.

Speaking first, General Vanerev gave an overview of how the drugs were to be taken from Afghanistan to America.

Mr. Sergie asked, "How much money will be raised?"

"If this goes as planned, we will have eighty-nine million dollars by winter," General Vanerev said.

Mr. Sergie and the other men at the table nodded approval.

Continuing, the general said, "It's not one hundred million, but I feel it will be enough. With that money, we'll have the ability to do what we must. I'll have time to get my army out of Afghanistan and back to Moscow by early next year. This will also give General Kavzo time to bring his commanders and others to our cause before we strike. We must all understand what is at risk here. If we're not able to stop our country's demise and be victorious in this mission, we'll all hang and our country will cease to exist."

Victor Krakov, head of the KGB Foreign Intelligence Branch, agreed with the general. "We must stop this lunatic before he destroys the Soviet Union. Gentlemen, this is the fight of our lives. What we do here will determine if our country survives or we become the dust of history. Most of us have fought in the last world war. We have always thought the defeat of Germany was our greatest success. General Vanerev made us all proud when he threw the defeated Nazi banner at the foot of Lenin's tomb. But history has once again asked us to defend our great country from destruction, this time from within. I'm prepared to give my life for my country if need be. But I'll not go down without a fight, and this is a fight we must make."

"General, how much time do you need to get back to Moscow, once your withdrawal begins?" asked General Damian Kavzo, former commander of the Far Eastern Military District. Kavzo had recently been ordered to Kazakhstan to quell the nationalist riots after Dinmukhamed Kunayev was replaced as First Secretary of the Communist Part of Kazakhstan.

"Six months minimum," Vanerev said. "Especially over the winter, it'll be difficult to get some of my troops out. I'll need at least through spring."

"That's my estimation too," Kavzo said. "So we're looking at next summer before we will be able to launch Operation Red Sword. I know my men, and they all see what's happening. When the time comes, we'll have overwhelming support from the military. Without that support, or if that support drops for any reason, we will fail. We will then all die traitors instead of patriots. Vadim and I have fought together for forty years. We are the oldest of friends. We have endured tremendous sacrifice, and we have watched our brave men fight and die for the Soviet Union. We will not let our country down, not when we are needed the most."

"I agree and we must make sure we have the continued support from our people," Karl Gopov, secretary of the Central Committee of Komsomol of the USSR said. "We must have the youth, the populace, and the unions on our side. We must be able to convince them when the time comes that we offer an improvement in their lives. Gorbachev has been trying to remove conservative managers, and this will ruin the Komsomol organization. We must be able to show that Western influence promotes nothing more than disloyalty to the party and hooliganism." A very deep thinker, Gopov was a welcomed member of Red Sword, as well as the chairman of the KGB in Latvia.

Finally, the fifth member of the inner circle of conspirators, Nikoli Sergie, chairman of the State Committee on Prices, spoke again. Having graduated from the Moscow Finance Institute, he was a renowned economist. He believed in a strong centralized government to maintain strength and stability for the USSR and didn't feel that Gorbachev's decentralization strategy was going to do anything but destroy them all. Holding the purse strings to the country's wealth made him one of the most powerful men in the Communist Party, and he knew it. He was not only an intelligent man but also an egomaniac. He felt he would make a much better leader than Mikhail Gorbachev, and he would try to prove that. In his mind, the world revolved around wealth and had nothing to do with honor and sacrifice. He would make sure the eighty-nine million dollars were well spent and asked, "General Vanerev, where will this money be hidden, and who will have access to it?"

"Mr. Sergie, those questions need answers. Where do you suggest the money be kept?" General Vanerev asked.

"It must stay overseas in an account that cannot be touched by any government. Right now, Luxembourg has the most secretive banking laws and rules in the world. Any bank there would be very secure. The Cayman Islands are second, but they are too closely scrutinized by the CIA. I would not advise any of them. And there is no bank in the Soviet Union that I would trust, too much corruption," Sergie said.

"I'll pass that to Yukorov. He can make sure we use a bank in Luxembourg," Vanerev said, looking at the others in the group and then to Krakov, who nodded his approval.

"If we have good luck," Kavzo said, "and keep this operation secret, I'm beginning to feel we have an excellent chance to save our country. We need this luck to continue."

General Kavzo had no way of knowing, but the coup god was about to smile on them. And it came the next day in the name of Mathias Rust. The young German landed a Cessna 172 single-engine airplane in Red Square. Minister of Defense, Marshal Sergei Sokolov was fired by Gorbachev. The Soviet impenetrable air defense had just been defeated by a teenager flying a rented plane. General Damian Kavzo was promoted to marshal and named the next minister of Defense. This placed Marshal Kavzo over all Soviet forces throughout the entire world on May 30, 1987.

Gorbachev had made it known; he wanted all Soviet forces out of Afghanistan as soon as possible. But Marshal Kavzo, now in command, would make sure General Vanerev was given enough time in Afghanistan to complete Red Sword.

Not everyone was so lucky. Gorbachev used this occurrence to purge several military officials who opposed his new liberal policies. To Gorbachev, this improved his grip on power. But it actually made it easier for members of Red Sword to recruit more military and KGB personnel who now wanted Gorbachev, if not dead, gone.

CHAPTER 14

Small Pieces

Monday, June 1, 1987

Davis was helping Clarence check irrigation lines on the many grape trellises. The small plastic drip lines would be used as the spring rains stopped. As he walked over to the holding pond used for this purpose, Davis's pager went off. Looking at it, he said to Clarence, "I need to place a call. Be right back."

"No hurry," Clarence said.

Getting back to the CJ, Davis opened the bag phone, pulled his notebook out of the backpack, and called the office number for Ray Taylor, US Coast Guard.

"Hello, United States Coast Guard, Special Agent Taylor. How may I help you?" he asked.

"Ray, it's Tony," Davis said.

"Hey, sorry it took a while to get back to you. They've been working on transferring all of our microfiche to computers, and it's taking longer than expected."

"No, problem. What did you find out on the *California Rose*?" Davis asked.

"Sixty-four-foot tug, diesel engines, purchased from Sacramento Tug, Corning, California, in January 1986 by Mary Rogers, co-owner of Supply Masters, Inc. The other owners are Harold Rogers Sr. and David Williams. Home port of Napa and company address of 1063 Almond Hill Lane, Napa, California. Former name of vessel was *Ruby Rebel*. No hits on Coast Guard, NADDIS or EPIC, so it looks clean," Taylor said.

"Okay, great. Thank you, Ray," Davis replied.

"There were a couple of things, though," Taylor said. "And they are probably nothing, but I'll throw them out there anyway."

"Go ahead. I always listen to my gut."

"Well, David Williams is an attorney who has an office address in Villa Park near Los Angeles. Now it's certainly not unusual for attorneys to partially own boats, but not usually a tugboat. Pleasure craft like a sailboat, sure, but tugboats? I just thought it was out of place."

"Okay, where does Harold Rogers Sr. live?" Davis asked.

"Dale Road, Corning, California. About one hundred miles north of Sacramento."

Where does Mary Rogers live?"

"She has a home address of May Road, Richmond, California."

"You thinking what I'm thinking, Ray?"

"Yes, that's the other thing. Who the hell lives on Almond Hill Lane in Napa?" Taylor asked?

"Think I'll do a drive-by, then go to the Napa County Tax Office, and look up that address. It'll have the owners listed," Davis said. "Hey, do you have a friend in DMV?"

"Yes, I do."

"Contact them. Get all those people's driver's license information, date of birth, addresses, what cars they drive, and their tag numbers. We may need that later on. Great work, Ray. If you ever need anything, you just let me know. Would be a pleasure working with you.

"Yes, you as well, Tony. And let me know who lives in Napa, if you don't mind."

"I sure as hell will. Thank you, Ray. Talk soon. Goodbye," Davis said and hung up. He thought about all the information Ray had given him, checking over what he'd written down and making any additions to his notes. Good start, he thought as he saw Clarence walking back towards the house.

"You need me anymore today?" Davis asked.

"No, we're done. It's almost four o'clock. You coming back tomorrow?" Clarence asked.

"If you don't mind, I have some errands to run. We have most everything ready, don't we?"

"Yes, we'll need to spray, but that's not for another month or two. So go ahead and take care of whatever you need to do. I'll see you when you get back."

"Thank you, you're a great guy. I don't care what Becky says."

Clarence laughed as Davis drove out of the ranch.

On Madrone Road, Davis turned right and then made a left on Route 12. In a mile, he turned right onto Trinity Road. He enjoyed that drive over the mountain to Oakville and then south to Napa. After he did a drive-by on Almond Hill Lane, he'd stop at his mother's house on Scenic Drive.

Going up over the mountain, Davis made the tires squeal several times on the CJ, coming out of the turns. Just before arriving at Oakville, Davis pulled over and got out his Northern California road atlas, finding Napa and then Almond Hill Lane. Davis saw that Almond Hill Lane was off Hagen Road, near the Napa Valley Country Club. Back on the road, he turned south on Saint Helena Highway and headed towards Napa. Almost into town, he turned left on Trancas Street and then again south on Silverado Trail. Coming to Hagen, he turned left and said, "Wow, nice homes."

Almond Hill Lane was on his left, and he drove slowly, checking the mailboxes for numbers. Finding 1063, he could see a large ranch-style home and a smaller home across the driveway. "Hmm," Davis said. "Two families perhaps."

Getting back out onto Silverado Trail, he turned west on First Street, on out to Browns Valley Road, and then to Scenic Drive. Parking the Jeep at 3309, he walked in the front door and yelled, "Anybody home?"

"We're out back, Nathan," he heard his mother say.

Walking through the living room and out the back door to the pool, he could see his mother and Bud in the hot tub that was connected to the pool.

"How are you guys doing tonight?" he asked as he gave his mother a kiss on the cheek.

"Great. Go get your trunks on and get in. The water's warm," his mother said.

"No, I need to get a shower. I've got Sonoma Creek mud between my toes," Davis said. "How are you, Bud?"

"Wonderful. Your mother and I are just wonderful," he said with that big Bud Yoder smile and laugh.

"Cool," Davis said and thought how heartwarming it was to see his mother happy with this really great guy.

"You mind if I stay tonight?" Davis asked. "I need to go to the tax office tomorrow."

"Of course, you can. Food in the fridge if you're hungry," Bud said.

"Thank you. I need to get cleaned up first," Davis replied.

Standing in the hot shower, Davis ran everything through his mind several times. Still nothing seemed to fit. Just a bunch of small pieces, he thought. After drying off, he put on his shorts and T-shirt and went back downstairs. In the kitchen, he got a piece of ham lunchmeat and a diet coke out of the refrigerator and then stepped onto the patio by the pool. Noticing there was no screen door covering the opening, he asked, "Don't you have bugs out here?"

"Not many. Not like back home," his mother said. "You'd be eaten up with mosquitoes back there. Here we have some, but not what you're used to."

"Good deal. Nice," Davis said

"Yes, it's a different world out here," his mother said.

THE NEXT MORNING, DAVIS GOT UP just in time to see his mother and Bud leave the house.

"You must've been tired. You don't normally sleep that long," she said.

"Clarence is working me to death."

"Who's Clarence?" his mother asked, walking into the garage.

"A guy I'm helping out. Have a good day," he said as his mother waved, getting into their white Cadillac as she and Bud left the home.

After getting another shower and putting on clean clothes, Davis picked up the Napa phone book and found the address for the Napa County Assessor's Office on First Street. It opened at 8:00 a.m., but it was still early, seven o'clock. Remembering Bud saying the Butter Cream was the best place to eat breakfast in Napa, he looked that up too. It was on Jefferson Street, only a couple of blocks up from the assessor's office.

Davis got in the CJ, drove the few blocks, and stopped a few minutes later. Liking the pink and white stripes on the sign that said Butter Cream Bakery and Diner, he walked in. It was packed with people, and it smelled of fresh pastry with bacon frying. Hungry, he found an empty seat at the counter and placed his backpack at his feet.

"What would you like to drink?" a waitress asked, handing him a menu.

"Black coffee, and I already know what I want."

"Okay, what would you like?" she asked.

"Two eggs over easy, ham, fried potatoes, and English muffin."

"Be right up," the lady said, writing on her pad as she walked away.

Looking around, Davis could tell why Bud told him to come here; it was a great little place that this community loved.

The waitress brought Davis's coffee, set the cup down, and placed silverware wrapped in a napkin on the counter.

"Thank you," he said.

"You're welcome."

Not much later, she returned with the breakfast and refilled his coffee cup. Taking his time, he enjoyed the meal, the atmosphere, and the people there. So very nice, he thought. After paying and getting back out onto the sidewalk, Davis slid onto the CJ's seat, pulled out, and was not surprised when his parking place was immediately taken.

"This little place is a gem," he said as he turned toward the assessor's office. Walking in the light-brown brick building, he asked the lady behind the counter, "How do I look up an address of a piece of property I'm interested in buying?"

"That's easy. Come with me," she said as she walked into the next room. "This is the map room. You find the property you're interested in on the map. It will have a parcel property number. Once you know that number, you find the ledger that contains that number, and you look it up. We run a little behind on updating the ledgers, but only by a month or so. If the property has been owned longer than that, the names listed as the owners will be current."

"Thank you," Davis said. "I can do that." He stood there, waiting until the lady returned to the assessors' counter, not wanting her to see what property he was looking at. Laying his backpack on an empty table, he took out his notebook, found 1063 Almond Hill Lane on the large map, and wrote down the parcel number. From the ledger shelves that covered three walls, he pulled out the large ledger that corresponded to the number. Thumbing through the pages, he finally found the number that also showed the property address.

He wrote down the owners' names, Doug and Sara Lawson, 1063 Almond Hill Lane, Napa, California. Placing the ledger back, Davis slid his notebook into his backpack. As he walked out the door, he thanked the lady for her help. Back in his Jeep, he pulled his bag phone out of his backpack and called Taylor's pager number. Not one minute later, Davis's bag phone rang. "That was quick," Davis said as he answered the phone.

"I was just sitting here at my desk, thinking about where to eat lunch," Taylor said.

"Where do you eat lunch? Do you have a cafeteria there?"

"Yes, we have a mess hall, pretty good food. You thinking about coming my way?"

"Yes, I'll be leaving Napa in five minutes."

"Okay, good. Just come to my office, and we can grab some lunch later. I have a pot of coffee on now. You got some information?"

"Yes, I do. Will see you in a couple of hours."

"Roger that," Taylor said.

I really like that guy, Davis thought as he pulled out of Napa and headed south. Arriving at the Coast Guard facility on Yerba Buena Island, Davis showed the guard his ID and parked next to the Quad buildings.

"What did you find out?" Taylor asked standing at the top of the stairs next to his office.

"Doug and Sara Lawson," Davis said.

Writing down Doug and Sara Lawson, Taylor said, "L-A-W-S-O-N?"

"Affirmative," Davis replied. "Run them through DMV too. There may be two families living there or another family member. Maybe a mother-in-law or somebody living in the spare house."

"Spare house?"

"Yes, there are two homes on the property. It's very nice. Whoever lives there has money. Once we get their data, we can then check criminal records through the National Crime Information Center. If need be, we can run it through the IRS and see where they work. This may not be anything, but it's still a good project."

"Yes, I agree. That tug is just a little hinky," Taylor said. "Let's eat. I didn't have breakfast."

"Sounds good."

CHAPTER 15

Money and Drugs

Monday, June 8, 1987

Colonel Petroff walked into the Kremlin feeling like a new man. His hair was cut, he was clean shaven, and he was wearing a crisply pressed uniform. He was back in the light and was never returning to that darkness. Being sober now, he knew exactly what Masha would have thought of his behavior. He pledged to himself he would now start living the life she would want him to live.

Saying good morning to Luba, he bent down, kissed her on the cheek, and walked on into his office and closed the door. Luba smiled. Taking his bug wand out of his briefcase, he swept the room, knowing it had been a perfect time for Yukorov to bug his office. Not finding anything suspicious, he placed the wand back in his briefcase and locked it. At his desk, he began going through the enormous amount of mail that was in his bin. He promised himself he would never be gone that long again. After two hours, he was finally able to clear his desk.

Sitting back, he tried to remember when he last contacted Buddy. His memory was still not clear about somethings and dates. But he was sure it had been over six months. The fact was Petroff had nothing else to tell his friend, other than he'd been drunk during that entire time.

"I need to get with Yukorov and see what's going on," he said softly and picked up his phone. Calling Yukorov's office, Petroff asked the secretary if the KGB agent was in the building.

"No, sir," she said. "He's in Afghanistan and will be back in two or three days."

"Thank you. Please inform him when he gets back to contact Colonel Petroff."

"Yes, sir, I will. Have a nice day, Colonel."

"Thank you," Petroff said and hung up.

IN KABUL, AFGHANISTAN, KGB STATION CHIEF Vladimir Yukorov and General Vadim Vanerev were discussing where to hide the money once it was received from the Americans.

"In discussion with the group," the general said, "we have determined that the best and safest place to keep the money is in Luxembourg. I need you to ask the American if he has experience with any of those banks. And if so, which one, and whom do we contact? Make sure you express to him how secret this communication must be."

"Yes, sir. I'll do that," Yukorov said. "General, I've been in contact with drug lord Afridi. He says they'll be ready by mid-July to transport forty-five tons of hashish to Karachi. From there it will be loaded onto the KGB vessel *Poliksena* and taken to the North Pacific where it will be transferred to the American's vessel. From there, it will take the American ten to fourteen days to get back into San Francisco and then unload it. After delivery to America, sometime in late September, our money will be released by the buyer."

"That's good, Vladimir," the general said.

"So far, General, everything is going according to plan. I'll be bringing Colonel Petroff up-to-date when I get back. I want to get his opinion on some of the operational aspects of what we are doing. I don't believe I'm overlooking anything, but I trust his opinion on tactical operations. I'll see what he says," Yukorov added.

"Up-to-date?" the general asked.

"Yes, sir. His wife died last fall. He's been going through a rough period."

"I'm sorry to hear that. Give my condolences. And, yes, talk to the colonel. I want to hear what he says."

"Yes, sir. I will. I'll also advise you as soon as I talk to the American about Luxembourg. Things will start happening quickly now since we're through the winter, and the snows have melted in the high country. The trucks can start transporting the hashish. One more thing, General," Yukorov said.

"What is it?"

"I need your permission to move Russian assets away from the travel routes. We can't have our Mi-24 helicopters targeting those trucks."

The general thought for a moment and said, "Yes, we must think of the greater good in all of this. Move whatever assets you feel will be a danger to our mission. If anyone questions your orders, tell them these orders have come directly from me. Understood?"

"Yes, sir. I do. Very well, General. I have more work to do. I'll advise as soon as I hear from the American. Good day, General."

The general nodded but didn't reply and turned from the KGB agent.

As Yukorov reached the door, he heard a bottle rattle as the general was opening his desk drawer. He continued to his office, calculating the time in California. It was 10:30 a.m. here in Kabul, making it 11:00 p.m. the day before there. Reaching his office, he picked up the phone and called Terrence George Valley's home number.

"Hello," Valley said as he answered the phone on Little Bluff Road.

"It's Vlad. We need to use a bank in Luxembourg to deposit the money. Do you have any experience with using them?"

"Yes, I do," Valley said, rubbing his face to wake up. "I've used the Bank of Paris in Luxembourg several times with no problems. We can have our money shipped from Canada to Luxembourg at any time."

"Why from Canada?" Yukorov asked.

"Because Canada doesn't have the currency reporting requirements the United States has. We can have US dollars delivered from the Federal Reserve Bank in New York to the Monarch National Bank also in New York. Monarch can then directly ship the money to a Canadian Money Exchange and from there anywhere in the world, even back if need be. The money can be electronically sent, or we can have cash or bearer bonds delivered. And the authorities have almost no way of tracing it."

"Good, then that won't be a problem," Yukorov said. "Remember, I need to speak directly with the money handler soon. I'll need the account numbers and to confirm what bank we are using."

"No problem. I've already told my contact that you'd be calling him. His name is Phillip DePantera, Monarch National Bank, New York, and this is his number," Valley said, giving Yukorov the telephone number for the bank financier of the largest drug syndicate in the United States and Canada.

"I'll contact DePantera tomorrow and tell him to expect your call," Valley said. "And make sure you use my name as George Hannah."

"All right, I will."

"Also, I have everything in the works here as far as the vessels," Valley said. "This is what we're planning to do. We have the tugboat, and we are in the process of obtaining a fifty-ton barge. We're going to place cargo containers on top of the barge with marine parts stored in them. This will appear as if we are supplying the parts to offshore vessels. The inside of the barge will be cleaned and painted to store the drugs. Once the drugs are inside the barge, the hatches will be welded shut so no Coast Guard Safety Inspection will be able to access the inner compartments of the barge. We can say we welded the hatches to prevent any water flooding in at sea. We feel that should be secure enough to prevent any discovery of the shipment by the Coast Guard."

"Is that the only people we need to worry about?" Yukorov asked.

"No, but if we're able to get the vessels back into the United States without being stopped by Customs, we'll be pretty safe. Out at sea, the Coast Guard is the main problem. At the border, it's Customs and somewhat the DEA. I've seen Customs cut open a teak deck on a five-million-dollar luxury yacht with a chainsaw, not find anything, and then just walk off. If they have any reason, they can cut the barge open to inspect it. But they have to catch us at the border. If they don't see us actually crossing the border, then they don't have a nexus. If they lose their nexus, they're not allowed to do shit."

"Okay, that sounds good," Yukorov said. "I've spoken to drug lord Afridi, and the hashish will be transported to Karachi by August 1. It will take a day or two to load the shipment into the *Poliksena*. The *Poliksena* can make twelve to fifteen knots and will then travel to Thailand. It can be in the Gulf of Thailand by the twelfth or thirteenth of August to pick up the Thai marijuana. Can your people deliver the Thai to the *Poliksena* then?" Yukorov asked. "It'll be going by callsign *Western Star*."

"Yes, I'll make sure they can," Valley said. "*Western Star*. Got it. The Thai vessels is the *Mala*, and its captain is Captain Saelao. They'll be operating on frequency 136.2. Give that to your captain. He can contact the *Mala* once he gets into the Gulf of Thailand. It should not take over a day to offload the Thai. So if the *Western Star* leaves Thailand on the thirteenth and can make twelve to fifteen knots, they should be able to arrive in the North Pacific around the first of September."

"Yes, I agree. Let's set September 5 as our rendezvous date. That way we have a few days to work with," Yukorov said.

"Yes, that'll be good in case of bad weather or something. September 5," Valley repeated.

"Also," Yukorov said, "you'll need to bring your barge plans to Hawaii so I can approve them before the *Poliksena* delivers the hashish. This is extremely important for us, and we cannot have any doubt of success. I'll need to approve your plans to hide the drugs before we let them be taken by your captain. My superiors demands that I do this."

"I understand, but this is going to be cutting it very close at a time when we'll be the busiest," Valley said. "Let's meet the first week in August in Hilo. That'll give us time to have the plans and the work completed if there needs to be any changes."

"Agree," Yukorov said. "That'll work. I'll start calling you more often, every couple weeks or so. We can then discuss any changes or problems."

"Yes, I think that's wise. As we get closer to the shipping dates, we'll need to be speaking more often."

"Yes, I agree," Yukorov said. "Goodbye."

"Goodbye," Valley said and hung up.

The next morning at 9:00 a.m., Valley called Monarch National Bank in New York.

"Monarch National Bank. How may I direct your call?" the operator asked.

"Phillip DePantera, please. This is George Hannah," Valley said.

"Just a minute, Mr. Hannah," the operator said.

After a couple of minutes, DePantera was on the line. "Good morning, George."

"Good morning, Phillip. You remember the Russian I told you about that will need to talk to you?" Valley asked.

"Yes, I do."

"Good. I spoke with him yesterday, and he'll be calling you soon. We also discussed using the Bank of Paris in Luxembourg. Do you see any problem with that?"

"No, I do not. They're still very secure, and we highly recommend that particular bank as well."

"Good," Valley said. "To reiterate, do you remember our pricing and your requirement to have Thai with the hashish?"

"Yes, just a minute," DePantera said as he pulled a file out of his desk with the name of Hannah on it. "To confirm, I'm buying one hundred tons of hash and twenty tons of Thai, the hashish from you for 1.3 million per ton and the Thai, nine hundred thousand per ton. However, the Russian needs to know only that I'm paying him 1.1 million per ton for the hashish. I'm also to tell him that I require the Thai or no deal. Do I have that correct?" DePantera asked.

"Perfect," Valley said.

Finishing the conversation with DePantera, Valley called Bergford Money Exchange in Toronto, Canada.

"May I speak to Steve Petrov, please? This is George Hannah," he said to the operator.

"One moment, please," she said.

A few seconds later, Petrov said, "Good morning, George.".

"Good morning, Steve. My vessel will be in the Gulf of Thailand by August 12. It's the *Western Star*."

"That'll be fine with us, George. I'll let my people know to be out there and waiting. Should not be any problem at all. And you said *Western Star*, correct?" Petrov asked.

"Yes, and they will be monitoring your frequency," Valley said.

"Very good, George. You have a nice day."

"You too, and thank you, Steve," Valley said as he hung up.

CHAPTER 16

Bigger Pieces

Wednesday, June 10, 1987

Taylor had paged Davis a few minutes earlier from his office, and when he called back, Taylor said, "I got the DMV information on the Lawsons."

"Good. What is it?"

"Doug drives a silver 1986 BMW 535i. No citations or accidents.

"Nice car," Davis said.

"Yes, expensive," Taylor said.

"Sara drives a white 1986 Lexus LS400. Again, no citations or accidents."

"Both nice cars," Davis said.

"There's nothing in NCIC on either. Do you want me to contact my IRS friend and see what they can come up with?"

Davis thought for a few moments and said, "No, my mother lives in Napa. Let me ask her and my stepfather if they know them before we do that. I don't want the IRS snooping into someone's business if they don't need to. That would piss me off if I weren't guilty of anything."

"Yes, I agree. If you want to ruin someone's day, tell them the IRS is looking up their ass. No one likes the IRS."

"If need be, we can always bring the IRS in later to look at bank records and tax returns," Davis said. "I'll check with my mother and see what she knows first."

"Okay. Let me know what you find out."

"Will do. Thanks, Ray," Davis said and hung up his phone while sitting in his Jeep on the west side of McAvoy Harbor. He had driven around the harbor roads and gotten a closer look at the *California Rose*. It's still here, Davis thought as he turned around at the chain-link fence gate, noticing a chain and padlock on it. I need to check out this location once a week to see if there's anybody around or changes to the vessel, he thought; so far, nothing. Heading back towards Route 12 and Napa, he planned to drive by his mother's store in Sonoma and ask her about the Lawsons.

An hour and a half later, Davis pulled into the rear of Yoder's Furniture Store on Broadway. Walking in the open, large, overhead door in the rear, he could see his mother and Bud relaxing in a couple of La-Z-Boy recliners on the display floor.

"Trying out the merchandise?" Davis asked.

"Yes, it's been slow this afternoon, so we're taking a break," his mother said with a smile. "Have a seat, Nathan."

Not seeing anyone else, Davis sat down on a couch next to the recliners and asked, "Do you know Doug Lawson from Napa?"

"Yes," Bud said. "He works at a bank in Napa, LendBest. He's a bigwig there. I think he is their chief appraiser. Nice guy, he's married to Sara."

"I don't know Doug," his mother said. "But Sara is very active in the Napa Church. I don't know her well, but know her if I see her. Why?"

"Well, I was thinking about trading in my Jeep for a truck, and Clarence said to talk to Doug Lawson at the bank in Napa." West didn't like lying to his mother and stepfather, but it was for their own safety. They didn't need to know the real reason he was asking.

"I would get rid of that thing too. Jeeps are not safe, and it makes too much noise," his mother said.

Davis laughed and said, "Yes, it does. I'll see. Not going to trade in anytime soon. But," he lied, "I'm thinking about it."

"You going to stay the night?" his mother asked.

"No, I need to get back to the city tonight. I have some paperwork that needs to be finished. I'll leave you guys to relax. You both look comfortable."

After giving his mother a kiss on the check and shaking hands with Bud, Davis said, "See you later," as he walked out the back of the store.

"Be careful, Nathan," his mother said.

"I will," he said climbing in his Jeep and revving the engine a couple extra times just for her.

Looking at Bud, she said, "He needs to get rid of that damn thing."

CHAPTER 17

NO LOOSE ENDS

Thursday, June 11, 1987

YUKOROV LANDED AT MOSCOW INTERNATIONAL AIRPORT at 3:00 p.m. and was met by his security detail. "Take me to the Kremlin," he instructed.

Seeing Colonel Petroff's car in the Kremlin parking area, he told his two guards, "Stay here. I'll be back shortly." He got in the elevator, bypassed the second floor where his office was, and continued to the fourth floor. Getting off the elevator, he walked into Petroff's office and was greeted by Luba.

"Hello, Mr. Yukorov. Would you like to see the colonel?"

"Yes. Is he in?"

"Yes, sir, just a moment," Luba said, walking into the colonel's office and closing the door behind her. Returning a minute later, she said, "Come in, sir. The colonel will see you now," and held the door open for the KGB agent.

"Come in, Vlad. How have you been?" the colonel asked, getting up from his desk and greeting the officer.

Yukorov could clearly see the colonel was back to his healthy self and once again had a spring in his step. Shaking hands, he said, "I'm doing well, Colonel. And I must say you look better."

"Thank you. Have a seat," Petroff said, motioning to a chair next to his desk and closing the door. "I do feel much better. I was in a poor way, and the recovery was difficult."

"Yes, I'm sure," Yukorov said.

"So, Vlad, what's the latest? I've missed much I know."

"Not a great deal, Colonel, but some. I had a couple of meetings with the general and confirmed some details from the American."

"Okay. How do things look at this point?" Petroff asked.

"Surprisingly good, Dimi. We're going to have forty-five tons of hashish ready to ship by August. The KGB vessel *Poliksena* will transport the drugs from Karachi to Hawaii. There, the American will receive the drugs and take them into San Francisco, probably in September.

"The American will need a very large vessel to carry that amount of drugs," Petroff said.

"A barge. The drugs will be hidden inside a barge and pulled back to America."

Petroff nodded his head and said, "Yes, that'll work well. How are they disguising the barge to not look suspicious?"

"There will be containers on top of the barge full of supplies for other vessels. It'll look like a resupply operation."

"Interesting. Anyone inspecting the vessel will have to look through all the supplies before looking elsewhere. By then, they'll have had enough searching and give up," Petroff said.

"Yes. I believe this is a very secure way to smuggle the drugs into America," Yukorov said.

"This all sounds good. Anything else?" Petroff asked.

"The committee has determined that the money must be held in a bank in Luxembourg. They apparently have the strictest secrecy laws for banking. I'm to call the money man in New York and make sure we are using a bank in Luxembourg. The American has used one there as well, and he agrees."

"I see," Petroff said. "While I was gone, I got to the point to where I wished Gorbachev had already been removed. You know why?"

"No," Yukorov said, studying the colonel's face.

"Because the vodka would be cheaper," Petroff said with a laugh.

Yukorov laughed as well and said, "Alcohol will make a man change his perception."

"Yes," Petroff said soberly. "I thought I was having a good time until I realized I was killing myself."

"Well, you're back now, Dimi. I need to get home, and take a hot shower from all this traveling," Yukorov said, standing. "I'll speak to you soon."

"Thank you for stopping by, Vlad," Petroff said, shaking hands with the cold-blooded killer as he was leaving.

Walking out to Luba's desk, the colonel sat down in a chair and said, "I want to thank you from the bottom of my heart for not quitting on me during my depression. I was not a very nice person then. I know how difficult it must've been for you."

"Colonel, you're a good man. I knew you would find your way back. I was not going to desert you when you needed me the most. We have always been friends, and you have always treated me with respect. You will always have my loyalty, sir," Luba said.

"Thank you," the colonel replied. "It's after four o'clock. Please take an early day. I'll not have anything else for you to do this afternoon."

"Thank you, Colonel. The flowers are blooming and calling me," she said, getting up from her desk and taking her coat. "Have a nice evening," Luba said as she left the office.

"You as well, Luba," the colonel said.

Returning to his desk, the colonel picked up his phone and called Yukorov's office. "Is Mr. Yukorov still in his office?" he asked.

"No, sir. He was here only for a moment and said he was going home. He was tired from traveling," the secretary said.

"Okay, thank you. I'll catch up with him tomorrow. Goodbye," Petroff said. He looked at his watch; it was 4:15 p.m. It'll be 8:15 a.m. for Buddy, he thought. Tanya would be at his home fixing dinner. He knew he had to go there, eat, and then return to the Kremlin for a more secure call later.

Fifteen minutes later, Petroff left the Kremlin, walked to the parking lot, and got in his car. Although the vomit had been cleaned from the back seat, the smell still lingered. Perhaps I should scrub it again, he thought, as he rolled down his window. Driving towards his home, he repeatedly glanced in his rearview mirror. Now he was sure of it; he was being followed. Way back, over a block away, he had caught only glimpses, but he was positive he was being followed by Sinesha's car.

Arriving at his home, he welcomed the smell of dinner that Tanya had prepared for him. She'd already left, but the note she always laid on the table made him smile. "Have a nice and relaxing evening, Colonel," it said. Removing his uniform jacket and laying it over one of the kitchen chairs, he sat down and enjoyed his meal. Finished, he placed his plate and silverware in the sink and rinsed them off, as Tanya had asked him to do. Reaching under the sink, he removed a plastic trash bag, picked up his jacket, and walked to the bedroom where he removed this shoes, shirt, and trousers. Folding them all, he placed the uniform and shoes into the plastic bag, tying it closed, and lay it on the floor.

In the spare bedroom, Petroff opened the closet and pulled out an old footlocker. Opening the combination lock, he looked at the tools of his old trade that he'd not practiced for many years as Russian Special Forces Officer. He picked up a switchblade knife that was closed, pushed the button, and the blade sprung open. Feeling the blade's edge, he knew it was still very sharp. "This will do."

He put on an old pair of trousers, a long-sleeved, dark pullover shirt, and an older pair of shoes. Petroff sat in his living room, thinking through what he was about to do. Patting the knife in his pants pocket, he knew that Masha would never approve. But for his life to be more secure and for him to be able to continue providing Buddy information that might save his country from a catastrophe, this needed to be done. He could not take any more risk with someone who knew him so well.

It was almost eight o'clock and getting dark when Petroff got up and took a small bottle of water out of the refrigerator. Carrying the plastic bag with his uniform to his car, he put it on the floorboard on the passenger side and laid the bottle of water on that side of the front seat. To make sure he was not being followed, he drove around town first in circles. Satisfied, he parked on the street down the block from Sinesha Orlov's home, walked up to her house, and knocked on the door.

As beautiful and sexy as ever, Sinesha opened the door, saying, "Hello, Colonel. This is a nice surprise. Would you like to come in?"

"No, I think it's best that I do not. But I owe you an apology, and I hope you can forgive me for my abrupt exit. I know you were trying to be kind."

"Your apology is accepted, Colonel. I know you were having a hard time."

"I hope we can still be friends," the colonel said. "Would you care to have a walk with me?"

"Well, perhaps some other time, but not tonight."

"That's okay, perhaps some other time when I'm not bothering you," the colonel said and prepared to leave, knowing women of her nature hated a man implying any type of emotional weakness and then walking away. That was a weakness Sinesha would not allow to be even suggested.

"Wait a minute, Colonel. Yes, I'll take a short walk with you," she said. "Give me a minute to get my coat." Not bothering to pick up her pistol, she would show this man. She proudly walked out her door and closed it behind her. Sinesha was a KGB assassin, and she would not allow any man to imply she was a frail woman.

The spring evening had a slight chill as the two walked around the block, making small talk about their relationship, the sex, and the alcohol. And the entire time, the colonel thought, she was there to kill me. That thought made it easier for what he was about to do. Coming to a darkened alley, the colonel glanced to make sure there were no other people on the street. There were none.

Putting his hand in his pocket, Petroff pulled out the knife and pushed the button to open the blade. At the same instant, he grabbed Sinesha's long black hair, jerking her head backwards to expose her neck. Trained killers don't scream, and she couldn't have even if she wanted to. The blade of the knife was now stuck through her neck as the colonel picked her up by her hair and the knife he now held in her throat. Quickly moving deeper into the dark alley, he shoved her face down on the pavement and cut from the inside out towards the front of her neck, severing all the major arteries and her windpipe. He wiped the blood-covered blade against her jacket, closed the knife, and walked back towards his car as her feet finally stopped kicking.

Driving towards the Kremlin, the colonel thought how, although he'd killed women before, that had been in combat; this was the first time he'd killed a woman with a knife. But any regretful thoughts were quickly dismissed when he reminded himself she was there only to kill him. To him, she deserved this death. Less than half a mile from the Kremlin, as he was crossing the Bolshoy Moskvoretsky Bridge, he tossed the knife out the car window into the Moskva River. Near Red Square, he pulled over and quickly removed his shoes, shirt, and pants in the car. Opening the door, he washed the blood from his one hand with the bottle of water.

Across the street, Petroff saw a homeless man and quickly put on his uniform and stuffed his old clothes and shoes in the bag. He got out of the car and walked over to the old man. "Here, old man, I have a gift for you," the colonel said, handing over the bag of old, blood-stained clothes.

"God, bless you, sir," the old man said with a smile, as he looked in the bag at the clothes, shoes, and bottle of water.

"God had nothing to do with this," the colonel said and walked back to his car.

Arriving at the Kremlin, he returned the salute to the guards that were still on duty as he walked up the stairs to the fourth floor. He could tell he was getting stronger climbing the stairs each day. Reaching his office, Petroff could also tell he was becoming very cold-blooded. He closed his office door, locked it, and thought, No loose ends; it'll look like she was killed by a junky.

CHAPTER 18

Lock, Stock, and Barrel

2:00 p.m., June 11, 1987

HAYDEN WAS BEGINNING TO ADDRESS the new border patrol class. As one of his many duties as the program director of FLETC, he would give each new class a quick overview of the facility and the many amenities offered while being a student there. To this old CIA undercover operative, this was a pain in his ass but a necessary one to maintain his cover as the special agent in charge of the FLETC Division of the CIA.

Feeling his pager going off, Hayden glanced at it while still speaking. The number displayed made him stop—1880, the date he had been shot in Kabul, saving the life of Russian Colonel Dimitri Petroff. Starting over, he finished the description of the cafeteria and its policies. He glanced at his watch, 1:00 p.m. He had sixty minutes to finish before Petroff would call Hayden's STU-II in his DOD office. He finished in six and in closing said, "*Bienvenidos a* FLETC," as he walked out of the classroom.

Jumping in his Jag, he called the Administration Building.

"Admin. How can I help you?" asked Delores, Hayden's receptionist.

"Cancel my classes for the rest of the day. I just got busy."

"Yes, sir," said Dr. Delores Mitchell, clinical psychologist of CIA FLETC.

At the DOD building, Hayden limped his way into his office and locked his office door behind him. Opening his safe, he retrieved the keys to open the STU-II cabinet door and the STU key. He slid the STU out, picked up the receiver to check for a dial tone, and satisfied, glanced at his watch; it was one fifteen. Getting ready for the call, he got his notebook out and wrote in the date and time on a new page. He was in deep thought when, forty-five minutes later at exactly 2:00, the STU rang. "*Moy dobryy drug*," Hayden said.

"My good friend," Petroff repeated in English, meaning both were in secure locations and could speak freely, using their old code from years before.

"I've been worried about you, Dimi," Hayden said.

"I'm good, my friend. But I have bad news. My Masha has died," Petroff said as tears swelled up in his eyes.

"My God, I am so deeply sorry, Dimi. I wish there were something I could do."

"She's in no more agony, and I'm comforted by that thought."

"We are now both alone, Dimi. Two old soldiers that deserved to die years ago, but we haven't. I'm sorry, my friend." Hayden now felt again his own grief over the loss of his wife, Sophia, a few years before.

"*Da*, Buddy. I wish I could speak to you longer, but I cannot."

"Yes, what do you have?"

"KGB vessel *Poliksena* will deliver forty-five tons of hashish in August or September to the American. The drugs will be hidden in a barge and taken to San Francisco. The barge will have containers on it to disguise it as a supply vessel. They'll also be using a bank in Luxembourg. That's all I have. Take care, Buddy," Petroff said, preparing to hang up.

"One question, Dimi. Who killed President Amin? Who pulled the trigger?"

"Why the question, Buddy?"

"I know a former CIA agent who knew Amin's killer. That agent now lives in northern California."

"Yukorov, Vladimir Yukorov, KGB, Zenyth, he's part of the coup group. They call themselves Red Sword. Buddy, that's who I get my information from," Petroff said. "I watched him shoot Amin," knowing this connection was a vital one.

"Damn. Got it, Dimi. That gives us our link here."

"Yes, it does. Goodbye, Buddy."

"Goodbye, Dimi, and prayers," Hayden said as he hung up.

Hayden reread his notes and made sure everything was correct. He also added that he needed to find out if the vessel Davis had found, the *California Rose*, could pull a barge. Hayden knew he needed to call the new director of the CIA, William Weatherby. The former director, William Casto, had died on May 6 from a brain tumor, and Weatherby had ordered briefings on all current high-value operations. Thorn was on top of the list. Hayden had spent several hours with the new director, informing him of the operation from the start and to its status at that point. He liked Weatherby, but he was not the old school OSS officer that Casto had been.

Hayden now found he no longer enjoyed calling headquarters as much. Thank God June is still there, he thought. Picking up the phone on his desk, he called CIA headquarters in Langley.

"Director's Office. How may I help you?" June McDonald, secretary for the director of the Central Intelligence Agency, said.

"Hi, beautiful," Hayden said.

"Hi, Buddy. When you coming to see me?"

"Not sure, baby. Is the director in?"

"Yes. Would you like to speak to him?"

"Yes, but tell him to call me on my STU, please, here at FLETC."

"I'll do that right now. Come and see me. I need to feel some soreness," McDonald whispered with a laugh.

"As soon as I can, baby, as soon as I can. Goodbye sexy," Hayden said and hung up his phone.

Hayden placed the STU key in and waited for it to ring. When it did, he picked it up, said, "Three, two, one," and turned the key at the same time as Weatherby did.

"Hello, Buddy," Weatherby said.

"Hello, sir. I heard from my source ten minutes ago. A KGB vessel called the *Poliksena* will deliver forty-five tons of hashish to an American vessel. The American vessel will then bring the drugs to San Francisco in August or September. The drugs will be hidden in a barge disguised as a supply vessel with containers. They're also going to funnel their money through a Luxembourg bank."

"That's good intel," Weatherby said. "But will that make them their one hundred million dollars?"

"No, not even close. About half."

Pausing to think, Weatherby then said, "That puts us in a quandary, doesn't it?"

"Yes, sir. If we take that shipment, our operation is exposed. The KGB will just change their shipping destination and crew next time. We'll only set them back six months, max. And then we'll have nothing to go on."

"Agreed," the director said. "We need to disrupt them after their supply of drugs is removed and before they make their money. How do we accomplish that?"

"I don't know. I'm not sure if it can even be done," Hayden said.

"Okay. I'll update Howard Baker, the president's chief of staff. You keep at it. Tell those boys to keep digging hard and deep. Do you think the vessel Davis found is involved?"

"We don't know that yet. Something about it doesn't add up, but nothing for certain. There's another piece of information."

"What is it?" Weatherby asked.

"Valley, Terrence George, one of our former agents. He now lives in Northern California, and he knows a member on the coup group that is KGB. Yukorov is his name," Hayden said. "They call themselves Red Sword."

"I know both of those names from the FBI. Where did Valley meet the Russian agent?" Weatherby asked.

"Afghanistan. He may have been moving drugs with the Russian," Hayden said. "Valley was supplying the mujahideen with Stingers through ISI."

"Yes, that's where I know those names. Valley was a little shady, and Yukorov was the station chief for the KGB in Kabul." After a pause, the director said, "Do you need me to place a team on Valley?"

"No, sir. Jack Reynolds has that covered. Valley lives on the end of a gravel road, and there's no place to surveille from without being burnt. We'll take care of him."

"Okay. Keep me informed of any changes. That's good work, Buddy. Stay on it."

"Yes, sir. Goodbye," Hayden said and he hung up the STU.

SITTING AT HIS DESK IN CIA HEADQUARTERS in Langley. Weatherby was trying to remember where else he'd heard of Yukorov's involvement while still the director of the FBI. "Bedford. That's it. Charles Bedford. Yukorov was his KGB handler in Mexico City," he said to himself.

AFTER ADDING TO HIS NOTES OF THE CONVERSATION with the director, Hayden called another number.

"Hello," Reynolds said, answering the STU in Vacaville.

"We need to key in. Three, two, one," Hayden said as both men turned their keys. "I bet you're enjoying sitting on your ass in Vacaville watching the *Lone Ranger*."

"Close, but no. I prefer *Laverne & Shirley* reruns," Reynolds said. "To tell you the truth, I'm getting bored out of my fucking mind."

"Well, this may help. I can tell you details about me fucking Melinda. Then you'll have something to fantasize about at night."

"Please, God, don't. I wouldn't be able to sleep with that image in my head—an old grey possum trying to fuck a beautiful swan," Reynolds said.

"Okay, maybe this will help. I heard from Petroff."

"Now, why does everyone feel the need to fuck with me? If it's not you, it's Davis. Just give me the fucking information straight out next time. I don't need the details of you violating some young woman. What do you have?"

Hayden relayed the same information to Reynolds that he had told the director and then asked, "Can the *California Rose* be used to pull or push a barge that's disguised as a supply vessel with containers on board?"

"Yes, that's exactly what they're built for."

"Do we have a barge located yet?" Hayden asked.

"No, we don't. And if they're going to use one in two or three months, they'd better be getting one soon," Reynolds said.

"Are we onto the wrong people?" Hayden asked.

"Perhaps, but there's no way of knowing. We'll just have to keep on this until we know otherwise or find something else."

"Okay, and this next bit of information is going to make you get a hard-on," Hayden said.

"Let's see," Reynolds said.

"Valley knows the KGB station chief from Kabul. And this particular Russian is not only part of the conspiracy, but he's also the one providing my source with information. Oh yeah, and remember when I told you that Greg Wolfe said Valley knew Amin's assassin?

"Yes, a Russian. Don't tell me."

"Yes. He's the guy that put the bullet in Amin's head. His name is Vladimir Yukorov."

"I'm getting a woody," Reynolds said. "Okay, so we know the KGB would never tell anyone unless they needed to know. The question is whether the KGB needed Valley for this operation. I'd say we need to assume he's involved until proven otherwise."

"Yes, I agree. He's on top of the list, and his standing keeps getting firmer," Hayden said.

"Hot damn," Reynolds replied. "If Tony is correct on this tug, then we have who we're looking for."

"Lock, stock, and barrel," Hayden said. "Get Davis on the barge. We need it found."

CHAPTER 19

Find the Barge

Noon, Friday, June 12, 1987

After getting off the phone with Hayden, Reynolds paged Davis with 10210501.

Davis had left the Hayward safe house three hours earlier and was driving down Solano Street in Corning when his pager went off. Seeing it was Jack wanting him to call his phone number with the last four digits of 0501, he pulled into the 7-Eleven parking lot, picked up the receiver of his phone, and called Reynolds.

"Hello," Reynolds answered.

"It's me, Jack," Davis said.

"Where you at?" Reynolds asked.

"I'm in Corning."

"Corning. I can be there in little over an hour. Get a room there and call me back. We need to talk."

"Roger that, will call you back in a little bit." Davis had just passed a Super 8 Motel. He turned around in the parking lot and headed back west on Solano Street. Walking into the motel, he said to the lady behind the counter, "I need a room for tonight."

"How many people, sir?" she asked.

"Just me."

"I'll need to charge you ten dollars more for early check in since it's before three p.m."

"That's fine," Davis said, handing the lady his credit card, and filled out the guest registration.

"May I see your driver's license, sir?" she asked.

"Yes," Davis said, showing his Oregon driver's license and then putting it back in his wallet.

"Okay, sir. Room 112. Park wherever you like."

"Who delivers pizza to the motel?" he asked.

"Marco's is just across the street, very good and fast. The number will be on a card in the room."

"Thank you. Have a nice day," Davis said as he walked out of the office.

Driving the Jeep down the side of the building, he parked in front of room 112. He picked up his phone and backpack, entered the room, and laid the phone on the small table and backpack on the floor. Then he called Reynolds.

"Hello," Reynolds said.

"Get off on the Solano Street exit. Super 8, half-block on your right. Room 112. How soon you coming?" Davis asked.

"Leaving now. Be there by one thirty."

"Okay, I'll order pizza. It'll be here when you get here."

"Sounds good."

Davis hung up his bag phone and walked to the air conditioning unit. "I like it cold," he said as he turned the thermostat to sixty-eight and pushed the cool button. Taking his 9mm out of the backpack, he laid it on the table as he sat down. He found the card for deliveries and called the number for Marco's Pizza.

"Hello, Marco's Pizza. How can I help you?" the cashier asked.

"I need to order a meat lovers pizza and two Pepsis. But I don't want it delivered until one fifteen. Can you do that?" he asked.

"Where are you located?"

"Across the street. Room 112 at the Super 8."

"Yes, that'll be no problem. Do you want to pay cash or give a credit card number?"

"I'll pay cash."

"Okay, sir. Your total will be twelve fifty."

"Thank you," Davis said and hung up.

Taking his notebook out of the backpack, he began looking at what he'd written over the past week. He wanted to make sure he told Jack everything he'd found out.

At one fifteen, there was a knock on his door. Peeping though the side window, he saw a young Hispanic boy holding a pizza box and a bag. Davis opened the door and asked, "Did you walk over?"

"Yes," the boy said.

Taking the pizza box and bag containing the two Pepsis, Davis handed the boy a twenty-dollar bill and said, "Keep the change. You're a hard worker."

"Thank you, sir," the boy said as he walked back towards the pizza shop.

Closing the door, Davis put the pizza box and bag on the table. He opened the box, picked up a slice of pizza, and took a big bite. "Damn, that's good," he said, opening one of the Pepsi cans and taking a drink.

Davis was glancing at his notebook again when he heard a truck pull into a parking place next to the Jeep. Walking to the door, he glanced out the window, saw Reynolds getting out of his pickup, and opened the door. Reynolds stepped in as Davis shut the door behind him.

"Pizza's still hot, and there's a Pepsi in the bag."

Reynolds took a slice and sat down at the table as he ate.

"What's going on, Jack?"

"The source called Buddy. Forty-five tons of hashish will be hidden in a barge and smuggled into San Francisco in August or September. The barge will be disguised as a supply vessel with containers on it. And Valley knows a KGB agent who's one of the conspirators."

"So if Valley is in on this, then I need to connect him to the *California* Rose. I also need to connect the *California Rose* to a barge, assuming the *California Rose* is also part of the operation and a barge does show up," Davis said.

"Yes, that's correct. You need to start a link chart, and I'll do the same. It's a lot easier connecting the dots with everyone involved and their connections if it's on a wall in front of your face," Reynolds said.

"I was thinking the same thing. We need to get everyone linked up," Davis said.

"Yes. Have you seen many barges in your travels?"

"Yes, a couple. Most of them have been down around the Concord and Pittsburg area where there are large industries and the oil refinery.

"Okay, keep an eye out because, if we're onto the right people, they'll have a barge showing up very soon."

Davis looked at Reynolds intently.

"What?" Reynolds asked.

"Tell me again about the barge and containers."

"The drugs will be hidden in a barge disguised to look like a supply vessel with containers on top."

Davis sat back in his chair and said, "Supply vessel, probably owned by a supply company?"

"Yes, more than likely and with containers on the barge to look like a supply vessel. So no one would suspect it carrying drugs," Reynolds said.

Handing Reynolds a clean sheet of paper and a pen, Davis said, "You're going to need these. The Coast Guard RAC Dale Case and one of his agents, Ray Taylor, have been especially helpful. I gave them the name of the *California Rose*, and Taylor ran it. Owner of the *California Rose* is Mary Rogers. She is co-owner of the company with Harold Rogers Sr. and David Williams. The home port of the *California Rose* is Napa. The address given for the company is 1063 Almond Hill Lane, Napa. Makes sense so far, right?" Davis asked.

"Yes," Reynolds said.

"Well, Harold lives here in Corning. Mary lives in Richmond. And David Williams who is an attorney lives near LA in Villa Park."

"Who lives in Napa at the company address?" Reynolds asked.

"The Almond Hill Lane address is a nice home, actually two, a big home and a smaller one like a mother-in-law place. This property is owned by Doug Lawson, a banker at LendBest in Napa, and his wife, Sara Lawson. Doug is well known in Napa and so is Sara. She is a big church goer. Can you run David Williams through the database and see what it shows up? I would love to know his story. I don't know about you, but my skin is starting to crawl."

"Yes, I'll give that name to Buddy and see what Langley can come up with," Reynolds said. "What else do you have?"

"Nothing else, other than the name of the company."

"What is it?"

"Supply Masters, Inc." Davis said, dragging out the word *supply.*

Reynolds looked at Davis. "Holy shit!"

At 2:00 p.m., standing at the Brandenburg Gate in West Berlin, President Ronald Reagan was giving a speech that he hoped would further unite the two great superpowers. Speaking of eliminating nuclear weapons and allowing more freedom, he directly addressed the general secretary of the Soviet Union when he said, "Mr. Gorbachev, tear down this wall!"

CHAPTER 20

Stalin's Birthday

10:00 a.m., Monday, June 15, 1987

YUKOROV WAITED UNTIL IT WAS 6:00 P.M. in Moscow before he dialed the number Valley had given him.

"Monarch National Bank. How may I direct your call?" the operator asked.

"I need to speak to Mr. Phillip DePantera," Yukorov said.

"Who may I say is calling, sir?" the operator asked.

"Tell the gentleman Moscow is calling."

"Yes, sir. Just a few moments please," she said. After a minute, she transferred the call.

"Hello, this is Mr. DePantera. How can I help you?"

"We have a mutual friend, Mr. Hannah. He gave me your number."

"Yes, and may I ask your name, sir?" DePantera asked.

"Yuk, my name is Mr. Yuk."

"Very well, Mr. Yuk. How may I assist you?"

"These conversations are extremely sensitive. Do you understand that?" the KGB agent asked in a veiled threat.

"Yes, Mr. Yuk. I'm fully aware of the confidentiality that's required here."

"Good, I need to know the bank we'll be using and the account number. I can then confirm all this before releasing the shipment."

"Yes, of course, Mr. Yuk. We'll be using the Bank of Paris in Luxembourg. I can provide an account number for you, in your name, and it's spelled, Y-U-K, correct?" he asked.

"Yes, that's correct."

"Confirmed. But first I need to know what eight-to-ten-digit code number you would like to have placed on the account. This way, you can call the bank at any time, give your name and code number, and have access to the account. The only other person that'll have that information, of course, will be me. I can then transfer money into that account and then check to make sure it has been received."

Thinking it would be easy to remember Stalin's birthday, Yukorov said, "12091879."

DePantera repeated, "That's 12091879," and then asked, "Is that correct?"

"Yes, it is."

"Very good. Now I can either call you back in a few minutes or place you on hold while I set up the account. What would you prefer?"

"I'll hold. You'll not have my contact information."

"Very well, please hold for a few minutes. I'll set this up and be right back," DePantera said.

Ten minutes later, DePantera came back on the line. "Okay, Mr. Yuk, the account is all set up, and this is the account number," DePantera said, giving the KGB agent the number, as well as the address and phone number to the Banque De Paris, Luxembourg. "Also, Mr. Yuk, when you call the bank, ask to speak to Mr. Andre. Tell him I set the account up for you. He's my personal contact at that bank, and he'll take exceptionally good care of you. And, Mr. Yuk, I've deposited one thousand US dollars in this account. You can confirm the amount whenever you wish."

"Very good. I'll do that," Yukorov said.

"One more item, Mr. Yuk. I have the ability to deposit money into that account. And I have the ability to place a hold on the money in that account. This way, when the shipment is received, the money will be released. Prior to that release, you'll have the ability to inquire how much money is being held in that account. Do you understand, Mr. Yuk?"

Yukorov didn't like being held over a barrel, but he had no choice. "Yes, I understand."

"Very good, Mr. Yuk. It's been my pleasure speaking and working with you. I look forward to a long and prosperous association. Do you need any other assistance?" DePantera asked.

"No, you've been very helpful. I'll check that account soon. Goodbye, Mr. DePantera."

"Goodbye, Mr. Yuk," DePantera said, and both men hung up their phones.

Thinking for a few minutes, Yukorov once more picked up the phone and called General Vanerev's personal number in Kabul.

"Hello," the general said, answering the phone on his desk.

"General, it's Vladimir."

"Yes, Vlad."

"General, I've spoken to the American. He is aware of and has used the Bank of Paris in Luxembourg. Today, I called the financier for the New York organization. He set up an account for us with the Bank of Paris in Luxembourg. I'll call and confirm that the account exists," he said.

"Very good, Vlad. You're making good progress."

"Yes, General, so far there have been no major problems. Things have been going well. General, do you want the account number and passcode?"

Thinking for a moment, the general said, "No, I don't need to know that right now, perhaps later."

"Okay, General. I'll keep you informed. Good night, sir."

"Good night, Vlad," the general said and hung up his phone.

AFTER GETTING OUT OF JAIL IN LA, Dude finally showed up at McAvoy Harbor. He'd been installing new radios and a radar on the *California Rose* and had finished earlier that morning. Then he, Carlin, and Willard took the vessel to Concord to get the fifty-ton barge. Bringing the barge into the harbor at McAvoy was no easy task. The barge was 110 feet long, thirty-five feet wide, and eleven feet tall. They had to use a smaller tug owned by Harold Rogers Sr. to assist getting the huge barge up against the dock.

Walking over the top of the deck with Carlin after getting the barge secured, Willard said, "This is like a small football field."

"Yes, it is," Carlin said. "We'll be able to make some money with this big boy. I have some jobs near Hawaii coming up where we'll need to supply vessels out at sea with parts. They pay big money too."

"That's great. I hope you hire me to go," Willard said. "I need a new truck."

"Don't worry, you'll be there," Carlin said. Although he knew Willard smoked pot and wouldn't say a word about bringing a load of drugs back in, for now, he needed to think it was a supply job.

DAVIS WAS PARKING AT YERBA BUENA ISLAND when Taylor pulled in. "You have a good weekend?" Davis asked.

"Yes, got to spend a little time with the wife. Mowed the grass. And we went to see a new movie that just came out."

"What did you see?"

"*Platoon,* hell of a movie, a bunch of killing, about the Vietnam War. Glad I missed that conflict."

"Yes, me too. That was fucked up. A lot of good people on both sides died."

Walking in behind Taylor, Davis shut the door to the office and said, "I know who Doug and Sara Lawson are."

"Who are they?"

"Bankers. At least Doug is, for LendBest in Napa."

"So that's where they get their money from," Taylor said.

"Yes, and they are well-thought-of. Big church goers and pillars-of-the-community type people."

"Well, that pretty much eliminates them," Taylor said.

"Yes, perhaps, but I'll keep watching the tug in case anything else comes up. But so far, you're right; it's been a dead end." Despite his words, Davis knew there was a small possibility things were just getting started.

CHAPTER 21

Get It Done

Wednesday, June 17, 1987

Carlin was happy to see Billy Little show up that morning in his green pickup. He needed someone who could engineer the work that needed to be completed on the barge.

"About time you show up," Carlin said as he shook hands with his cousin.

"Been busy, Carlin. You know how it is running whores."

"No, I wouldn't know," he said with a laugh. "Most of those women are crazy, and you fit right in."

"I'm telling you, it's damn good pussy," Little said with a laugh. "Okay, what do you have in mind?"

"I need to tow that barge to Hawaii, load it up with forty-five tons of hashish and ten tons of Thai, and bring it back here. I need enough fuel to get to Hawaii, as well as keep the drugs hidden so no one can find them."

"Wow, that's a crazy amount of drugs. How many compartments are there in the barge and how big are they?"

"Six compartments. The four inner compartments are fifteen feet long, thirty-five feet wide, and eleven feet high. I've figured it up. There's about 5,800 square feet in each of the four inner compartments. The end compartments will not be used since they are accessible from the outside. From what I've been told, a bag of hash will take up about the same amount of space as a bag of concrete, about two and a half square feet, and weigh about fifty pounds each. If we have forty-five tons of hash, that's ninety thousand pounds and about eighteen hundred bags. Eighteen hundred bags will take up 4,500 square feet. So one compartment will hold the forty-five tons of hashish easy. Another compartment can hold the ten tons of Thai."

"Damn. How much money you making on this?"

"Two million. They don't know it yet, but they're going to pay me half up front before I risk my ass in bringing this back in."

"I can't blame you there. You'll be taking the risk. Those other people can run if this goes bad. You'll be stuck on this damn boat with the Coast Guard pointing guns at you. What are you going to do? Jump overboard and drown yourself?"

Carlin looked at Little and said, "I need you to make sure the drugs cannot be found. I'm thinking to keep enough tools in a container on top to where we can cut open the deck over the compartments, drop in the bags of hash or boxes of Thai, and then reweld the deck and paint over it."

"Yes, that'll work if we can waterproof the compartments. Will need to see what we have once we get inside."

"There are top hatches on each side of the compartments. You can go down in from there. We can weld the hatches shut once we have the drugs loaded," Carlin said.

"That sounds good. Let's get it done," Little said as he walked towards the barge with a flashlight in hand. Going from one compartment to the next, Little opened up each hatch on the top side of the barge. He leaned down in, shined the light into each corner of the compartment, and checked out the condition of the walls and floor, trying to see how much water, if any, was on the floors. "Some rust and water, but not too bad," Little said to Carlin. "We'll need to sandblast the inside and clean it thoroughly, reseal the seams with good waterproof caulking, and then repaint with a high-quality marine paint. We can use one compartment for fuel. Run a nipple up to the deck surface under a cover. Use two other compartments for the drugs. I think that should work fine and will take care of most of the problems. The big thing is to keep the fuel and drugs dry. If you get salt water in your fuel, that'll be a pain. If the drugs get wet, they'll need to be dried out."

"I've been thinking about that," Carlin said. "I'm going to tell Valley to make sure the drugs are vacuum sealed if they can. That way, even if a box or bag gets damp, it's still no problem."

"That's a good idea, and most good packers are doing that now anyway," Little replied. "The drugs are normally hermetically sealed, so moisture isn't a problem. But you need to check with him to make sure."

"That'll save a worry of mine if they are. I'll mention that to Valley. I need to get this work done as soon as possible. Who can we hire?"

"I know a few guys I can get, all family members or close friends. They're good hard workers that will keep their mouths shut. We should have all this completed in a month or so. After we get the inside done, then we can decide how many containers you'll need on top to carry all the tools and parts," Little said.

The next day, Little had three more men working with Willard on the barge and the *California Rose*. The once quiet west side of McAvoy Harbor became a busy worksite overnight.

CHAPTER 22

Carlin Rogers

9:00 a.m., Saturday, June 20, 1987

Davis was drinking his morning coffee and looking at the link chart he'd created and pinned on the wall in the kitchen. The three-by-four-foot piece of drafting paper was starting to take shape with what little he knew. "I need to add more names, places, and dates," he said. "The only problem is I don't know any more names, places, or dates." I need to hit the road again and see if I can find anything else, he thought. He took another sip of the hot coffee and put the cup in the sink.

By ten fifteen, Davis was heading east across Interstate 580 out of Hayward and then north on Interstate 680. Almost to Walnut Creek, he turned onto Highway 24 towards Pittsburg. I doubt if anything's going on today at McAvoy, but it's worth a look, he thought, as he got off the highway in Pittsburg and took Willow Pass Road. Then on around to Port Chicago Highway, he drove into McAvoy Harbor.

"Holy shit!" Davis said as he made the loop at the end of the harbor road, looking across to where the *California Rose* was tied up. There was now a large barge next to it with half a dozen vehicles parked on the road next to the tug. He could see a couple of men standing on the barge as he made the loop.

"Holy shit," he said again as he drove back around to McAvoy Café. Going inside, Davis sat on the side bar where he could look back outside towards the docks.

"What would you like to have?" the lady asked behind the counter.

"You serving breakfast or lunch?"

"Honey, whatever you want," she said.

"Bring me two buttermilk pancakes, three eggs over easy, sausage with English muffin."

"Links or patties?"

"Links and black coffee, please."

"Just a few minutes, sugar," she said as she walked away.

That should take the cook long enough for those guys to break for lunch, Davis thought. He would make sure he ate slow. Ten minutes later, the waitress came back with a huge plate with the pancakes, eggs, and sausage all on one and the English muffin on a smaller one. She placed both in front of Davis and refilled his coffee.

He was only about half-done with his meal when he watched an old green pickup and a red crew cab pickup come from the direction of the *California Rose*. Pulling into the restaurant, two men got out of the green truck and four men out of the red truck. The driver of the red truck was a very large, blondish-haired man with sideburns. All six entered the building together and took two booths off to the side. The large man and another man took one booth, and the other four men took the second booth. After the waitress took their orders, the men began to talk among themselves.

Davis ate his meal as he listened to their conversation. One man in his early twenties laughed often and was particularly loud. Davis heard someone call him Willard. The large man didn't speak much. When he did, he spoke softly to the man across the booth from him, giving Davis a couple of glances.

One of the men in the four-man booth said, "Billy, we're going to need more grit for the sandblaster."

"How many more bags do you think you'll need?" the man identified as Billy asked, sitting in the booth across from the large man.

"We have one more compartment to do after this one. We've used thirty bags, and we have five left, so another ten would be a plenty. That would give us some extra," the man said.

Willard then spoke up and said, "Gerald is the sandblasting king!"

The waitress started delivering the men's food to them as they all quieted down to eat. "Hurry up, fellows. I don't pay you to sit here and eat," the big man said, indicating he was in charge of the crew.

"How many checks?" the waitress asked.

"Just one," the big man said.

"Thank you, Carlin," Willard said.

"Shut your mouth and eat, Will," the man now identified as Carlin said as the waitress laid down his bill.

"Would you like anything else?" the waitress asked Davis as she returned to the bar.

"Yes, just one more cup of coffee, and then I need to get out of here. The breakfast was delicious," Davis said, knowing Carlin and a couple of the other men were now looking his way. "I'm stuffed. Those pancakes were excellent," he said as she refilled his coffee cup.

"I'm glad you liked 'em," she said, laying down his bill.

Davis sat there and enjoyed his coffee as the men began to get up and walk out the door. Watching the large man, Carlin, walk up to the bar, Davis said, "Morning."

"Morning," Carlin said to Davis, as he laid down several bills. "Keep the change," he said to the waitress.

"Thank you, Mr. Rogers," the waitress said as he turned to walk out the door and get back into his truck.

"That's one big man," Davis said to the waitress.

"Yes, he is, and super nice too."

Davis paid for his meal and said, "Keep the change. This was pleasant, and the food was great."

"You're welcome," the waitress said.

"By the way, I'm Tony. Nice meeting you."

"Joan. Nice meeting you too."

Taking the last few drinks of coffee, Davis left the café and got in his CJ. As he drove towards Hayward, Davis went over every detail in his mind that had just occurred. He now not only had the barge together with the *California Rose*, but he also had a man by the name of Carlin Rogers. While everything was still fresh in his mind, he would document all he'd learned and call Jack later.

Arriving at the Hayward safe house, he immediately went to the link chart on the kitchen wall. Adding Carlin Rogers's name to the middle of the chart, he drew a line from the *California Rose* to him. Then another line from Mary and Frank Rogers under Supply Masters, Inc., back to him as well. Adding "barge" next to *California Rose*, he then wrote Willard, Billy, Gerald, and two question marks for the two unidentified men underneath the vessels. Next to "barge," Davis wrote, "Sandblasting, 3 compartments?" Figuring if they had used thirty bags of grit already, with five remaining and needing ten more, there had to be three compartments they were getting ready.

Next to "Carlin Rogers," Davis wrote, "red Ford crew cab." He didn't know the license plate number since he hadn't been able to see it from where he'd been sitting. And he hadn't wanted to appear obvious trying to look at it. Next to Billy, he wrote, "old green Chevy pickup." Off to the far right on the chart he added the name "Valley," and wondered when he was going to be able to draw another line to him and from where. Taking out his notebook, he wrote down everything that had happened from the time he first saw the barge to the point of his leaving McAvoy. Putting "June 20, 87" at the top of the page, Davis realized it was West Virginia Day. "It sure as hell is," he said.

Then he picked up his bag phone, called Reynolds's pager number, and entered 10210499, meaning to call Davis's bag phone with the last four numbers of 0499. Two minutes later Davis's phone rang. "Hello," he said.

"Tony, it's Jack," Reynolds said.

"We really need to meet tonight, and we need to use a really nice phone when I get there," Davis said.

Reynolds thought for a few moments and said, "Come to Vacaville and get off the first exit, Alamo Road. Go back under the interstate, and there's a Big Lots up there on the left. Park in the parking lot, and I'll find you."

"I'm leaving in ten mikes," Davis said.

CHAPTER 23

Hitting the Fan

3:00 p.m., Saturday, June 20, 1987

Davis drove the Jeep into the Big Lots parking area, went to the far side of the lot, and waited. Seeing Reynolds's dark-blue F-350 crew cab pull up, Davis grabbed his backpack and got out of the CJ.

The side passenger window was down, and Reynolds said, "Get in the back."

Davis jumped in the back of the crew cab and lay down, holding his backpack.

"We shouldn't be seen together," Reynolds said.

"Yes," Davis replied.

"What do you have?" Reynolds asked.

"Everything. We're in business, Jack. Have you ever heard the name Carlin Rogers?"

"No, who is he?"

"The big man that's working on the barge tied up to the *California Rose*. What do you want to bet he's related to Mary and Harold Rogers Sr., owners of the tug and Supply Masters?"

"Fuck me," Reynolds said, as he drove up to the safe house on Barbera Court. He opened up the remote garage door and drove in while Davis lay still until he heard the door completely close.

Getting out of the truck, both men went upstairs to the living room where Reynolds opened the picture of Mt. Shasta and then the safe. Hearing an audible metallic click as the bookshelf moved to partially open, Davis said, "Your place is a whole lot cooler than mine, Jack."

Reynolds opened the bookshelf, exposing the inner room, desk, chair, STU, and cabinets.

"Way cooler than mine," Davis said.

Reynolds sat down and pulled out his large legal pad that he wrote on and said, "Go." Listening to Davis describe the events of the day, he wrote down every word.

Davis finished saying, "That's it."

Reynolds began to reread all he had written. When he'd gone over it twice, he looked up at Davis and said again, "Fuck me! Okay, what do you need?"

"I need Buddy to run Carlin Rogers. I need to know what size of underwear he wears and the brand. I need everything. Like I said, he's a large man, and just something about him made me think he's an ex-con."

"Why?" Reynolds asked.

"I've been around thousands of cons, and he had that air about him. No tats on his hands or neck that I could see, but I bet he has a record somewhere. One more thing about him, he's a professional. He has that confidence, you can just tell, an extremely cautious man. And with David Williams being an attorney, there has to be a connection there somewhere."

"Okay, let's get Buddy on the horn," Reynolds said, as he paged Buddy to the STU.

It was almost 6:30 p.m. on St. Simons Island. Melinda Hicks was sitting with Buddy Hayden at the Rafters blues bar. Hayden had been giving a lot of thought about retiring after this case was concluded, and he was seriously considering asking Melinda to marry him.

"What would you say if—"

Hayden's pager went off. Glancing at it, he thought, Fuck! "Honey, we need to go now. I need to go to the office for a while."

"What would I say about what?" she asked.

"Some other time, baby. We need to go," he said, as he waved for the waitress to take his credit card.

Hurrying back to Melinda's house, Buddy apologized for the abrupt night and kissed her as he hurried to get back in his Jag. He glanced back at his pager again to make sure of the number that had been put in by Reynolds, 1033707. Knowing 10-33 was emergency in ten codes, Hayden said, "What the fuck kind of emergency, Jack?" He sped to Glynco and the DOD building, got in his office, locked the door behind him, opened his safe, and got out his keys for the cabinet and STU. Dialing the Vacaville STU number at area code 707, he heard Reynolds say "Three, two, one." Then both men turned their encryption keys, and Reynolds pushed the speaker button on.

"What's going on, Jack?" Hayden asked.

"Buddy, Tony is here, and I have you on speaker," Reynolds said.

"Hi, Tony," Hayden said.

"Hello, Buddy," Davis said.

"Listen to this," Reynolds said. "We have a barge at the *California Rose* location, and they are working on it with at least six men. We have a name, Carlin Rogers. We need that name run. Davis feels he's an ex-con. And see if there are any connections to David Williams, the attorney out of LA."

"Who is Rogers?" Hayden asked.

"He's running the crew at the site," Davis said. "They're sandblasting the inside of the barge, at least three, maybe four compartments that they're going to refurbish or paint. There'd be no other reason to sandblast."

"How big is the barge?" Hayden asked.

"Over one hundred feet long, and I would say close to forty feet wide and pretty damn tall, ten to twelve feet, a big one," Davis said. "Is there any way you can run those names now?" he asked as Reynolds looked at Davis and nodded.

"You guys stand by. I'll call you back in less than thirty minutes," Hayden said and hung up the STU on his end.

Reynolds pushed the speaker button off and looked at Davis. Both men said not a word as thoughts a thousand miles an hour rushed through each of their heads.

"Valley?" Reynolds said looking at Davis.

"No, not yet," Davis said, knowing Reynolds was asking if there were any connections.

HAYDEN CALLED CIA HEADQUARTERS IN LANGLEY.

"How may I assist you?" the operator asked.

"Access code 717647," Hayden said.

"Phrase please?" the operator asked.

"Sophia's love."

"How may I help you, sir?" the operator asked.

"I need a tech supervisor stat."

"Yes, sir. One moment please."

Thirty seconds later, a man said, "Hello. How can I help? Do you need this call encrypted?"

"Yes. Three, two, one," Hayden said as he turned his key on the STU. "This is Buddy Hayden FLETC. Whom am I speaking to?"

"This is Ted Jackson. We've met before at FLETC."

"Okay. Ted, I need a stat run on the following names and possible locations. David Williams, Los Angeles, and Carlin Rogers, use Napa, California. Also run a vessel for me, the *California Rose*, Napa, California. Cross reference them all."

"Roger that, give me a few moments here. Let's see what we have," Jackson said.

Hayden could hear the computer keys being rapidly tapped, and after a few moments, Ted said, "Hmm, you've got some interesting fellows. You'll need to see this yourself, Buddy. Is your computer secure there at your office?"

"Yes, it is. Send all that you have to me," Hayden said.

"Hmm, this just keeps getting better and better," Jackson said as he went through the CIA database on the men. "Okay, I've sent everything that I have on this system. I'll check a couple other places and see if I can come up with any additional information. This is going to impress the hell out of you. If I get more, I'll contact you. Take care. Signing off," Jackson said.

"Thank you," Hayden said as both men hung up their STUs. As the information began to come through to Hayden's DOD computer, he sat there, looking at screen after screen. As he printed every page off, he could only say, "Motherfuck me," as he read and reread the information.

Picking up the STU, he called Reynolds back. When Reynolds answered, Hayden said, "You guys don't move. I'll be there in the morning," and hung up.

Reynolds once again pushed the speaker button off and looked at Davis. "The shit's about to hit the fan," he said.

Buddy Hayden was studying the documents he'd just printed out. "Dear mother of God," he said. Putting the documents in a folder, he picked his briefcase up off the floor, unlocked it, and laid the folder inside. From the back of the briefcase, he pulled out a small address book and thumbed through the pages until he found the number he was looking for, picked up his phone, and called Weatherby's home number. Getting the answering machine, Hayden said, "Buddy Hayden," and waited.

"STU in one minute," Weatherby said.

One minute later, Hayden dialed the director's STU number.

"Three, two, one," Weatherby said as both men encrypted their phones and then, "Go. What do you have?"

"Davis found a barge with the *California Rose*. There's a crew of men working there now. It's being run by Carlin Rogers," Hayden said.

"I know that name," Weatherby said.

"I thought you would. He was cellmates with Charles Bedford at Lompoc and helped him escape. Took him to Idaho and hid him out with his girlfriend in a cabin on some mountain."

"Yes, I remember him. What else?" Weatherby asked.

"Part owner of the company that owns the tugboat is David Williams, attorney David Williams, Charles Bedford's former attorney. Guess who was Bedford's KGB contact in Mexico City?" Hayden asked.

"I know that one. It was Vladimir Yukorov."

"Yes, and he knows Valley," Hayden said.

Weatherby thought for a few moments as he added it all up and said, "We can't let any of this out. If I were still the director of the FBI, I'd be pissed if I weren't briefed on this. I no longer sit in that chair. We keep this super tight; no one is to know. How much faith do you have in Davis?

"Explicitly, he's trade craft all the way. If any of this ever gets out, it won't be from him. Matter of fact, if anything ever leaks, I'd want him to plug it."

"Okay, superb work, Buddy. What are you doing next?"

"I fly to Sacramento tomorrow. I'm going to the safe house in Vacaville to brief Jack and Davis who are there now. I want to brief them in person."

"All right. I'll go to the White House on Monday and brief Chief of Staff Baker. And I pray there are no White House leaks. Good work, Buddy. Keep me informed and tell those men they'll continue as is until this is completed."

"Yes, sir. I will," Hayden said and hung up the STU.

Director Weatherby thought, I'm not going to break up or interfere with this team; they're too damn good.

Hayden called the number for the CIA Lear jet hangar at Glynco Jetport.

"Bobby," the voice said.

"Buddy Hayden, FLETC. I need to get to Sacramento Executive in the morning. Get that baby fueled up and have me a car in Sacramento."

"No problem, Buddy. What time do you need to be there?" Bobby asked.

"Noon," Hayden said.

"Okay, we lift off at seven a.m. We'll be bucking a head wind."

"I'll be there. See you at seven," Hayden said and hung up. For another thirty minutes, Hayden sat in his office chair, thinking what all this meant. He was positive, if this first shipment was going to make Red Sword only half the money needed, the CIA special agents would have to let it come into America unhindered. Hayden wanted to call Bob Klass on this but decided not to. The special agent in charge of the US Customs Service in San Francisco should have no knowledge of allowing forty-five tons of drugs walk into the United States under his watch. Hayden wouldn't put Robert Klass in that predicament.

Having made that difficult decision, he then smiled to himself and said, "Goddamn, Davis," as he got up and headed back to Melinda's place to pack his clothes.

CHAPTER 24

Only the Best

Sunday, June 21, 1987

Hayden couldn't sleep as he lay in bed next to Melinda. He'd been watching the clock since 4:00 a.m., and she was watching him.

"Will you ever be able to tell me what's going on?" she asked.

Hayden looked at her but couldn't immediately answer, as he was shoving different scenarios through his brain. A few moments later he said, "No."

"Okay. What were you going to ask me in Rafters yesterday?"

"If you'd marry me," Hayden said truthfully, looking at her.

"Bullshit! I know that's not true," she said with a laugh.

Hayden then looked at the beautiful sexy blond bombshell he was in love with resting next to him. Lying through his teeth, he said, "Honestly, I was going to ask you what you thought about me growing my beard back."

Melinda looked into the steely eyed man with a grin on his face and said, "If we were married."

As Hayden was getting out of bed he said, "If I didn't have to leave, I'd be fucking you about now."

"Well, don't be in such a hurry," she said as she pulled the comforter down to show her large breast.

Laughing, Hayden walked into the bathroom to take his shower.

After getting dressed and with his suitcase and briefcase in his hands, Hayden stood by Melinda. Wearing only a black thong, she opened the door. "Be careful," she said as she kissed him.

"Be back in a couple days," Hayden said as he headed for his Jag and the jetport. Arriving twenty minutes later, he drove up to a side gate at the airport where a guard was posted. He showed his ID, and the guard said, "Good morning, sir. They're waiting for you."

"Thank you," Hayden said as he drove to the hangar where the Lear jet was waiting outside. Parking the Jag to the side, Hayden walked over to the jet and began climbing the stairs where he was greeted by a man at the top. "Good morning, Buddy," the man said.

"Good morning, Bobby. Get this thing in the air."

"Yes, sir," Captain Bobby Taylor, CIA senior pilot, replied.

Taking a seat, Hayden yelled to a man in the right pilot's seat, "Good morning, Steve."

"Good morning, Buddy. Buckle up. We're lighting this candle," Steve Wilson, CIA co-pilot, replied.

Five hours later, Davis heard Bobby say, "KSAC control, November-zero-niner-Zulu turning final for runway two-zero."

"Ten-four, November-zero-niner-Zulu, you're cleared to land runway two-zero," the tower said.

Bringing the jet to a stop, Captain Taylor got out of his seat and opened the left side door. "How long do you need us to wait?"

"Be out of here tomorrow, Bobby," Hayden said walking down the steps. Stopping at the bottom he turned and said, "Thanks."

"You're welcome, Buddy. See you when you get back here," Taylor said.

Walking towards the hangars, Hayden saw a man standing next to a Thunderbird.

"Keys are in the ignition, sir."

"Thank you," Hayden said as he got in the car. Looking at his watch, it was 12:06 p.m. "Right on schedule," Hayden said as drove towards Vacaville. As he was coming into the town, he called Reynolds's mobile phone.

"Hello," Reynolds said.

"Open the garage door and move your vehicle over to the side. Be there in five mikes."

"Already done. Will open the garage door in four."

"Roger that," Hayden said and hung up his phone.

Five minutes later, Hayden was pulling into the garage at 143 Barbera Court. Waiting until the garage door was closed before getting out, Hayden exited the vehicle and grabbed his cases off the back seat. "Gentlemen," Hayden said looking at Reynolds and Davis standing at the bottom of the steps as he limped up. He walked into the living room, setting down the suitcase and laying the briefcase on the bar, and then shook hands with Reynolds and Davis. Looking around the room, he made sure all the blinds and shades were closed, and they were.

"Take a seat," Hayden instructed as he sat down on a stool at the kitchen bar and opened the briefcase. Taking out a folder, he opened it, and glanced at the contents. "I spoke with Director Weatherby yesterday and informed him of what has been uncovered. He wanted me to advise you that this team will stay intact until resolution of this affair, one way or another. I'll give a brief summary of what has transpired, and please interrupt me if I misstate any of this. This must be exact. If any of my information doesn't jive with what you know, say so. This is all from CIA data banks."

The men nodded for Hayden to continue.

"We have a tugboat, the *California Rose* in McAvoy Harbor near Pittsburg. We now have a barge with the *California Rose*. The *California Rose* is owned by Supply Masters, Inc. out of Napa, California. The officers of Supply Masters, Inc. are Mary Rogers, Harold Rogers Sr., Sara Lawson, and attorney David Williams."

"One minute. I didn't know about Sara Lawson being an officer of Supply Masters," Davis said.

"Yes. She's the secretary of Supply Masters. Her maiden name is Rogers," Hayden said.

Davis smiled and said, "There you go!"

Continuing, Hayden said, "We now have Carlin Rogers working on the barge tied to the *California Rose.* Supply Masters is located at an Almond Hill Lane address in Napa, and the owners of this address are Doug and Sara Lawson. Doug is a member of LendBest Bank in Napa. So far is that correct?" Hayden asked.

"Yes. Go on," Davis said.

"Carlin Rogers has been incarcerated most of his adult life. His last stint was at Lompoc Federal Prison near LA for counterfeiting. His cellmate was convicted Russian spy Charles Bedford. In December 1979, Rogers was paroled. In January 1980, Bedford broke out of Lompoc, was transported to Bonners Ferry, Idaho, by Rogers, and was placed with Rogers's former girlfriend, Gladys Wymes. Bedford and Wymes robbed seventeen banks in the Pacific Northwest over an eighteen-month period. It's suspected that Bedford and Rogers were trying to accumulate enough money to buy a boat to smuggle Bedford out of the country and to Russia. This was never proven, but it's felt that Rogers was to buy the boat," Hayden paused looking at the men as none spoke.

Continuing Hayden said, "KGB Agent Vladimir Yukorov was Charles Bedford's handler in Mexico City, where he was selling the secrets to the Russians. When Bedford was arrested in 1977, David Williams was his attorney. It's suspected that Williams is or was on the KGB payroll. Yukorov and Terrence George Valley of the CIA were working together in Afghanistan to smuggle small amounts of drugs into the US during 1984 and '85. Vladimir Yukorov was the KGB assassin that killed Afghan President Amin, his son, and mistress. He especially hates women and kills them every chance he gets. His mother was a prostitute." Hayden looked up from his papers and said, I wouldn't ever let him know you have a wife or girlfriend," and then continued reading from his notes. "Yukorov is also the person who is supplying my source with information on Red Sword. Carlin Rogers is brother to Harold Rogers Sr. and ex-husband of Mary Rogers. Sara Lawson is Sara Rogers Lawson and is Carlin and Harold's sister. Gentlemen, we know the cast to this movie."

Nobody spoke as the three men looked at each other.

Then Davis said, "If Carlin Rogers helped Bedford escape, then Yukorov would know Carlin Rogers, especially if he was going to be involved with buying the boat to smuggle Bedford out of the country. We can assume that Bedford had been in contact with the KGB after his escape and that Yukorov would have been at least informed of the escape, if not actually assisting to smuggle Bedford out of the country and back to Russia. That's why Carlin Rogers is involved with this. That's why David Williams helped start Supply Masters and purchase the *California Rose*. Yukorov, and I would say Valley, made all this happen, although we still don't have a connection of Valley to Rogers or the vessels."

"Yes, you're correct, Tony. And I think it's just a matter of time until we tie in Valley," Hayden said. "But we now must address what we are going to do next. If they bring in forty-five tons of drugs, that will make only half of their money. The question we have is, will that be enough, or will they be forced to bring in a second load to make the amount of money they want? We know Gorbachev wants the Russian army out of Afghanistan. However, I do not see the members of Red Sword pulling the plug on their source of revenue until they've got their money—or more importantly, think they've got their money. I believe they'll be forced to bring in another load or they'll not have enough money to run with this coup. Once they bring in the next load, whenever that may be, that's when we jump. We must allow the Russian army to begin its withdrawal from Afghanistan before we take the drugs and stop the payment." Hayden paused. "The timing of that may be an impossibility, but we have no choice."

"You're saying we let them bring in the first load," Davis said. "You're actually saying we guarantee that they bring in the first load. We protect that first load and them up to the point where we take the second load. But we must wait until the Russians begin their pullout before we even take the second load. So until all that happens, if it happens, we are running interference for them."

"Yes. If we expose ourselves and take down the first shipment, what will that do?" Hayden asked.

"Yes. I see your point. But damn the second-load timing. For them to pull out of Afghanistan is nothing we'll have any control over," Davis said.

"Right, none," Hayden said. "We'll have to rely on their wanting to get out of Afghanistan as soon as possible to get back to Moscow. One way we can assist them in feeling comfortable to do that is to make sure this first run goes as smooth as possible. No fuckups. Hopefully, that'll give them the confidence to pull the plug early to leave Afghanistan on the next run. Once the order is given and the Russian army starts out of Afghanistan, there'll be no going back. So we need only a couple of days difference in them leaving and us taking the drugs and stopping the money. We may just have that window in the amount of time it takes for the drugs to be shipped from Afghanistan to here."

"Yes," Reynolds said, nodding his head. "I see what Buddy's saying. If we take down the first shipment, they'll not stop. They'll only shift tactics, locations, and crews. We'll have accomplished nothing and have nothing to go on. We'll be back to square one."

"This is the other part of that scenario," Hayden said. What would the public think if it ever found out that the Customs SAC let forty-five tons of drugs walk into the United States under his control?

"Fuck," Davis said. "You do realize, if we don't tell him, I'm the one he's going to kill if he gets wind of this."

"Yes, I do," Hayden said. "My advice to you is to do whatever you have to do to keep him from ever finding out."

"Fuck," Davis repeated and then said, "All right."

"He's got a weak spot if you have to fight him," Reynolds said.

"And what would that be?" Davis asked.

"Hit him on that scar as hard as you can before he caves in your skull by body slamming you headfirst into a metal trash can," Reynolds said with a smile.

"Yeah, that's good, Jack," Davis said. "That's real fucking good."

"We keep it tight; he'll never know. Jack, do you have anything to drink in this place?" Hayden asked.

"Yes, in the fridge."

Opening the refrigerator, Hayden picked up a bottle of Jack Daniels. "How much did this cost you, ten bucks?"

"No, not quite," Reynolds said with a laugh.

"You always were a cheap date," Hayden said as he got three glasses out of the cupboard and poured a shot of whisky in each. He carried them into the living room, giving one glass to each man saying, "You sons of bitches did it. Only the best."

All three men stood and clicked glasses saying, "Only the best," and drank the whiskey.

Davis spoke up and asked, "Do you have a picture of Valley?"

Hayden returned to the folder and pulled out a three-by-five black-and-white picture of a man in a suit and handed it to Davis. On the back was Valley, Terrence George, dob 110937.

Handing it back to Hayden, Davis said, "Got it."

CHAPTER 25

Ready to Go

Wednesday, July 1, 1987

THREE OF THE INNER COMPARTMENTS of the barge had been completely sandblasted and recaulked; one was painted. Rogers, Little, and Valley were well pleased with the work, and so far, there were no water leaks into the areas. They would use the painted compartment to hold twenty-five thousand gallons of diesel fuel, needed to resupply the *California Rose* at sea. A hose and filter were laid in the bottom of the compartment, and the hose ran to a nipple under a cover on the deck for easy refueling when the time came.

Valley informed Rogers and Little that both the hash and Thai would either be wrapped in plastic or hermitically sealed in plastic bags. But the extra precautions were well worth the effort. The barge had a ribbed floor of steel beams. They decided to take several sheets of plywood and rolls of plastic with them. These would be stored in the containers, chained to the topside of the barge. After the hole was cut in the deck, the plywood and plastic would be placed on the floor of the two compartments that were going to be holding the drugs. This would ensure dryness as it would lift the bags of hashish and boxes of marijuana six inches off the bottom of the barge.

"I like it," Carlin said.

Carlin and Little measured out from the side onto the top of the barge exactly where they were going to need to cut the hole over the compartment to lower the drugs. The hole would be two feet by four feet to allow for a makeshift ramp to slide the drugs into the one compartment. To access the next compartment, they would open a wall hatch and lay down a set of rollers. The lighter boxes of Thai marijuana would go in the far compartment first, and then the heavier bags of hashish would go in the compartment directly underneath the hole in the deck.

"I like it too," Billy Little said, with Valley agreeing.

While in prison, Carlin had begun to read the King James Bible, and he especially liked Job 24. To Carlin, this passage described the inequity of his life and why he stayed in a life of crime. In his mind, the rich and affluent were the real criminals, and they were never held accountable for their sins or crimes. Carlin was bitter, and felt he deserved what he could take from these rich people. To him, smuggling drugs was just another way of getting over on the man.

He started keeping a ledger of expenses for this endeavor and advertised that this was a contract job of going to Hawaii to supply marine parts to vessels owned by Seattle Salvage. On top of the ledger, he named this contract Job-24. No one would understand or suspect that he was talking about a Bible passage, and this was his payback.

The Russian Airforce colonel and his lieutenant both found it unusual having orders relayed by the KGB station chief. But they weren't going to question the authority of Vladimir Yukorov when he said, "This is directly from General Vanerev." Having the Mi-24 squadron starting to patrol areas near Herat in the north and away from Kandahar didn't make much sense to them, but they weren't saying shit. They both knew this was the man that executed President Amin. And the orders to move patrolling grids starting July 19 were given.

Yukorov got back to his office in Kabul, closed his door, and called a number in Kandahar.

A man answered, "Hello."

"Tell Ayub that the roads are clear starting July 19," Yukorov said.

"Who is this?" asked the man.

"Tell him I control the skies and they are clear after July 19," Yukorov said and hung up.

The man hung up and walked into the next room.

"Who was that?" drug lord Ayub Afridi asked.

"He wouldn't say. But he said the roads are clear starting July 19 and that he controls the skies," the young man named Zaman said.

"That was the Russian," Afridi said. "Bring me the phone. I need to call Karachi."

VLADIMIR YUKOROV LEFT KABUL THAT EVENING and returned to Moscow, arriving back at his home near midnight. He felt good about the developments and would go over them with Colonel Petroff in the morning to make sure he wasn't overlooking anything.

At the Kremlin the next morning at 7:00 a.m., he was surprised to see Colonel Petroff's car there. Stopping on the second floor at his own office—his secretary had not yet arrived—he laid his coat and hat on his chair. Then he took the stairwell up to Colonel Petroff's office on the fourth floor. Luba had not arrived either, and Yukorov knocked on the colonel's door, saying "Hello."

Recognizing Yukorov's voice, the colonel said, "Come in, Vlad. The door's unlocked."

Yukorov opened the outer door, seeing the inner door was opened and the colonel was sitting at his desk, doing paperwork.

"Come in, Vlad," Petroff repeated. "Have a seat," he said, as he threw the last bit of documents into his shredder bin. "How's Afghanistan?"

Yukorov sat down in the large leather chair against the wall. "Good. I need to ask your opinion on something."

"Sure. Close that door," Petroff said, motioning to his inner door.

Swinging it closed from his seat, Yukorov said, "Afridi is ready to move the hashish. This past week, with the general's permission. I changed the Hind's patrolling areas to the northern border. This moves them away from the travel routes that Afridi will be taking. What else do you recommend be done?"

"How many patrols do the special forces have out?" Petroff asked.

"Minimal, but they could be a problem if they become aware of drugs being transported," Yukorov said.

"You'd better send them on a wild-goose chase because those boys will fuck things up if given the chance. They are exceptionally good at what they do. I know there will be teams out doing nothing but lying in the rocks and watching the roads leading into Pakistan."

"That's a good idea. I'll contact General Vanerev and mention this to him. He'll have a better understanding of whom to contact and what to say."

"Yes, I believe something should be done because if not, we could have an event that derails everything," Petroff said.

"Thank you, Colonel. I'll go call the general now and relay this information," Yukorov said as he got up to leave.

"Very well, Vlad. Anything else new?" the colonel asked.

"No. But we're getting awfully close to our first shipment. Five maybe six weeks away. I'll be talking to the captain of the *Poliksena* again this week. He needs to be ready," Yukorov said. "Talk more later."

Petroff nodded as Yukorov left his office. He doesn't know yet, or he's better at hiding it than I thought he'd be, Petroff thought.

Yukorov walked down the two flights of stairs to the second floor and his office.

His secretary, Teresa, had arrived. "There's a folder on your desk, sir," she said.

"Thank you," he said and shut his office door while walking in. Sitting down at his desk, he picked up the large, sealed folder marked URGENT. He opened it, pulled out another folder, and then opened that one. Even as a cold-blooded killer, he wasn't prepared for the picture on top of the other documents—a color photo of Sinesha Orlov with her throat cut, her black eyes glazed over in death. Yukorov didn't speak but quickly read the other documents and the police report indicating she was possibly killed by one of the drug addicts in that area or by a customer who refused to pay for her services. The police report wrote her off as just another junkie prostitute killed in the alleys of Moscow. The family had requested cremation, and Sinesha's ashes had already been thrown into the Moskva River during the third day of the Vietnamese funeral ceremony. Her mother cried from the bank and prayed that this unlucky death would not bring more misery to her family.

Yukorov didn't buy it. She was an expert in hand-to-hand combat and would make quick work of every junkie in Moscow. For an angry customer, she would never have met one in an alley, and that was where she was killed. He was positive. Looking at the pictures and where the blood had squirted as it gushed from her neck, he could tell she was killed right there, and it was by a professional. The knife wound in her neck was not done by slashing. It was done by someone trained in the arts of death. The cut mark was from a knife being shoved through the neck and then cutting from the inside out. Yukorov had seen that cut many times on men and women, and he had been the one holding the knife.

CHAPTER 26

Final Preps

11:00 a.m., Thursday, July 2, 1987

Yukorov placed Sinesha's folder in his desk drawer. I don't have time to worry about that now, he thought. But his mind kept going back to Petroff, and he thought, I'll bring it up to him later. Taking a small address book out of his coat pocket, he glanced in it, picked up the phone, and dialed a number in Luxembourg.

"Good morning. Bank of France, Luxembourg. How may I direct your call?" the operator asked.

Looking at his notes, Yukorov said, "I need to speak to Mr. Andre."

"Just a moment, please. I'll transfer you to his extension," the operator said.

The phone rang twice and was picked up. "Hello. Mr. Andre. How may I help you?"

"Mr. Andre, my name is Mr. Yuk. I was given your name by Mr. DePantera of the Monarch National Bank in New York."

"Yes, Mr. Yuk. How can I help you?"

"I need to verify an account and the balance."

"That's no problem. I remember the account in your name, Mr. Yuk. And if you can please give me your code number, I can provide that information."

"It's 12091879."

"Confirmed, Mr. Yuk. Yes, your account is active with a balance of one thousand American dollars," Andre said.

"Thank you, Mr. Andre. Have a nice day," Yukorov said and hung up the phone. Next, he dialed the back number for General Vanerev's office at Army Headquarters in Kabul.

"Hello," the general said.

"Good morning, General. This is Vlad."

"Good morning, Vlad. What did the colonel have to say?"

"He mentioned the Spetsnaz Teams, sir. He thinks we need to redirect them elsewhere."

"Good. Then he is thinking clearly. I wanted to make sure about Colonel Petroff after losing his wife. Sometimes men in despair can change. I've already given Spetsnaz a stand-down order for six weeks. They've been deployed for several months, and they need a rest. I did that knowing it was the right thing to do for my men. So there's no guilt with that order."

"Yes, sir."

"Anything else, Vlad?"

"Yes, sir. I contacted the Luxembourg Bank, and we do have an account there. It is active with a balance of one thousand dollars, as the financier in New York told me it would have. So we are good there as well, General."

"Very good. Keep me updated with any changes. I'll notify the others," the general said.

"Thank you, General. I'll do that," Yukorov said and hung up. Then he dialed the ship-to-shore number for the *Poliksena*.

"Hello," a voice said in the communications room of the KGB spy ship.

"I need to speak to Captain Faucher. This is Yukorov."

"Yes, sir. I'll get him," the radioman said.

A few minutes later, the phone was picked up by Captain Babin Faucher, a French national the KGB paid to operate the *Poliksena*. Having worked for the KGB for almost ten years, he could care less about national boundaries or loyalties. He liked the money and the excitement. But he especially liked living and knew his life would not be worth one franc if he ever told Yukorov he wanted out of the business. He knew way too much for Yukorov to ever let him leave and live.

"Vlad, any instructions?" Faucher asked in his French accent.

"Yes, write this down," Yukorov said. "You must be in Karachi by the first of August. As we discussed before, you will be taking on forty-five tons of product there. From Karachi, you will go to the Gulf of Thailand and pick up an additional ten tons of product. I need you in the gulf by August 12 or 13. The vessel you're to meet there is the *Mala* with a Captain Saelao. They will be on frequency 136.2. From there, travel to the North Pacific and rendezvous with the American vessel the first week in September. We are trying for September 5. I'll provide more information on the American vessel later. For right now, you be in Karachi on the first of August.

"Yes, sir, we'll be there," the captain said.

"I'll be in touch, Captain," Yukorov said and hung up.

General Vanerev stared at the small flag of the Soviet Union on his desk. Picking up his phone, he called a number in Moscow at Znamenka 19, the main building of the Ministry of Defense.

"Marshal Kavzo's office. How may I help you?" the secretary said.

"This is General Vanerev. Is Marshal Kavzo in please?" the general asked.

"Yes. Sir. Would you like to speak to him?"

"Yes, I would," Vanerev said.

A few minutes later, Marshal Damian Kavzo, minister of defense, said, "Hello, Vadim. How are you doing in Kabul?"

"Very good, sir. Do you have a minute to speak?" Vanerev asked.

"Yes, General. I'm alone in my office," he said.

"Sir, everything's in place, and we will start transporting to Karachi in two weeks. I have secured that area of the country so there will be no intervention. Also, the bank account has been confirmed in Luxembourg."

"Very well, Vadim. Things are going as planned," the marshal replied. He paused for a moment and then said, "General Vadim

Vanerev, I am your superior officer, and I'm ordering you to continue with operation Red Sword."

General Vanerev was silent for a moment and then asked, "Sir?"

"General Vanerev, do you understand what I have just ordered?" the marshal asked.

"Yes sir," Vanerev said, knowing what his lifelong friend had just done.

"Very well, General. Continue with your orders, and report back to me," Kavzo said. He then added, "I want you to document this order as it came from me today. Goodbye, Vadim."

"Goodbye, sir," Vanerev said and hung up his phone. Sitting and thinking for a couple of minutes, he then picked up a clean sheet of paper and did as his superior officer and old friend had ordered. After writing down the date, time, and order, Vanerev folded the piece of paper and put it in an envelope, sealing it. On the outside of the envelope, he wrote "Order" and placed it in his desk drawer. Marshal Kavzo had just given General Vanerev a possible get-out-of-jail-free card while signing his own death warrant if this operation failed. Only very honorable men are capable of such courage, General Vanerev thought, as the final preparations of Red Sword were underway.

CHAPTER 27

100 Percent

Monday, July 20, 1987

For centuries, Afghan farmers grew, cultivated, and harvested cannabis resin, called garda. To collect this powdered residue, the dried cannabis plants are beaten on a rock or across a barrel or drum to separate the buds and leaves from the branches. Next the buds and leaves containing the resin are hand crushed over a sieve to remove as much debris as possible and allow the powdered resin to fall through. The remaining garda, in its powdery form, is then pressed into a gooey paste called hashish. The hashish paste is spread evenly in a small, plastic-lined twelve-by-six-inch wooden mold that's a half-inch deep.

Once the gooey hashish paste is spread throughout the mold, it's completely wrapped in the same plastic before being removed. This product is one sole of hashish and weighs about two pounds. As the hashish dries and cools wrapped in the plastic, it becomes firmer and is packed with four other soles in its own plastic wrap. Five of these small bundles of five soles each are placed in a burlap bag, which weighs approximately fifty pounds. Each burlap bag's wholesale value on the streets of America and Canada in 1987 was eighty thousand dollars. Broken down into retail dosage units, it's worth three times that.

Drug lord Ayub Afridi had been collecting stores of hashish for months. Some of it had been harvested as far back as the fall of 1985. For weeks, the bundles of hashish had been carried out from the most remote tribal areas by mules and, if there were roads, by vehicles. Having collected over 120 tons in his Kandahar warehouse, he was now organizing his transportation to the various locations for shipping all over the world. Today, the largest segregated amount of drugs to be shipped would be inspected by the buyer.

"*As Salaam Alaikum*," Yukorov said, as he entered Afridi's warehouse in Kandahar, placing his hand over his heart.

"*Wa Alaikum As Salaam*," Afridi replied.

"Are you ready to transport to Karachi?" Yukorov asked.

"Yes, as soon as you inspect. Then the final loading will be done, and the trucks will go into Pakistan and then on to Karachi. We can be there easily by August 1."

"Show me," Yukorov said.

Afridi and one of his lieutenants led Yukorov into a separate room, filled to the ceiling with burlap bags.

"How many?" Yukorov asked.

"One thousand eight hundred bags, forty-five tons of hashish," Afridi replied.

"Open one bag for me. Show me what you have," Yukorov said.

Afridi spoke in Urdu to the other man, who took a knife out of his belt sheath and sliced open one of the bags. Taking a separate plastic bag out, he sliced it open to reveal five individually plastic wrapped soles of dark hashish. Afridi took one and handed it to Yukorov, saying, "The finest hashish in the world."

"Okay. Where will it be stored in Karachi before we can get it on the vessel?"

"I have a warehouse there near the docks. It's secured by my own armed men. It will be safe until loaded onto your vessel."

"You make sure it is," Yukorov said. "If this goes as planned, I want another forty-five tons this fall."

"Yes, I can do that. I should have enough already here. And if not,

I'll have more brought down from this year's harvest. Either way, I can do it."

"Good," Yukorov said. "I have removed all Soviet military from your travel routes into Pakistan. You'll have no problem from them."

"We have watched your special forces teams leave. And we have checked to make sure the routes are clear. We'll have no problems. We leave tomorrow," Afridi said.

Two days later on July 22, 1987, General Secretary Mikhail Gorbachev proposed to President Ronald Reagan the elimination of all nuclear and conventional ground-launched ballistic and cruise missiles with ranges of 500 to 5,500 kilometers. They would call this the Intermediate-Range Nuclear Forces Treaty, or INF Treaty. It wouldn't be praised by western countries or signed by either leader until December 8 of that year. But there were immediate voices of outrage in the Kremlin and the main building of the Ministry of Defense in Moscow. The target on Gorbachev's back had just gotten bigger and brighter.

On Friday, July 24, Valley drove to McAvoy Harbor after Carlin Rogers called and said, "I need to see you today, and it's important." Arriving there, Valley met Rogers in the wheelhouse of the *California Rose*.

"What?" Valley asked in a loud voice.

"You heard me. I'm not taking all the risk and not getting paid for it. I want one million dollars up front, in cash, or this boat does not move," Rogers said.

"That's not what we agreed to, you son of a bitch," Valley remarked.

"You call me a son of a bitch one more time, and I'll break your back. I'm the one taking all the risk. You guys, including that big Russian fucker, are just sitting back and watching me run the gauntlet. Now, I don't have any problem sticking my neck out. But you motherfuckers are going to pay me first, half up front, in cash."

"We don't have time for this," Valley yelled. "We have to be in Hilo in two fucking weeks."

"You make it happen, or this entire operation goes down the fucking toilet," Rogers said.

Valley could see he was dead serious. Trying to calm down and think for a few moments, Valley said, "Okay, wait here. I'll go use the payphone at the restaurant and see what I can do. Goddamn it."

Rogers watched Valley leave the *California Rose*, get in his new, tan Ford F-250, and drive towards McAvoy Café. "Fuck you," Rogers said, watching him leave.

"You motherfucker," Valley yelled as he hit the steering wheel driving towards the restaurant.

Tony Davis was sitting in his favorite spot in McAvoy Café and was just finishing his breakfast of buttermilk pancakes and eggs when a tan pickup hurriedly pulled into the parking area. He didn't recognize the driver wearing the ballcap until he opened the door and walked up to the cashier.

He said in an agitated voice, "I need five dollars in quarters."

Davis continued eating his breakfast as Valley got the change and walked back outside to the payphone booth.

"Must not be having a good day," Davis said to the waitress.

"No, he's pissed," she said.

Slamming the door shut on the phonebooth, Valley inserted a quarter and dialed a number in New York City. When a computer voice said, "To complete your call, please deposit two dollars and twenty-five cents," he put in nine of his remaining nineteen quarters. The call went through, and the line began to ring.

"Monarch National Bank. How may I direct your call?" the operator said.

"Phillip DePantera, please. This is George Hannah," Valley said.

"Just a moment please," the operator said, placing Valley on hold.

"You motherfucker," Valley said looking back towards the *California Rose*. Valley paid no attention to the brown CJ leaving the parking lot.

"George, how are you doing?" DePantera asked when he came on the line.

"I need a favor, Phillip. I need one million in cash released for me to Bergford," Valley said.

"Well, George, I'm sure I can make that happen, but it's going to cost you of course. Hold on one minute. Let me get my folder out. . . . Yes, this is what I'm willing to do. I'll pay you eight hundred thousand per ton for the Thai. And I want all twenty tons of it, too," DePantera said, knowing he would save himself one hundred thousand dollars per ton, or two million dollars total.

Valley thought for a minute, figuring Rogers making him pay the one million up front just cost him one million dollars in the end.

"Fuck, okay. It's a deal," Valley said. "How soon can you send it to Bergford?"

"George, I'll have it in Toronto tomorrow. You can make your customary arrangements after that," DePantera said.

"Okay, thank you, Phillip," Valley said.

"My pleasure, George. It's always nice doing business with you," DePantera said. Hanging up his phone, DePantera smiled.

Valley looked back towards the *California Rose* and again said, "You motherfucker!" Then he called a Toronto number and fed it the rest of his quarters.

"Bergford. How can I help you?" the receptionist asked.

"Robert Duvet or Steve Petrov. This is George Hannah," Valley said.

"Just a moment, sir. They're both in," she said as she put Valley on hold.

After a minute, Valley heard, "Hello, George. This is Bob."

"Hi, Bob. Hey, I'm on a payphone and running out of minutes. But I'm having one mil transferred to you tomorrow from New York. I'll need it brought to me in California in two weeks. Can you do that?" Valley asked.

"Yes, of course, George. Twenty thousand sound good to you?" Duvet asked.

"Yes. I'll let you know more specifics later. But you be ready to travel when I need you. Thanks, Bob," Valley said.

"No problem, George. Talk soon."

Hanging up the phone in the phonebooth, Valley again said, "You motherfucker." He got back in his truck and drove back to the *California Rose* where Rogers was standing next to his truck.

"You get it taken care of?" Rogers asked Valley, as he sat in his truck.

"Yes, now there will be no more fucking surprises," Valley said looking at Rogers.

"You get my money, I'm good."

"I got your fucking money. But I'm not giving it to you until the Russian approves your plans and designs on the barge when we're in Hawaii in two weeks."

"All right," Rogers said. "Then we set it up to where, once he gives his approval, that money is released to Billy while you and I are still there."

"Agreed," Valley said.

TONY DAVIS DROVE OUT OF MCAVOY HARBOR and pulled into the Kroger parking lot in Pittsburg. After paging Reynolds to his bag phone, Davis sat there, enjoying the warm sun with the top down on the Jeep.

When the phone rang, Davis asked, "Do you remember the no show in the picture at Vacaville?"

"Yes," Reynolds said.

"He's no longer a no show."

"Probability?"

"One hundred percent."

CHAPTER 28

Closer Looks

2:00 a.m., Sunday, August 2, 1987

Davis had been staying at a distance anytime he went into McAvoy Harbor, but he needed to get a closer look at the *California Rose* and barge. Leaving the CJ in Hayward because of the loud headers, he took the Mustang and got to McAvoy Harbor about two in the morning. He parked to the side next to some boats lining the parking area. Reaching down to the light switch, he turned it counterclockwise all the way until it clicked. With the night vision goggles Reynolds had given him in Maine, Davis stepped out of the Mustang and quietly closed the door. He stood next to the car for several minutes, looking at everything, not moving, and not making a sound.

There were lights still shining on one of the yachts in the harbor, but everything else was dead quiet and dark, just the way he liked it. Davis walked past the café and towards the gated area near the *California Rose*. Getting to the chain-link fence and gate, he found it locked with a chain and padlock. Putting on the NVG headset, Davis began to climb the fence slowly and quietly until he got to the top. At the top of the gate, he stopped for a few moments to make sure no one was around. Not sensing any danger, he lowered himself to the ground and walked up the road a hundred yards to where the two vessels were tied to the dock.

Davis stood there by the vessels for a few moments, listening. Nothing. Quietly climbing onto the *California Rose*, he discovered all the doors and windows were locked. Leaving that vessel, he climbed up on the barge where four twenty-foot containers had been placed. Slowly, he opened the double door on the first container and then turned on the infrared light on the NVG so he could see in the pitch black. Checking all four containers, Davis found assorted tools, air wrenches, a cutting torch, welder, and barrels of oil and gasoline in two of the containers. Another container held cans of red paint, sheets of three-quarter-inch plywood, two-by-eights ten feet long, four-foot rolls of plastic sheeting, water hose, electrical extension cords, air compressor, generator, and rolls of steel cables. The final container was empty.

Closing the last container door, he walked to each surface hatch on the barge. One contained a fuel nipple underneath a covered hatch lid. Wanting to inspect that compartment, he opened the other side hatch and climbed down inside. Without the infrared light on the goggles, it would have been impossible to see. But he could, and everything glowed a light-green color. The walls, ceiling, and floor had been freshly painted white he thought since it looked so bright with the goggles. Leaving that compartment, he inspected the other five. Two more of the middle compartments had been sand-blasted, cleaned, and recaulked but not painted. The other three compartments had been cleaned but still had considerable rust on the surfaces.

Satisfied with what he had found, Davis quietly climbed down off of the barge and walked back towards the café. After climbing back over the gate and back to the Mustang, he stood and, once again, looked around. It was still very dark and perfectly quiet. No one had any idea that CIA Special Agent Tony Davis had been inside the hidden compartments of the barge that would be used in the largest drug smuggling operation in history. Getting in the Mustang, he drove back to the safe house on Newport Street in Hayward.

DRUG LORD AFRIDI HAD NO PROBLEM TRUCKING the forty-five tons of hashish to his Karachi warehouse. Half of the shipment had already been loaded onto the *Poliksena*, and the other half would be completed today.

"I'll leave first thing in the morning," Captain Faucher told Afridi.

"Good. How long will it take you to reach the rendezvous location?" Afridi asked.

"I can be there in a month. I can make 15 knots if the water is smooth. And I think we're going to have good weather for most of the trip."

"That's good. I'll see you for the next shipment," Afridi said, shaking hands with the captain.

"Yes, see you later," Faucher said. Then he turned to yell at one of his crew, "Hurry up. We sail in the morning."

7:00 a.m., Monday, August 3, 1987

YUKOROV WAS SITTING IN HIS OFFICE IN MOSCOW and had confirmed his reservations for the Hukilau Hotel in Hilo for Thursday night. Picking up his phone, he called Valley's number in El Dorado, California.

When the phone rang, Valley glanced at the clock. It was 8:00 p.m. on Sunday. "Hello," he said.

"We meet on Friday, the seventh. The Hukilau Hotel in Hilo at noon. Bring the plans for the barge. I want you and the captain there," Yukorov said.

"We'll be there. Everything's ready here."

"Good. See you in Hilo."

Valley called Rogers's mobile phone.

"Hello," Rogers said.

"I just got off the phone with the Russian. We meet in Hilo on Friday at a hotel. I'll get us both tickets to fly out Thursday and each a room at the Hukilau Hotel where he's staying. We can fly back on Saturday. Bring your drawings of the barge."

"What about my money?"

"I'll call the couriers in the morning. They can fly in on Wednesday, and we can meet them at a hotel near the airport in Sacramento. Make sure Little is with you. He'll need to meet Robert Duvet and Steve Petrov from Bergford. Once Yukorov approves the barge design, I can call them from Hilo and tell them to release the money to Billy. Does that sound good to you?"

"Yes, that'll work."

"I shouldn't have to tell you but will anyway. With that much cash, you'd better be damn careful about who sees it. The IRS has strict laws about cash deposits, and a bank is required to report any deposit over ten thousand dollars. So unless you want the IRS sniffing up our asses, be damn careful."

"Don't worry. I have that covered," Rogers said.

"How?" Valley asked. "I'm in this with you up to my neck. So how do you have that covered?"

"My sister, Sara, is married to a banker in Napa. I have arrangements with him to take care of the cash. Once Billy gets the cash, he's to give it to Sara. She'll give it to Doug, her husband, and he'll deposit it into my accounts."

"Okay. That sounds good. I know you wanted cash this time, but there's a better way for some of your money. You can get bearer bonds. It's the same as cash and is a lot easier to handle. You just have to make sure you don't lose them. They're nothing more than a sheet of paper. And whoever has them, owns the listed value of the bond."

"Let me see how this goes first. If it seems to be a problem, then I'll have bonds next time," Carlin said.

"Okay. I'll call Duvet and Petrov in the morning. I'll get back to you on what room and hotel they'll be in on Wednesday. Have Little with you," Valley said.

"Okay. I'll wait for your call," Rogers said and hung up.

THE NEXT MORNING, VALLEY CALLED BERGFORD Money Exchange.

"Good morning. Bergford's. How may I direct your call, please?" the operator asked.

"Robert Duvet or Steve Petrov. This is George Hannah," Valley said.

"One moment please. Mr. Petrov's in," the operator said, putting Valley on hold for a few minutes.

"Good morning, George. Steve here," Petrov said.

"Good morning, Steve. I need you and Bob to fly to Sacramento on Wednesday. Can you do that?' Valley asked.

"Yes. We have been waiting for your call. We'll fly the private jet to Executive Airport Wednesday morning. I've already reserved a room at the Westin for the entire week, room 232. How about we meet in that room at two p.m.?" Petrov asked.

"That'll work. I'll have two men with me. The person getting the money and another man who you'll release the money to once I call you from Hilo on Friday," Valley said.

"Okay, George. We'll see you Wednesday at the Westin, two p.m., room 232."

"Yes. Goodbye, Steve, and thanks," Valley said. Then he called Rogers back. After stating where to meet on Wednesday, he said, "You can see your money, and I can introduce Billy to Bob and Steve."

"All right. That sounds good. Billy and I'll meet you there."

"Everything's coming together. Who you taking with you on the *California Rose*?" Valley asked.

"I'm taking Dude, Willard, and my brother's son, Jim. I'm sure Dude and I can handle any problem that comes up. He's more experienced running the boat, and I want him there on the first trip. The boys can help with whatever we need."

"Great. I'm starting to get excited," Valley said.

"Yes, let's hope this goes smooth and no one's on to us," Rogers said.

"I'll start more surveillance. But so far, I've seen nothing that alerts me. I think we're good."

"Damn, I hope you're right."

CHAPTER 29

Money in the Bank

2:00 p.m., Wednesday, August 5, 1987

Carlin Rogers parked his red Ford crew cab in the parking lot of the Westin Sacramento at exactly 2:00 p.m. "Let's go see what a million in cash looks like," he said to Billy Little.

Getting out of the truck, they walked into the hotel and took the stairs to the second floor. Rogers knocked on the door of 232. Seeing the security peephole go dark, he knew he was being looked at. He heard the deadbolt being unlocked and then the chain being removed. The door opened with Valley standing behind it. Walking in, Rogers saw two men in suits, both in their late thirties.

"Carlin, Billy, this is Robert Duvet and Steve Petrov," Valley said introducing the men in the suits.

"Where's my money?" Rogers asked.

"First, they need to pat you down," Valley said.

"What?" Rogers said.

"Just let them fucking pat you down, Carlin. This is their safety protocol."

Rogers and Little raised their arms as Petrov patted both men down for weapons.

"They're clean," Petrov said to Duvet.

As Duvet bent over to pick up the large metal suitcase that had been sitting on the far side of the bed, an Uzi submachine gun swung out from under the suit jacket.

Rogers looked at Little and said, "Make sure you don't bring a gun when you come back here on Friday."

"No, shit," Little said.

Duvet laid the suitcase on the bed and opened it, spinning it to face Rogers. "Gentlemen, this is what one million dollars looks like," Duvet said in a French accent.

"Goddamn," Rogers said. "Isn't that pretty?"

Duvet closed the case and relocked it, placing it back on the floor near his feet.

"Satisfied?" Valley asked, looking at Rogers.

"When can I count it?" Rogers asked.

"When it's yours," Petrov said. "As soon as we receive instruction to do so by Mr. Hannah, we'll release the case to Billy as planned. After that, we will immediately leave and head back to Toronto."

"All right. That'll work," Rogers said. "Thank you, fellows. Hope to do business with you again." Rogers turned and walked out of the room followed by Little.

"I'll be out in a minute," Valley said to Rogers and Little. Turning to the other two, Valley took two bundles of one-hundred-dollar bills out of his coat pocket. Giving one to each man, he said, "Ten thousand each. Thank you, gentlemen. I'll call you from Hilo on Friday."

"Thank you, George. Pleasure doing business with you, as all ways," Petrov said as Duvet nodded.

Valley shook hands with both men and left, joining Rogers and Little in the parking lot.

"How much did that cost you?" Rogers asked.

"Whenever they deliver cash or bonds, it's a set fee, ten thousand each," Valley said.

"Well, that was worth it to me," Rogers said, smiling.

"What are their backgrounds? Most people don't carry Uzis," Little said.

"Both are former Canadian Special Forces, Joint Task Force 2. They have no trouble protecting their money. Don't ever fuck with them. Carlin, I'll see you at SFO tomorrow at noon. We fly to Hilo and meet the Russian the next day. Stay that night, get drunk, and fly back Saturday."

"Fuck, that sounds good," Rogers said. "And I don't get drunk."

Rogers took Little back to his home in Chico, dropped him off, and then drove to his place on Almond Hill Lane in Napa. Arriving there, he parked his truck and went inside the big house where Doug and Sara lived.

"Hello," he said to his sister, who was in the kitchen.

"Hey, how did the meeting go?" she asked.

"Very good. The money was there in a metal suitcase. All one million dollars of it in cash!"

"My Lord! So everything's okay?"

"Yes. So this is how it'll work. When I'm in Hawaii on Friday, the people who brought the money will release it to Billy. I told him to keep one hundred thousand. You're to get nine hundred thousand dollars in cash."

"Dear Lord."

"Once Billy brings the suitcase to you, you take out two hundred thousand and keep it for me. Hide it somewhere. Take the remaining seven hundred thousand, and get it deposited over the next few weeks into both Supply Masters' accounts. Doug knows what to do, so make sure he's in charge of the deposits. I don't want the IRS looking into what we're doing. I also told Billy the same—don't be doing anything stupid with the money."

"Yes. Doug knows what he's doing. And the bank president, Daniel Henderson, will also be helping with the deposits."

"The bank president?"

"Yes. Doug explained your situation, and he agreed. He would never turn down depositing almost a million dollars into his bank," Sara said. "He's very professional but a greedy man."

"Okay. Just make sure none of this gets out, or we're all toast," Rogers said. "I'm going over to my place. I need to make sure my drawings are accurate before we leave in the morning. Good night."

"You hungry? You can eat with us when Doug gets in."

"No. Billy and I drove through Burger King, but thanks," Carlin said, as he walked out the backdoor and across the driveway into his house.

The next day at noon, Sara's white Lexus pulled up to the International Terminal at SFO. "Be careful, Carlin," she said.

"I will. Be here Saturday at five p.m. to pick me up," Rogers said.

"Don't worry. I'll be here. Just look for my car."

Rogers got his suitcase off the back seat and walked into the terminal. Glancing over against the wall, he saw Valley leaned up against a window smoking a cigarette.

"You ready?" Rogers asked.

"Let's do it," Valley said as he walked towards security, handing Rogers his tickets.

It was almost seven in the evening by the time Valley and Rogers got to the Hukilau Hotel in Hilo.

"You hungry?" Rogers asked as they were getting to their rooms.

"Yes. Let me drop my bag, and let's go downstairs for some dinner," Valley said.

"Good. I'm starving."

While eating in the bar area, Valley said, "I'm surprised he isn't here now."

"Just as well. I don't like the fucker. And I'll enjoy my burger more, if I don't have to look at him," Rogers said, taking a sip of his Budweiser.

At that moment, Yukorov was upstairs fucking a Hawaiian prostitute after he had called an escort service to come to the hotel. Finishing, he said to the young Hawaiian girl, "Get dressed and get out."

"Why the hurry? You paid for the night," the raven-haired beauty said.

"Because you remind me of someone."

"So you're still in love with her?"

"No, never was. She got her throat cut for running her mouth, though," Yukorov said, looking keenly at the young girl.

With that, the prostitute quickly dressed and left the room.

11:45 a.m., Friday, August 7, 1987

THE NEXT MORNING, VALLEY AND ROGERS were sitting at a corner table in the bar area when Yukorov walked in. Sitting down beside them at the next table over, Yukorov said, "Let me see the plans."

Rogers picked up the rolled-up drawings and handed them to the Russian. Yukorov took off the rubber band and rolled the plans out on the table. He looked at them for several minutes, reading how the shipment was to be placed into the barge and welded.

"What's the draft on the barge loaded?" he asked.

"About nine feet loaded, five empty," Rogers replied.

Yukorov looked at Rogers, nodded and asked, "How many knots can you make loaded?"

"We can make about six knots loaded coming back. That'll also depend on the tail wind, which can help some. We may get another knot or two if the wind is right."

Rolling the drawings and descriptions back up, Yukorov turned his chair and handed the plans back to Rogers and said, "I like your plans. The plywood and plastic are good ideas. The containers on top loaded with tools is another particularly good idea. I don't see how this can fail." Yukorov took an envelope out of his jacket pocket and gave it to Rogers. "This is how you contact my vessel, callsign *Western Star*. The coordinates are listed where you will rendezvous north of Hawaii. Radio frequency is 161.7. We are planning for September 5. Make sure you're there. What callsign are you going by?" Yukorov asked Rogers.

"My callsign is *Ulu*," Rogers said, remembering the big sailboat he had often seen in the San Francisco Bay. Rogers had no way of knowing, but the *Ulu* belonged to the *San Francisco Chronicle*'s night editor.

"Okay, monitor the frequency listed for the *Western Star*, and they can contact you on that frequency as well as callsign *Ulu*," Yukorov repeated.

"Yes," Rogers said. "I'll stay on that frequency, and I'll be there by September 5."

Standing up, Yukorov shook hands with Valley and Rogers, said, "Good luck," and left the room.

"Not much for words today," Rogers said.

"His head's in a noose, and the only way he lives is if we deliver," Valley said.

"Okay, make the call."

Valley pulled out his mobile phone and called Petrov's number.

"Hello," said Petrov.

"Steve, release the money to Billy, and thanks."

"He's here now. He wants to talk to Rogers."

Valley handed the phone to Rogers and said, "Billy."

"Hello," Rogers said.

"I got the money. I'm going to Sara's now," Little said.

"Good. I'll see you when I get back. Sara knows what to do. You get going," Rogers said, handing the phone back to Valley.

"Steve?" Valley asked.

"Yes, go," Petrov said.

"Thank you. I'll be in touch. Goodbye," Valley said and hung up.

In room 232 of the Westin Sacramento Hotel, Billy Little picked up a metal suitcase holding one million dollars in sequentially serial-numbered, uncirculated, one-hundred-dollar bills, walked out the door, and headed to 1063 Almond Hill Lane, Napa. He arrived at Sara and Doug Lawson's residence at 4:00 p.m. and knocked on the side door.

Sara opened it and gave her cousin a big hug. "How are you doing, Billy?" she asked.

"Scared shitless, traveling with this much money."

Putting the suitcase on the kitchen table, he looked at Sara and asked, "You ready?"

"Yes, open it," Sara said.

Little opened the case, and both stood there gazing at the enormous amount of cash, all in one-hundred-dollar bills, wrapped in one hundred bundles of ten thousand dollars each.

"Oh my God."

"Do you have a paper sack I can have?" Little asked.

"Yes, I need one too," she said, getting them from between the refrigerator and the counter. She handed one to Little, who placed ten wraps of hundreds in the bag and rolled the top shut. Sara placed twenty bundles of wrapped hundreds in her bag and placed it in the cupboard over the sink.

"I've never had one hundred thousand dollars in cash before," he said, looking at Sara.

Sara gave Billy another big hug and said, "Shut the case, please, and put it in my car."

Little closed the suitcase, carried it into the garage, and placed it on the backseat of the Lexus.

"I need to get to the bank. Doug is waiting on me," she said, getting in her car.

"I'm going home and stopping at a liquor store. I'm getting shitfaced tonight," Little said.

"You make sure you're safe in showing any of those hundreds," Sara replied.

"I will," Little said as he walked towards his old green truck. Getting in, he thought, I'm going to buy me a Lincoln.

IT TOOK BILLY LITTLE'S BANK IN CHICO only one week before it sent its first FinCEN Suspicious Activity Report (SAR) to the Financial Crime Enforcement Network of the IRS and the Department of the Treasury. Little had gone to his bank on a daily basis and deposited nine thousand dollars in uncirculated, sequentially serial–numbered, one-hundred-dollar bills, ninety-one-hundred-dollar bills for each deposit. He did that for seven straight days. He spent the other thirty thousand dollars on a new white Lincoln Town Car, paying cash. When the dealer deposited the cash that evening in the bank, a teller sent an IRS form 8300, indicating the three hundred one-hundred-dollar-bills being deposited.

IT WOULD TAKE FOUR MONTHS, between, August 7, 1987, and December 11, 1987, for Sara and Doug Lawson, Daniel Henderson, president of LendBest, Robert Powers, owner of McMillian Winery in Napa, and others to deposit seven hundred thousand dollars into the two accounts of Supply Masters. By the end of December 1987, FinCEN had also received several SARs from other banks in Napa. Special Agent Rich Cain of the IRS was now looking at Supply Masters, Inc. He was very carefully building his currency structuring case against all involved. He didn't know where the money was coming from, but it didn't matter to him. His case was already solid.

Friday, August 7, 1987

VLADIMIR YUKOROV FLEW BACK TO MOSCOW that evening. In his KGB office, he called the ship-to-shore number for the *Poliksena*.

"Hello," the radioman said.

"Get me the captain," Yukorov ordered.

"Yes, sir. Just a minute."

A few minutes went by, and finally the phone was picked up. "This is Captain Faucher."

"Babin, it's Vladimir. I talked to the American captain this morning. His callsign is *Ulu,* and he will monitor frequency 161.7. He will be at the coordinates by September 5."

"Good. We have the hashish on board and heading towards Thailand," Faucher said.

"Where are you now?"

"We are rounding past Sri Lanka. We'll be in the Gulf of Thailand by the twelfth."

"Okay. When you get there, contact the *Mala* as instructed. Get the Thai onloaded as quickly as possible and get to north of Hawaii as soon as you can get there."

"Yes, sir," Captain Faucher said as Yukorov hung up.

CHAPTER 30

Outbound

5:00 p.m., Saturday, August 8, 1987

Rogers and Valley flew back to SFO and were talking outside the terminal when Sara Lawson pulled up.

"I've got about ten days before I have to leave. I'll make sure everything is ready and nothing is missed," Rogers said.

"Good. I'll meet you in Hilo when you get there. Let's stay at the same hotel since it's close to the airport and docks."

"Yes, that's good. I'll plan on refueling in Hilo and picking up some more food for the return trip. If the weather's good, we should be able to find the other vessel pretty easy," Rogers said.

"Okay. I'll talk to you later this week," Valley said, as he walked towards the shuttle for the parking garage.

"All right," Rogers said as he got in the car with Sara.

"Carlin, all I can say is, oh my God," Sara said as he shut the door.

"You have any problems getting the money in the bank?"

"No, it'll take a few weeks, but we've started the deposits," she said. "Doug doesn't want to take a chance in making a big deposit. So we're making deposits of less than ten thousand dollars each."

"All right. Did Billy get his money?"

"Yes. He took one hundred thousand. He put it in a paper sack at my place and left."

"In another six weeks, I'll have another million to put in the bank," Rogers said to his sister.

"Oh my God," Sara said as she drove from SFO.

"Get me home. I need some sleep, and then I need to get to McAvoy Harbor."

Sunday, August 9, 1987

The next day, Rogers was on the *California Rose* looking at his marine chart for San Diego to Aleutian Islands and Hawaii Islands. Following the coordinates that Yukorov provided, of 38 degrees north, 155 degrees west, he would meet the *Western Star* 1,080 nautical miles due north of Hilo Hawaii. "That should make it easy," he said. Figuring on travelling light and fast, he could make the 2,500 nautical miles to Hilo in eleven or twelve days. Once there, he would stay one night, refuel, and then head north to meet the *Western Star*. He figured he could do all of that by September 5 and be there to receive the hash and Thai. Getting back to San Francisco would be a little slower since the barge would be loaded. But he thought he should still make it by the third week in September if all went as planned. Rogers double-checked his calculations. Yes, he was sure. He would leave McAvoy Harbor on the eighteenth of August and head towards Hilo.

For the remainder of the week, Rogers kept Dude, Jim, and Willard busy checking and re-checking everything on the two vessels. The engines of the *California Rose* were purring like a kitten after Dude spent two days tuning the twin Cummins diesel engines. Satisfied with all the work, Rogers ordered Willard to stay on the *California Rose* until they left. Rogers wanted no surprises, and he couldn't get rid of that unsettling feeling that they were being watched.

2:00 a.m., Tuesday, August 11, 1987

DAVIS DROVE ACROSS THE RAILROAD TRACKS on McAvoy Road and gently pulled to a stop beside the bait shop at the entry of the harbor. Turning off the Mustang, he sat there for a few minutes and made sure no one was around and then got out of the car, walking the winding road past the café and towards the loop. He stopped halfway there when he saw a light on in the tugboat and an old pickup truck parked next to it on the locked road. Somebody's staying on it now, Davis thought, turning and walking back towards his car. That's security, and they're leaving soon.

1:00 p.m., Tuesday, August 11, 1987

THE *POLIKSENA* HAD GOOD WEATHER and arrived in the Gulf of Thailand on the eleventh.

Turning to frequency 136.2 on his marine radio, Captain Faucher called, "*Mala*, *Mala*, *Mala*, this is *Western Star*, *Wester Star*, *Western Star*. Over."

"*Western Star*, this is *Mala*. Give me your coordinates. Over," Captain Saelao said.

Faucher gave his current location to the *Mala* and waited.

"*Western Star*, *Western Star*, I'm thirty nautical miles to your northwest. I'll be at your location in three hours. Stay at your location and I'll come to you. Over."

"Affirmative, *Mala*, I'll stay on station and wait for your arrival. Over," Faucher said. Then he turned to First Mate Simeon and said, "Get everything ready. We have a thousand boxes of Thai to take on."

The tall blond-haired, blue-eyed, thirty-four-year-old Frenchman was a ladies' man and liked his wine when in port, but out at sea, he was an extremely hard worker. The men respected him and obeyed his orders as if they came from the captain. Always wearing coveralls, the six-foot three-inch man was not hard to miss.

Three hours later, Simeon was yelling at the men to tie the *Mala* tight against the boards that were used as bumpers on the *Poliksena*. The ocean was calm and flat as the onloading began. The crane and net on the *Poliksena* were extended over to the *Mala*'s fantail and lowered. Once the net was full of boxes of Thai marijuana, the crane picked them up and brought them over to the *Poliksena* where they were stored in the compartments below deck.

It took seven hours to load the 667 boxes. But with Faucher's calculations, there were only seven tons of marijuana.

"We were to get ten tons," Faucher said.

"This is all they had for me to bring. They said they'll make it up on the next shipment. They didn't want to send such a large load on the first run," Saelao said.

"Okay, tell them to have thirteen tons next time. The total of twenty tons must be made."

"I will tell them, Captain," Saelao replied.

"Okay, let's have a drink."

Faucher shared a bottle of wine with Captain Saelao after the loading was completed.

"I'll see you again in a few months, my friend," Faucher said.

"Yes, good luck," Saelao replied as he returned to the *Mala*, and both crews cast off.

Returning to the wheelhouse of the *Poliksena,* Captain Faucher said to Simeon," Let's get to Hawaii and turn that radio to 161.7."

"Yes sir," Simeon said.

"This nice weather will not hold out forever. Let's take advantage of it. We have twenty-four days to get there. We should be able to make it in twenty-one," Faucher said.

THAT AFTERNOON DAVIS PAGED REYNOLDS.

"Tony, what's going on?" Reynolds asked.

"They're keeping someone on the tug now. I was there at two this morning, and it's occupied."

"No other reason than for security," Reynolds said.

"Yes, I agree. I think they're leaving soon. Looks like everything's in place, and the containers are chained down to the deck of the barge. One morning, they're just going to be gone."

"Well, this is what we've been searching and waiting on. We need to make sure this goes smoothly for them. That's the only way we're going to get an incredibly lucky break if, on the next load, the Russians pull the trigger early on leaving Afghanistan."

"I understand," Davis said.

"This is one of those occurrences in intelligence work that you'll never be able to talk about, not for at least thirty years, if then," Reynolds said.

"Roger that. I'll go up there every couple days until I find them gone. Then we'll just have to wait until they come back."

"That'll work. Do you think they'll come back to the same spot?"

"I'm not sure. They could do it right there, but I'd want more room to work; I'd move to a location where the trucks had more room to maneuver. It would go quicker for them. Where they're at now, all their dicks would be hanging out for hours," Davis said.

"Okay, keep me informed of any developments."

"Will do."

2:00 a.m., Monday, August 17, 1987

ON THE THIRD SUCH NIGHTTIME VISIT, Davis walked to the McAvoy Harbor Road loop and counted three trucks at the *California Rose* locations. He heard a generator running and saw lights still glowing on the barge and tug.

"They're leaving soon," Davis softly said and walked back to the Mustang parked at the bait shop. Arriving back at the Hayward safe-house at 3:00 a.m., he paged Reynolds.

His phone finally rang. "They're leaving today or tomorrow, Jack."

"Why?"

"Three vehicles there at two a.m., and they're still working with lights strung and a generator running."

"All right. I'll advise Buddy later in the morning. What're you going to do now?"

"Sleep a couple of hours, and then I'm having buttermilk pan-cakes and sausage at the McAvoy Café."

"All right. Play it cool."

"Roger that," Davis said as he hung up. "I need some sleep," he said, as he kicked off his shoes and lay down on the bed. As usual, he was out in less than a minute.

Waking, Davis looked at his watch. It was 9:15 a.m. "I need to get back up there," he said, pulling his Nikes back on. He walked out of the house and got in the CJ, firing up the 360 engine, and headed north. It was 11:00 a.m. when he walked into the McAvoy Café.

"Good morning, Joan."

"Good morning, Tony. What would you like today?"

"You know I can't pass up those pancakes, eggs, and sausage."

"English muffin, too?"

"Yes, please."

"I'll get this started," she said as she poured Davis a cup of black coffee.

"Anything new going on?" he asked.

"Yes, the Rogers crew will be leaving tomorrow. Said they're going to Hawaii to deliver parts to a company. Be gone about a month."

"Well, that's good. They should be making some good money."

"Yes, they spend a lot of it here."

"Nice," Davis said.

Davis enjoyed his late breakfast and was pleased no one from the crew showed up to eat. I don't want to be seen any more than I need to be, he thought. Paying for his meal and leaving a tip, he said, "Thank you, Joan. See you later."

"Thank you, Tony. Have a nice day," she said as he left the café.

Driving the Jeep back across the railroad tracks, Davis looked to the left at the old gravel plant. "There's where I would unload."

2:00 p.m., Tuesday, August 18, 1987

The next afternoon, later than usual, Davis pulled into the McAvoy Harbor, hoping the *California Rose* was gone. The fewer times Carlin Rogers and Terrence George Valley saw his face, the better this thing was going to turn out. Turning around at the loop, he saw no sign of the *California Rose* and barge. "Here we go," he said.

Leaving McAvoy Harbor, he pulled over at the old gravel plant's entrance. The chainlink fence gate was locked. Davis climbed the fence and dropped down to the other side. Walking towards the water, he liked what he saw. The area was the size of two football fields to turn around in. "This would be perfect for large trucks."

Walking over to the water's edge, he saw old pilings next to the bank where gravel barges, in prior years, had been tied up to unload the gravel. If the water was deep enough there for a gravel barge it will certainly be deep enough for a barge loaded with drugs, he thought. "This is where they're returning to," he said as he left.

As he climbed back over the fence and drove down Port Chicago Highway, Davis searched both sides of the road for a place to hide when they came back. A quarter-mile down the road, there was Acme Steel on the left. Coming out of the rear of the building, Davis could see a railroad track that extended back towards the gravel plant.

"That'll work," he said. Pulling over, he paged Taylor and waited. Hearing his phone ring, he said, "Hello, Ray."

"Whose day are you ruining?" Ray asked with a laugh.

"Nobody's yet. Can you do me a favor?"

"Sure. What do you need?"

"Are you notified when a vessel leaves the Bay Area?"

"Yes. They'll check in with VTS, vessel tracking service, and give their destination. What do you need?"

"The *California Rose* left this morning, and I'd like to know when it comes back."

"So you're still looking at that tug, huh?" Taylor asked.

"Well, yes, in a way. But more as a learning experience. When the time comes, I want to know what's all available if we ever get a real case."

"I'll give VTS a call and put the *California Rose* on their lookout list."

"That's not publicized, is it?" Davis asked. "I don't want anyone getting their tits in a bind over me trying to learn."

"No. I'll tell them this is just an exercise and to notify me of any contacts."

"Cool. Great, Ray. Thank you. I'll come that way soon, and we can have lunch again."

"Sounds good. I'll call you as soon as I hear any contacts on the *California Rose*."

"Thank you." After hanging up, Davis paged Reynolds. After a couple of minutes, Davis answered his phone, "Hello."

"They gone?" Reynolds asked.

"Yes. I'll be notified by the Coast Guard when they return, that is if they check in with the vessel tracking service. Will see," Davis said. "I figure we'll have three maybe four hours, once notified before they can make it from Golden Gate to Pittsburg. I've found a place to surveille from. You game?"

"Absolutely," Reynolds said.

"Okay. They're to be gone a month. So we have plenty of time to prepare."

"You need anything right now?" Reynolds asked.

"No, I'm good. As soon as I'm notified by the Coast Guard that the *California Rose* is inbound, I'll call you. Let's meet at the CVS in Concord on Clayton Road. We can take your truck from there. It'll blend in better than the Jeep or Mustang where we need to park."

"I'll be ready. I can leave this place in two minutes and be in Concord in an hour. I'll let Buddy know what's going on. Good job, Tony."

"Thanks. Will be talking to you, Jack," Davis said. Driving back to Hayward, he thought, At least so far, this has gone smooth. But, from being a cop for many years, he knew it could all turn to a world of shit in a heartbeat.

AT THE SAME TIME, CARLIN ROGERS WAS TALKING TO JIM ROGERS and Willard Butler in the small galley as the *California Rose* was leaving San Francisco behind. "We're bringing back a load of drugs. If you guys can keep your mouths shut, I'll pay you both fifty thousand dollars each. You in?"

Both boys said, "Hell, yes!"

CHAPTER 31

Hilo, Hawaii

5:00 p.m., Sunday, August 30, 1987

After reeling up the slack in the winch cable and maneuvering the *California Rose* alongside of the barge, Dude pushed it up against the dock where Carlin, Jim, and Willard cinched it and the *California Rose* up tight.

"Good job, Dude," Carlin said, giving the thumbs up to Dude still in the wheelhouse.

Walking back on board the *California Rose*, Carlin used the radio-telephone and contacted KMI on channel 809. KMI was AT&T's West Coast radiotelephone station. Once on KMI, Carlin called Valley. "We're here and tied up."

"Great. I have you a rented truck here at the hotel. I'll be down in a few minutes," Valley said from his room at the Hukilau Hotel. "They're here, honey," he said to his girlfriend, Julie.

Driving to the dock in a rented black Thunderbird, Valley meet Carlin on the barge.

"Any problems?" he asked.

"No, but I want a bigger boat next time. That backend was under two feet of water with the heavy waves," Carlin said.

"Fuck that," Valley said. "I'll continue to fly."

"I did break a hydraulic line and bracket that'll need to be repaired by a shop here somewhere. Nobody's open on Sunday, so that's going to cost us a day. I can't leave until I get it back."

"When you take it in tomorrow, pay them extra for a rush job," Valley said.

"I will. But we still can't leave until I get it back and hook it up."

"How about you and Dude come with me, and we can get some dinner," Valley said.

"Yes, I'm hungry. Give me a minute. I'll tell the boys what to do while we're gone."

Arriving at the hotel, Valley gave Carlin the room keys for the two additional rooms he reserved and the key for the rented truck.

"Truck's on the back end of the building. Look for the orange Chevy," Valley said.

"Thanks. Me and Dude will take one room, and the boys the other. Let's get something to eat, and I can go get Jim and Willard in a little while."

After dinner, Dude went to the hotel room, and Carlin found the truck. Driving it back to the dock, he picked up the boys, and they all went to the hotel.

"Restaurant's on the first floor. Be ready to leave at nine a.m.," Carlin said in the elevator, giving them the key to their room. "I need to get some sleep," he said, heading to his room where Dude was already snoring.

Opening the door to their room, Willard said to Jim, "I've never been to Hawaii. We need to hit a bar tonight."

"Oh, hell, yes," Jim said.

At 2:00 a.m., Jim Rogers was pounding on Carlin and Dude's door.

"What the fuck do you want?" Carlin asked, seeing it was Jim.

"Willard's in jail."

"Jail! What the fuck for?"

"We walked to a bar down the street. Willard got drunk and started a fight with the bartender. He called the cops, and Willard was arrested. They let me come back to the hotel."

"That stupid son of a bitch."

"The cop told me to tell you that you can bond him out in the morning."

"That stupid son of a bitch. You get the fuck to your room and stay there," Carlin said.

Shutting and locking the door, Carlin got back in bed.

"Don't kill 'im. We're going to need him," Dude said from the next bed, and then added, "That stupid son of a bitch."

9:00 a.m., Monday, August 31, 1987

CARLIN WAS AT THE POLICE STATION bonding Willard out and paying the two-hundred-dollar fine.

"I'm sorry, Carlin. I've never been to Hawaii before and wanted to see a bar," Willard said.

"From now on, you don't do anything without asking me first. Not one goddamned thing. Do you understand?"

"Yes, I'm sorry."

Pulling into the dock, Carlin said, "Go get the damaged hydraulic hose and bracket, the dirty laundry, and Jim. He and Dude are already on board."

"Okay," Willard said. "I'm sorry, Carlin."

"Listen to me, and I'm going to tell you this only once. I love you as my own son. But if you fuck up again, I swear to God, I'll kill you myself. Now go do what I said."

Willard got out of the truck and climbed onto the *California Rose*.

After putting the dirty clothes, broken line, and bracket in the back of the truck, Jim and Willard got in with Carlin. Driving back into Hilo, Carlin dropped the two off at a laundromat and said, "I'll be back in two hours to get you. Be ready."

Carlin then went to a marine machine shop that was recommended to him by a fisherman on the dock.

"What can I do for you?" a man in the shop asked.

"I need this hydraulic line and bracket fixed today. If it costs more money, I can pay. But I need it fixed today. I sail tomorrow," Carlin said to the man.

Looking at the bracket he said, "This will need to be welded, but no problem. Give me until this afternoon, and you can pick it back up. I close at five," he said.

"Thanks, I will be back by four thirty," Carlin said and left.

Driving back to the dock he was met by Valley and Julie.

"Those fucking boys," Valley said angerly.

"Yes, I took care of it. They'll be all right,"

"Did you tell him if you wouldn't kill him, I would?" Valley said.

"You're not killing shit. I took care of it."

"Okay, but stupid shit like that will get us all sent to prison."

Rogers turned towards Valley and said, "I took care of it. Now drop it."

"All right. When can you get underway?" Valley asked.

"First thing in the morning. The line and bracket will be repaired by this afternoon. Will only take an hour or so to get it hooked back up. In the morning, we head north."

"All right. I'm leaving this afternoon. I'll see you back in Pittsburg. Are you still going to the old gravel plant?"

"Yes, just next door. I have a key to the gate. Billy will have a crane on a barge there waiting. It should be quick work to get the trucks loaded and out of there."

Shaking hands, Valley said, "Good luck, Carlin."

As Valley left in the Thunderbird, Dude walked over to Carlin and said, "The fuel truck will be here this afternoon. I'll have the tug filled and another five thousand put in the barge."

"All right, you take care of things here. I need to go get the boys and then go to the grocery store for some more food. Anything you want special other than that fucking baloney you always eat?" Carlin asked.

"Yes, this time buy the whole damn loaf. I can cut my own."

"You do realize that baloney is made from assholes, tongues, and dicks?"

"Just buy the whole damn loaf," Dude said.

After picking the boys up from the laundromat, Carlin drove to the KTA grocery store and filled up three carts of food.

"This should be enough to get home," Willard said.

"Yes, it should with only three eating," Carlin said, looking at Willard while standing in line at the checkout counter.

Willard saw the glare and didn't reply.

Dropping the boys and the groceries off at the vessels, Carlin went back to the repair shop.

"Is it ready?" he asked the man.

"Sure is. Did it rip the line when the bracket failed? the man asked.

"Yes, it did."

"Thought so. I rewelded it heavy. You shouldn't have any problems with it now."

"I'm grateful," Carlin said, paying the man the sixty dollars for the repair. Getting back in the truck and then pulling out of the lot, Carlin said, "Finally, let's get the hell out of here."

CHAPTER 32

MOTHER SHIP

8:00 a.m., Tuesday, September 1, 1987

WITH THE REPAIRS MADE, VESSELS REFUELED, and all on board, the *California Rose* left the dock at Hilo, Hawaii. Once off-shore, Carlin ordered Willard and Jim to extend the cable attached to the barge 1,200 feet. Operating the winch on the main deck, the two watched the line spool out as the tug pulled away from the barge. When it reached the 1,200-foot mark on the winch housing, Willard stopped the unwinding and locked the winch spool in place.

"Twelve hundred feet," he yelled back to Carlin and Dude in the wheelhouse.

Slowly tightening up on the cable catenary, the men could feel the *California Rose* start to dig in as the barge began to move with the vessel.

"Okay, we're at long tow," Carlin yelled. "Secure the hatches."

If nothing else broke, the *California Rose* and barge would be at the rendezvous point in four days, making it the morning of September 5.

GENERAL VADIM VANEREV WAS SITTING in the locked Kremlin office of the KGB. Present also were KGB Officer Vladimir Yukorov, KGB

Head of Foreign Intelligence Victor Krakov, Secretary of Central Committee of Komsomol and the KGB Head of Latvia Karl Gopov, Chairman of State Committee on Prices Nikoli Sergie, and the Soviet Minister of Defense Marshal Damian Kavzo.

Yukorov was addressing the assembly of men. "Gentlemen, this coming Saturday, September 5, the KGB vessel *Poliksena* will rendezvous with the American vessel *California Rose.* They are meeting one thousand nautical miles north of Hawaii. Transferring of the forty-five tons of drugs from the *Poliksena* to the American barge will begin then. Offloading will take two or three days, depending on how calm the weather is.

"A hole in the deck of the barge will be cut to lower the drugs into the hull. Once offloading is completed, the shipment will be secured by welding the hole in the deck. This new welded area will be repainted, and a twenty-foot container will be pushed on top of the area and chained down. There are four containers on top of the barge. All of them contain tons of marine parts, oil, fuel, cables, tools, and food. If the *California Rose* is stopped and boarded while returning to the United States, either by the Coast Guard or navy, the boarding party will find nothing suspicious and will have no way of finding the drugs. This design by the American captain, I believe, is ingenious and will look like every other supply vessel operation."

The men of Red Sword nodded.

Yukorov continued, "It will take approximately twelve days for the *California Rose* and barge to return to the US, give or take a day, depending on the weather. So during the week of September 20, the vessels will return to America. The removal of the drugs will be conducted at a hidden site fifty miles east of San Francisco. The loading of the trucks will take two or three days. Once the trucks are loaded, the money will be released to our account in the Bank of Paris, Luxembourg. We will have 49.5 million dollars."

General Vanerev looked at group and said, "We'll be halfway there. Go on, Vlad."

"Even after we pay the American 4 million and the drug lord 1.35 million, we will still have 44.15 million dollars on the first run.

Gentlemen we're going to make another run later this year and one next spring, if need be. The deal with the drug lord is for one hundred tons. But he'll sell whatever he has once he knows the shipments are safe, and I think this is foolproof. Any questions gentlemen?"

No one asked a single question. Nodding, Marshal Kavzo stood, shook hands with the other men, and walked out of the room. He was quickly followed by Gopov, Sergie, and Krakov.

Once the two were alone, General Vanerev asked Yukorov, "How much chance do we have to succeed?

"Ninety-five percent, General, if no one's watching us."

"Nope, not a sound," Taylor told Davis after being asked if the USCG VTS had heard from the *California Rose*.

"All right. How about lunch? I'll buy this time," Davis said, sitting in the Jeep at McAvoy Harbor.

"Cool. See you when you get here," Taylor said.

"Okay, see you about lunchtime," Davis said and hung up. Feeling his pager go off, he saw that Klass had paged him.

"Good morning, Bob," Davis said, after calling Klass's phone.

"Anything new?" Klass asked.

"No, nothing. I'm looking at different areas now. More upstream towards Sacramento."

"You're not going to like this, but this fall you will need to go to FLETC for criminal investigator training for eight weeks."

"When Bob?"

"Not sure of the exact dates yet, but it should be around November 1. I should know more in a few days."

"Well, fuck."

"Yes, I know. But you must go, or your cover is shit."

"Okay, let me know when as soon as you can."

"Will do. Let me know if you find anything," Klass said and hung up.

"Fuck," Davis said. I can't tell him why I can't go, he thought. "Fuck!" he said again. If he were going to be away, at least Taylor would still keep Davis informed of any travel of the *California Rose*.

And if need be, he could fly back in a few hours. "Fuck!" he said. Davis pulled out of McAvoy and headed for Yerba Buena Island and lunch with Taylor.

Daylight, September 5, 1987

"*Western Star*, *Western Star*, *Western Star*, this is *Ulu*, *Ulu*, *Ulu*. Over," Carlin said in the microphone. There had been no reply for the past thirty minutes of trying to reach the mother ship. Carlin checked the frequency to make sure it was on 161.7. It was.

"Are you sure we're at 38, 155?" Carlin asked Dude.

"Yes, I'm sure."

"Recheck your figures."

"I said I'm sure."

"I said to recheck your fucking figures," Carlin said, looking at Dude.

Carlin had not said anything up to this point, but Dude, Jim, and Willard had been smoking weed every day, and they were all high. Everyone was high, except Carlin who didn't do drugs.

After a few minutes, Dude said, "I may have made a mistake. Can you check these calculations?"

"What?" Carlin asked. "You sons of bitches are all high. No more fucking drug use on this boat. If I smell one more whiff of weed, I'm throwing all of you assholes overboard." Looking at the calculations Carlin yelled, "No more fucking weed. You are off three hundred fucking miles! We're not at 38, 155. We're at 38, 150. You didn't calculate the drift. No more fucking weed. Get this thing turned west, Dude. No more fuckups!" Carlin yelled.

It didn't make much difference. The *Poliksena* had hit a storm north of Wake Island, and it had also lost a day in the turbulent North Pacific. Hurrying to catch up on schedule, Captain Faucher had increased his engine speed to 1,800 rpms and would be at the rendezvous point by mid-day on the sixth. That night the vessels made radio contact, and it was confirmed that the new rendezvous point would be one hundred miles closer to the *California Rose*. Carlin liked that. He'd have time to swing around to the barge and be ready when the *Poliksena* arrived.

The next morning at daylight Dude bowed the *California Rose* to the side of the barge, and it was secured. Dude stayed in the wheelhouse while Carlin, Jim, and Willard climbed onto the barge. A container was moved over with a winch, and with the cutting torch, a two-by-four-foot hole was cut in the deck above the number four compartment. After placing plywood and plastic over the floor inside the barge, a slide was built with two-by-eights and plywood. This was also covered with plastic to protect the boxes and bags when they would be slid down into the barge.

The wall hatch between compartment four and three was opened, and sections of rollers were placed through the opening to slide the boxes of Thai from compartment four to compartment three where they would be stored. Carlin and crew had everything ready.

1:00 p.m., Sunday, September 6, 1987

The *California Rose* and *Poliksena* found each other.

"Affirmative, *Wester Star*. I'll position the barge against your port side over," Dude said.

"Acknowledged. *Ulu* will standby for your positioning. Over," Faucher said.

"All right, Dude. Let's do it right the first time," Carlin said.

It took both crews over an hour to get the vessels secured up against each other and tied off. But the water was smooth, and the offloading would soon begin.

The much shorter Captain Faucher stood with Carlin on the barge. He looked like a midget next to the big man. But his dark greying hair and weathered face showed he'd spent many years at sea. Looking at Carlin he said, "They shorted us on the Thai."

"How much?"

"Three tons, but they said they'll give us thirteen tons next trip."

"I know someone who's going to be pissed. But if they make it up next trip, that should be all right."

"They said they would."

Before the offloading began, Carlin told Jim to go back on the *California Rose* and listen to the radio and watch the radar for any surface vessels in the area. Captain Faucher returned to his ship to do the same, and he told Simeon to start the offload. Simeon had done this many times, and he kept both crews hustling.

The crane boom and net of the *Poliksena* was loaded with boxes of Thai marijuana first and then extended over to the deck of the barge where they were unloaded. Willard and one of the *Poliksena* crew members got down into the barge forward compartment number three. Two of the *Poliksena* crew members got down into compartment number four at the bottom of the slide. Two other *Poliksena* crew members stood on the barge and unloaded the net, handing the boxes to Carlin, who slid them down into the first compartment. Once the boxes were down below deck, they were shoved across to Willard on the sections of rollers where he and the other man stacked them up. Dude stood next to Carlin with a hand counter and clicked as every box passed.

It was well past midnight when Dude said, "Six hundred sixty-seven," after all the boxes of Thai had been loaded into the barge.

"Okay, let's call it a night. Everyone's beat," Carlin said.

Shaking hands with Simeon and the other crew members of the *Poliksena*, Carlin said, "Thank you, fellows. Will see you in the morning."

It took all of Monday and most of Tuesday to load the 1,800 bags of hashish into compartment number four of the barge. Both crews were exhausted after carrying that many fifty-pound sacks. Finally, the offloading was complete, and the *Poliksena* left after thankful handshakes and slaps on the back.

As the *Poliksena* pulled away, Captain Faucher called Yukorov's mobile phone and said, "The offloading is complete."

"*Khorosho*," Yukorov said, pleased. After hanging up, he called General Vanerev. "They've completed the offload, General. The American is heading back to San Francisco."

"I wish I could pull my troops out now. If this goes smoothly and we get our money without any problems, the next time, I'm moving my troops as soon as I can."

"Yes, sir. I believe this will go as planned."

Carlin told Dude and Jim to get the *California Rose* headed back towards San Francisco. He and Willard stayed on the barge and finished up. They welded support tabs underneath the deck hole, the deck plate was laid back into position where it had been cut out, and then they rewelded it. After the weld cooled, it was wire brushed and repainted. Using a hand winch, the men pulled the container back over the spot and chained it back down to the deck.

Being well after dark, Carlin called the *California Rose* on the handheld radio. "We'll stay here tonight in the empty container. After daylight, swing back around and pick us up. Over."

"Will do. Get some rest. Jim has first watch. I'll relieve him at two a.m. Over," Dude said.

"All right. See you in the morning. Over," Carlin said and put the radio down next to his sleeping bag, lying on the floor of the container. "I'm fucking tired," he said to Willard, who'd already passed out and was starting to snore.

CHAPTER 33

Inbound

9:00 a.m., Friday, September 11, 1987

Luba handed a cup of coffee to Yukorov as he sat in Colonel Petroff's office.

"Thank you," Yukorov said.

"You're welcome, sir," she said, turned, and shut the inner door behind her as she walked back to her desk.

"When did you get a coffeemaker?" Yukorov asked the colonel.

"Last week. I've been spending so much time here late in the day I thought a coffeemaker was a good idea."

"I think so too," Yukorov said and then added, "The first shipment has been delivered to the American's ship."

"When?"

"Couple days ago. They're on their way back in. They should get there in a week or ten days.

"That's really good. Is the general pleased?"

"Yes, but he wishes he could start his troop movement now."

"That'll take some time once he starts. Not easy to move a hundred thousand troops quickly," the colonel said.

"If this goes smoothly, next time he's going to order the withdrawal when the next load of drugs is delivered to the American captain. He's tired of waiting."

AT EIGHT THAT EVENING, PETROFF RETURNED to the Kremlin after eating dinner with Tanya. He saluted the guards as he walked in, saying, "Good evening, men."

"Good evening, Colonel," the two guards said.

After Petroff went into the stairwell and started climbing towards his office, one guard said, "I've never seen an officer work as hard as the colonel does. He's here all hours of the day and night. What a great man."

In his office, Petroff locked the doors behind him and once again swept the room for bugs. Finding none, he placed the wand back into his briefcase and then called Buddy Hayden's pager, putting in 1880.

HAYDEN WAS SITTING BUTT-ASS NAKED in a chair at Hick's house while she was doing a striptease for his lunch break. "You are one sexy bitch," Hayden said stroking himself.

"Yes, I'm a fucking hot slut," she said, as she rubbed her nipples and slid her hand over her panties she had pulled up into her crotch. "Is daddy going to fuck me hard for being a naughty girl?"

"Oh yes, daddy's going to pound you hard, baby."

Melinda moved her fingers out of her crotch and slid them into Hayden's mouth when he heard his pager go off.

"God damnit!" he mumbled with Hick's fingers still in his mouth. "Where're my pants?" Getting up, he picked his pants up off the floor and looked at the pager. "God damnit. I have to go."

Thirty minutes later, Hayden walked into his office at the DOD building and locked the door behind him. Getting the STU ready, he wondered what information Petroff would have. He already knew the *California Rose* and barge were missing. After a half-hour more, the STU rang.

"*Moy dobryy drug*," Hayden said.

"My good friend," Petroff replied. "Buddy, the drugs have been delivered to the American vessels. They will arrive in seven to ten days."

"All right. How are you doing, my friend?" Buddy asked.

"I'm good, Buddy. It was hard, but I'm now doing much better."

"You're in my prayers, Dimitri."

"Thank you, my friend. Goodbye," Petroff said and hung up his phone.

Hayden dialed Reynolds in Vacaville.

"Hello."

"The offload from the *Poliksena* to Rogers has been completed. They'll arrive back in San Fran in seven to ten days."

"Okay. I'll pass that info to Tony. He has a place picked out to surveil he thinks they'll use to unload. I'll join him when the vessels arrive. He's to be notified by the Coast Guard when the *California Rose* contacts VTS. We should have three or four hours to set up."

"That sounds good. Make sure you guys are not burnt. This offload may take a couple of days to complete. Be prepared to stay two or three days once you get set up. I know you know this, Jack, but be equipped. I need to stress again at this point we are protecting Rogers and Valley. This needs to go down without a hitch."

Roger that," Reynolds said. "I'll have plenty with me and will make sure Tony does too. I'll give him a call now. Talk later," Reynolds said.

"All right," Hayden said.

After hanging up with Hayden, Reynolds called Davis's bag phone.

"Hello," Davis said.

"Tony, it's Jack. Buddy heard from the source. The vessels will be back in seven to ten days. The offload from the mother ship has been completed."

"Today's the eleventh, so sometime around the eighteenth to the twenty-first. That's next weekend or later," Davis said.

"Yes. How sure are you on the offload site?"

"Not sure at all. But that's where I'd go."

"Okay, we go with that. You've been right on so far. No need to mess with success."

"I do have a problem, Jack."

"What?"

"Klass told me that in November, I'll need to go to FLETC for criminal investigator training."

"For how long?" Reynolds asked.

"Eight weeks."

"Fuck."

"That's what I said. But he said if I don't, it'll mess with my cover story. I can't tell him why I can't go. He'd kill us all."

"Fuck," Reynolds said. "Even if Buddy would stop this at FLETC, Bob would know something's up. He would know it came from Buddy to keep you here, and he'd want to know why."

"The good part of this is the Coast Guard will keep me informed if the *California Rose* moves. If it does, I can always jump on a flight and get back here in a few hours. Buddy can smooth it over with the instructors, and Klass will have no way of knowing I skipped class."

"Fuck. I still don't like it. But we have no choice. We have to keep your cover intact. Sooner or later, that's going to come up, and it needs to be airtight," Reynolds said.

"Okay, a day at a time. Hopefully, nothing goes on while I'm at FLETC anyway," Davis said.

Davis and Reynolds had no way of knowing, but that November and December, all hell was going to break loose.

CHAPTER 34

VTS

10:00 p.m., Sunday, September 20, 1987

DAVIS HAD BEEN ASLEEP MAYBE FIFTEEN MINUTES when his bag phone rang.

"Hello," he said.

"Tony, it's Ray. The *California Rose* just checked in with VTS and said it was inbound to Pittsburg."

"Okay, thank you, Ray. Maybe tomorrow, I'll ride up and take a look at it. Anything else going on? Davis asked.

"No, same ol', same ol'."

"Well, thanks for calling, Ray. You have a good night."

"You too, Tony. Good night."

Throwing the covers off, Davis jumped up and grabbed the clothes he'd had lying on a chair next to the bed for the past week. He put on the black long-sleeve turtleneck poly top, jeans, and Danner boots and then called Reynolds's phone.

"Hello."

"Jack, we're on. Taylor just called. The *California Rose* is inbound to Pittsburg."

"Okay, meet you at the CVS in Concord in an hour."

"Roger that."

Grabbing his backpack, Davis placed the phone and pistol inside and ran out the door, jumped in the Mustang, and headed north to Concord. Fifty minutes later, he could see Reynolds's truck off to the side and pulled up beside it. He got out, taking his pack, locked the Mustang door, and got in the passenger side with Reynolds.

"I hope you've got food and water because I'm not sharing shit," Reynolds said as he drove the truck out of the parking lot towards Pittsburg on Highway 4.

"Is a frog's ass watertight?" Davis asked.

"What?" Reynolds said.

"Haven't you ever watched the old *Hee Haw* TV series?"

"What?"

"Lily Tomlin on *Hee Haw*. Didn't you ever watch it?"

"Fuck no. I think I was in Vietnam getting shot when you were picking your nose and watching *Hee Haw*."

Laughing, Davis said, "Lily Tomlin answered a question one time saying, 'Is a frog's ass watertight?' meaning yes, like "Is the pope Catholic?" Davis continued with a laugh. "Okay, get off on Willow Pass Road. Go back under the highway, go a half-mile, and turn left onto Port Chicago Highway."

Reynolds followed the directions.

Then Davis said, "Up ahead on your left is the Shore Acres Shopping Center. We park there."

Pulling in, Reynolds parked on the far end, facing the road and said, "What now?"

Pointing to the north, Davis said, "Up that way, quarter-mile, is McAvoy Harbor. To the right of the entrance to McAvoy is an old gravel plant. That's where I would unload the barge. If it's deep enough for a gravel barge, it's deep enough for a barge full of drugs."

"Good point," Reynolds said.

"We cross the road here. Go around that building, and there's an old railroad track behind that curves back towards the gravel plant. We'll be within 150 yards of it."

"Okay, let's do it," Reynolds said.

Both men looked around, but no one was out at 11:00 p.m. on a Sunday night. Grabbing their packs, the two hurried across the road and started through the field below the building. Once out of range of the streetlights, they stopped and put on their NVG, stored in their packs. Losing some depth perception with the NVG, the men slowed their walk as they went through the pitch-black field. Neither wanted to step in a hole and sprain an ankle.

Reaching the railroad track, Davis said, "Out there another hundred yards, the gravel plant will be at our ten o'clock."

"I can see some lights over there," Reynolds said.

"Yes, those are at McAvoy. To the right of that where it's dark is the gravel plant."

Getting to where Davis thought was a good spot, they crossed the tracks and sat down in the high brush.

"Straight in that direction," Davis said, pointing his hand with fingers close together, "is the gravel plant. I think they'll come here to offload."

With the NVG, Reynolds could see Davis pointing in the pitch black.

"I'm taking these off," Davis said, pulling off the goggles. "I need my eyes to adjust."

Reynolds did the same, putting the goggles away, and pulled out a pair of binoculars from his pack.

"You got binocs?" Reynolds asked, as he held an old large pair of M19 7x50 power binoculars.

"Yes," Davis said, looking at Reynolds's relic. He pulled out a small 10 power Zeiss and put the strap around his neck. Reaching again into his pack, Davis pulled out a small tube of black face paint cream. "You need any of this?" Davis asked.

"No, I have my own," Reynolds said, reaching into his pocket and pulling out a stick of camo paint in a metal case with two end caps

"How old is that shit?" Davis said, squinting his eyes, finally adjusting to the darkness.

"Probably before you were born," Reynolds said as he rubbed the hard black stick against his face.

Davis softly laughed as he took a small amount of the cream out of the tube, rubbed it between both hands and then spread it all over his face, neck, and back of his hands, finishing before Reynolds had his forehead completed. "Are you sure you don't want some of this?" he whispered to Reynolds.

"No, I'm good," he said.

Davis chuckled in the dark, watching the old warrior rub his skin off with the Vietnam War–era camo stick.

"Fuck you," Reynolds whispered, rubbing the paint stick on his face and trying to get comfortable.

"Seriously, Jack, how old are you?"

"Forty-three."

"You know, I used to love crawling around in the woods at night. But I'm thirty-three, and I'm starting to think, I'm too fucking old to be doing this," Davis said looking at Reynolds.

"Buddy and I had this same conversation a few months ago. We're both going to hang it up after this."

"What are you going to do?"

"After I got shot up in Nam, they put me with the 1/11 Armored Cavalry Regiment. They basically let me ride for the remainder of my tour. This may sound odd, but I kinda liked it. I've been thinking about going back to school and getting a degree in safety."

"You going to do that in Maine?"

"No, Carol wants to be closer to her mother in Frederick, Maryland. So I'll see what develops."

"When you get to that point, check out WVU. If I'm not mistaken, they have degree programs in safety," Davis said.

"Hmm, I will," Reynolds said, looking at Davis.

2:00 a.m., Monday, September 21, 1987

After about three hours, Reynolds and Davis watched a vessel light turn towards them out in the delta.

"What do you think?" Reynolds asked.

"The timing is about right," Davis said.

Both men watched as the vessel light got closer.

"That's the *California Rose*," Davis said, looking through his binoculars.

The barge was close behind the tug as the vessels came into the gravel plant area.

"That's new," Davis said.

"What?" Reynolds said.

"I couldn't see it before because of the darkness, but there's small barge already there with a crane on it. That wasn't there the other day."

Voices could be heard as the *California Rose* shoved the barge it had been towing up against the bank, pinning it there. The crew then tied both vessels to the pilings.

Davis and Reynolds lay there, watching and listening. But there was not much activity after the vessels arrived. Hours later, after daylight, a vehicle began down Port Chicago Highway and onto McAvoy Road. It stopped at the gated entrance to the gravel plant.

"That's Sara Lawson's Lexus," Davis whispered. He looked at his watch. It was seven o'clock. "And that's Carlin Rogers opening the gate," Davis said.

Davis and Reynolds watched the big man get in the car and it pull up to the tug and barge. Then a woman and Rogers got out of the car and talked to three other men. At times voices could be heard but not what was being said; it was just too far.

"We need a directional mic," Reynolds said.

"Yes," Davis said. "I thought you were bringing it," he whispered, looking at Reynolds.

"Fuck you," Reynolds whispered back.

After a short while, Sara Lawson, Carlin Rogers, and another man got in the car and left.

"Wonder where they're going," Reynolds said.

"I don't know, but I bet things start picking up."

An hour later, several vehicles drove into the gravel plant.

Both men watched through their binoculars.

"That's Carlin Rogers in the red crew cab," Davis said. "And that's

Billy Little in the old green truck. And looky there. That's Terrance George Valley in the tan pickup."

Behind those vehicles were two tractor trucks, one black and one tan. The black truck was pulling a lowboy trailer. The tan truck was towing a flatbed trailer. All the vehicles pulled up to the barge area.

"The two young men getting out of Valley's truck, I don't know who they are. You see the tall boy on the barge, blond hair?" Davis asked.

"Yes," Reynolds said, looking through his binoculars.

"That's Willard. Don't know his last name. Getting up on the barge now, the big man is Carlin Rogers, and the guy getting up behind him is Valley," Davis said.

"Yes, it is. Look at that fucker," Reynolds whispered. "You know, he's definitely a risk to our operation. Those other guys aren't trained, but that son of a bitch is a highly trained operator. If we get the chance, and if we can do it without alerting Rogers too much, we need to off his ass."

"All right. You just tell me when."

"Better idea, though, I need to take him someplace and speak to him for several days."

"Butterfly, butterfly," Davis softly sang, sitting there in the high weeds.

Reynolds glanced at Davis, chuckled, and said, "That didn't hurt that much, you fucking pussy."

"No, it actually didn't. I was too mad to feel anything. I wanted to kill all you sons of bitches."

Reynolds softly laughed as Davis looked at him and smiled.

"What the fuck are they doing now?" Reynolds asked, seeing a dark blue tarp being raised on the barge.

"Putting up a tarp so no one can see them unload the drugs into the containers. Those trucks are going to carry those containers away."

"I bet you're right."

FOR THE REST OF THE DAY CARLIN ROGERS, Billy Little, Terrence George Valley, Willard Butler, Jim Rogers, the two truck drivers, and the two other men removed the 1,800 fifty-pound sacks of hashish and 667 twenty-one-pound boxes of Thai marijuana and placed all into three of the containers on the barge. Fortunately for Davis and Rogers, it was a genuinely nice sunny day of seventy degrees with moderate wind off of the water.

BY 3:00 P.M., REYNOLDS WAS TRADING DAVIS beef jerky for peanut butter crackers. Each had four bottles of Gatorade in their packs.

"That goes good together," Reynolds said.

"Yes, it does. Who would've thought that?"

"And the Gatorade tops it off," Reynolds said as Davis laughed.

"I bet you Billy wishes he had some. He's been standing guard at that gate for hours," Davis said with a chuckle.

"Yeah, the poor fuck got guard duty," Reynolds said. "That always sucks. I've got to piss out some of this Gatorade."

"Go ahead and piss yourself. I'll never tell," Davis said.

"Don't think so. I'm going to crawl over there and piss lying on my side," Reynolds said, as he crawled about ten feet into the high brush. After relieving himself, he crawled back and said, "Doctor says my prostate is enlarged. That's the reason, I have to piss so often. He says I need a TURP procedure, whatever the fuck that is."

"I know what that is," Davis said.

"What is it?"

"I don't know what TURP stands for, but the procedure described to me is they strap a man down on a bed, wipe the end of your dick with some type of antiseptic, and then run a quarter-inch drill bit up your dick until it bottoms out. They have to pull it in and out a few times to cut out all of the tissue that's blocking the urine flow," Davis said, looking at Reynolds.

"Fuck that," Reynolds said, looking at Davis.

"I hear it's highly successful. And don't worry. They shove a handful of gauze in your mouth so you don't bite your tongue off or chip your teeth."

"I'd rather piss myself," Reynolds said as Davis laughed.

"You should've seen the look on your face," Davis said, quietly laughing as tears ran down his cheeks.

"Fuck you," Reynolds whispered.

After dark, Reynolds and Davis watched Willard and another man get in the red Ford crew cab with Carlin Rogers and leave. An hour later, Carlin returned by himself. The two truck drivers got in their cabs and stayed there. Valley and the two men with him left the area in the tan pickup. By 10:00 p.m., all was quiet on the *California Rose* and barge.

"I think they're done for tonight," Davis said.

"Yes, I agree," Reynolds said, pulling an old poncho liner out of his pack. "We need to get some sleep."

"Yes," Davis said pulling an ultralight sleeping bag with Gore-Tex liner out of his pack. "I got first watch. You get some sleep, pappy. I'll wake you at 0200."

"Fuck you," Reynolds said as he tried to curl up in the old liner and go to sleep.

Davis chuckled as he watched the old warrior drift off to sleep, his body jerking as he went.

CHAPTER 35

Money Is Released

3:00 a.m., Tuesday, September 22, 1987

Davis let Reynolds sleep until he couldn't keep his eyes open any longer. Lightly shaking him, Davis said softly, "Jack, wake up."

Stirring and then opening his eyes, he said, "We catch any walleyes?"

"No, but I've been watching an old carp snore all night."

Stretching in his poncho liner, Reynolds looked at his watch. "It's three o'clock."

"Yeah, I thought you needed your sleep, you old fuck."

"Fuck you. Okay, I'm on. Get some sleep. I'll wake you as soon as something happens."

"Okay," Davis said as he slid into this bag. "If I snore, just roll me over onto my side."

"You snore and I'm kicking you in the fucking back," Reynolds said as Davis laughed.

It was turning daylight at 6:30 a.m. when Davis began to wake to the sound of birds in the reeds along the water. Looking at his watch, he sat up, rubbing his eyes and face. "Nothing?" he asked.

"No," Reynolds said.

Taking a drink of Gatorade, Davis said, "I really need to piss," and he crawled to the side to relieve himself.

"If you need to take a dump, go about thirty yards farther."

"I think I'm good, but with that beef jerky and those peanut butter crackers, I may just start building pressure soon," Davis replied.

Reynolds chuckled as Davis crawled back to his spot.

"I think they'll be out of here early this morning," Davis said.

"Yes, I think so too. I wouldn't stay here any longer than necessary."

At seven, Valley's tan pickup pulled up to the gravel plant entrance. One man got out and unlocked the chain, opened the gate, and then swung it closed after the truck pulled in. Davis and Reynolds watched Valley talk to the two truck drivers who had gotten out of their rigs. After a short conversation, all the men went into the *California Rose.* A half-hour later, a small silver car pulled up to the gate, and two men got out. They walked into the area, and the silver car left.

"That's Willard and the other guy from yesterday," Davis said. "I don't know who's driving the car. Looks like a female."

The two men boarded the *California Rose.* A few minutes later, Carlin, Billy, Valley, and the two truck drivers were looking at the crane on the small barge. Carlin then got in his truck and left again.

"Where the fuck is he going?" Davis said.

"I don't think that crane can pick up one of those containers if it's loaded. Maybe empty, but not loaded," Reynolds said.

"Well, they'd better shit one out pretty quick then."

An hour later, Carlin returned with a wheeled crane and operator following him. The operator positioned the crane hook over one of the containers. But after several tries, the crane was not able to lift the heavy load.

"They're fucked if they can't get those containers off that barge," Reynolds said.

"They sure are. God damnit, I didn't think I would be rooting for a bunch of drug smugglers, but come on, boys!"

Carlin left again with the crane and operator following him. An hour later, Carlin returned, and this time, a huge wheeled crane followed him with the same operator. The flatbed trailer and truck were put in position and the large crane placed two containers on its bed. The truck driver and Carlin chained the containers down while Billy was again watching the gate entrance. After the flatbed was loaded, it pulled out of the way. The lowboy trailer was then backed up and the crane placed one container on its bed. This was also chained down by the driver. Davis and Reynolds watched as the work was completed and then the men entered the *California Rose.*

IT WAS NOON WHEN CARLIN GAVE THE CRANE OPERATOR five one-hundred-dollar bills and said, "Thank you. That was more work than I expected."

"You're welcome. Would have gone easier if we could've unloaded the containers first," the man said.

"Yes, but that's not possible. Those are sealed loads and can't be opened until they get to the buyer."

"Sure is heavy for marine parts, but thanks for the work," the operator said as he left to take the crane back to Alfred's Crane, located two miles away.

"Okay," Valley said, "let's make the call."

"All right," said one of the truck drivers.

Valley called a number on his mobile phone.

"Good afternoon. Monarch National Bank. How may I direct your call?" the operator asked.

"Phillip DePantera, please," Valley said.

"Who may I say is calling, please?" the operator asked.

"George Hannah," Valley said.

"Just a minute, sir," she said and put Valley on hold.

A few moments later, DePantera said, "Hello, George."

"Good afternoon, Phillip. I have a gentleman here that needs to speak to you," and handed the phone to the truck driver.

"Mr. DePantera, the trucks are loaded."

"What's the count?" DePantera asked.

"Forty-five tons of sacks, and seven tons of boxes," the driver said.

"Let me speak to Mr. Hannah, please."

Handing the phone back to Valley, DePantera asked, "Seven tons of Thai, George?"

"Yes, they shorted us on the first run. They said they'll make it up with the next shipment of thirteen tons," Valley said.

"Okay. George, the one payment to your Luxembourg account will be adjusted accordingly. The other payment to your account will be per our agreement. And Mr. Yuk's payment will be according to our agreement as well. I'll transfer the money today, and it will be available tomorrow."

"Thank you, Phillip. As always, it's a pleasure doing business with you. I'll advise as soon as I know about the next shipment."

"Very good, George. Let me speak to my driver, please."

Valley handed the phone back to the truck driver.

"Yes, Mr. DePantera."

"Earl, you may proceed. If you have any problems, let me know. I'll see you in a few days," DePantera said.

"Yes, sir. We'll leave now," the truck driver said and hung up the phone, handing it back to Valley.

Shaking hands with Valley and Carlin, the two truck drivers got in their trucks and pulled out, heading north towards Seattle. From Seattle, the trucks would continue into Vancouver, British Columbia. There, the trucks would be met by members of the BC Chapter of the Hells Angels motorcycle gang. The Hells Angels now dominated organized crime in Canada and were the muscle, distributors, and enforcers for the drug syndicate out of New York and Toronto.

After the trucks left, Little walked back to the *California Rose* where Carlin and Valley were talking.

"I'll take Willard and Jim back to the hotel," Carlin said. "Willard has his truck there. He can take Jim home."

"Okay. I'm going home and calling the Russian," Valley said. "He can check his account tomorrow and make sure the money's there." Looking at Carlin, he asked, "Have you decided how you want your next payment?"

"Yes, I want bearer bonds, four two-hundred-thousand and two one-hundred-thousand."

"Okay, I'll have those delivered to you. It'll be the same people as before."

"That'll work."

"I'll double-check and make sure we left nothing after you guys leave," Billy said as all three men were shaking hands.

"We fucking did it! We fucking did it!" Valley said.

Yes, we did," Carlin replied.

REYNOLDS AND DAVIS WATCHED AS WILLARD and the other young man threw two duffle bags in the back of Carlin's truck, get in with Carlin, and leave. The other man and Valley got in his truck and also left. Billy Little looked around for a few minutes, got in his truck, and drove out, locking the gate behind him.

Carlin dropped Willard and Jim off at the Motel 6 in Pittsburg, telling them, "I'll call you around the first of October. We'll meet then, and I'll have your money."

"Thank you, Carlin," both boys said as he drove away.

Walking to Willard's truck, Jim said, "He'll kill us if he ever finds out we took five bricks of hash."

"You keep two and I'll keep three. That sound all right with you?" Willard asked.

"Yes, I'll never smoke two bricks in a year."

"I'm selling some of mine. I have a friend in Longview that'll sell it for me," Willard said.

"Just be careful nobody finds out. Carlin and Billy will both fucking kill us," Jim said.

"They'll never know. Get in. I need to get you to Santa Rosa. Then I'm heading home to Fairview."

STILL LYING IN THE HIGH BRUSH, Davis said, "You know what they're thinking about now, Jack?"

"That they're rich?"

"Yes, but they're really fucking thinking they got away with it."

Reynolds looked at Davis, and both men smiled.

"Do you know what?" Davis said.

“What?”

“We’re the ones that really did it,” Davis said, extending his hand towards Reynolds.

Reynolds took his hand, shook it, and said, “Yes, we did. Let’s get the hell out of here. Police the area.”

Making sure nothing was let behind, they picked up their packs and walked out, retracing their route back to the road and crossing it to Reynolds’s pickup.

Arriving back at the Concord CVS, Davis got out Reynolds’s pickup. As he was getting in the Mustang, he said, “I’m going to go get some sleep. See ya, Jack.”

“See ya, Tony. Great job. I’ll call Buddy, and then I’m sleeping for the next two days.”

CHAPTER 36

International Drug Money

3:00 p.m., Tuesday, September 22, 1987

Terrence George Valley arrived at his home on Little Bluff Road after dropping his oldest son off at his home in Placerville. Walking into the house, he went straight to his liquor cabinet and took out an unopened bottle of Redbreast 27 Irish Whiskey. For the first time, took the cap off and smelled the top of the bottle. "Damn, that smells good," he said as he sat down in his favorite chair in the living room. Putting the bottle to his lips, he took a huge drink before lowering it. "Goddamn, that's good, and I'm fucking rich."

Picking up his phone he called Moscow, Russia, knowing it was 11:00 p.m. there.

"*Da*," the sleepy voice said, answering the phone.

"Wake the fuck up," Valley said.

"I'm awake. Did you make it?"

"Yes, no problems. I talked to the buyer. Your money will be in your account tomorrow."

"Wonderful, I'll call the general tomorrow after I confirm the money's in the account."

"When you confirm your money, you tell Mr. Andre that he's to transfer four million into the account of Mr. Hannah. He'll know what account you're referring to. That way, I can pay Carlin."

"I'll do that."

"Okay. As soon as you can, we need to start working on the December shipment," Valley said.

"Yes, I'll set it up with Afridi. He's mentioned he wants to load the next shipment in Karachi by the end of November."

"One other thing, we only got seven tons of Thai. So your payment will be 350,000. But I was told the next shipment will be thirteen tons."

"You wouldn't be fucking me, would you?" Yukorov asked.

"No, this is straight up. If we don't get the thirteen tons next time, I'll give you the name of a man I want you to visit.

"I will if we don't get the correct amount next time."

"Okay, how do you want to receive your money? I can have two Canadians deliver cash to you if you wish."

Yukorov thought and said, "Yes, but not in Russia. Can they fly to Kabul?"

"Yes, they can fly to Kabul. Is that where you would like to meet them?"

"*Da.*"

"Okay, I'll set that up. They'll fly in on a private jet. You'll have to meet them off the tarmac and on their plane."

"I can do that."

"I'll provide them with your mobile phone number so they can contact you directly to select a date. It'll take a few days for me to set this up, but it can be easily done."

"Okay, I'll be expecting their call. I can fly to Kabul at any time," Yukorov said.

"Good, I'll check my Luxembourg account tomorrow afternoon to make sure the four mil is in there. I'll then contact the Canadians and advise them to contact you. I'll be in touch."

"All right. Goodbye," Yukorov said.

"Goodbye," Valley said and hung up. Laying the phone down, Valley said, "Goddamn," and took another big drink of Redbreast 27.

CARLIN ROGERS ARRIVED AT ALMOND HILL LANE and went into Sara and Doug's house. Sara was sitting on the couch in the living room reading her Bible. Carlin walked in and sat down on the chair next to her. He could tell she was upset.

"What are you reading?"

"Ecclesiastes 12, verses 13 and 14."

"I can't remember it. Can you read it to me, please?"

"Okay," she said. "'Now, all has been heard. Here is the conclusion of the matter. Fear God and keep his commandments holy, for this is the sole duty of man. For God will bring every deed into judgement, including every hidden thing, whether it be good or evil.'"

Carlin looked at his sister who now had tears in her eyes.

"It'll be all right, Sara. Read Job 24. I think it's a better scripture," he said as he got up and walked out of the house.

DAVIS ARRIVED AT THE SAFEHOUSE IN Hayward and walked into the kitchen, taking the blue bag of Crown Royal off the refrigerator. He took the bag off the bottle, unscrewed the cap, and took a big drink. Coughing, he put the cap back on and the bottle back on top of the refrigerator. "I need to sleep," he said as he walked towards his bedroom.

AT THE VACAVILLE SAFEHOUSE, REYNOLDS TOOK THE KEYS for the STU out of the safe and popped open the bookcase door to the hidden room. Picking up the receiver, he called Hayden's pager. He entered, 1024707, indicating assignment complete and the Vacaville area code.

BUDDY HAYDEN'S PAGER WENT OFF AS HE AND MELINDA were sitting down to a romantic candlelight dinner at his home. Hayden had grilled filet mignon on the back patio, Melinda's favorite. Watching Buddy's eyes get big when he looked at this pager, she said, "We can warm them in the microwave when you get back."

"Holy shit," Hayden said as he kissed Melinda and ran out of the house, forgetting about the diamond ring in his pocket. Arriving at the DOD building, he limped in as fast as he could, shut his office door behind him, and locked it. He got his STU key out and dialed Reynolds.

"Three, two, one, go," Hayden said as the men keyed in their STUs.

"Went off without a hitch. They showed up night before last and got everything loaded in three containers yesterday. This morning, they got a big crane and loaded one container on a lowboy trailer and two containers on a flatbed, and away they went."

"Damn, that's great news. You didn't take any pictures or collect any evidence that could be embarrassing later on, did you?" Hayden asked.

"No, none. Like it never happened." Reynolds said.

"All right. I'll advise the director."

"We do have one bump."

"What?" Hayden asked.

"Klass wants Davis to return to FLETC in November for CI training."

"Well shit," Hayden said. After thinking a few moments, he said, "We can't stop that, or Bob will want to know why."

"I agree, but it can still work. Davis's Coast Guard buddy will advise him anytime the *California Rose* moves, that is, if they keep checking in with VTS, and up to this point they've been consistent."

"Okay, let's play this by ear. If Davis needs to get back out there in a hurry, I can put him on the company jet. He'll be there in six, seven hours tops. I can cover him here for any absences."

"All right. We'll see how it goes," Reynolds said.

"Did you see Valley?"

"Yes, in the flesh. I don't like him being around. He's too sharp, and it wouldn't take much to alert him."

"What are you suggesting, Jack?"

"We need to take him out of the picture if we can. He's the one big jeopardy to our mission. I've thought of killing him, but that wouldn't be the best thing. We need to take him somewhere and have a long chat."

"Let's think about that for a while. Perhaps something will come up where we can wrap him up," Hayden said.

"Roger that."

"Goddamn, Jack. I know you and I contributed to this, but that damn Davis continues to do a hell of a job."

"Yes, he does."

"Listen, you guys rest up and get back to work. Great job and tell Davis to watch out for Valley. We don't need Valley fucking things up for us. My steak is getting cold. I need to get back to the house. I'll talk to you later, Jack," Hayden said and hung up. The director can wait until tomorrow, he thought as he headed for his Jag.

VALLEY WOKE UP EARLY THE NEXT MORNING. After fixing his coffee, he sat down at the kitchen table, opened a notebook, and started making a list of payments—the people paid or needing to be paid, the amounts, what they were for, and how the transfers were to be accomplished. He knew what everyone was making and their cost, and he wanted to see just how much money everyone was going to make. Of course, he started with himself.

V

Receive

9M	Hash, 45 tons, 200k per ton; Luxembourg account, DePantera
5.6M	Thai, 7 tons, 800k per ton; Luxembourg, DePantera
4M	Shipping, Luxembourg, Yukorov
18.6M	Total receiving

Payments

2.1M	To Steve Petrov: Thai, 7 tons, 300K per ton; DePantera to transfer to Bergford
1M	To Rogers: bearer bonds (200K x 4 and 100K x 2); DePantera transfer Bank of Paris bearer bonds to Bergford; Duvet and Petrov deliver
350K	To Yukorov: Thai, 50K per ton; DePantera transfer to Bergford; Duvet and Petrov deliver to Kabu
20K	To Duvet and Petrov, deliver to Rogers
20K	To Duvet and Petrov, deliver to Yukorov
3.49M	Total payments

Total

$15,110,000 Net total

"Oh my God," Valley said when he wrote his net total. Thank you, all you potheads in Canada and the US, he thought. He decided he'd make what payments he needed to make, but he'd wait a few weeks before having any of his cash delivered. I want things to cool down for a while, he thought. He then continued with the others involved.

ROGERS

Receive

2M	1M cash from me and 1M bonds (200K x 4 and 100K x 2); DePantera will transfer cash; Duvet and Petrov deliver bonds

Payments to crew

100K	Billy
50K	Dude
50K	Willard
50K	Jim
250K	Total payments

Total

1.75M Net total

YUKOROV

Receive

49.5M	Hash, 45 tons, 1.1M per ton, DePantera
350K	Thai, 7 tons, 50K per ton, me

Payments from 49.5M

4M	To Me
1.35M	To Afridi for 45 tons hash, 30K per ton
5.35M	Total payments

Total

44.15M Net total, plus 350K personal

DEPANTERA

Receive after selling retail

175.5M	Hash, 45 tons, 1.3 M per ton x 3
18.9M	Thai, 7 tons, 900K per ton x 3
194.4M	Total receive

Payments

58.5M	Hash, 49.5M to Yukorov, 9M to me
5.6M	Thai, to me
64.1M	Total payments.

Total

130.3 M Net total.

After completing his calculations, Valley said, "Now that's a payday, 130 million dollars! I bet those people would really like to thank all those stupid-ass potheads."

CHAPTER 37

Check's in the Mail

9:00 a.m., Wednesday, September 23, 1987

Davis slept in late, two hours past his usual seven o'clock rising. Sitting at the kitchen table, he was drinking his coffee and looking at the link chart on the wall. "I need to add a few unknows," he said, thinking of the two young men who had been with Valley, the two truck drivers, and the woman in the small silver car who dropped off Willard and the other guy.

As he took another sip of coffee, his bag phone rang. "Hello," he said.

"Tony, it's Klass. I got your dates for FLETC. You need to be there from November 1 to December 31."

"I don't suppose I can postpone that, can I?"

"No, not unless you have a very good reason."

"Not really."

"The good part of this is you'll miss all the heat."

"Yes, that's a good thing. It's hotter than seven hells there. Will you make the travel arrangements?"

"Yes, the secretary here will take care of all that for you. You won't even have to come to the office. I can mail the tickets out to you in plenty of time."

"Thank you," Davis said.

"You find anything else out?"

"No, not much going on anywhere. But I'm keeping my fingers crossed."

"Okay, keep looking while you can. I'll get your travel itinerary taken care of. Talk to you soon. Goodbye," Klass said.

"Thanks, Bob. Goodbye," Davis said and hung up.

9:45 a.m., Wednesday, September 23, 1987

TERRENCE GEORGE VALLEY NOW HAD HIS LIST of what needed to be done as he called Monarch National Bank in New York. "Phillip DePantera, please. This is George Hannah."

"One moment, sir."

A minute later, DePantera said, "Good morning, George."

"Good morning, Phillip. Has the money been transferred?" Valley asked.

"Yes, it has. This was taken care of yesterday afternoon."

"Thank you. I need you to do the following for me, similar to past arrangements."

"Okay, what are they?"

"I need one million in Bank of Paris bearer bonds, payable *au porteur*, four two-hundred-thousand and two one-hundred-thousand bonds. I need them sent to Bergford. They will deliver them for me."

"I can have those ordered and overnighted by air to me in two days and sent to Toronto the same day by courier." DePantera said.

"That's good. I also need 2.1 million transferred to Bergford; that's the payee."

"All right. Anything else?"

"Yes, I need 350 thousand in new one hundreds, also sent to Bergford. They'll deliver those for me, as well."

"To confirm, you want all this to be debited out of your BOP, Luxembourg account?" DePantera asked.

"Yes, that's correct."

"Very good, George. Can I help you with anything else?"

"No, you've been extremely helpful, Phillip. I'll talk to you soon. Goodbye."

"Goodbye, George," DePantera said as he hung up.

Valley then called Bergford in Toronto, Canada.

"Steve Petrov, please. This is George Hannah."

"Let me get him, sir. Hold the line, please," the receptionist said.

"Hi, George. Did everything work out?"

"Almost, they sent only seven tons of our product."

"Yes, they informed me of that yesterday. However, they assured me they'll make it up on the next shipment. Is that all right with you, George?"

"Yes, Steve, that'll be fine. Everything else went as planned."

"I like to hear that. Has New York taken care of their end?" Petrov asked.

"Yes, they have. I've already sent 2.1 to you. I also need you to deliver a couple of items that I'll have sent to you."

"Thank you, and what are they and where do they go?"

"Six bearer bonds need to come out here to me. Four two-hundred-thousand and two one-hundred-thousand, one million total."

"Okay, same twenty thousand for service?"

"Yes, the same. The next item, 350 thousand in new bills, will need to be taken to Kabul, Afghanistan, to a Mr. Yuk. This is his mobile phone number," Valley said as he gave Yukorov's number to Petrov.

"We'll need an additional twenty thousand service payment with our usual fee for that, George, if we're going to Kabul."

"Agreed," Valley said. "I'll pay you sixty thousand when you make the delivery of the bonds here."

"That'll work, George. When do you want us to come to you? After we make your delivery, we can then fly on to Kabul."

"How about the first of October? That should give everyone plenty of time to be ready. Fly into Executive as before and get a room at Westin. Let's meet at noon," Valley said.

"I'll do that, George. I'll get the same room, 232. If it's different, I'll let you know. If you don't hear from me, it's the same room at noon on the first," Petrov said.

"Very good. Thank you, Steve. See you in a week. Goodbye," Valley said and hung up.

Valley looked at his clock, 10:00 a.m. "Hmm," he said, "nine p.m. in Moscow." After dialing Yukorov's number, he let it ring several times and was about to hang up when the line was picked up.

"*Da*," Yukorov said in a slurred voice.

"You drunk?"

"Terrence, my good friend! *Da*, I'm drunk."

"Listen, you drunk fuck. Did you transfer the four million to my account?"

"*Da*, Terrence, I did." Yukorov could barely speak.

"Good. I'm sending you the 350 thousand in October. They'll contact you."

"*Da,* Terrence," Yukorov said as he hung up the phone.

Laughing, Valley said, "That drunken fucker won't even remember we spoke."

Valley next called Rogers.

"Hello," Carlin said.

"Your bonds will be here in a week."

"All right."

"I'll have them here at my place on October 1. You'll have to come here to get them. Let's meet here at two p.m. Remember this: those six sheets of paper are the same as carrying one million in cash. The payee is *au porteur*, which means whoever is holding them owns them."

"I understand. I'll keep them in a safe place."

"When you get here, we can have a beer. What do you say?"

"Yes, that'll be fine. I need to meet the crew and pay them. I can do that in Placerville, and it should only take an hour. But before I go shoveling out any more money, I want that other million in my hands."

"You'll have it. Okay, meet me here at two. Talk soon. Goodbye," Valley said.

"Goodbye," Rogers said and hung up. Those bonds will be okay, he thought. I'm putting them in a safe until I buy me a larger boat.

After checking the phonebook, Rogers called the Motel 6 outside Placerville on Route 50.

"Motel 6," the receptionist said.

"I need a room for October 1."

"How many people will be staying?"

"Just me."

"What's the name? And I need a credit card to hold it."

"Carlin Rogers," Rogers said and gave the credit card number.

"Okay, Mr. Rogers, you're all set. Room 219 is reserved for October the first. Check in's after two o'clock."

"Thank you," Rogers said and hung up.

Next, he called a number in Grass Valley, California.

"Hello."

"Dude, on October 1, I need you to meet me at the Motel 6 on Route 50 near Placerville. Be there at exactly 4:30 in the afternoon, not before and not after. Room 219."

"All right, I'll be there at 4:30 sharp, room 219."

"Okay, see you then."

Next Rogers called Willard's apartment in Fairfield.

"Hello," a woman said.

"Tammy, is Willard there?"

"Yes, just a minute, Carlin."

"Hello," Willard said.

"I want you at the Motel 6 on Route 50 near Placerville at exactly 4:45 on the first of October."

"Okay, let me write this down. Motel 6, Placerville, 4:45, October 1."

"Yes, I'll have your money."

"That's great. I really appreciate it. I'm going to by a new truck and Tammy a car."

"Okay, you're a hard worker, Willard. I appreciate your help. I'll see you then."

"Okay, Carlin. Thank you," Willard said and hung up.

"If he finds out you took that hash, he's going to be upset," Tammy said.

"He's not going to find out, so quit harping on it."

Carlin then called Jim Rogers and told him to be at the motel at 5:00 p.m. sharp. Jim agreed to be there on time.

Although satisfied with these plans, Rogers couldn't completely relax. By now any danger was surely over, but deep inside, he still worried about dragging his family into something that could cause all their lives to be ruined. Nonetheless, for this amount of money, he felt it was worth the risk.

CHAPTER 38

Payoffs

Noon, October 1, 1987

VALLEY KNOCKED ON THE DOOR AT the Westin Motel, room 232, at exactly 12:00. Steve Petrov opened the door.

"Hello, George. I got the 2.1. Thank you," Petrov said.

"You're welcome. I always enjoy doing business with you gentlemen," Valley said, shaking hands with Petrov and then Duvet. "Let me do this first," he said as he took six bundles of wrapped one-hundred-dollar bills, ten thousand dollars each, out of his jacket pockets. He handed three to Petrov and three to Duvet.

"Thank you," Duvet said.

"You're welcome," Valley said.

"Okay, here are your bonds," Petrov said, handing Valley a large envelope.

Opening up the envelope, Valley pulled out the bonds and laid them on the bed, side by side. "They look awesome. Every time I look at bearer bonds, they just look incredible," Valley said. "Thank you, gentlemen. Have you been in contact with Mr. Yuk?"

"Yes, we leave here within the hour and fly to Hawaii, refuel there, and then onto Afghanistan. We'll meet him late tomorrow evening at the Kabul airport," Petrov said.

"Excellent. Well, I'll not keep you fellows. As always, it's my pleasure. Oh, yeah, I forgot. Just before Thanksgiving, I'll have you bring me two mil in new one-hundreds. I'm going to surprise Julie with a new Porsche for Christmas, and I'd like to have some cash in my safe. I've been blowing through a bunch with building my new house."

"No problem, George. We'll put it on our schedule," Petrov said, looking at his pocket calendar. "How about the Saturday before Thanksgiving, the twenty-first? Plan on meeting here, same room at noon?"

"Yes, excellent. I'll have the money transferred to you a couple days before. You gentlemen have a safe flight," Valley said, shaking hands with the men and then leaving the room.

ROGERS WAS GETTING READY TO LEAVE his house in Napa. He reached under his bed and pulled out the paper sack containing the two hundred thousand dollars Sara had kept for him. Taking out fifty thousand, he shoved those five wrapped bundles of hundreds under his mattress. Putting the remainder of the cash in a gym bag, he got in his truck and started towards Valley's place on Little Bluff Road. Two hours later, he turned off of Route 50 and headed down the gravel road to the home. Pulling in, Rogers parked his truck and knocked on the downstairs door.

"Come on in. We're upstairs," Valley yelled.

Entering the downstairs garage, Rogers walked up the stairs to the living quarters.

"Welcome," Valley said, shaking hands with Carlin. "You want a cold beer?"

"Yeah, that'd be good. I need to be in Placerville by four o'clock. Going to meet the boys and pay them."

"Okay, you have some time. You can be there in about twenty minutes," Valley said. "I bet you're wanting to see these," he added, picking up the large envelope from the dining room table and handing it to Carlin.

"Yes." Opening it, Carlin looked at the six bearer bonds. "Wow, one million dollars in six pieces of paper."

"Yes, so don't lose them."

"That won't happen. I need to buy a new boat. That *California Rose* may seem like it's fairly good size on the delta, but you get it out at sea, and it's too fucking small."

"Do you have one in mind yet?"

"No, Billy's looking for me right now. He's going to contact Sandbar Marine in Olympia, Washington. They're a vessel brokerage and may have what we're looking for. Billy knows the owner, Dick Parker.

"How much do you think one will cost?"

"Probably two; I doubt if it'll be over that."

"It's money well spent," Valley said.

"Yes, and I can make some righteous money with it too. Hire out for some companies that need vessels moved or even dredging. I'm also going to buy that barge. For this next run, I need to cut the deck open and put some fuel tanks down inside it. Chuck Stevens is not going to let me do that, leasing it. We got some seawater in the fuel on this past trip, and that was a problem. Putting tanks inside the barge takes care of that issue, as well as provides more cover for the drugs. The Coast Guard will see it as another fuel barge. They won't want to cut into it and blow themselves up.

"Good idea," Valley said. "We're going to need to do one if not two more runs for the Russian. After that, let's start running some of our own. That's where the big money is. I may even get another plane. I used to own a DC-6 but sold it in '85 after doing a fly into Arizona with some weed from Mexico. But I'm tired of working for someone else. I say you and I and Billy start making some big money in forming our own organization. We have the money worked out; we have the buyers. I know the drug lords in Afghanistan, and I can get us weed out of Thailand. And we now have the vessels to transport. What do you say?"

"I'm all in," Carlin replied. "I know Billy will be too. We also have the workforce, and they're all family who will keep their mouths shut. I don't need Dude anymore; I learned plenty piloting the *California Rose* to Hawaii and back. Willard and Jim are now rather good wheelmen too. Speaking of, I need to get going to pay the guys. Thanks for the beer," Carlin said, shaking hands with Valley, and left.

ROGERS ARRIVED AT THE MOTEL 6 outside Placerville and checked into room 219, carrying the gym bag of cash into the room. He put five stacks of hundreds into the top drawer of the dresser and sat down on the bed and waited. At 4:30 p.m., Bill Smart arrived and knocked on the door.

Carlin opened it. "Come on in, Dude," he said, closing the door behind the man. "I appreciate all your help. Look in the top drawer," Carlin said, pointing at the dresser.

Dude opened the drawer and said, "Hello, beautiful," as he took the fifty thousand dollars and put it in his pockets. "You going back out for another load?"

"Yes, I think. But I may not need your help. However, if I do, I'll certainly call you."

"No trouble. Keep me in mind if you need me."

"I certainly will. Thank you," Rogers said as the man left the room.

One down, Rogers thought as he put five more stacks of hundred-dollar bills in the dresser. Willard and Jim came at their appointed times and received their money the same way Dude had. The boys had never seen that much money before, and Carlin warned them both to be very careful where they spent it. Both said they would. Carlin also told both boys that he was buying a larger boat and possibly two more trips were being scheduled, one in December and the other in May or June of 1988. He ended by warning them to keep their noses clean. They both assured him they would.

Leaving the Motel 6, Rogers drove to Sonora where he'd rented a home on Snell Street. He liked this getaway where he didn't have to speak to anyone. It was a quiet little community in the foothills of the Sierra Nevada Mountains. And no one had any idea that the big polite man that moved in was the runner for the largest hashish smuggling organization in the world.

On October 3, Jim Rogers went to the Chevrolet dealership in Santa Rosa, California, and purchased a used 1981 Corvette for $11,700. That evening when the dealership deposited the cash with the local bank, a bank employee filled out an IRS Form 8300 since the deposit was over the ten-thousand-dollar limit. It was noted on the IRS form that the deposit was 117 new, uncirculated, sequentially serial-numbered, one-hundred-dollar bills.

On October 9, Willard Butler went to the Ford dealership in Davis, California, and purchased a new 1988 Ford Ranger pickup and a new 1988 Ford Festiva for $23,800. That evening when the dealership deposited the cash with the local bank, a bank employee duly filled out IRS Form 8300, which was sent to the IRS with a special notation of the 238 new, uncirculated sequentially serial-numbered one-hundred-dollar bills that were deposited.

Within a week, the special agent in charge of the Internal Revenue Service in San Francisco was reading alerts he'd received on possible illegal activities. He glanced at the information before him and thought, What's the possibility of two different people passing new sequentially serial-numbered Benjamins, not only from the same Federal Reserve Bank in New York but also from the same batch and both buying cars within a week of each other and being less than one hundred miles apart?

Calling for his secretary, the SAC knew this needed to go to one of his best agents. "Cathy, give this to Rich Cain. Tell him to follow up on this and let me know what he finds out. This has bad shit written all over it, and it might be connected to his Napa investigation."

CHAPTER 39

A Mother's Love

October 1987

In early October, Willard called his mother, Irene Kasper, and told her to come to his apartment in Fairfield. While there, she saw several thousand dollars in one-hundred-dollar bills and two soles of hashish. Having been married to Carlin Rogers, she knew full well his criminal past and the many years he'd spent in prison for various offenses. She was best friends with Gladys Wymes, who'd hidden convicted Russian spy Charles Bedford and later robbed banks with him. She feared her son was heading down the same path as her ex-husband, and it worried her greatly. Willard was her only child, and she grieved over the direction he was traveling. When she returned to her home in Spokane, she confided in her new husband, Daniel. She decided if there was any possible way, she would try to keep her son out of prison.

October 14, 1987

Carlin and another sister, Debra Rinehart, opened a joint bank account at a different bank in Napa and began depositing many of the one-hundred-dollar bills that had not yet been deposited into LendBest. Getting his cash into a bank was taking longer than he expected, and he didn't like it. He wanted all that cash in a bank account where he had access to it. Over the next two months, almost two hundred thousand dollars were deposited into this joint account. From September to December 1987, there were only three days that a deposit was not made into one of the three accounts associated with Rogers. All the deposits were for less than ten thousand dollars to avoid the IRS currency transaction reporting requirement.

Saturday, October 24, 1987

BEFORE LEAVING FOR FLETC, Davis had his favorite breakfast of buttermilk pancakes, sausage, eggs, and English muffin at the McAvoy Café. After eating, he drove around the loop and saw the *California Rose* and barge were back, tied up in their previous location. No one was around, and he took his time driving back down to Hayward. He really enjoyed the weather in Northern California and dreaded going back to Georgia. Hopefully, he thought, everything will be nice and quiet while I'm gone.

November 1, 1987

MIKHAIL GORBACHEV RELEASED *PERESTROIKA; New Thinking for Our Country and the World*. With obvious fanfare from the western countries, Gorbachev felt good about changing his country for the good of the common Russian. The Russian generals and members of the intelligence community felt they were being betrayed by Gorbachev. They also felt the USSR would no longer exist if drastic measures weren't taken and taken soon.

Monday, November 2, 1987

AFTER THE PREVIOUS YEAR OF NON-STOP TENSION, Davis, Hayden, and Reynolds were trying to relax for a few weeks.

Davis was sitting in Criminal Investigator Class #806 at the Federal Law Enforcement Training Center in Glynco, Georgia. Since arriving, he'd spoken a couple of times with Hayden. Davis enjoyed the time with his classmates, especially Willy Wojack, a big hulk of a man for the Customs Service from the Keys in Florida. No matter how hard Davis tried to beat him in agility drills, Willy always won.

Davis even asked Willy, "How in the hell can you get that big of a body to move so fast?"

November 8, 1987

DRUG LORD AFRIDI AND CAPTAIN BABIN FAUCHER completed the loading of forty-three tons of hashish on board the *Poliksena* tied to the dock in Karachi. Faucher told Afridi that he was expecting forty-five tons, but Afridi explained that was all he had. The *Poliksena* was to leave the next day and rendezvous with the *Mala* off the coast of Thailand in approximately twelve days, picking up the thirteen tons of Thai marijuana then.

November 16, 1987

WILLARD WAS ARRESTED BY THE OREGON STATE POLICE for driving while revoked. An impoundment search found four pounds of hashish he was taking to his friend in Longview, Washington, to sell. Carlin Rogers was notified and bailed Willard out of jail. But Willard was also wanted in Colombia County for parole violation and was transferred there. Rogers again bailed him out of jail and hired an attorney. Willard took a quick plea deal that was offered from a busy prosecuting attorney. He agreed to attend a drug rehab center at the Mt. Hood Medical Center for three weeks in lieu of going to trial and possibly prison. The prosecuting attorney didn't have time for this petty shit, and the impoundment search done by the troopers had its problems.

Carlin Rogers was furious and also very alarmed. With the Oregon State Police now in possession of the two soles of hashish, surely they were wondering how the hell someone like Willard

Butler could possess four pounds of hash worth almost seven thousand dollars. Rogers immediately notified Valley.

"What do you think?" Rogers asked.

"I think we're still good," Valley replied. "He's not going to tell where he got it, and they have no way of finding out."

"He should be out by early December. I think we can still make that run," Rogers said.

"Does he need to go with you on that trip?"

"Yes. I'm afraid if I cut him out now, he'll be just pissed enough to talk."

"Okay. I'll tell Yukorov you may be a day or two late but we'll be there by December 20. Is that good?"

"Yes, that should work."

"Anything on the new boat yet?" Valley asked.

"No, we'll have to make the run this time with the *California Rose*. Maybe before next year's run I can find a new boat."

"Okay, we're still a go then, correct?"

"Yes, as long as nothing else happens, we're good," Rogers said.

After the men hung up, Valley wondered if maybe he shouldn't use his phone at the house as much in case it was being listened to. I can use the phone at Poor Reds BBQ if I need to, he thought. "Naahhh," he said, "we're good."

November 19, 1987

In the morning, Irene Kasper sobbed when she heard from Willard in the drug rehab center. She'd known it'd only be a matter of time, and it was now hitting her in the face. In desperation, she looked up the phone number for the FBI in Seattle.

"Yes, I'd like to report a drug smuggling operation that involves the Russians."

"Would you like to speak to someone, ma'am?" the agent on call asked.

"Yes, please send someone to my house on 1010 North Summit Boulevard in Spokane."

Noon, Thursday, November 19, 1987

SAC Robert Klass called Hayden at FLETC. "We have a problem. I have a Customs agent out of Sacramento, Mike Murphy, who's going to obtain a warrant for Valley for his part in a 1985 marijuana smuggle into Arizona. He was indicted in Arizona last week."

"When are they making the arrest?" Hayden asked.

"They'll have the warrant early next week, probably by Tuesday."

"We need to talk to Valley first, especially if they're going to pop him anyway. Rogers and the Russians will see that indictment in Arizona as the reason for his arrest, nothing more than coincidental bad luck and nothing to do with Afghanistan," Hayden said.

"Yes, I agree. How do you want to do this?" Klass asked.

"You forget you told me. I'll have Jack and Tony take care of this. We need Valley only for a couple of days, and then we'll drop him off for Murphy.

It was 4:00 p.m. when Davis was at Paula's #1, sitting at the bar, talking about old times with Paula, and laughing when Hayden walked in.

"Buddy!" Paula said.

"Tony, we need to go," Hayden said as Davis turned on his stool.

"I got your beer. You go," Paula said.

Following Hayden out to the parking lot, Davis asked, "What's going on?"

"You need to fly back to Sacramento in the morning. We're taking Valley. Customs is getting an arrest warrant for him on a smuggle he did in '85. Flew a plane full of weed into Arizona. I want Jack talking to him for a couple of days before we turn him over to Customs. I'll pick you up at five a.m. How did you get here?"

"Taxi," Davis said.

"Okay, jump in. I'll get you back to your dorm," Hayden said as both men got in the blue Jag.

The next morning, as he drove Davis to the Glynco Jetport, Hayden said, "We have a company jet here. They'll have you in Sacramento by noon. Jack will pick you up and take you to Hayward. Once there, get your tac gear and car. After you and Jack take Valley, Jack will question him for a couple of days. You drive back to Executive Airport, and the company jet will bring you back here to FLETC. When you land here, a taxi will take you back to your dorm. Once you graduate, forget your domestic flight home. I'll fly you back to Executive and your G-ride."

"All right."

"Be ready for Valley. He's a trained killer."

"Roger that," Davis said as he got out of the Jag and climbed the steps into the Lear jet.

"Bobby Taylor," said the man at the top of the steps. "I'm the captain."

"Tony Davis," he said, shaking hands with the pilot, and took a seat.

Saturday morning, November 21, 1987

Two special agents from the FBI knocked on Irene Kasper's door. They stayed for two hours, taking notes and asking questions. When they concluded their interview, both agents assured her they would look into the information she had given.

After leaving the residence, the junior agent asked the other, "Do you believe all that shit she said?"

"Fuck no! Russian spies and the KGB! She's a fucking squirrel!" the senior agent said.

"What're you going to put in the 302?"

"That she's obviously mentally ill," the FBI special agent said, who was an accountant before joining the bureau four years earlier.

"Okay, I'll concur," the junior FBI special agent said, who was an attorney and just graduated from Quantico.

6:00 p.m., Saturday, November 21, 1987

Valley couldn't have been happier arriving at his home on Little Bluff Road. He'd met Petrov and Duvet at the Westin earlier in the day and picked up his two million in cash. He then drove to the Porsche Dealer in Rocklin and looked at the new convertible models that Julie loved. Walking in the house and to his bedroom, he turned on the light, threw his briefcase on the bed, and opened the case. He stood and stared at the contents—two million in layers of sequentially serial-numbered one-hundred-dollar bills still in their wrappers—and he began to laugh. His laughter came to a sudden stop when he heard the bedroom door close behind him. As he turned towards the sound, he reached for a pistol in the back of his pants.

"I wouldn't do that."

He saw a man wearing all black come into view, pointing a 9mm at his chest.

"On your face or die right here, right now," the man in black directed.

Valley slowly pulled his hand back out in front, knelt down, and lay prone on the carpeted floor next to the bed. As he did, the door opened, and he could see another set of legs walk into the bedroom.

"Cross your legs and put your hands behind your back," the man in black further directed Valley. He then added, "If you don't do exactly as I say, I will kill you."

He then felt the man in black place one knee on his neck while handcuffing his wrists together.

Pulling the pistol from Valley's belt, the man in black searched the rest of him, saying to the other man, "He's clean."

Valley saw the other man's feet got closer, and he felt a gloved hand press his head against the floor and a sharp needle stab in his neck.

Reynolds was injecting 75 milligrams of propofol into Valley's jugular vein, saying, "You know where you're going for the rest of your life, asshole, and you deserve to be there. But first you are going to tell me everything I want to know."

Valley didn't hear it all. After "asshole," he was unconscious.

Reynolds then spoke into his wrist mic, "Target secure. Get him out of here."

Thirty seconds later, Special Agents Dave South, Juan Rodriquez, and Eric Harmon dressed in black entered the house. They placed a black hood over Valley's head and dragged him to a waiting panel truck outside being driven by Special Agent Mike Callahan.

"Don't ask where he's going," Reynolds said as Davis took off his balaclava and sat down on the bed next to the briefcase.

"Never entered my mind," Davis replied, closing and fastening the briefcase. Handing it to Reynolds, Davis said, "Let's get out of here before we draw attention. I need to get back to FLETC."

"Affirmative," Reynolds said, shaking hands with Davis as they left the residence. Climbing into the passenger seat of the panel truck, Reynolds asked Davis, "You need a ride?"

"No, I'm parked nearby," Davis said as he walked toward a dirt side road next to the property.

"Good job, Tony," Reynolds said as he was closing the door.

"Be talking to you, Jack," Davis said as he walked into the familiar darkness.

8:00 a.m., Monday, November 23, 1987

Davis was sitting in class at FLETC as an attorney for the government explained the Racketeer Influenced and Corrupt Organization Act of 18 USC.

I know exactly who that can be used against, Davis thought.

2:00 p.m., November 23, 1987

Irene still had not heard back from the FBI and the agent who had been the lead on the interview. He refused to call her back after she called the office several times. She was now pissed. Sitting down at her desk, she typed out a brief one-page description of the smuggling organization. She included the names of Carlin Rogers, Billy Little, Willard Butler, Jim Rogers, and William Smart. One important piece of information that was not mentioned was the vessel name, *California Rose*.

Irene took the letter to CVS in Spokane and made five copies. Being married for many years to a criminal husband, she had learned a few tricks. After getting home, she addressed six envelopes, one each to the CIA, FBI, DEA, Customs, IRS, and California Tax Department. Before folding the last letter to the tax department, she took a pen and wrote "Please do something," on the bottom, a final plea from a distraught mother.

Putting all the envelops in a larger envelope, she made it out to a maildrop company. After receiving the letters, the maildrop company would send the individual letters to several different parts of the West Coast to be mailed from there, making every letter non-traceable. At the post office in Spokane, she paid the clerk and watched as they put the large envelope in a pile of others. Walking back to her car, she wondered how long it would take for the whirlwind to begin. If she couldn't keep her son from going with Carlin, she would at least expose the organization so Willard didn't have a job.

CHAPTER 40

Delays

10:00 a.m., Tuesday, November 24, 1987

For the previous sixty hours, Terrance George Valley had talked freely about his wall safe combination, where he kept all his cash, his bank accounts, smuggling activities, his contacts, his suppliers, his money men, his girlfriends, and everyone he knew in the KGB and the Rogers organization. He spilled the beans on everything he'd ever known, and he never knew he did it.

Putting Valley back in the chair in his living room on Little Bluff Road, Reynolds opened the man's mouth and placed a dissolving film of LSD on his tongue. Waiting a minute, he then poured some Redbreast whiskey into his mouth and on his shirt and laid the bottle on the floor to run out. "Have a nice trip," Reynolds said.

Picking up the phone in Valley's kitchen, Reynolds called the US Customs Office in Sacramento. After the standard greeting, Reynolds said, "Tell Special Agent Murphy that Valley is at his home on Little Bluff Road and he's drunk. Tell Murphy right now." Hanging up the phone, Reynolds walked down the stairs and out of the house, leaving the front door open.

That evening, Carlin Rogers got a call from Julie, Valley's girlfriend.

She was in tears and afraid. "TG's been arrested. What should I do?" she asked.

"Who arrested him?" Rogers asked.

"Customs. He was indicted in Arizona for flying an airplane with drugs. But he doesn't make any sense when he talks. He called me from the jail and wanted me to call you."

"What do you mean, he doesn't make any sense?" Rogers asked.

"He told me I reminded him of a girl he was in love with in high school. I don't understand what's going on!"

"They probably rang his bell when they arrested him. I want you to pack your clothes and get the hell out of town. Don't tell anyone where you're going. Call me back in a week and not before," Carlin instructed and hung up.

Carlin then called his sister, Sara at her home. "How are the deposits going?" he asked.

"Slow, but getting there."

"I've been thinking. How about spreading the money around to have it deposited?"

"What do you mean?"

"I'm sure you have many employees at LendBest who can be trusted. Give them some of the cash, have them deposit it into their personal accounts, and then write a check to the Supply Masters account at LendBest. Wouldn't that work?"

"Yes, that would work. We don't have any CTR requirements with checks. We do have several employees we could trust to do that. I'll tell Don to ask them to do that tomorrow.

Wednesday, November 25, 1987

Forty-two thousand dollars in new, sequentially serial-numbered one-hundred-dollar bills were deposited into the personal accounts of several associates of LendBest, all at the Bank of America in Napa. Over the next few weeks over two hundred thousand dollars in personal checks from these same associates were deposited into the Supply Masters, Inc. account at LendBest. All the checks had "Loan Payment" on the memo line, except for one check, and it said "Rogers."

The *Poliksena* received the thirteen tons of Thai and was now underway towards the rendezvous point in the North Pacific. Yukorov called General Vanerev to inform him that the KGB spy ship would be meeting the American's vessel around December 20.

"Thank you, Vladimir. However, it's already too late to start withdrawal of my troops. The roads are already blocked with the heavy snows we've received. It's good we'll have the money. As soon as the weather breaks in the spring, I'll give the order to move."

"Yes, sir. I'll let you know as soon as this money is released to our account."

"Thank you, Vladimir. Goodbye."

"Goodbye, sir," Yukorov said.

It was late afternoon when Yukorov called Valley's home number. He was going to tell him that he'd met Petrov and Duvet in Kabul and received his $350,000 and that the *Poliksena* was on its way. Valley's phone rang several times before it was picked up.

"Hello," a male voice said that Yukorov didn't recognize.

"Who's this?" Yukorov asked.

"Who's calling, please?" the voice asked.

"I need to talk to Mr. Hannah."

"He's not here. He's being held at the Sacramento County Jail."

Yukorov immediately hung up.

"Who was that?" Special Agent Mike Murphy asked the agent who answered the phone.

"Didn't give his name and hung up."

"Okay. Let's finish searching this place and get the hell out of here. It looks like this place has already been searched," Murphy said.

Yukorov looked for Carlin Rogers's mobile phone number that Valley had given him and called the number.

"Hello," Rogers said.

"This is Vlad. Has Valley been arrested?"

"Yes, Customs arrested him for a smuggle he did in 1985. He flew some weed into Arizona, and Customs indicted him there."

"Are we compromised?" Yukorov asked.

"I don't think so," Rogers said. "This was all out of Arizona." In actuality Rogers had no fucking idea, but he was willing to roll the dice. Just to be safe he said, "I think we should lay low until spring and run the next shipment then."

"My boat's on the way," Yukorov said.

"Tell them to turn around and keep the drugs six months. We can restart after everything cools off in the spring."

Yukorov thought it really didn't make any difference since the general couldn't move troops now anyway. "Okay, I'll contact you in February. We make more plans then, agreed?"

"Yes, that'll work for me."

"*Blyad!*" Yukorov said in disgust. "Goodbye."

"Yes, goodbye," Rogers said and hung up, not knowing what the fuck he meant.

Yukorov hated to call the general but he had no choice. "General, there's been a delay with the American vessel. He says he'll be ready by spring, and there will be no further delays."

"All right, Vlad. It makes no difference at this point. We'll plan on resuming in the spring, and I want to be starting out of Afghanistan by the end of May. Whatever you have to do, Vlad, you make sure this next shipment goes as planned. I've decided I'm pulling the troops out as soon as we deliver to the American ship. We're wasting time sitting here in Kabul while Gorbachev writes books and profits on the demise of our country."

"Yes sir, I'll make it happen," Yukorov said, as the general hung up.

Yukorov then made a ship-to-shore call to the *Poliksena.* "Get me the captain."

"Hold one minute, sir."

"This is Captain Faucher."

"Babin, it's Vladimir. You need to turn around and bring the shipment back to Karachi."

"Why? What happened?"

"The American is having boat problems and will not be able to meet us until spring."

"Confirmed. The weather is getting rough too. It's a good time to head back to port. I'll leave the shipment onboard. It'll be fine stored here until spring," Faucher said.

"Very good, Babin. Let me know when you get back to Karachi." Yukorov hung up and called Monarch National Bank.

"Good morning. Monarch. How may I direct your call?" the operator asked.

"Mr. DePantera, please. This is Mr. Yuk."

"One moment, sir," she said.

"Good morning, Mr. Yuk. How can I help you today?" DePantera asked.

"Hannah's been arrested. We have cancelled this shipment and will restart in the spring."

"What's my exposure?" DePantera asked.

"I don't believe either of us is exposed. This was an old case that caught up with him. He had flown some packages into Arizona in 1985," Yukorov said.

"I know the shipment you are referring to."

"One more thing, Mr. DePantera. I was to be paid fifty thousand dollars for each ton of Thai that I delivered for Mr. Hannah. I will still need to get paid for using my ship to transport that to the American," Yukorov said.

"I see, Mr. Yuk. I believe that can still be arranged. You have my word."

"So, we're still good for the next shipment in the spring?" Yukorov said.

"Yes, Mr. Yuk. The agreement that we have is still intact. How many tons will be coming this time?"

"There are forty-three tons of hashish and thirteen tons of Thai already on my ship. It'll set sail to the American in April."

"Very good, Mr. Yuk. We shall proceed with our arrangement then."

"All right, Mr. DePantera. I'll contact you in March or sooner."

Very well, Mr. Yuk. I'll let Mr. Petrov know what has happened as well. We'll talk in the spring. Thank you. Goodbye."

"Goodbye, Mr. DePantera," Yukorov said.

After getting off the phone, DePantera thought about the 8.6 million dollars he had just saved with Hannah being out of the picture with the hashish. If he needed to pay Mr. Yuk 650 thousand dollars for the Thai, no problem. He would see what kind of deal he could get off Mr. Petrov, who he knew was providing the Thai to begin with. "Everyone needs to get paid," he said.

Yukorov sat at his desk in the Kremlin looking at his phone. He felt an uneasiness and thought he was overlooking something important. But he just couldn't put his finger on it.

Picking up the phone, he called Colonel Petroff's home.

"Hello," Petroff said.

"Good evening, Colonel. I apologize for the late call, but I was wondering if you could come to the Kremlin for a few minutes. I have some pressing matters that I'd like to speak to you about."

"Yes, Vlad. Give me forty-five minutes and I'll be there," Petroff said, wondering what was going on. Yukorov had never asked him to come to the Kremlin before.

Arriving at the Kremlin, Petroff went to the second floor and the KGB office. "What's going on, Vlad?" Petroff asked as he opened the inner door of the office, walked in, and sat down in a chair.

"One of the Americans has been arrested, and the current shipment has been cancelled until spring. I was wanting to run this by you to make sure I'm not missing something. I don't feel good about this."

"Tell me what happened."

"The former CIA agent has been arrested for smuggling with a plane in 1985. At least that's what I've been told. I don't believe in coincidences, and this has given me concern."

"I agree. If a trained intelligence agent's been arrested, what did he miss to end up behind bars?" Petroff asked, knowing he had to go with this for his own cover.

"*Da*."

“Okay, worst-case scenario. Let’s say someone knows what’s going on in America. What can they do to us?” Petroff asked and then said, “Pretty much nothing.”

“Yes, but there’s another thing that happened that doesn’t fit either.”

“What’s that?”

“We had an intelligence officer killed here in Moscow under very unusual circumstances.”

“That’s unfortunate, but what does that have to do with this operation?” Petroff asked, knowing exactly whom Yukorov was referring to.

Watching Petroff’s reactions very closely, Yukorov said, “You’re right. It has nothing to do with this.”

“So what’s the next plan?” Petroff asked.

“We start again in the spring. The general wants to be pulling out of Afghanistan by the end of May.”

“I don’t like coincidences either,” Petroff said. “But this may be all that it is. Just bad luck on the part of the American. Does this affect us getting our money?”

“No, I’ve spoken to the buyer. They’re still wanting this to proceed.”

“Well, that’s all we care about. If someone in the US gets arrested, I don’t care, as long as we can still complete our mission.”

“Yes, you’re right, Dimitri. I can always depend on you to put things in a clearer prospective.”

“Vlad, I think you need to get some sleep. You look tired, and a good night’s rest will help you see this better.”

“You’re right. I haven’t been sleeping much, three to four hours a night. One more thing, Dimi. Do you remember when I said I had contingencies?”

“Yes, I do.”

Reaching in his desk, Yukorov pulled out an envelope and handed it to the colonel.

“What’s this?”

“Contingencies.”

Looking in the envelope at the fifty thousand dollars, Petroff said, “Thank you, my friend.”

Standing, Yukorov shook hands with the colonel and said, "Thank you."

With that, the colonel left the Kremlin.

Yukorov closed down his office and went home to get some desperately needed rest. The colonel's right; I do need sleep, he thought.

Petroff drove to his home and went inside as usual. He saw no one following him, and he waited there for an hour before driving back to the Kremlin at 2:00 a.m. Going into his office, he shut and locked both doors. Taking the bug wand out of his briefcase, he swept his office for listening devices. Not finding any, he placed the wand back into his briefcase, locked it, and set it on the floor. Picking up his phone he called Hayden's pager.

At 6:30 p.m. in Georgia, Buddy was finishing up at his DOD office after a long day of welcoming new classes and making sure the coming graduations of other classes went smoothly. Feeling his pager buzz for the fiftieth time that day, he grudgingly looked at it. He saw 1880 and knew if he didn't call the colonel right back, he would be there another hour waiting on him to call. Getting the STU out, he called Petroff's number. He let it ring once, hung up, and called it right back.

Hearing it being answered, Hayden said, "*Moy dobryy drug*."

"My good friend," Petroff said.

"What's going on, Demi?"

"The December trip has been cancelled; it will be in May. Goodbye, Buddy."

"Goodbye, Dimi."

Well, that makes sense, Hayden thought and said with a smile, "They don't know whether to shit or go blind now." Hayden grabbed his things, turned off his light, and walked out of the office.

CHAPTER 41

FIRESTORM

Thursday, November 26, 1987

CARLIN KNEW HE NEEDED TO LAY LOW for a few weeks, and the Sonora house was a good place to do that. He also instinctively knew he needed to hide the *California Rose* and barge. But he didn't want to expose himself to do it. After thirty years of being on the other side of the law, he knew when to stay hidden. Carlin contacted his older brother Harold Sr.

With the help of three other men, Harold moved the *California Rose* and barge fifteen miles to a hidden island on the remote Sevenmile Slough near Rio Vista. Not contacting VTS when the move was made, it was like the *California Rose* and barge just up and disappeared.

December 4, 1987

CONGRESS PASSED AND SIGNED THE NATIONAL Defense Authorization Act of 1988-1989. This created Section 380 under Title 10, which included the following:

At the same time as the President submits the budget to Congress each year . . . , the Secretary of Defense shall submit to Congress a report containing the following:

(A) A detailed list of all forms of assistance under this chapter that is proposed to be made available by the Department of Defense to civilian drug law enforcement and drug interdiction agencies (including the United States Customs Service, the Coast Guard, the Drug Enforcement Administration, and the Immigration and Naturalization Service) during the fiscal year in which the budget is submitted.

With this new US Code, and in conjunction with Section 371 of Title 10, passed in 1981, the United States Military was now able to begin what was called Joint Task Force FIVE, or JTF-5. It was located on Coast Guard Island, Alameda, California. With additional listening stations in Hawaii and Alaska, JTF-5 had the ability to triangulate and locate any vessel of interest anywhere in the Pacific Ocean that utilized the KMI ship-to-shore communication service. This was a top-secret listening operation, and unless you had a top-secret clearance, you were not allowed in.

December 8, 1987

GENERAL SECRETARY GORBACHEV AND PRESIDENT REAGAN signed the INF Treaty during a ceremony at the White House in Washington, DC. The treaty was set to become effective on June 1, 1988. To the Soviet military, once the agreement became effective, it would basically gut the Soviet nuclear arsenal. The growing ranks of discontent were now palpable in the Soviet military and the KGB. Gorbachev must go.

IN THE SECOND WEEK IN DECEMBER, Willard was released from the drug rehab center in Oregon. He was happy to be home and drove to Sonora to personally apologize to Carlin. He was clean now and wanted to stay that way.

"I'm sorry, Carlin."

"Willard, you must start using your head and stay off the junk. There will not be another run until next spring, and you're partially to blame for that. We lost a lot of money, boy," Carlin said.

"It won't happen again, I promise."

"You and Bill grew up together. I used to love to watch you two wrestle and play. I love you like my own son, but you have to stop fucking up. I'm not going back to prison again, and I need you to stay out of trouble or that's where you're heading."

"I promise, Carlin."

"Okay, get a local apartment here in Sonora so you'll be close to me. In a few weeks, I want you working on the barge and getting it ready to go in the spring. I'm still looking for a larger tug and should find one by then."

"Okay, Carlin. Whatever you need me to do, I'll do it."

11:00 a.m., Tuesday, December 22, 1987

HAYDEN CAME TO THE INDOOR FIRING RANGE looking for Davis and spoke to the instructor, who told Davis over the loudspeaker to secure his weapon and back off the firing line.

"What's going on?" Davis asked.

"Come with me," Hayden said and drove Davis to the DOD building. The men went into his office, and Davis closed the door behind them.

"We have a major problem," Hayden said, handing Davis a letter.

Davis read the letter and said, "Holy shit! Where'd this come from? Who the fuck wrote this?"

"It was sent to Langley, the director faxed it to me late last night. Keep that one. I already made copies and faxed one to Jack. This morning, Bob Klass called me and said Customs received a letter too. He made the point that we're looking at the right people, but we missed the load mentioned in this letter. Bob wondered if they got another ship since you last checked the *California Rose*."

Davis looked at Hayden, who continued.

"The director is checking with the FBI to see if they received anything. We don't know how many of these have been circulated.

The ones received have been xeroxed, no originals, no handwriting. They're all anonymous and untraceable."

"Fuck. The whole world's going to be looking at this," Davis said.

"Yes, and we need to put a lid on it ASAP. You need to find out who the hell sent this and fast."

"Fuck," Davis said. "I'll be here until the thirty-first when I graduate."

"Yes, but that's only a week away. When you get back there, find out who the hell is doing this. God only knows what else they're planning to do. They could completely fuck this entire operation and everything we've done in the past year."

"Can I use your phone?" Davis asked.

"Sure, who are you calling?"

"Coast Guard."

"Hello, United States Coast Guard. How may I help you?" Taylor said as he answered his phone on Yerba Buena Island.

"Ray, it's Tony."

"Well, how the hell are you and how's FLETC?"

"I'll be glad to get out of here. We graduate next week."

"That's good. I never cared much for the area."

"Ray, could you do me a favor?"

"Sure. What is it?"

"Can you do a drive-by for me of McAvoy Harbor and see if the *California Rose* is still there?" Davis asked.

"No problem, but I don't think it's moved. We've had no notifications from VTS, and the *Cal Rose* has been pretty good about checking in when they operate."

"Yes, you're probably right. But you need to get out of the office for a few hours anyway."

"Ha, you got that right. I'll drive by there later this morning. Do you want me to page you after I do?"

"Yes, please. Let me know what you find out. Also eat lunch in the café. They have great burgers and fries."

"Will do. I'll page you later. Goodbye."

"Goodbye. Thanks, Ray," Davis said and he hung up. "As soon as I hear back from him, I'll let you know," Davis said to Hayden.

At 2:15 p.m., Davis's pager buzzed in class. Glancing at it he got up and walked out of the room. Going to the secretary's office at the front of the building, Davis asked, "Can I use your phone?"

"Yes, go ahead," she said.

Davis called Taylor's phone. "What did you find?"

"She's gone. I checked with VTS, and the *Cal Rose* hasn't checked in since back in September."

"Okay. Did you have lunch at the café?"

"Yes, it was excellent. When you get back, can you do me a favor?"

"Sure. What is it?"

"Can we have a talk about the *California Rose.* What do you say?"

Davis thought for a moment and said, "Yes, let's do that. I'll be back after the first. Thank you, Ray. I need to get back to class."

"No problem. See you when you get back," Special Agent Ray Taylor replied.

Walking back to the class, Davis thought, I need to level with him, especially now that we have the letters.

On December 31, Davis graduated as the FLETC Distinguished Graduate of Criminal Investigator Class #806. Davis was the only member of the class to achieve honors in all three major areas of study: academics, firearms, and physical fitness. Davis said his good-byes and called a taxi.

"Where do you need to go, sir?"

"Glynco Jetport."

Six hours later he was getting in the Mustang at Executive Airport in Sacramento. Davis paged Reynolds and waited there. A minute later his bag phone rang. "I just landed. Did you get the fax from Buddy last week?"

"Yes. Stop by Vacaville. Let me know when you're five minutes out, and I'll open the garage door."

"Roger that. See you in an hour," Davis said and headed towards 143 Barbera Court.

Arriving at the Vacaville safe house, Davis shook hands with Reynolds and said, "Good to see you, Jack. I can't stand Georgia anymore."

"Yes, glad you're back. Who the hell do you think is writing these letters?" Reynolds asked.

"I have no clue," Davis said. "But I've been thinking on the way here. It's somebody with a big hard-on for Rogers. Whoever it is, they know the organization inside and out. Have Buddy run Rogers for any more previous marriages other than Mary and for girlfriends, disputes, lawsuits, creditors, and whatever else he can think of. If anything turns up, run that person for all contacts. We're missing a link. Could be revenge or jealousy. Get Buddy on this. I need that information now."

CHAPTER 42

Please Do Something

9:00 a.m., Saturday, January 2, 1988

Davis had been adding to his link chart at the Hayward safe house—Billy's last name as Little and Willard's last name as Butler. He also added Jim Rogers to the unknown next to Willard. All that new information came from the anonymous letter given to him by Hayden. It wasn't much but was still important pieces. Picking up his phone, he called Taylor's mobile phone.

"Wake the hell up. If you come to McAvoy Harbor Café, I'll buy you breakfast," Davis said.

"I'll take you up on that. I don't have anything planned this morning. See you at ten thirty."

At 10:30 a.m., Davis met Taylor in the parking lot. Shaking hands, Davis said, "How the hell you been?"

"Been good. Weather's starting to turn a little wet so not much going on."

Walking into the café, the men took a seat at the bar off to the side, facing back towards the harbor.

"Good morning, Joan," Davis said.

"Good morning, Tony. Haven't seen you for a while."

"Been traveling for a few weeks. Bring me two of my favorites.

This guy will eat one."

"Will do," Joan said, bringing out two cups and filling them with coffee.

"What did you just order me?" Taylor asked.

"The best buttermilk pancakes you'll ever have."

Taking an envelope out of the inside pocket of his London Fog jacket, he handed it to Taylor. "Read that, but we need to keep this conversation at a whisper."

Taylor took the letter out and read it. "Jesus, where'd you get this?"

"The CIA. But there are more out there, Customs has one. I need to find out who wrote it."

"No wonder you wanted me to check on the *Cal Rose.* A Rogers owns it, and another Rogers is in the company. Are they related to Carlin Rogers?"

"Yes, brother to Harold Sr., ex-husband to Mary, and brother to Sara Rogers Lawson," Davis said.

"No shit! Are you saying that this is true?"

"Yes. And that trip when they checked into VTS was a drug run. We have nothing to prove that, but they're supposed to have another run coming up this spring. We take that one down. Ray, I trust you, and I need to ask you to do something."

"What do you need?"

"I need you to keep this to yourself for the time being. I'll brief your RAC soon, but I need to find the source of these letters first. They have valuable information that we'll need."

"I can do that as long as you're able to share this with Case eventually."

"I can and will. Let me find this source first before this becomes a shit show."

"That'll work," Taylor said as both men shook hands.

Joan brought the two breakfasts out to the men. Afterwards Davis and Taylor were standing in the parking lot next to their vehicles.

"Let me know if the *California Rose* contacts VTS or if she's sighted anywhere. I don't know if Rogers is aware of the letters, but they obviously moved from here for a reason," Davis said.

"Will do," Taylor replied.

Both men shook hands again and left McAvoy Harbor.

Davis drove towards Vacaville as he called Reynolds. "Any information from Buddy?" he asked.

"Yes, I'm getting faxes from him. How soon can you get here?"

"Leaving McAvoy now. Be there in an hour."

Parking in the garage at the Vacaville safe house, Davis went inside and then upstairs with Reynolds. In the STU room, Reynolds handed Davis four pages of printouts. Turning, Davis sat down in the living room on the couch and read the information.

"Hmm, Carlin's been married twice before. The last is Mary, and the previous is Irene Steadman. She'd been previously married to a Jeff Butler, then to Carlin Rogers, and now Daniel Kasper. She must be Willard's mother."

"Yes, but you wouldn't think she'd rat out her own son," Reynolds said.

"No, but her husband might if he doesn't like Carlin," Davis said.

"True. So Daniel Kasper goes on the list."

"Yes," Davis said. "I need to pick a local law enforcement brain where these people live. I need to contact the Napa County Sheriff's Office and talk to whoever's in charge of their drug team. You have a phone book for Napa County?" Davis asked.

"No, I don't."

Davis picked up the phone in the STU room and dialed 0.

"Operator. How can I help you?" she asked.

"Napa County Sheriff's Office," Davis said.

After writing down the telephone number the operator provided, Davis called it.

"Napa County Sheriff's Office. How can I help you?" the man said.

"Yes, whom am I speaking to?" Davis asked.

"This is Deputy Miller."

"Miller, my name is Tony Davis. I'm a special agent for the Customs Service, and I'm on the Organized Crime Drug Enforcement Task Force. Who's in charge of your drug unit, and how do I get ahold of him?"

"That would be Sergeant Chris Decker. He's not here. But if you call back on Tuesday, he'll be here then."

"Okay, Miller, leave a message for Decker that I'll call him on Tuesday. Also give him my pager number," Davis said, giving the deputy the number.

"Will do."

"Thank you," Davis said hanging up. Looking at Reynolds, Davis said, "If he's any good at all, he'll know all the players and should be able to provide some gaps in our information."

Tuesday, January 5, 1988

Davis called Sergeant Decker of the Napa Special Investigations Bureau and made an appointment for the following day at 10:00 a.m.

The next day at their meeting, Davis said, "Thank you for seeing me," as he shook hands with the very polite Decker.

"Absolutely. What can I help you with?" Decker asked.

"I'm with OCDETF out of the city. I'm also a former state trooper, and I know the real work is done by the local, county, and state officers out in the field. I'm sort of the liaison for the task force, and I like to meet all the people involved with the different departments. If you guys need anything at all, just let me know. We have lots of federal money that we can provide for operations and equipment if you need it."

"That's great. We can always use some help at times."

"Also, we've received information on some local people that may or may not be involved with a smuggling organization, possibly based here out of Napa."

"Supply Masters?" Decker asked.

Surprised, Davis said, "Yes, we received an anonymous letter about them."

"I did too. It actually went to the State Tax Department. They forwarded it here to me," Decker said. Digging in the left drawer, he pulled the letter out from his desk. "Here it is," he said, handing it to Davis. "I've checked out all the people listed, and they do exist and live here. But I don't have the resources to do anything else with it. They're talking about an international drug smuggling operation, and I'm a county sheriff's deputy."

Looking at the letter, Davis saw it was the same letter the CIA and Customs had received with two big differences. It was not a Xerox, and on the bottom, it had "*Please do something*" in someone's handwriting. Davis felt the hair on the back of his neck rise up.

"Can I keep this?" Davis asked. "I think this is the same information we received, but I'd like to compare them side by side to be sure."

"No problem. Go ahead and take it. Let me know what you find out," Decker said.

"Thanks, and if you ever need anything, you just let me know," Davis said. "Been a pleasure meeting you, Chris."

"You too, Agent Davis."

Davis walked back out of the Special Investigations Bureau, got in the Mustang, and said, "Holy shit!" Picking up his phone, he called the Customs office in San Francisco.

"Hello. US Customs Service. How may I direct your call?" the operator said.

"Louise, it's Agent Davis. Is Klass in?" he asked.

"Hi Tony. Yes, he is. Hold on one minute."

"Bob Klass," the SAC said when he picked up the phone.

"Bob, its Tony. I received a copy of the same anonymous letter from the Napa County drug task force," Davis said.

"Shit! That means a wider distribution than we knew about."

"Yes, but this one went to the state tax department. It was forwarded to Sergeant Chris Decker by them. So the local police may not know anything about it."

"That could be a blessing," Klass said.

"Yes, one more thing. This one was signed."

"Signed?"

"Yes. Not with a name but with "Please do something." It's as good as a signature."

"Wow. What do you need?"

"I need a stack of the Customs summons. I'm going to go to the areas where Rogers's former wives and current husbands live and check bank signature cards. I need those summons for it to be legal."

"I'll priority mail them to Hayward today. You'll have them tomorrow."

"Thanks. I'll let you know what I find out. That brings me to the other question. If I find this person, what are we willing to offer them for their assistance?"

"Money for starters. We have plenty we can access for this kind of cooperation," Klass said.

"There must be a gripe there somewhere. When I find them, if I can find them, I'll see what they want. Thanks, Bob."

"Good luck, Tony," Klass said.

CHAPTER 43

Signature Cards

Monday, January 11, 1988

Davis received the blank Customs summons in the mail at the safe house in Hayward. Armed with the summons, he began to visit every bank in Richmond, looking for the account of Mary Rogers, Carlin's ex-wife, and registered owner of the *California Rose*. Davis didn't realize how many banks were actually in Richmond. Finally at the Mechanics Bank, he introduced himself.

Walking up to a teller Davis showed his ID and badge and said, "May I speak to the bank manager, please?"

"Yes, sir. Just a moment," the lady said and walked back into an adjacent office.

Walking out, she was followed by man in a grey suit.

"Hello. I'm Mr. Wilson," he said.

"Hi, I'm Special Agent Davis. May we speak in private?"

"Yes, come this way," Mr. Wilson said as he directed Davis around the counter and into his office. "What can I help you with?"

"I'm looking for the bank account of Mary Rogers, with a date of birth of July 29, '49. I know you cannot provide that information without a summons. I'll provide one to you, if she has an account here. But I don't want to waste your time, if she doesn't," Davis said, pulling out the yellow Customs summons.

"Let me check. . . . Yes, she does," the manager said.

"Okay, all I need to see is her signature card," Davis said as he filled out the summons and handed it to Mr. Wilson.

"Just give me a minute and let me get it."

Coming back a few minutes later, the bank manager gave the document to Davis. Looking at it and handing it back to the manager, Davis said, "Thank you. That's all I need to see. I appreciate your assistance, and my appearance here is strictly confidential. Have a good day." Davis got up and left the bank.

One down, Davis thought as he got into the Mustang. Davis had looked at the distinctive writing on the anonymous letter so many times, all he needed was a glance to tell if the signature card matched. Knowing the CIA and Customs Service letters were postmarked from Rainier, Oregon, and Longview, Washington, Davis spent the next month going from bank to bank looking for the account of Daniel Kasper.

Starting in Rainier, Oregon, there were only a couple of banks, and none had Daniel Kasper's account. Longview, Washington, however, had almost fifteen banks, and it took a couple of weeks for Davis to find out none of those had Daniel Kasper's current account.

But one bank manager had known Daniel Kasper in the past, and speaking to Davis, he said, "Yes, he did have an account here a couple of years ago, but he moved to Spokane."

"Thank you," Davis said, as he left the bank and drove the six hours to Spokane, Washington. After he got there, Davis realized the area had almost thirty banks.

"Goddamn," he said, as he looked at the banks and addresses in the Yellow Pages at the Best Western Motel off Interstate 90. He tore out three pages of banks and placed them in his folder.

Over the next four days, Davis showed his badge more times than an agent would do in two careers, and he still hadn't written one summons.

2:00 p.m., Thursday, February 18, 1988

In the afternoon of the fourth day in Spokane, the nice lady bank manager said, "Yes, Daniel and Irene Kasper have their accounts here."

"Wonderful," Davis said as he filled out the summons with carbon copy and handed the top sheet to the lady. "Can I see Daniel's signature card please?"

Returning after a few minutes, the bank manager handed the document to Davis. Glancing at it he said, "Well shit. Excuse me, but that's not what I'm looking for."

"I'm sorry," the lady said. "Is there anything else I can help you with?"

"No," Davis said and then changed his mind. "Yes, may I see Irene's signature card please."

"Okay, be back in a moment."

Davis knew this was another wild-goose chase until she handed the signature card of Irene Kasper to him. Even as his heart pounded and the hair rose on the back of his neck, he said, "Nope. Thank you anyway. What's their address?"

"It's 1010 North Summit Boulevard," she said.

"You wouldn't happen to have a telephone number for them, would you? I'll need it for my report when I get back to the city."

"Yes, I do," she said, as she gave Davis the number.

"Well, I would like to thank you for your cooperation, and I'm sorry that I took up so much of your time. Also, my visit today is strictly confidential."

"Of course, my pleasure to help. Have a nice day," the bank manager said.

"You too," Davis said as he left the bank.

Davis walked to the Mustang and looked at his road atlas for Spokane and North Summit Boulevard. Then he drove up Route 2 and turned west on Maxwell Avenue. Winding up around Maxwell, he came to North Summit Boulevard, turned left, drove a couple of blocks, and pulled over onto the side of the street. There were no cars in the driveway of 1010. Studying the light-green home, he called the telephone number of Daniel and Irene Kasper.

"Hello," a raspy voice said.

"Hello, is this Irene?" Davis asked.

"Yes, it is. Who's calling?"

"Is this a good time to speak?"

"It might be if you tell me who the hell you are."

"Irene, my name is Tony Davis. I'm a special agent for the US Customs Service. Do you mind if we speak?"

"I don't know what we would speak about. So it would just be a waste of our time."

"I first want to say I'll not hurt you in anyway. We may be able to help each other."

"I don't think we have anything to talk about. And I'm not sure how you could help me."

"I would like to speak to you about the letters you sent about Carlin," Davis said.

Irene didn't say a word.

Davis repeated, "Again, I'm not here to hurt you, and I think I can help you if you help me."

There was a long pause as Davis watched the house in case she tried to leave. If he needed to, he was prepared to arrest her as an accomplice to the drug smuggling. He knew it wouldn't ultimately stick, but it would give him a chance to talk to her. That wasn't needed.

"When would you like to talk?" she asked.

"Are you busy now?"

"No. Come on over. I live at 1010 North Summit Boulevard."

"Yes, I know. I'm sitting outside your driveway; I'm pulling up now." Less than a minute later, Davis got out of his vehicle and knocked on the door.

A slender woman in her forties opened it.

"Hi, I'm Tony Davis," he said holding up his ID and badge.

Taking the ID and looking at it, Irene said, "Come on in. Have a seat."

Davis sat on the couch as Irene handed back his credentials.

"How'd you find me?"

"By your signature card at the bank. I matched it to the letter you sent to the California Tax Department and wrote on the bottom 'Please do something.'"

"Oh," she said. "That was a mistake, wasn't it?"

"Either that or a blessing," Davis said. "How can I help you?"

"I didn't do that for me. I did it for my son, Willard. If I help you, you must promise me in writing that he'll never go to prison."

"If you will excuse me, let me get my phone and writing pad out of the car. And we'll find out right now, together, if that's possible."

"Okay," she said.

Davis went out to the Mustang, got his bag phone and notebook, and came back into the home. He opened the notebook and wrote down her request. "Anything else you want me to ask for?"

Irene thought for a moment and said, "Yes, one hundred thousand dollars."

"Okay, let's see what we need to do," Davis said, as he called Bob Klass's mobile phone.

"Klass," Bob said when he answered his phone.

"Bob, I'm sitting with the author of the letters we received. She has two requests before she'll help us."

Special Agent in Charge Robert Klass paused and asked, "What does she want?"

"Number one, she has a son, Willard Butler, that's involved with the Carlin Rogers smuggling organization. She wants it in writing that he'll not go to prison if we arrest him on information that she will provide to us. Is that correct, Irene?" Davis asked looking her.

"Yes," she said.

"What's number two?" Klass asked.

"She wants one hundred thousand dollars in cash."

"I can make both of those happen. I need to talk to the US Attorney. Can you bring her here?" Klass asked.

"Will you go with me to San Francisco?" Davis asked Irene. "I'll drive us there, and then I can fly you back to Spokane."

"Yes. Let me call Dan," she said as she got up and walked into the kitchen to use her own phone.

"I can be there tomorrow afternoon, Bob," Davis said.

"Where the hell are you?"

"Spokane, Washington."

"Jesus, okay. What's Willard's birthday?" Klass asked.

"Irene, what's Willard's birthday?" Davis asked loudly.

"October 2, 1961," she yelled back.

"Ten, two, sixty-one," Davis told Klass.

"Okay, get her here. We need to do a debrief and assign her a confidential informant number."

"Roger that. We'll be on our way within the hour," Davis said and hung up.

Irene came back into the living room after finishing her call to her husband.

"Are we good?"

"Yes. Let me pack a small suitcase and we can go."

CHAPTER 44

Mary Williamson

11:00 p.m., February 18, 1988

Davis and Irene talked for the next eight hours before they stopped for the night at the Holiday Inn in Klamath Falls, Oregon.

Getting them both rooms, Davis asked, "Is seven too early for you in the morning? We can meet in the lobby."

"No, I'll be ready," Irene said. "Goodnight."

"Goodnight," Davis said as he went to his room down the hall. In his room, Davis paged Reynolds. Two minutes later, the bag phone rang. "Hello, Jack," Davis said.

"What's going on, Tony? You doing any good?"

"I found the author."

"What? Where?"

"Spokane. It was Willard's mom. I have her with me. I'm in a hotel in Klamath Falls, Oregon. I'm taking her to Klass in the morning. He's setting up a deal with the United States Attorney for immunity from prosecution for Willard. We'll make her a CI."

"How did you find her?"

"I matched the writing on the bottom of the letter I got from Sergeant Decker from Napa County to a signature card at a bank. I called her up and she agreed to talk."

"Man, that's good investigative work," Reynolds said.

"Perhaps, but I had some luck too. I ran into a bank manager in Longview that happened to know her husband had moved to Spokane."

"That's still good work. What's next?"

"If Klass can swing the deal with the US Attorney, we'll debrief her and then get her on a flight back to Spokane. Advise Buddy. Klass will have his hands full for the next few days."

"Will do. Good work, Tony. Goodbye."

"Thanks. Goodbye," Davis said and hung up.

Friday, February 19, 1988

DAVIS AND IRENE WERE HEADING TO SAN FRANCISCO by 7:00 a.m. At 2:15 p.m., Davis pulled into the parking garage on Montgomery Street. Putting his hat and glasses on, he hurried Irene across the street, while he limped, hoping no one was watching. Inside the building, Davis knocked on Klass's door.

"Come in," the SAC said.

Davis entered with Irene following him into the room. There were ASAC Sherman, SSA Waskovic, and another man with reddish-blond hair that Davis didn't know.

"Good afternoon. This is Irene Kasper," Davis said.

Klass came over and shook hands with Irene and then introduced the other men. The man Davis didn't know was introduced as Assistant United States Attorney Earl Swedish, the lead AUSA for the Organized Crime Drug Enforcement Task Force.

"Please, let's all have a seat," Klass said, directing everyone to the large meeting table in his room. "Mr. Swedish, if you would, please explain to Mrs. Kasper what you are willing to do."

"Yes, Bob. Thank you. Mrs. Kasper, it's my understanding that you possess information that pertains to an international drug smuggling operation involving your ex-husband, Carlin Rogers, and others. Is that correct?" Swedish asked.

"Yes. I do," Irene said.

"And I understand you are willing to fully cooperate with the government, specifically with Special Agent Davis of the Customs Service.

"Yes."

"For guarantees that your son, Willard Butler, who is also part of the Rogers organization, will not be fully prosecuted nor be sent to prison for any crimes involving those drug smuggling activities. Is that correct, Mrs. Kasper?" Swedish asked.

"Yes, if it's in writing and I receive one hundred thousand dollars."

"Yes, ma'am, it is in writing, and you will be authorized a confidential informant payment of one hundred thousand dollars," Swedish said. "Your cooperation will be secret under the Freedom of Information Act Exemption 7D. This exemption prevents your confidential informant status from being exposed. Do you understand everything I just explained to you?"

"Yes, I do."

"Do you enter into this agreement freely and on your own accord?" he asked.

"Yes, I do."

"Very well," Swedish said, handing a folder to Irene. "This is our agreement with you. Please take a few minutes and read it fully. If you have any questions, feel free to ask me."

Irene took the next ten minutes and read the document twice. Afterwards, she signed the document, which was witnessed by Swedish and SAC Klass.

"Thank you, Mrs. Kasper. You have the government's word that your son will be taken care of in the event that he's arrested pertaining to any information that you will provide. In the actuality that he is arrested, you do understand that for his safety and yours, he cannot be just set free. That would put a target on him and you. He may have to spend some time in jail until he makes bond or until the case is resolved. But he will not go to prison," Swedish said.

"Yes, I understand that. I just don't want my only son to spend the biggest part of his life in prison the way his stepfather has," Irene said.

"I understand," Swedish replied. "Nice meeting you, Mrs. Kasper, and again, thank you. Gentlemen, have nice day," he said, preparing to leave.

"Thank you," Davis said, shaking hands with the AUSA.

"My pleasure. When you get this case moving along, bring it to me, and we'll put it on OCDETF," Swedish said.

"Yes, sir," Davis said as Swedish left the room. "Irene, I need to debrief you now," Davis said. "Bob, can I use the meeting room?"

"Yes, you'll not be disturbed. I'll be in shortly, but no one else will be in that room," Klass said.

"Follow me, please," Davis said as he led Irene into the meeting room next to Klass's.

OVER THE NEXT FEW HOURS, Irene explained her life with Carlin—his counterfeiting and how he came to be cellmates with convicted Russian spy Charles Bedford in Lompoc Prison; how Carlin had helped Bedford escape and took him to live with Gladys Wymes on Katka Mountain in Idaho; how Gladys had told her that Bedford and Carlin were trying to buy a boat to smuggle Bedford out of the country to a Russian ship; how they were planning to get the money to buy the ship by robbing banks; and how Willard told her that Carlin had met with the KGB in Cali, Columbia, in 1986 to set up the drug smuggling operation.

Davis was to later learn that this one statement in her letter to the different agencies, mentioning the Russians, caused all the recipients to doubt its veracity. Every agency with the exception of the CIA had an experienced agent put this letter in File 13 simply because they didn't believe it or know what to do with it. The IRS did later acknowledge the letter's importance after receiving disturbing Suspicious Activity Reports and IRS Form 8300s from banks in Napa, Santa Rosa, Fairview, and Chico.

Irene also said how Willard confided in her that there was going to be another drug trip during last December, but with him and Valley being arrested, it was cancelled. However, there was going to be another run in May or June of '88, and Carlin was getting a bigger boat. She informed Davis that she had no idea where the *California Rose* was but said, "Willard does, and you can follow him from his apartment in Sonora to find it."

SAC Klass came into the room, carrying a zippered bag with long straps like a purse. "Irene, can you please take the money out of the bag and count it?" Klass asked.

Taking the ten paper-wrapped bundles of ten thousand dollars each, she counted the money. "One hundred thousand dollars," she said.

"Yes, now if you will, please sign this saying you received this money. This payment will not be reported to the IRS," Klass said.

After Irene signed the document, Klass and Davis witnessed it with their own signatures.

"How will I get this on the plane?" she asked.

"Don't worry. I'll get you past security and onto the aircraft," Davis said.

"I have one more document that I need to file out, and I need to ask you a question, Mrs. Kasper," Klass said.

"Okay."

"I need you to tell me a name that you want to go by. This name will be on your documentation along with your confidential informant number, which is SF743. What name would you like me to use?" Klass asked.

"Mary Williamson," Irene replied.

"Bob, I have pretty much all I need here. Irene and I have exchanged contact information, and we'll stay in contact weekly if not more often. Can you get her a flight out of SFO to Spokane? I'll take her down there and get her headed home," Davis said.

"Yes, give me fifteen minutes," Klass said and left the room.

"Do you have any questions for me, Irene?" Davis asked.

"Yes. Where're you from, Australia?"

"No," Davis said with a laugh, "West Virginia, but I've been asked before, if I was from Australia. I guess it is a little different accent. Is there anything else?"

"I trust you, Tony. I expect you to help me when the time comes.

Because we both know how this is going to end up. And I don't want Willard sitting in the same cell with Carlin for the rest of his life."

"You have my word, Irene. I'll keep Willard out of prison, one way or another. That will not be an easy task, once this goes down, but I'll think of something."

"Thank you," Irene said, giving Davis a hug.

Klass came back into the room with the plane ticket and gave it to Irene.

"Thank you, for your cooperation. Tony will take care of whatever you need. If you ever have any problems, and you cannot get in touch with him, you call me," Klass said, handing Irene his business card.

"Thank you, Mr. Klass. You don't know how much I appreciate what you and Agent Davis are doing for me and Willard. One thing I will ask is he is never told while I'm still living that I did this."

"Mrs. Kasper, I can assure you that he will never be told," Klass said. "Goodbye, Mrs. Kasper."

"Goodbye, Mr. Klass," Irene said.

ARRIVING AT SAN FRANCISCO INTERNATIONAL AIRPORT, Davis parked by the curb and placed his red light on the dash. He took Irene into the United terminal and walked with her to security where he bypassed the screening. Showing his ID to the officer, he signed in and entered "SA Davis, USCS" and "Mary Williamson" in the log of authorized personnel. After walking with her to the gate, he sat with Irene until boarding time.

"You know, I called the FBI," she said.

"When?" Davis asked, somewhat surprised.

"The week before I wrote those letters. Two agents came to the house from Seattle. I told them just about everything I've told you."

"What did they say?"

"They said they would look into it. But they wouldn't call me back. I think they thought I was crazy or something."

"Davis laughed with Irene and said, "Well you have to admit it is a wild-ass story."

"Yes, I guess it is," she said.

It was finally time for her flight to board. With a thank you and hug, Irene boarded the flight with her small carryon suitcase and one hundred thousand dollars.

With Irene as confidential informant, or CI, SF-743, Davis began an official Customs Service investigation into the smuggling activities of Carlin Rogers and others. Now being forced into the open, he would need to be mindful of the United States Attorney and the other agencies that would have interests in this case. Davis needed to make sure he maintained the lead on the case so it would not spiral out of control. To do that, he'd have to stay one step ahead of everyone else—and to find the *California Rose* and fast.

CHAPTER 45

New Arrangements and Locations

Tuesday, February 23, 1988

Yukorov now knew he had only one person to rely on to make sure the shipments went through. He never told General Vanerev that Valley had been arrested. Instead, he decided to put all his trust in Rogers. He knew this had its risk, but what else was he to do?

Calling Rogers he said, "Will you be ready in May?"

"Yes, I've found a larger tug. I'll have it and the barge ready by the first week in May."

"Good. Our new rendezvous point will be 38, 150. You'll not need to go out as far, and you'll be able to get back into San Francisco faster. We want this completed as soon as possible," Yukorov said.

"Understood. And since Valley is no longer involved, I want his two million dollars, as well as my own two million dollars," Rogers demanded.

Yukorov had no other choice but to agree. "Yes, I agree. I'll pay you four million dollars. We can have the same men who brought me money deliver it to you from Toronto, but only after I'm paid."

"Yes, I know those men. That'll work for me," Rogers said, knowing he had no chance of getting any upfront money from the Russian.

"Very good, Captain. Let's plan on the rendezvous date of May 12. Is that agreeable with you?" Yukorov asked, remembering the general wanted to start out of Afghanistan by the end of May. The offloading would take two or three days, so he figured everything would be completed by the fifteenth.

"Yes, I'll be able to meet then. The new tug is faster and can do twelve knots traveling light."

"Okay, we'll use the same callsigns and same frequencies on the radios. You will be meeting the same ship and crew, callsign *Western Star*. You will still use callsign *Ulu*. Is that agreeable?"

"Yes, we'll keep everything the same as last year. There will be no mistakes that way."

"Very good. Also, Captain, after the exchange, I'll have my vessel shadow you until you get closer to shore. That will be in case you have any problems.

"That's fine. I don't mind the company."

"Good, you'll need my contact number in case you need to call me," Yukorov said, giving Rogers his mobile phone number.

"I usually call you the big Russian fucker to Valley, but what do you want me to call you since we're now business partners?"

"Call me Vlad," Yukorov said with a laugh.

"Okay, Vlad, I'll talk to you later."

"Yes, Captain. Goodbye."

"Goodbye," Rogers said.

Getting off the phone with Rogers, Yukorov called Monarch and asked to be connected to DePantera.

"Hello, Mr. Yuk. How are things progressing?" DePantera asked.

"Good. My vessel will meet the American captain on or about the twelfth of May. He should be back in San Francisco by the third or fourth week in May."

"That is good, Mr. Yuk. To confirm, you are bringing forty-three tons of hashish. I will pay 1.1 million per ton for the hash, or 47.3 million American dollars. And I will pay you for the thirteen tons of Thai at fifty thousand per ton, or 650 thousand dollars. Is that correct?"

"Yes, but only pay for the hashish to the account in Luxembourg. I will have the men from Toronto deliver the 650 thousand to me."

"Yes, of course, Mr. Yuk. Is there anything else I can help you with today?"

"No. I will inform you when my ship departs from the American vessel."

"Very well. Have a nice day, Mr. Yuk. Goodbye."

"Goodbye, Mr. DePantera," Yukorov said and hung up.

DAVIS AND A TEAM OF TWO OTHER CUSTOMS AGENTS, Art Curia and Matt Dike, had been watching Willard at his Sonora, California, apartment for over a week. The agents had been so exposed sitting along the road that Davis took a chance and asked a man and his wife if the agents could use their home to surveil from. Amazingly, the parents of two small children agreed to let the agents in each day and sit in their living room to watch out the front window.

Finally on Tuesday, March 8, at 8:30 a.m., Willard got in his new black Ford Ranger pickup, California license plate, 3K02157, and left the apartment. He first drove around Sonora in circles to make sure he wasn't being followed, as Carlin had instructed.

Davis and the other two agents, all in separate cars, kept changing eyeball position and keeping Willard in sight to make sure he didn't think he was being followed by the same car. Almost losing him a couple of times in traffic, they managed to stay on him. Willard finally headed out of town, traveling west on Route 4. Turning north on Interstate 5 in Stockton for a few miles, he then turned west again on Highway 12. After crossing the Mokelumne River Bridge, Willard turned south on the Jackson Slough Road.

Davis told the other agents over the radio that he would take the eyeball and they should pull off. "I don't want all three cars on this narrow gravel road," Davis said.

Staying well behind the black truck, Davis pulled down to another bridge where it crossed the Sevenmile Slough and stopped before crossing the bridge. He looked to the east and saw a sign that said Owl Harbor. Looking to the far end of the dock, a quarter-mile down the slough, he could see Willard's pickup parked there. Davis watched as Willard got into a small boat that was tied to the dock and motored to the *California Rose* and barge. The vessels were tied to an island in the middle of the slough. Standing on the back of the tug and helping Willard out of the small boat was Carlin Rogers.

"Got ya," Davis said as he left the area. It was 10:30 a.m. Pulling back onto the highway, he radioed Art and Matt that the target was there, adding, "Thanks for your help and 10-22."

Driving back towards Rio Vista, Davis called Taylor. "Hey, you going to be in your office around noon?"

"Yes, come on down."

"Okay, be there about noon. Is the RAC in today?"

"Yes, he is. Do you want to have lunch with us?"

"Yes, I found the *California Rose* and the author of the letters. We need to talk."

"Great. I'll see you in a little while."

Davis drove to the Coast Guard station, and they all went to the cafeteria to eat. After getting their meals, they sat at a table reserved for officers off to the side.

Taking Irene's letter out of his pocket, Davis handed it to RAC Dale Case USCG.

After reading it, Case said, "Damn, this is factual?"

"Every word," Davis said.

"What's the status and timeframe?" Case asked.

"The status is ongoing and picking up. I found the *California Rose* this morning in the Sevenmile Slough after following Willard Butler from his home in Sonora. Carlin Rogers was on the vessel when Butler arrived. It's moored to the barge out in the middle of the slough, and the two are tied to an island, about a hundred feet from the bank. They're using a small boat with outboard to go back and forth. The timeframe is this spring, May or June for their next run, and they're to be purchasing a larger vessel."

"How can we help?" Case asked.

"How do you track a ship at sea?" Davis asked.

"They make a satellite tracking device, but you'll need a federal court order to plant it."

"Where do you get one?"

"I'm sure the Customs Service has access to them. They're not big, about the size of a large walkie-talkie," Case said.

"Okay, I'll check into that," Davis said.

"What are you going to do now?" Taylor asked.

"I'm going fishing. There is absolutely nowhere out there to surveil them from except the water. I'll look into the satellite tracking device. If I can find one, I'll let you guys know when I'm going to plant it. Ray, you up for a little nighttime surveillance?"

"Heck yeah! You just let me know when."

"Thanks, fellows. We'll have to play this by ear," Davis said.

Thursday morning, March 10, 1988

DAVIS PICKED UP HIS BOAT ON MADRONE ROAD and drove towards Sevenmile Slough. Before crossing the Mokelumne River Bridge on Highway 12, he pulled onto Brannan Island Road and stopped at B&W Marina where he'd seen a boat launch. He walked into the office.

"Hello," a smiling lady said, standing behind the counter.

"Good morning," Davis said. "Can I launch my boat here?"

"Five dollars a day to launch, or twenty dollars a week to use a slip," said the lady.

"That sounds good. I'll rent a slip," Davis said, laying down a hundred-dollar bill. "Sign me up for five weeks," he said, giving his name and the description of his boat.

"You fishing?" the lady asked.

"Yes. I live in Hayward. It's a lot easier to leave the boat here than drag it back and forth. Do you have a gas pump here?" he asked.

"Yes, you'll find Marvin around the dock somewhere. He's the owner and can get you the gas."

"That's great. I'm Tony," he said extending his hand.

"I'm Susie. I'm married to Marvin. Nice to meet you, Tony," she said, shaking his hand.

"Thank you," Davis said.

"You're welcome. See you later."

Davis left the building and looked at everything. I like this area, he thought. It was a beautiful morning as he backed the boat trailer down into the water at the launching dock. Climbing onto the trailer tongue after the small vessel started to float up off of the trailer, Davis unhooked the hand winch strap from the eyebolt on the front of the boat. He held onto the rope that was tied to the eyebolt, jumped back onto the dry launch pad, and pulled the boat over to the dock where he tied it to one of the dock cleats.

Getting in the CJ, Davis pulled the trailer up into one of the parking slots for trailer and vehicle. Back at the boat, he untied it and climbed in, being careful not to step on the two fishing poles he'd purchased a few weeks before at a fishing shop near Sonoma Plaza. He sat down on the far seat. The old Johnson motor started easily with two pulls on the rope handle, after placing the choke on. Pushing off, Davis began to idle his way towards the end of the dock and the open water of the Mokelumne River. As he pulled around to the boathouse, he saw the Chevron gas pump and an older man sitting in a lawn chair.

"Need fuel?" the man asked.

"Not yet, but you must be Marvin," Davis said as he pulled over and held the dock with his hand.

"That's right, owner, operator, and slave to Susie," he said with a laugh.

"Well, at least you can laugh about it," Davis said, smiling. "I'm Tony. Nice to meet you, Marvin."

"You, too. What're you up to today?" Marvin asked. "I hope you don't mind, but I'm a little nosy about people coming and going around here. Had some things stolen, and that really pissed me off. I keep a shotgun in the shop and my pistol with me." Raising the front of his shirt to where Davis could see a small grip.

"Thirty-eight Colt Cobra?" Davis asked.

"Well, I'll be damn. Yes, it is. How'd you know that?"

"I have one exactly like it. Interesting story too. Used to belong to Sheriff Robert Ellis in Marshall County, West Virginia. He was killed in a car wreck, and the widow gave his gun to my father, who was his doctor. Later, my father gave it to me."

"Damn," Marvin said. "That was bad luck."

"Yes, it was. I don't know how it happened. I was only fifteen or sixteen at the time in 1970."

"You can never be too careful," Marvin said.

"Isn't that the truth. Okay, Marvin, nice talking to you. I think I'll go drown some worms," Davis said as he pulled away from the dock.

"You too, Tony. Talk later."

Davis turned down the river, thinking he would hug the right shoreline for the two miles until he got to the San Juaquin River. Casting out a shallow-running Rapala, he slowly trolled with the 35 HP motor idling at its slowest speed without stopping. Anyone watching would honestly think he was fishing because that was exactly what he was doing, as well as getting a closer look at some international drug smugglers involved with conspirators trying to kill Russian leader Mikhail Gorbachev. But nobody would ever even consider such a wild-ass thought.

Coming to the mouth of the river, Davis turned up the San Joaquin and then into Little Potato Slough where he found numerous islands before turning around and starting back down towards the river. He reached down and picked up his six-gallon fuel tank to see how much gas he'd used. Not even half, he thought, feeling the weight and hearing the fuel slosh. He had two tanks in the boat, so he didn't think there was any danger of running out of fuel. Coming back out onto the river, he hugged the left bank going downstream for a couple more miles. I need this to look good, he thought. Crossing the San Joaquin below Sevenmile Slough, he began the slow idle back upstream that was even slower against the current.

When he finally came to the slough, Davis turned into the waterway and began his slow troll towards the *California Rose*. Pulling his camera out of his backpack that was lying on the floor of the boat, he hurriedly took one picture after seeing no one around and then shoved the camera back into the bag. Slowly, he got closer to the vessel and saw the tug was tied to the barge, which was moored to an old piling on the island.

Davis fished his way up past the *California Rose* to Twitchell Island Bridge, turned around, and then headed back out of Sevenmile Slough. Once again seeing no one around, he quickly took a close-up picture of the vessels as he was going by.

When he got back to B&W, Marvin was still sitting at the boathouse.

"Can I use any slip?" Davis asked.

"Yes, any that's empty. Help yourself."

Davis pulled the boat into an empty slip, tied it up, and got out.

"Did you catch anything?"

"Yes, but only a couple small bass," he lied. "That's a lot of water out there. Do you have many oceangoing vessels come up this far?"

"Not many up this far. It's normally just river craft with shallow drafts. Big vessels may get grounded if you're not paying attention. Now over on the Sacramento River, there are some large craft that go all the way to Sacramento. But not many on this side of the delta, at least not up this far."

"I was just wondering, seeing that tug tied up on Sevenmile."

"I don't know what it's doing up here," Marvin said. "It's been there a couple months. Every now and then, you'll see it on the river, but not often."

"I see," Davis said. "See you later, Marvin."

"See ya, Tony."

CHAPTER 46

OCDETF

Monday, March 14, 1988

Davis was asked to come to Assistant US Attorney Earl Swedish's office in the Federal Building in San Francisco.

"Come in, Agent Davis," Swedish said. "Nice seeing you again."

"You too, sir," Davis said, shaking hands with the AUSA.

"I would like to introduce you to Special Agent Rich Cain of the IRS."

"Hello," Davis said, shaking hands with the IRS agent.

"Hello," Cain said. "We may be on to the same target."

"Gentlemen, have a seat, and Rich, fill Tony in on what you've found out."

"Okay, last fall we started getting SAR reports from banks in the Napa area. We then got some from a Chico bank and then IRS forms 8300 from a couple different banks. I've identified the company that some of the SARs are associated with, and it's Supply Masters, Inc. out of Napa."

"I see," Davis said.

"It's my understanding that you have a CI that has information about drug smuggling from this same company."

"Yes, I do. I think we are onto the same people. Are you aware of the anonymous letters that were sent last November, detailing this organization?" Davis asked.

"Yes, I have the letter the IRS was sent. And I understand several agencies got the same letter."

"Yes, that's correct. I also got one of the letters from Napa County Sheriff's office. That letter had some handwriting on the bottom of it. I was able to match the writing to a signature card at a bank in Washington State."

"That's what I've heard. Good work. What do you think about us exchanging information and coordinating this through OCDETF?"

"I think that's a great idea and needs to be done at this point," Davis said. "I found the vessels last week. It looks like they're getting them prepared for the next drug run in May or June."

"Excellent," Swedish said. "I think we need to write this up and present it to the OCDETF Committee for acceptance. What do you guys think?"

Both agents agreed.

Cain said, "If we make arrests, I think it would be better if we keep the drug case separate from the money case."

"Yes, I agree with that," Davis said.

"I do as well," Swedish stated. "For this to be presented properly to the court, that would need to be done. Okay, I'll present it that way to the committee, and I'm sure they're going to recommend these investigations go forward as an OCDETF case, especially with both lead agents having your own initial cases and you both already being on OCDETF. This'll be a slam dunk for the committee. Okay, gentlemen, let's start coordinating this as of today."

"That sounds good to me," Davis said.

"I agree," Cain replied.

"Okay, what do you guys need? Anything I can do?" Swedish asked.

"Yes. I need an order to plant a satellite tracking device on the *California Rose*," Davis said.

"Bring me the paperwork, and I'll make sure it's signed off on," Swedish said.

"I'll do that," Davis replied. "Rich, let's exchange contact information."

Information was exchanged, and Cain gave Davis contact information for another IRS agent in case he couldn't be reached.

"This is Mike Hagers's information too. Good agent and he's easy to work with. Some say I'm not at times."

Davis chuckled and said, "I'm a results kind of guy too, and I hear you are good. We won't have any trouble. I don't candy-coat much either. I've already been working with the Coast Guard. How about I set up a meeting for this Friday, the eightieth, and we all have a sit down?"

"I'll be out of town, but contact Mike. He and another agent, Bill Basler, can meet. Go ahead and set it up and let them know," Cain said.

"I'll do that. We can meet at the Coast Guard facility. I don't like coming to the federal building any more than I have to. Too many eyes here."

"Yes, good idea," said Cain.

"It's been a pleasure, gentlemen," Davis said, shaking hands with the men, and then he left the federal building. Getting to his car, Davis called the Customs office. "Hi, Louise. Is the SAC in?"

"Yes, Tony. Hold on."

"Klass."

"I just had a meeting with AUSA Swedish and IRS Agent Rich Cain. This case is going to OCDETF."

"Will that cause you any problems?" Klass asked

"No, none that I can't take care of. Will you notify Harvey what's occurred?"

"Yes, I'll take care of that."

"How do I get a satellite tracking device? I need to put one on the *California Rose*. Swedish already said to bring him the paperwork and he'd get it approved."

"We have them, but they're in LA. We have a tech guy there that does the install. His name is Barry Frank. I'll contact him and have him send us a go-by for the court order. Tomorrow I'll have it, and we can change the wording for our vessel. Should be easy to do."

"Okay. I'm running out of time fast. We have six to eight weeks max before this thing goes down. With the tracking unit, we'll know exactly where they are returning to. I suspect it will be back to the same place. But right now, that's up in the air, and we must know for certain."

"Understand. I'll page you when I know more," Klass said.

"Thanks. I'll be fishing for the next few days. I need to get a long look at what's going on up there."

"All right. Let me know what you find out."

THAT SAME DAY, CARLIN ROGERS AND his sister, Debra Rinehart, were in Olympia, Washington, buying a much larger tugboat named the *Valiant Venture*. This was a true oceangoing vessel that could make fifteen knots if running wide open. It was located at its home port of Long Beach, California. They purchased the vessel for $168,000, completing the deal by giving the owner, Dick Parker of Sandbar Marine, a $100,000 bearer bond from the Bank of Paris, Luxembourg, and a check from Supply Masters, Inc. for $68,000. Carlin would fly to Los Angeles in a few weeks and bring the new vessel back to Sevenmile Slough, and he was excited.

Tuesday and Wednesday, March 15 and 16, 1988

DAVIS FISHED THE SEVENMILE SLOUGH'S UPPER END near the Twitchell Island Bridge, staying over one hundred yards from the *California Rose*. No one paid any attention to him, a fisherman that merely came and went.

Carlin Rogers showed up late on the fifteenth but was there all day on the sixteenth. He had three men working on the barge and tug—Willard Butler and two other men Davis later learned were Bill Rogers, Carlin's son, and Scott Dawn, a friend of Bill's. Being far enough away and using a telephoto lens, Davis was able to take almost one hundred pictures those two days.

On the evening of March 16, Davis was leaving the slough when Carlin Rogers yelled at the fisherman in dirty clothes wearing an old floppy camo boonie hat, "You catch anything?"

"No, not yet," Davis replied.

What Rogers couldn't see was the West Virginia State Police patch on the inside of the old boonie hat that was being worn inside out.

Thursday, March 17, 1988

DAVIS, WITH THE HELP OF SSA HARVEY WASKOVIC, finished the application for a federal court order authorizing the installation and use of the satellite tracking device in accordance with Title 21, United States Code, Section 952(a). The only problem was a tracking unit would not be available until the first of April. At that time, Customs Technician Barry Frank would bring it to San Francisco.

Friday, March 18, 1988

DAVIS MET IRS AGENTS MIKE HAGERS and Bill Basler and USCG Agents Ray Taylor and Dennis Robins at Coast Guard Headquarters on Yerba Buena Island.

"They're getting ready to go soon," Davis said. "They have four or five men working down inside the barge all day. It looks like they're painting the inside from the material and buckets they're carrying onto the barge."

"What has the CI said?" Taylor asked.

"Not much, only that they'll be leaving soon. The other thing is they're talking about getting a bigger boat. I hope the hell they don't because I'm getting an order to install a satellite tracking device on the *California Rose*. The device is supposed to be here by the first of April. If they get another tug at the last minute, we're fucked in tracking it or knowing where it'll come back to," Davis said and then asked Hagers, "How's your case going?"

"Cain is pushing us hard to get all the documents we'll need for the money case. It appears to be solid now. But we still don't know all the players and connections."

"Who do you have?" Davis asked.

"We're trying to figure out what the relationships are between

Rogers, Little, a man named Terrance Valley, Willard Butler, Jim Rogers, and Sara and Doug Lawson."

"I can help with that," Davis said. "Rogers and Little are cousins. Butler is Carlin Rogers's former stepson. Jim Rogers is Carlin's nephew; his father is Harold Rogers Sr., Carlin's older brother. Valley is an outsider, but an organizer from way back that knows them all—Carlin, Little, Willard, and Jim. Sara is Carlin and Harold's sister. She is a Rogers. Doug is her husband and is the chief appraiser at LendBest. This is an almost exclusive family operation."

"What do you know about Mary Rogers, the owner of the *California Rose*, and David Williams, part owner of Supply Masters?" IRS Agent Bill Basler asked.

"You'll like this part," Davis said. "Mary is Carlin's ex-wife, no biggie there. But Williams is an attorney from Villa Park. He helped form Supply Masters because he was contacted by Valley who knew Williams was the attorney for convicted Russian spy Charles Bedford. Carlin Rogers helped Bedford escape from Lompoc Federal Prison and was trying to buy a boat to get him out of the country. Williams knew Rogers through Bedford. Rogers was recommended to Valley, but we don't know by whom. US Marshals arrested Rogers for helping Bedford escape but couldn't prove it, so they cut him loose."

"Do you think the KGB is involved with this?" Hagers asked Davis.

"No way. They wouldn't have any interest with any of these people. This is just another drug smuggling organization run by a bunch of ex-cons," Davis lied.

March 23, 1988

AUSA Swedish signed the Application for Court Order, authorizing the installation and use of the satellite tracking device on the *California Rose*.

Davis made a call to Customs Tech Barry Frank in LA. "Barry, I need you to hurry the hell up."

"I'll have one free in the next week, and I'll fly up as soon as I get it."

"Barry, are you married?

"Well, yes."

"Do you still like her?"

"Yes, most of the time. Why?"

"Okay, just imagine your wife has been kidnapped by human traffickers and rapists. And the only way you're ever going to keep her from being violated and see her again is if I put that tracking device on this boat. Do you understand what I'm saying to you, Barry?"

"Yes."

"I hope you do because this is that important."

"Are you serious?" Barry asked.

"Not really. But if I don't get that unit on this vessel up here, someone important somewhere is definitely going to be fucked."

THAT EVENING, DAVIS CALLED IRENE IN SPOKANE.

"How're you doing?"

"I'm doing fine. I talked to Willard. He says Carlin is buying a new boat soon and they have a job with a salvage company out of Seattle. They're going to take marine parts to Alaska.

"Alaska?"

"Yes, that's what he says. But it could just be noise they're putting out."

"I think so. I don't think they're going to be any place near Alaska."

"I've been thinking. If you arrest the crew, Willard will have to be put in jail with the rest of them."

"Yes. There won't be any way around that."

"Yes, I know. What happens if this goes to trial and he's found guilty with the rest of them?"

"That's the problem. There probably will have to be a trial, and it'll be a sham trial for him. If he's found guilty, the judge will set aside his guilty verdict. If he's sentenced, then the sentence will be set aside per your agreement with the United States Attorney. The thing is, when that happens, everyone's going to know that either he talked or someone else talked to get him out. That will point straight at you."

"That's what I've been thinking about. But to tell you the truth, I don't care who finds out. I'm his mother. I don't need any other reason. If someone wants to be mad at me, that's their problem."

"Yes, I understand. Hopefully, we can figure a way around this. The one thing on our side is the judge in charge of the case will know about our agreement. He may be able to shield this somehow," Davis said, knowing that was a big if but possible if they got the right judge.

CHAPTER 47

WETSUIT

Thursday, March 31, 1988

EARLY THAT MORNING, DAVIS PICKED UP THE BOAT from B&W Marina and took it to Madrone Ranch. Seeing Clarence, he asked, “Would you happen to have any flat black paint?”

“What’re you going to use it on?”

“The boat. Don’t ask me why because I can’t say.”

“Okay. No, but I do have some olive-drab paint.”

“That’s even better. Could you do me a big favor? Paint that entire boat inside and out this morning with olive drab, motor included. I don’t have time to do it. And I’m going to need it very soon. It doesn’t have to be pretty.”

“Is this like some secret shit?” Clarence asked.

“Kind of.”

“Yes, I’ll do it.”

AT 1:00 PM, FEDERAL MAGISTRATE ESTER MYERS signed the court order authorizing the installation and use of the electronic tracking device on the *California Rose*.

Two days later on April 2, Customs Tech Barry Frank was flying to San Francisco with the device, telling Davis, “I’m not going to let anyone get fucked if I can stop it."

"That devise may just keep someone alive, Barry. That's what this is all about, and don't ever tell anyone I said that."

That same day, Yukorov called the *Poliksena*. "Babin, are you ready to sail?"

"Yes, Vlad, we can leave within the hour if you give the order."

"Very well, Captain. You will rendezvous with the American vessel at 38, 150 on May 12. Also, Captain, I want you to follow the American vessel back towards San Francisco until you feel you should not get any closer. If anything happens, I want you to take over the shipment with force if necessary. We cannot allow this shipment to fall into the hands of the Coast Guards. Do you understand, Babin?" Yukorov asked.

"Yes, I understand. After we offload to them, I'll follow them back towards the coast and then return to Karachi. And if needed, I have plenty of weapons on this vessel. All my men are KGB trained marksmen."

"Okay, Babin. Let me know as soon as you make contact with the American. That's important. Good luck, Captain," Yukorov said and hung up.

Looking across the desk at General Vanerev, Yukorov said, "This is it, General. They'll be underway in an hour."

"Finally. I'll give the order to withdrawal from Afghanistan as soon as the shipment is delivered to the American. And I'll advise all my senior staff to be prepared to leave by May 15. We should have enough men back in Moscow by August to remove that idiot from power."

"Yes, General. I fear for our country too," Yukorov said.

At 7:00 p.m., Davis picked up the newly painted olive-drab boat and took it back to B&W Marina. Meeting Taylor there, Davis got in the Diplomat, and Taylor drove to Sevenmile Slough to see if anything was going on at the Rogers worksite. After crossing the Twitchell Island Bridge, they could see lights on the *California Rose*. Taylor passed the parking area and drove on around the bend, where he parked off the road. Getting out of the Diplomat, they walked back up in the dark.

"Sounds like they're having a party," Taylor said, hearing music playing on the vessel.

"Yes, I think so," Davis said as both men lay down on the levy. Davis looked at the vessel through his binoculars. "I see Willard but don't recognize the other men or the woman. Take a look. They're smoking weed and snorting coke," Davis said, handing Taylor the binoculars.

"Sure as shit," Taylor said.

"How cold is that water?" Davis asked.

"Why?"

"Because I want to hear what they're saying. I'm going to swim out to the boat," Davis said as he took his wallet out of his jeans pocket.

"That water is nothing but snowmelt out of the mountains, you know, like Donner Pass kind of snow. I bet the water temp is close to forty degrees, maybe slightly higher but not much," Taylor said.

"Okay. I'll see how far I get," Davis said as he slipped his boots and socks off. Wearing only jeans and a black turtleneck poly top, Davis slid down the bank and into the water. "Goddamn," Davis said softly as he felt the frigid cold of the water. Slowly swimming with only his head out of the water, he got only halfway when he turned around and started back towards the shore. Crawling out of the water, Davis lay back down on the levy next to Taylor.

Snickering, Taylor said, "Fucking cold, ain't it?"

"Goddamn! I would've been yelling at Willard to help me out of the water and onto the *California Rose*," Davis said with a laugh. "I was getting ready to sink like a rock when my arms and legs stopped working. I need to find a wetsuit."

"Well, we aren't doing any good here, and you're going to catch pneumonia if you don't get warmed up."

"It's not that bad," Davis said, shivering with his teeth chattering.

Both men quietly laughed as they got up and walked back to the car.

"Goddamn!" Davis said. "Turn on that fucking heater!"

Fortunately for Davis, Customs SSA Don Campbell had a wetsuit, goggles, and flippers that he loaned to Davis. "This is great. Thanks, Don."

"Remember, when you first get in the water, it'll be cold for a few minutes as the water gets in between your skin and the suit. Then it'll warm up to your body temperature," Campbell said.

"Thank you. The water in the delta is like ice."

Davis went to a dive shop in San Francisco and purchased a small waterproof float bag. "Can you put items in that bag and float it in front of you as you swim?" Davis asked the salesman.

"Sure. What items and how much do they weigh?" the salesman asked.

"Model 39 9mm Smith and Wesson, camera, night vision goggles, and a suction cup. About five pounds," Davis said.

"Yeah, sure," the salesman said, laughing.

Davis smiled.

8:00 p.m., Saturday, April 2, 1988

Davis met Customs Tech Barry Frank at the CVS parking lot in Concord. Frank had rented a car at SFO after flying in from LA and drove up.

"Hello. Nice to finally meet you, Barry."

"You too, Davis."

"Show me?" Davis said.

"This is it," Frank said, pulling what appeared to be a large walkie-talkie out of a soft-sided tool bag. "We'll need to wire it up to the vessel's electrical system and then run an antenna to the top outside."

"What does the antenna look like?"

Frank pulled out a small coil of one-eighth-inch round black cable and said, "It's not very big and can be easily hidden with other antenna cables."

"Okay. Throw everything you're going to need in the Mustang. We leave your car here. I have my boat at a marina that's four miles from the vessel. Let's do a drive-by and make sure no one's there tonight. Last night they had a party on the boat."

"All right," Franks said as he put his bag in Davis's car and got in.

Driving by B&W Marina, Davis said, "Over there's my boat in one of the slips. Down the road four miles is the vessel." As he drove down Brannan Island Road and started through a right-hand turn, Davis said, "The vessel is moored to an island straight ahead. If we can't see any lights, no one's on the boat."

They got closer, driving to Twitchell Island Bridge and back towards the vessel's location, and neither man could see any lights on the *California Rose* or in the dock parking area.

"We're good," Davis said, looking at this watch. As he drove back to B&W, he said, "Three Coast Guard agents will join us tonight. I want them looking at the inside of that boat and telling me what they see."

At 10:30 p.m., USCG RAC Dale Case, SA Ray Taylor, and SA Dennis Robins arrived at the B&W parking lot where Davis introduced them to Frank. They decided Taylor would maintain security of the area while the other four agents installed the satellite tracking device on the *California Rose*. If it looked like someone was coming, Taylor would blow his car horn and wave at the person like he knew him.

Half an hour later, the agents, all wearing dark clothing, boarded Davis's olive-drab boat and headed towards the tug. Wearing his night vision goggles, Davis ran the Johnson motor wide-open to get to the vessel. Arriving twenty minutes later at the *California Rose*, Davis held the side of the gunwale as Frank, Case, and Robins got onboard. Then Case held the small boat and tied it off as Davis climbed on.

Still wearing the NVG, Davis told the three men to stand still as he checked all the doors on the *California Rose* to gain entry. They were all locked. Returning to his bag, he got the large suction device used to pull dents out of car bodies. Climbing up to the second deck, he walked out around the wheelhouse on the four-inch lip, holding onto the top of the tug. The first window he tried to slide down with the suction device was locked from the inside. The second window was not. After sliding down the window, Davis crawled through the opening into the wheelhouse and unlocked the door from the inside. With a slight whistle, Davis turned on a small flashlight, and shined the light on the stairs as the men climbed up into the control room.

"What do you need, Barry?" Davis asked.

"I need you to stay out of my way," he said.

While Frank was taking apart the console of the vessel in the wheelhouse, Case, Robins, and Davis were looking at the chart of the North Pacific and the Hawaiian Island, lying on the center counter. There were no markings on the chart to indicate any previous or future travel.

"That sure is a lot of water," Davis said.

"Yes, and finding a vessel out there sometimes is almost impossible," Case said.

"Do you see anything out of the ordinary on the vessel?" Davis asked.

"No. If we were doing a safety inspection, I've seen nothing that would make me suspicious," Case replied.

"Okay, fellows," Frank said. "I need someone to run this antenna up through the hole in the ceiling with the other wires."

Robins was the tallest and threaded the cable up through the roof's rubber-grommeted hole along with the other cables. Davis climbed up to the top of the tug and pulled the cable through until Frank said to stop.

Back in the wheelhouse, Davis listened to Frank's instructions.

"Okay, it's like this. When the engine is turned on, the tracker will go live. As long as the key switch is in the on position, the tracker will be sending a signal several times an hour. Let's go up on top, I need to conceal the antenna."

At 1:00 a.m., the men were getting back in the olive-drab boat and shoving off from the *California Rose*. Taylor never had to blow his car horn once, and the men were able to leave without anyone knowing they were ever there.

"Thanks, everyone," Davis said once they were back to the slip at B&W. "Ray, I'll give you a call tomorrow."

"Sounds good. Talk to you tomorrow," Taylor said as the three men got in Taylor's car and left.

"You ready to go?" Davis asked Frank.

"Yes, whenever you are."

While driving Frank back to his car in Concord, Frank wrote in Davis's tablet how to contact NASA to receive coordinates of where the tracking device and vessel were anyplace in the world. The accuracy of the location would be within one hundred meters.

THE NEXT MORNING AT DAYLIGHT, Davis was dressed to fish and was slowly trolling up the Sevenmile Slough. Getting up to the *California Rose*, he quickly boarded the vessel to make sure nothing was left behind during the night and to splash water on the two windows to remove suction marks.

April 4, 1988

DAVIS MET TAYLOR AT THE COAST GUARD Vessel Tracking Service on Yerba Buena Island. Lieutenant Commander Mick Shider gave Davis a tour and explained how the VTS service worked.

"If a vessel meets the criteria and is moving anywhere in the Bay Area or up in the delta, they are required to check in with us here."

"What percentage of vessels actually do it?" Davis asked.

"Of the ones required to check in, probably 80 percent."

LCDR Shider showed Taylor and Davis the log where the *California Rose* had departed San Francisco, August 18, 1987, and returned on September 20, 1987.

"Let's keep our fingers crossed they keep dialing in," Davis said to Taylor.

Saturday morning, April 9, 1988

DAVIS DROVE TO THE SEVENMILE SLOUGH, and the *California Rose* was nowhere to be seen. Davis called Taylor and asked him to check with VTS and see if the vessel had checked in.

A few minutes later Taylor called back. "She checked in this morning at eight a.m. for a radio check but gave no destination."

"All right. Let me call Frank and see if she's been bouncing a signal off the NASA satellite, and I'll call you back," Davis said and then contacted Frank.

"Let me check my system," Frank said, "and see if I have any notifications from NASA. . . . No, none. There's nothing coming from the *California Rose*."

"Shit!" Davis said. "Can you check with NASA, please, and make sure they're listening to that particular tracker?"

"Yes. I'll let you know what I find out."

"Thanks, Barry," Davis said hanging up.

Calling Taylor back, Davis said, "Not a word on the tracking device. Barry will check with NASA and make sure they're listening to our tracker."

"Do you think they found it or it's not working?" Taylor asked

"I don't know, but I need to find out."

"Okay, I'll swing by there in the morning and see if she's back. I'll call you after I get there," Taylor said.

"Okay. Thanks, Ray. If I don't get a call back from Frank by tomorrow evening saying the device is working, I'm swimming out and taking a look if and when she shows back up," Davis said, and both men hung up.

10:45 a.m., Sunday April 10, 1988

Taylor was at the *California Rose* worksite. Calling Davis, he said, "She's still not here. But she called VTS this morning and said she was enroute from Port Chicago to Twitchell Island."

"Okay, the barge is still there, correct?" Davis asked.

"Yes, it's still here. So they must be local somewhere."

"Yes, if they called VTS, they must still be here," Davis said.

"Hold on," Taylor said. "You're not going to believe this, but she's coming in right now, pulling a barge with a crane on it."

"Wonderful. I'm going to have an ulcer before this is all over," Davis said.

"Yes, me too," Taylor said with a laugh.

"Okay. You available tonight?" Davis asked.

"Yes."

"I need to get on that boat and make sure that tracking device is still there. Let's meet at eleven tonight at B&W parking lot."

"Okay, I'll be there," Taylor said.

At 11:00 p.m., Davis picked Taylor up at the B&W Marina parking area and drove to Twitchell Island Road near the *California Rose.* Pulling down the road past the parking area, Davis parked the Mustang off to the side. He got out of the car, grabbing the wetsuit and float bag out of the trunk.

"You swimming tonight?" Taylor asked with a chuckle.

"Yep," Davis said, smiling to Taylor.

Getting up on the levy, they saw no lights on the tugboat.

Davis took off his shoes and jeans and put on the wetsuit. Checking his float bag, he confirmed he had his 9mm, night vision goggles, camera, and suction cup. "I'll be back," he said as he slid down into the icy water. After the initial chill from the water coming into the suit, he immediately felt better as the water, trapped between his skin and the rubber, began to warm. After pulling on the goggles and flippers, Davis began a slow swim out to the vessels, pushing the float bag in front of him. There still were no lights or noise coming from the *California Rose* as he got nearer. Reaching the tug, Davis laid the float bag over the gunwale and pulled himself upon the deck of the vessel. He stood still for a few moments to make sure no one was there.

"Crazy fucker," Taylor whispered to himself, watching Davis through a pair of binoculars. There was just enough moonlight to barely make Davis out standing on the fantail of the *California Rose.*

Not sensing any danger, Davis took off the goggles and flippers and put on his night vision goggles. Climbing to the top of the vessel, he checked to make sure the antenna cable was still in place, it was. He then climbed along the side of the vessel's wheelhouse and looked into the window. He could see the antenna cable next to another cable going into the back of the console.

I see nothing disturbed, Davis thought. Quietly climbing back down, he placed the night vision goggles back into the float bag, pulled the goggles and flippers back on, and slipped into the black water and darkness. Back at the levy bank, he slid the goggles up onto his forehead and pulled the flippers off and climbed up to where Taylor was lying.

"How'd it look?" Taylor asked.

"Just as we left it. I saw nothing disturbed," Davis said. "Let's get out of here."

CHAPTER 48

VALIANT VENTURE

Monday, April 11, 1988

AT NOON, BARRY FRANK CALLED DAVIS, "They're getting a signal from the *California Rose*. They hadn't put that device on their lookout list, but it is now and it's working."

"Great. Thank you, Barry," Davis said.

Davis called AUSA Swedish and IRS Special Agent Bill Basler, advising them the satellite tracking device had been installed and was working.

Afterwards, Davis called Taylor, "Frank called and said the tracker is being received by NASA. Apparently, they hadn't put that particular device on their lookout list. It's now being monitored."

"Great," Taylor said.

THAT EVENING, IRENE CALLED DAVIS.

"Carlin bought a ranch in Corning and has moved there along with Willard and some others. Willard said Carlin is leaving in a day or so to go to LA to get a new tugboat. On the way back, he is stopping at Moss Landing to get a crane barge."

"Has anyone mentioned a specific date when they're leaving for the next run?" Davis asked.

"No, but it's very soon. Three to four weeks at the most."

Friday morning, April 15, 1988

Carlin, his son Bill, and Willard flew to LA. That afternoon they climbed aboard the *Valiant Venture* and headed back towards San Francisco. The next day, they stopped in Moss Landing and hooked up to a two-pilot house barge, capable of moving a very heavy crane, and headed north.

9:00 a.m., Sunday, April 17, 1988

When entering San Francisco Bay, the *Valiant Venture* got its cable that was attached to the barge entangled with a navigation buoy. Carlin Rogers had no choice but to call the Coast Guard and ask for assistance. Patrol Vessel 41403 traveled from Coast Guard Headquarters at Yerba Buena Island to the *Valiant Venture*, and was able to untangle the cable from the buoy. At 1:00 p.m., the *Valiant Venture* arrived at Sevenmile Slough with the crane barge in tow.

Monday morning, April 18, 1988

Davis put on his fishing clothes and drove to B&W Marina. Getting in his boat, he slowly trolled the four miles to Sevenmile Slough and turned into the waterway. "Fuck," he said. The *California Rose* and barge were no longer moored to the island. They were now on the roadside of the slough, and the *California Rose* was tied to the drug barge that was tied to a smaller crane barge against the bank.

Two hundred feet further up the slough, a much larger red-and-white tugboat was tied to another small barge against the bank. Just above the larger tug on Brannan Island Road, six vehicles were parked on the waterside of the road. Davis knew only two of the vehicles. "Fuck," he said again. Trolling up the slough, he read the name on the red-and-white tug, *Valiant Venture.*

Davis turned around at the Twitchell Island Bridge and trolled back out of the slough. Reaching the San Juaquin River, he reeled in the fishing lure and laid the pole on the floor of the boat. He then opened the throttle fully on the old Johnson motor, running it as hard as it could go the four miles back up to B&W Marina. After tying up in the slip, Davis walked to the CJ where he called Taylor's mobile phone. "We've got a problem. There's a new large tug at the worksite. It's named the *Valiant Venture*. Can you run that name and see where it came from and who owns it?" Davis asked.

"I sure can. I'm traveling right now, but I'll have that tomorrow."

"Thanks, Ray. I'll come to your office in the morning." Hanging up, Davis said, "Fuck, I'm going to need another tracking device."

Davis next called Reynolds's pager and put in his bag phone number. Sitting in the marina parking lot, he waited for Reynolds to call. When his phone rang, he said, "Jack."

"Yes, Tony, go."

"Rogers got a new tugboat, a big one named the *Valiant Venture*."

"How much of a problem does that create?" Reynolds asked.

"I have a satellite tracking device on the *California Rose*. I don't have one on the *Valiant Venture*."

"Can you get one?"

"Maybe, but I'm running out of time. And we were lucky as shit to be able to plant the one on the *California Rose*."

"What do you need me to do?"

"Give that name to Buddy, and see what he can turn up. Coast Guard's running it for me too, and I'll have that information tomorrow. But I want to see if there's any deep information on that vessel."

"Will do. Keep me informed," Reynolds said.

"All right, Jack. Talk later," Davis said, and both hung up.

"Fuck," said Reynolds and then dialed Hayden's number.

Morning, Tuesday, April 19, 1988

Davis pulled into Coast Guard Headquarters and then walked into Taylor's office. "What do you have?" Davis asked.

"Previously named *Southern Venture*. Purchased on March 14 by

Debra Rinehart Rogers, Dale Road, Corning. Bought it from Dick Parker, Sandbar Marine, Olympia, Washington. Previous homeport of Long Beach, California. *Valiant Venture*'s registered homeport is now San Francisco and hailing port is Corning. No previous Coast Guard violations."

"Okay, can you give me a printout of that information?" Davis asked. "I have a query in with another agency, and we'll see what they come up with too."

"Sure. What are you going to do now?" Taylor asked.

"I need to get back out to Sevenmile and see what they're doing. There's a little bar near the vessels, called Spindrift. I need to check and see if they serve food. If so, some of the crew will be going there. I just have to be careful I don't get a face to face with Carlin. He may recognize me from McAvoy."

"Okay. Let me know when I can help."

"If the crew is going to the Spindrift, we need to get out there some Friday or Saturday night, hang out with them, and see what we can learn."

"I'm all for it. Let me know."

"Thanks, Ray," Davis said as he left.

For the next three days, Davis fished up and down the Sevenmile Slough. Taking several photos of vehicles, people, and Carlin Rogers when he had his back turned, walking on the deck of the *Valiant Venture.*

Sunday evening, April 24, 1988

Irene called Davis. "I heard that Harold Rogers Sr. is working on the *Valiant Venture* and barge. Supposedly they're getting ready to go to Alaska and deliver equipment."

"What are the odds of that?" Davis asked.

"Zero," Irene said. "They're going after drugs."

Getting off the phone with Irene, Davis called Reynolds's mobile phone.

"Hello," Reynolds said.

"Jack, it's Tony. I just got off the phone with the CI. The crew is putting out disinformation about going to Alaska and delivering equipment."

"That means they're leaving very soon," Reynolds said.

"Yes, I agree. What did Buddy say about the vessel?"

"Interesting information. The *Valiant Venture*'s previous name was *Southern Venture*. It was involved with drug smuggling back in 1979 in the Gulf of Mexico. In 1982, the *Southern Venture* transited the Panama Canal and changed its name to *Valiant Venture*. It was owned by Sandbar Marine, Olympia, Washington. Sandbar's original company address was 3033 May Road, El Sobrante, California. That address on May Road is the same address of Mary Rogers, Carlin's ex-wife. Rogers purchased the *Valiant Venture* from Dick Parker, owner of Sandbar Marine in Olympia. He's a boat broker with a history of providing vessels for smuggling organizations dating back to 1980. So it looks like the company is only a shell company for smugglers," Reynolds said.

"Good info, Jack. Tomorrow I'm putting together an application for another tracking device. I've spent the last few days on Sevenmile. But I can't see what I need to see from the water, and it would be easy to get burnt on the road if you're in a car."

"What are you going to do?" Reynolds asked.

"I'm going to ask Customs if they have access to a surveillance van. I may be able to do that if I park far enough away. I'll need a high-powered telescopic lens for pictures. I'll check and see if they have one. Rogers and crew still haven't loaded the containers on the back of the barge. When they do, we'll know their leaving is imminent, and then I'm going to rent a small plane and fly over the area for pictures. We'll need them for aerial surveillance once they go to sea."

"You can fly?" Reynolds asked.

"Yes, I've been taking some lessons. I have my privates now."

"How many hours do you have logged?"

"Forty-seven hours."

"You just got your check ride completed?"

"Yes, two weeks ago up at Clear Lake. I'm certified now."

"You have just enough hours to be dangerous. You make sure you double-check yourself on everything when you're flying."

"I'll remember that, Jack. I've already almost been blown into a fence while doing touch-and-goes up at Angwin."

"Remind me not to fly with you until you have over one thousand hours. Okay, Tony, let me know if I can help. I know how things can get screwed up in a complicated operation. My advice to you is to keep focusing on the mission. We need to stop the payment to the KGB. To do that, we only need to seize the drugs."

"Roger that. I'll talk soon," Davis said.

8:00 a.m., Monday, April 25, 1988

Davis went to speak to Taylor on Yerba Buena Island. "If we can't get a tracking device on the *Valiant Venture*, is there any way to track its location out at sea?" Davis asked.

"Yes, we have a possibility. It's a new joint operation between the military and law enforcement. They've started a new command center on Coast Guard Island outside Alameda. They call it Joint Task Force FIVE."

"What can they do for us?"

"To start, they have listening posts in Hawaii, Alaska, and Alameda. If they're listening to a vessel, they can triangulate their location out at sea."

"That would be great. I need to visit them at some point. Can you get me in?" Davis asked.

"Sure, our RAC can take us over and get us introduced. After that, we could come and go as we need to."

"Damn, that's great Ray. That's our ace in the hole."

"What're you going to do now?" Taylor asked.

"I'm going to the SAC office and start working on the new application for a court order for another tracking device. I'll call Frank and see if he can get one."

"Fuck," Taylor said.

"Yes. I'll see you later, and thanks, Ray," Davis said as he left.

Driving over the Oakland Bay Bridge, Davis called Customs Technician Barry Frank's mobile phone.

"Hello."

"Barry, it's Tony. Can you get another tracking device? I now have another ship I need one on."

"I think I can. We have another one coming free in two days," Frank said.

"Great. As soon as you get it, ship everything to me. I watched how you did the first one. I can wire this one up. I'm getting another court order application ready today."

"Are you sure you can wire it up?" Frank asked.

"Yes, I can."

"Okay, I'll ship it to the SAC office in two days. All I need to do is check it when I get it, and then it'll be on its way."

"Great, thank you. I'll talk to you later," Davis said and hung up. As he drove up the Embarcadero, Davis put his dark glasses and hat on. Getting out in the parking garage, he limped across the street to 1700 Montgomery Street and took the elevator to Suite 445.

When he got out of the elevator, Davis said, "Good morning, Louise."

"Good morning, Agent Davis," she said as she pushed the unlock button on the glass door.

"Is the SAC in?" Davis asked.

"No, he's TDY in DC for the next month," she said.

"Shit," Davis said as he walked to SSA Waskovic's office and then knocked on the door.

"Come in."

Opening the door, he found ASAC Paul Sherman and Waskovic talking, "I don't mean to interrupt," Davis said, "but should there be any trouble getting a second court order for another tracking device?"

"No. Why? What happened to the first one?" Waskovic asked.

"Nothing, but I now have another boat."

"Do you need any help on the order?" Waskovic asked.

"No, but I would like for you to read it before I take it to the AUSA."

"No problem. Bring it to me when you get it done."

"So you really think there'll be a shipment of drugs coming in?" Sherman asked.

"Yes, sir, I do. So far, the CI has been spot-on."

"Okay. Let me know if you need anything. Klass will be gone for a month, and he said to support you if you need anything," Sherman said.

"I do have one question," Davis said.

"What is it?" Sherman asked.

"Where the hell do you get socks that yellow?"

"Get the hell out of this room," Sherman said as Waskovic laughed.

"Seriously, do we have a surveillance van?"

"Yes, it's in the basement of the parking garage," Sherman said.

"How do I get it?"

"Harvey can check you out on it. When do you need to take it?" Sherman asked.

"This afternoon."

"Okay, when you're available, Harvey will get you the keys and fill you in on the electronics."

"Does it have a long telephoto lens?"

"Yes, it's about two feet long," Waskovic said.

"Great. I'll be back, Harvey," Davis said, leaving the office and going to his own. He pulled up the copy of the application for the tracking device order for the *California Rose* on the computer. It was easy to change the names and dates and add the new information of Rogers purchasing the *Valiant Venture.* Reading it several times, he was satisfied, printed it out, and took it to Waskovic to read.

"Looks good to me," Waskovic said, after reading it twice.

"Okay. I'm going to the Federal Building now. I want AUSA Swedish to get this approved ASAP. I'll be back after a while, and you can brief me on the van."

"Okay. I'll be here," Waskovic said as Davis left.

Davis drove to the Federal Building and presented the application to Swedish.

After reading it thoroughly, Swedish told his secretary, "Get this to AUSA Lee, and have him finish it up with the cover sheet and memorandum of points and authorities."

"Yes, sir," she said, taking the document.

"I need to tell you something," Swedish said. "DEA Senior Special Agent Tom Banning thinks this is a wild-goose chase. He feels this case should not be on OCDETF."

"I'll prove him wrong, sir," Davis said.

"How can you be so sure?" Swedish asked.

"The CI's son was arrested with four pounds of Afghanistan hashish by the Oregon State Police. Where would he get that?"

"I hope you're right. In the next couple of weeks, I'll arrange a meeting with Banning, and let's discuss this."

"Let me know when, sir. I'll be here."

"Okay, I'll have the secretary call you when you can pick this up and take it to the federal magistrate."

"Thank you, sir. Goodbye," Davis said as he left the AUSA's office and drove back to the Montgomery Street parking garage. Picking up his phone, he called the Customs number. "Louise, let me speak to Waskovic," Davis said.

"Yes?" Waskovic said.

"Do I need to come back up, or can you meet me in the garage?"

"I'll be right down. Go to the basement, and I'll meet you there."

"Roger that," Davis said. Getting out of the Mustang, he walked down the stairs to the parking garage basement and saw a light grey van sitting against the wall. The windows were black tinted to prevent anyone from looking in, and it had a large sliding door on the right side. "Perfect," Davis said. He was going to park the van up the levy from the *Valiant Venture* and open the sliding door on the side towards the slough. He would then put out a couple of fishing poles, so anyone driving by would think someone was just fishing.

Waskovic arrived with the keys and unlocked the van. Opening all the doors, he showed Davis the inner panel that slid closed behind the two seats.

"If you have this inner panel closed, no one can see in the back. Also, there are sensors on all four corners. It'll tell you if anyone is closer than ten feet. If the lights flash on this panel, someone is near," Waskovic said, pointing to an array of electronic devices in the back of the van. "This may be your best option," Waskovic said, pulling a large tripod and camera out of a closet. Setting it up in the center of the floor, he then placed a two-foot-long telephoto lens on the front of the camera. "This can make something one mile away look like you can touch it," Waskovic said.

"That's exactly what I need," Davis replied. "Can I take pictures out the back window?"

"Yes, right through the glass, and no one can see what you're doing."

"Cool."

"If you want, you can connect a harness from this recorder here," Waskovic said, pointing at a monitor, "to the camera and record your pictures here too. Also, if you roll up the roof vent, it's actually a video recorder that you can watch on this monitor and record to these tapes. It only has slight telephoto properties, though, and if you are very far away, it's useless. It's directional, but not the best quality."

"Cool shit," Davis said. "Yes, I think the tripod and camera are my best option."

"Okay, I'll sign you out with it," Waskovic said, handing Davis the keys. "Oh, one more thing. It's not bulletproof."

"Thanks," Davis said.

CHAPTER 49

Are You Out of Your Fucking Mind?

7:00 a.m., Tuesday, April 26, 1988

Wearing his old fishing clothes, Davis pulled the surveillance van to the side of the road over a thousand feet from the Rogers worksite. After opening up the side door, he cast out both of his fishing poles and shoved the rod ends into the dirt to hold them upright. He then set out a lawn chair and Coleman cooler with beer and ice. Anyone driving by would be able to see the fishing-pole setup.

After making sure all the doors were secured, he placed the tripod in the middle of the floor and attached the camera with telephoto lens. Zooming into the worksite, the telephoto lens made the pictures look like he was standing on the road next to the *Valiant Venture* and taking pictures. "Wow," he said. "This'll work just fine."

By nine o'clock, a total of fifteen vehicles were at the worksite, taking up every bit of room on both sides of the road. A short time later, a tractor trailer, pulling a lowboy trailer, arrived, carrying three freight containers.

"Holy shit," Davis said, as he took picture after picture of everyone and everything that was happening. The initials SMI were on the fuel tank of the tractor trailer. "Got to be Supply Masters, Inc.," Davis said. The containers were removed from the lowboy by the crane on the small barge and placed on top of the drug barge deck.

A water tanker from Three Sands Company arrived and pumped water into the bow compartment of the barge. I need to ask Taylor why they'd do that, Davis thought. Shortly before noon, Carlin Rogers arrived and carried a brown leather bag and two nautical charts onto the *Valiant Venture*. Throughout the day, several vehicles drove by the surveillance van, including Rogers, but no one stopped.

The following day, Davis was in the same spot with his fishing poles out. During the morning, three more containers were brought to the site by the same truck and trailer. Again, they were loaded onto the drug barge by the small crane.

That afternoon, Davis was paged by AUSA Swedish. "I got your order ready. Stop down and pick it up."

"I'll do that in the morning. Thanks."

"Anything new?"

"Yes, I'm watching them now. In the past two days, they've loaded six freight containers onto the barge. They're leaving very soon."

"How are you watching them?"

"I'm in a surveillance van about a thousand feet away. I have a tripod set up with camera and telephoto lens. I'm taking lots of pictures. I'll be down in the morning. Thank you, sir."

Thursday, April 28, 1988

Davis picked up the court order for installation and use of the tracking device on the *Valiant Venture* from the AUSA's office. He needed to have the federal magistrate sign it the next day, but he still hadn't received the tracking device from Frank. Calling Frank, Davis asked, "Barry, did you ship it?"

"Yes, yesterday. You should have it tomorrow. They couldn't guarantee an overnight since it was late in the day. If it doesn't show up, call me back."

"I will. Thanks."

Friday, April 29, 1988

FEDERAL MAGISTRATE ESTER MYERS signed the court order, and then Davis waited in his office at Customs office for the mail to arrive.

In the afternoon, Louise walked in carrying a package. "This is for you."

"Great," Davis said, taking the package and opening it. "Awesome," he said, as he left the office. Getting in the Mustang, he called Taylor. "I got it. Can you meet me tonight at B&W?"

"Sure. What time?"

"Seven and bring some friends."

"I'll bring Dennis and Wayne."

"Great. See you at seven."

AT 7:00 P.M., TAYLOR ARRIVED WITH Special Agents Dennis Robins and Wayne Amos.

"You guys have a pair of binoculars?" Davis asked.

"Yes," Robins said.

"Okay. Ray, you come with me. One car will drive down past the worksite every hour. We'll alternate the drive-bys so they don't get suspicious. Whoever is not driving use the binoculars as you go by and try to get a better look. There are three men on there right now, and it looks like they are there for the night," Davis said.

Surveillance of the *Valiant Venture* continued until 2:00 a.m., Saturday.

"They're not leaving," Amos said.

"God damnit, I know," Davis said. "Okay, let's call it a night. Can you guys come back this evening?"

"Yes, we'll be here," Taylor said.

"Great. See you guys back here at seven tonight," Davis said as the men left the area.

Davis drove back to the Hayward house and got a few hours' sleep, but his mind was still working. Upon wakening, he had an idea that could work, and he called the local California Highway Patrol Detachment.

"Yes, I need to speak to an officer please," he told the man who answered the phone.

"Yes, this is Sergeant Stevens. How can I help you?"

"Sergeant, this is not a prank call. I'm a special agent for the US Customs Service. I'm assigned to the federal task force in San Francisco."

"Yes, sir. How can I help you?"

"I need the number to your colonel in Sacramento."

"What's this in reference to?"

"This is a drug case I'm working on, and I'm going to need your help. But I first need to speak to your colonel because this will have to come from him."

"He won't be in today, but you can reach him at this number on Monday. His name is Colonel Lanier," the sergeant said, giving Davis the number.

"Thank you, Sergeant. I'm also a former West Virginia state trooper. You be safe."

"You too, and you're welcome, sir."

7:00 p.m., Saturday, April 30, 1988

DAVIS MET TAYLOR, RAC CASE, AND ROBINS back at B&W Marina.

"Good evening, Dale. So Ray dragged you out?"

"Yes, and I wanted to see how this is going."

"I have a question first. A water tanker put three loads of water in the front compartment of the barge. Why do you do that?" Davis asked.

"That's a ballast for stability, especially if you're going to have much weight on the top. It keeps the barge nose down and from rolling over in rough seas," Case said.

"Okay, thanks. Well, for how it's going, so far, not good. I'm sure Ray has filled you in on what's happened up to this point. But they're keeping someone on the *Valiant Venture* twenty-four hours a day. I have the tracker and the court order, but if they don't leave, we're fucked."

"Yes. We do have JTF-5 as a backup. But it won't be near as good as having a tracker on the vessel," Case said.

"Okay, let me tell you what I did this morning. I got the number to the CHP colonel in Sacramento. I'm going to call him tomorrow."

"What are you thinking?" Case asked.

"As a state trooper, whenever you have a fuel tanker wreck, it's mandatory protocol to evacuate everyone within a mile radius. They do that because of the BLEVE explosion in Kingman, Arizona, in 1973. That was a tanker on a train. When it exploded, it killed over a dozen people and injured almost one hundred. It rocked houses five miles away."

"What are you thinking?" Case asked again in a slow serious tone.

"If we can't get the crew to leave the vessel, I'm going to wreck a fuel tanker in the levy ditch near the worksite. California Highway Patrol will come in and evacuate everyone off the boat and make them stay over a mile away."

"Will they let them leave in the boat?" Robins asked.

"No, and that's something I need to talk to the colonel about. They must not let them do anything but immediately leave the vessel and evacuate the area."

"Damn," Taylor said. "You don't need me riding with you, do you?"

"No, but I'll have water in the tanker. It won't explode. I know the plan can work. CHP will give us a couple of hours to install the tracker. That's my plan if I can get approval and the money off ASAC Sherman to lease the truck. I'll ask the colonel to find me a truck out of this area."

"Ballsy," Case said.

"Let's hope these guys get off the *Valiant Venture* so I don't have to be in a wreck."

Case got in the Mustang with Davis, and the two cars took turns driving by the worksite. Two men were on the *Valiant Venture*, and they didn't leave. At 10:00 p.m., Carlin Rogers arrived at the site. With the help of a crewman, he carried a mattress onto the *Valiant Venture*.

"These boys are leaving soon," Case said.

"Yes, we're running out of time, quickly," Davis replied.

At 11:00 p.m., Rogers left. As soon as he did, the crewmember that helped him carry the mattress onto the vessel drove to the Spindrift bar in a brown Cherokee Jeep with a Nevada license plate.

Calling Taylor on the radio, Davis said, "Ray, that crewman went into Spindrift. Dale and I are going in. If the other guy leaves the *Valiant Venture*, come and get us."

"Roger that," Taylor said.

Parking the Mustang, Case and Davis went into the Spindrift. The crewman was sitting at the bar, and Davis sat down next to him. Case went to a table in the back and sat down.

A waitress came up to Davis and said, "I need to see your ID."

"Well, I'm way over eighteen, lady. Bud light bottle, please," Davis said, showing his Oregon driver's license.

The crewmember next to him laughed.

Looking at him, Davis laughed and said, "I haven't been carded in years. What's your name? I'm Tony Davis."

"Ron Carriage," he said, shaking hands with Davis.

"Where you from, Ron? Haven't seen you around here before."

"I'm from Nevada. I just got here a couple of days ago. I'm working for an old friend."

"You working nearby?"

"Yes, I'm a welder and working on the barge down the road."

"Cool. What are you welding?"

"Fuel tanks. We put six on the barge, a bitch. They cost twenty-one thousand dollars. We had to cut the deck open to get them in."

"Wow, six tanks. You about done?"

"Getting close. Another week and the vessels leave for Alaska."

"You guys need any help? I've been out of work for a month," Davis said.

"No. Unless you're family or a close friend of the boss, he won't hire you."

"Well shit," Davis said as he finished his beer. Laying down a five-dollar bill, Davis got up off the stool. Taking a last drink, he said,

"Nice meeting you. You take care," and walked out of the bar and back to the Mustang.

Case followed after about five minutes and got in the car as Davis pulled out.

"Could you hear?" Davis asked.

"Yes. Whatever we do, we better be doing it in the next four or five days."

At 1:00 a.m., Ron Carriage left the bar and went back to the *Valiant Venture*. Both men were still on the vessel when Davis called off surveillance at 2:00 a.m., Sunday, May 1.

Davis got to the Hayward safehouse at 3:30 a.m., took a drink of Crown from the bottle on top of the refrigerator, and went to bed.

It was 10:00 a.m. before he woke back up. He spent that Sunday morning at home and went over all his paperwork and documentation to see if he'd missed anything. Looking at the *Valiant Venture* on the link chart, he said, "If we can't get a tracking device on you, we are in deep shit." Thinking about JTF-5, he knew they would be beneficial when the time came. But that also presented a problem: he didn't want anyone knowing about the case unless it was absolutely necessary. This was a strictly need-to-know operation, and just yet, they didn't need to know.

That evening, Davis put his West Virginia baseball hat on backwards and headed the CJ north towards Sevenmile Slough. The warm evening air felt great in the open Jeep and hearing the headers made him smile. At nine thirty, he passed the worksite. The same brown Cherokee Jeep that Ron Carriage was driving the night before was still there. Although Davis couldn't see anyone, the lights were on in the *Valiant Venture*. I need to go to plan B, he thought, as he looked where he could roll the tanker truck into the levy ditch.

9:00 a.m., Monday, April 2, 1988

DAVIS CALLED THE HEADQUARTERS of the California Highway Patrol in Sacramento.

"Good morning. California Highway Patrol," a man said.

"Good morning. This is Special Agent Tony Davis of the Organized Crime Drug Enforcement Task Force in San Francisco. I need to speak to Colonel Lanier."

"May I tell him what this is in reference to?"

"Yes, I need his help on a major case, and the assistance I need must come from him. I'm also a former West Virginia state trooper."

"Hold the line, sir. I'll get him."

After a few minutes, the colonel picked up the phone. "This is Colonel Lanier. How can I help you?"

Good morning, Colonel. My name is Special Agent Tony Davis of the US Customs Service. I'm assigned to OCDETF. I'm also a former West Virginia state trooper. It is because I'm a former state trooper that I'm calling."

"Yes, go ahead," Lanier said.

"Colonel, I'm working on an especially important case where an international smuggling organization is preparing to bring in a multi-ton load of hashish and marijuana into the San Francisco area. We have documented that they've already successfully brought in a prior load in September 1987. That shipment was fifty-two tons of narcotics."

"Fifty-two tons?" Lanier asked.

"Yes, sir. Fifty-two tons of hashish and marijuana."

"Go on," Lanier said.

"I have planted a satellite tracking device on the vessel that they used last year. The problem is they purchased another larger vessel that they intend to use this year, and they're keeping crewmembers on it 24/7. This vessel is parked in a slough south of Sacramento. It's tied beside the slough road, within thirty yards of it."

"What do you have in mind, Agent?"

"I must get those men off that vessel for an hour while I plant another tracker on it. Being a former trooper, I know if a gas tanker is wrecked, we must evac everyone within a mile of that tanker. Is that your protocol as well?"

"Yes, it is. Goes back to the Kingman, Arizona, mishap."

"Yes, sir, the BLEVE explosion."

"That's correct," Lanier said.

"Colonel, if I roll a gas tanker full of water in the ditch near that vessel, could you come in there and evacuate everyone off that boat?"

"Absolutely, we would. When are you planning to do this?"

"In the next day or two. I'm running out of time; they're planning on leaving by the end of the week. One more thing, if you could, can you find me a tanker? I can't trust anyone around here and take a chance on the word getting out," Davis said.

"Let me make a couple of phone calls. What's a good call back number for you?"

Davis gave Colonel Lanier his phone number. Thanking the colonel, he hung up.

Thirty minutes later the colonel called back. "I found you a tanker, but it's going to cost you."

"How much?"

"Sixty-five thousand. They require that because of the expected damage to the rig when you run it in the ditch."

"Okay, Colonel, let me go see if I can get the money. I feel this would work. What do you think?"

"Yes, this would be a good ruse. We would evacuate everyone for a mile. You would have plenty of time to get on that boat."

"Thank you, Colonel. I'll call you back by this afternoon, one way or the other."

"Good luck, Davis," the colonel said.

AT 10:30 A.M., DAVIS WAS ENTERING ASAC SHERMAN'S OFFICE. "Good morning, Paul," Davis said.

"Good morning, Tony. How's everything going?"

"I received the extra tracking device for the *Valiant Venture*, and I have the court order signed by the federal magistrate. But there are crewmembers staying on the boat day and night."

"Well, that fucks things up, doesn't it?" Sherman said.

"Yes, sir. But I have a plan."

"What is it?"

"This morning, I spoke to the CHP colonel out of Sacramento, and he agrees this will work."

"Oh fuck. What're you thinking about doing?"

"I'm going to lease a gas tanker, run it into a ditch, and have CHP come out and evacuate the area."

"WHAT?" Sherman asked.

"It's standard CHP protocol to evacuate a mile-radius area anytime there's a gas tanker accident. It's in response to an incident that occurred in Arizona a few years back where several people were killed."

"You? You are going to wreck a gas tanker?"

"Yes, it'll have water in it, and I need you to authorize me sixty-five thousand dollars to lease the truck."

Sherman looked at Davis and said, "Are you out of your fucking mind? No, I will not authorize that, and that's final."

Davis looked at Sherman's yellow socks and asked, "Do you even own a pair of black socks?"

"Get the hell out of my office."

Davis looked at Sherman and walked out of the building. Getting in the Mustang, he called Taylor. "You in your office today?"

"Yes. Come on over."

Sherman sat at his desk and said, "Crazy fucking rookie." Looking at his socks, he said, "I like 'em."

CHAPTER 50

Don't Shoot the Guy in the Black Wetsuit

11:00 a.m., Monday, May 2, 1988

Driving to Yerba Buena Island, Davis called Colonel Lanier of the CHP. "I got shot down on the money, Colonel."

"Damn. I was excited about this too."

"Yes. I appreciate all your help. Colonel, if you see something on TV in a few weeks, you'll know who did it, another trooper."

"I'll be watching. Good luck, Davis."

"Thank you, sir."

Walking in Taylor's office, Davis said, "Sherman shot me down. Won't give me the money to lease the gas tanker."

"How much do you need?" Case asked.

"Sixty-five thousand."

"Wow, that's way past what we could do here," Case said.

"What's plan B?" Taylor asked.

"That *was* plan B. Now go to plan C. I'm going on the vessels one more time. Perhaps we can find a way to plant the tracker on the barge."

"When are you doing that?" Taylor asked.

"Tonight. You want to meet me at B&W at midnight?"

"Heck, yeah."

"Dale, does the Coast Guard have a rifle with a star scope?" Davis asked.

"Yes, it does."

"Do you think we could borrow it tonight? I'm going to be on the vessel with known smugglers, and it'd be nice to have Ray back me up."

"That's not a bad idea. Yes, I'll sign it out to Ray," Case said.

"Cool. I like that shit," Taylor said.

"Just remember, don't shoot the guy in the black wetsuit wearing the night vision goggles," Davis said.

AT MIDNIGHT, TAYLOR WAS GETTING IN DAVIS'S MUSTANG and putting a gun case between his legs.

"Three-o-eight?" Davis asked.

"No, 458, one of Vietnam's relics."

"Holy shit. Really, don't shoot me with that fucker, please."

"Don't worry. If I do, you won't know it," Taylor said with a laugh.

Davis didn't.

Pulling around Brannen Island Road, the agents could see the *Valiant Venture* now tied up to the drug barge. A light was on in the wheelhouse, and Carriage's Cherokee and a white Ford pickup were parked along the road. The *California Rose* was two hundred feet up the slough, tied to the small barge.

"Let's go over to Twitchell Island, and I'll swim back across," Davis said.

"Long swim, over three hundred feet," Taylor said.

"Yes, but I can't start from this side."

After going over the Twitchell Island Bridge, Davis drove down the levy road across from the worksite. Pulling over out of sight from the *Valiant Venture*, he parked the car. Taylor got the rifle out of the case, and Davis carried the wetsuit, goggles, flippers, and float bag back up the road. Lying down on the levy, Taylor turned on the star scope mounted on the rifle.

"Take a look. Pretty neat?" Taylor said, handing the rifle to Davis.

Looking through the scope, Davis could make out the dark areas of the *Valiant Venture* and barge surprisingly well. "I like that. Good quality optics," he said.

"Yes, not bad," Taylor said, taking back the rifle and laying it on the ground.

After putting on the wetsuit, Davis checked to make sure the float bag was securely closed.

"You got everything you need?" Taylor asked.

"Yes, I got the tracker, antenna, 9mm, NVG, suction cup, plyers, screw drivers, electrician's tape, tester and Leatherman," Davis replied.

"Good luck."

"I never asked you this before, but are there sharks in this water?"

"Fuck, yes. This is still saltwater up this far," Taylor whispered.

"Fuck, and remember don't shoot me," Davis said, as he slid down into the black water.

Putting on his goggles and flippers, Davis began a slow swim across the slough, pushing the float bag in front of him. I feel like a jitterbug on a bass pond, Davis thought as he skimmed across the top of the water, expecting at any moment to be jerked underneath the surface and eaten by a big fucking fish.

He looks like a big seal swimming across the water, Taylor thought, as he watched Davis get closer to the *Valiant Venture*. Sharks do eat seals, he thought, as he looked through the star scope at Davis's head and the float bag. "I hope he left the keys in the car," Taylor said softly.

Getting to the *Valiant Venture*, Davis slowly raised himself up on the gunwale on the back of the vessel, took off his goggles and flippers, and laid them on the deck. Then he took the NVG out of the float bag and put them on. Turning on the infrared light switch, he could see clearly for several yards. Out came the 9mm with holster and belt, which he placed it around his waist and tightened it. Sliding his left arm through the goggle strap and heel straps of the flippers, he picked up the float bag handle and walked across the deck.

The light was still on in the wheelhouse as he walked across the fantail of the *Valiant Venture* and climbed upon the top of the barge. Davis was walking around a container when he found a hole in the deck of the barge with an aluminum ladder extending down inside.

Quietly climbing down the ladder, Davis could see two large fuel tanks. Both looked to be at least fifteen feet long, six feet wide, and six feet tall. Thousands of gallons of fuel, Davis thought.

Climbing back up out of the barge, Davis thought he was just about in the middle of the barge length wise, as he looked in both directions. Then he began opening each container door very slowly to not make any noise that would awaken the sleeping men inside the vessel. Each container had an assortment of tools, same as the last time he'd checked before the 1987 run. Getting to the last container towards the bow of the barge, he began to open that door very slowly when something large in the container fell with a bang!

"Fuck," he said as he latched the door shut.

"Fuck," Taylor said as he heard the sledgehammer fall that Willard had leaned against the side of the container a few days before.

"What the fuck was that?" Jim Rogers said, waking up in his bunk in the *Valiant Venture.*

"What?" Carriage asked.

"I heard a bang on the barge," Rogers said, getting up and pulling on his pants.

"I didn't hear anything," Carriage said.

"Get your clothes on and come with me," Rogers said, picking up the pump shotgun that was kept on the vessel.

Carriage got up and turned the light on next to the bed.

"Fuck," Davis hissed as he saw the light turn on inside the tug.

"Fuck," Taylor said as he racked a .458 cartridge into the barrel of the Winchester Model 70. "Get the fuck out of there, Tony," Taylor whispered.

Rogers and Carriage climbed up the stairs to the wheelhouse and opened the back door of the tug. Stepping from the *Valiant Venture* onto the barge, both men used flashlights as they searched for the source of the noise.

"What did it sound like?" Carriage asked.

"Something heavy, metal to metal," Rogers said.

Checking between the six containers, they worked their way to the front of the barge.

Taylor watched as Davis slid down the forward tie line and into the water as a flashlight got closer to him. He moved slowly underneath the angled bow of the barge so he wasn't visible to the men standing on the deck ten feet above him.

"I'm shooting the first fucker that fires a gun on that barge," Taylor said, as he flipped the safety off on the sniper rifle.

Looking over the edge, Rogers said, "I don't see anything."

"It was probably a racoon. Let's go back to bed," Carriage said as he walked back to the *Valiant Venture*.

"Yeah, probably," Rogers said as he turned and got back on the tug.

"You lucky fuckers," Taylor whispered, flipping the safety back on.

Davis stayed underneath the bow of the barge for a few more minutes as he put his goggles and flippers back on. After placing the NVG in the float bag without getting them wet, he began to swim back towards Taylor.

Climbing up the levy where Taylor lay, Davis said, "They have huge fuel tanks in the barge." As he took off his gun belt and holster he said, " I'm going to have to take this pistol entirely apart to get the saltwater out."

"Do you realize how close I came to shooting one of those fuckers?" Taylor asked.

Laughing, Davis said, "I figured I was safe as long as those guys were the only ones shooting. I decided if you opened up, I was swimming to the bottom of the slough."

Taylor laughed and said, "Big fuel tanks, huh?"

"Yes, two of them in one compartment. Could be more. And there's no place to put the tracker on the barge; there's no electricity. Let's get the hell out of here," Davis said as he started back towards the Mustang. As they walked back, Davis asked Taylor, "Were you getting ready to smoke one?"

"Fuck yeah! Safety off and finger on the trigger."

Davis and Taylor chuckled.

"We need to do a flyover. I have a good camera you can use," Davis said getting in the car.

"What do you mean, flyover?" Taylor asked.

"I can fly. I can fly a little, but I can't fly a little *and* take pictures at the same time."

"Dear Lord. When?" Taylor asked.

"Not today. How about tomorrow? I can pick you up at the Napa Airport, say ten a.m.?"

"Oh fuck. Okay, I'll be there."

"I'll meet you on the tarmac where they park the small planes."

"Dear Lord," Taylor said again.

CHAPTER 51

Into the Fog

9:00 a.m., Wednesday, May 4, 1988

Davis rented a Cessna 152 from Santa Rosa Flight Center and flew to the Napa County Airport.

It was 10 a.m. when Taylor climbed into the right seat. "You do know how to fly this thing, correct?" Taylor asked.

"Yeah, like riding a bike," Davis said. "Here. Put these headphones on so we can hear each other scream," he said as he gave the plane full throttle, making the engine roar for takeoff. "Pretty windy today. Taking off is easy. Getting us back down will be the problem," he yelled, looking at Taylor.

"Dear Lord," Taylor said, making the sign of the cross on his chest as the plane left the ground.

Flying towards Pittsburg, Davis turned northwest into the wind to fly over Sevenmile Slough.

"We're going to be able to do only one pass, so take as many pictures as you can. More than one pass, and we'll look suspicious," Davis said.

"Roger that," Taylor said, getting the camera ready and opening his side window.

Flying up the San Juaquin River at two thousand feet, Davis began to drop altitude and said to Taylor, "There it is, up ahead. Do you see the turn in the road?"

"Yes, I got 'em," Taylor said, taking off his seatbelt so he could turn in the seat.

Davis slowed the engine and dropped to one thousand feet as he started up Sevenmile Slough. Taylor had the camera pointing out the side window as he began to repeatedly snap the shutter. When they got past the worksite, Taylor turned back in his seat and gave the thumbs up.

"We've done all we can do," Davis said.

"Yes," Taylor said, nodding his head.

"Did you notice anything different today?" Davis asked.

"Yes, they switched places with the tugs," Taylor replied.

"Yep, the *Valiant Venture* is now in tow position," Davis said.

"Yes, it is."

An hour later, the wind was blowing with such a crosswind that Davis had to land the airplane almost sideways at the Napa Airport.

"What are you doing?" Taylor asked. "We're sideways."

"Yes, we have a bad crosswind. I'll have to crab it in."

"Oh, dear Lord," Taylor said, gripping the seat with his hands.

6:30 a.m., Friday, May 6, 1988

Taylor called Davis and said, "Five minutes ago, the *Valiant Venture* notified VTS that it was going to sea. Robins is driving to the Richmond–San Rafael Bridge to take pictures as they pass underneath."

"Fuck. I'll drive to the Golden Gate overlook and watch them leave. You want to go?" Davis asked.

"Yes, I'll meet you there in an hour. We don't know exactly where they're at."

An hour later, Davis and Taylor were leaning against the front of the white Diplomat, looking at the Golden Gate Bridge.

"I have to admit I never in my wildest dreams every thought I'd be here," Davis said.

"Yes, an amazing view," Taylor replied.

"Ray, I come from a little town called Moundsville, West Virginia, and spent a lot of my time in a smaller town called Cameron. Population of Cameron is about a thousand people. When I was in high school, I loved the movie *Dirty Harry* filmed here in San Francisco. I even thought at the time of being a police officer. But I never dreamed I would be a police officer in San Francisco."

"Life is very strange, my friend," Taylor said.

"Ray, I'm going to tell you something, and I need you to take this to your grave."

"I will."

"Ray, if we can pull this off, it will be the largest drug seizure in history. We are looking at close to fifty tons of narcotics."

"How do you know this?"

"That I can't say, but it's the truth. The fuckers that are doing this go way back. And the international significance of this is enormous."

"International? Hmmm. The hair is starting to rise on the back of my neck," Taylor said.

"Welcome to the club, brother," Davis said.

"She just passed underneath the bridge," Taylor and Davis heard Robins say on Taylor's Coast Guard radio in the car. Opening up the door, Taylor picked up the mic and said, "Ten-four, 10-22. and thanks."

"Ten-four," SA Robins said.

"Okay, she'll be coming in the next hour. She just went under the Richmond–San Rafael Bridge."

"She'll be going through about ten o'clock," Davis said, looking at his watch. "I need copies of those photos as soon as possible."

"No problem. We develop our own film at headquarters. I can have them for you Monday."

"Great."

At 10:02 a.m., the *Valiant Venture* and barge passed underneath the Golden Gate Bridge. It continued on a westerly course as long as Taylor and Davis could see it.

As it disappeared into the fog of the Pacific Ocean and out of sight, Taylor asked, "Do you think we'll ever see her again?"

Davis pointed at the Golden Gate and said, "If I'm to have a nexus, we're going to meet that bitch right there when she comes back in. I need to go to JTF-5. Can we do that on Monday?"

"Yes. Case is at JTF-5 today. I'll get him to go with us."

"Great. I'll be at your shop early Monday morning, and we can go from there," Davis said. "Let me know if any more information comes in this weekend."

Shaking hands, Taylor said, "I will as soon as I get it."

Davis left the Golden Gate overlook and went to the Customs office. Walking into SSA Waskovic's office, Davis said, "The *Valiant Venture* and barge just left San Francisco. I was not able to get the second tracker on it. Do we have access to Customs aircraft to do a search at sea?"

"Yes, we have a P-3 Orion reconnaissance aircraft at the Corpus Christi Air Group," Waskovic said.

"Okay. How long does it take them to get here?"

"A day max. I've worked with that crew before, and they are very professional. If you need them to fly a mission, let me know, and I'll make the call."

"Great. Thanks Harvey."

9:00 p.m., Saturday, May 7, 1988

Taylor called Davis. "I just got word from VTS that the *Valiant Venture*'s next port of call will be Eureka, California."

"Can we get the Coast Guard's P-3 to fly the coast and check for us?"

"Yes, I'll ask Case to request it."

"Thanks, Ray. I'll notify Eureka Customs." Davis hung up and called Customs Communications, Sector, in Los Angeles. "Sector, this is Alpha 27141. I need you to notify alpha units at Eureka to be on the lookout for motor vessel *Valiant Venture*, a sixty-seven-foot red-and-white tug pulling a barge. If sighted, please notify me ASAP."

"Will do, Alpha 27141."

10:00 a.m., Sunday, May 8, 1988

A COAST GUARD P-3 RECONNAISSANCE AIRCRAFT left Alameda Air Station and flew the northern California coast from San Francisco to Eureka. The *Valiant Venture* and barge were nowhere to be seen.

That evening, Davis called Irene Kasper. "They left Friday morning. What's the latest you've heard?" Davis asked.

"I heard they're to return to San Francisco in fifteen days. That makes it the twenty-third," Irene said. "That information came from a friend of a friend, and I'm not sure how accurate it is."

"It's better than nothing. Thanks. Let me know if you hear anything else," Davis said and hung up.

CHAPTER 52

That's Classified

9:00 a.m., Monday, May 9, 1988

AUSA Swedish called Davis and asked him to come to his office for a meeting with DEA Senior Special Agent Tom Banning. Arriving at the office, Davis shook hands with Swedish and was introduced to Banning.

"Good morning," Davis said.

"Gentlemen, we need to clear the air on any issues that may be arising out of this joint investigation," Swedish said.

"Yes, sir. There are no problems from my end. I've been working with the Coast Guard and IRS agents that are involved with this case," Davis said.

"You have no DEA agents working on this," Banning said.

"Sir, I believe there are DEA agents assisting the IRS with their end of the investigation. And when the time is right, I'll be asking for help from anyplace I can, including the DEA. Currently, the agents involved have been able to handle everything. Additional bodies at this point would only get in the way and jeopardize the investigation," Davis said.

"Your premise is that this organization, if there even is an organization, is attempting to bring multi-ton loads of hashish into San Francisco," Banning said.

"Yes, sir."

"Do you realize there is zero corroboration from the intelligence community that there has ever been a multi-ton load of hashish brought into the West Coast, let alone San Francisco?"

"Yes, sir, I realize that, but the IRS believes there has been structuring of a million dollars, and one of the crew has been arrested with soles of hashish."

That money could have come from any number of sources, and the soles of hashish don't prove they came from a multi-ton smuggle," Banning said.

"That is correct, sir."

"Then how in the hell do you think this is happening? You're wasting OCDETF resources on a wild-goose chase."

"Sir, this is happening as we speak. And perhaps our intel is not as good as we think it is."

"Do you think the DEA, FBI, Customs, and the CIA are asleep at the wheel on this?" Banning asked.

"No, sir. But perhaps they've missed this."

"I think this case is horseshit, Davis. And you'll not be wasting DEA's resources."

"Sorry you feel that way, Tom. Gentlemen, it's been a pleasure, but I have work to do," Davis said as he left the Federal Building.

Davis drove to Coast Guard Headquarters.

"What have you been doing today?" Taylor asked.

"Just got my ass chewed by DEA Banning in Swedish's office."

"What for?"

"He thinks this case is, in his words, horseshit."

"He's a prick. He's one of those big-feeling fuckers that likes to hog cases, and if he's not involved, he badmouths it. He gives the DEA a bad name."

"Well, I think we can forget about any help from them if we need it."

"Fuck him. We don't need their help. Coast Guard, Customs, and the IRS are plenty capable of handling any case without his pompous ass," Taylor said.

"You know this guy?"

"Yes, we worked several cases with DEA. And usually, it goes pretty good between the agents. But let him stick his nose in it, and it goes to shit."

"Okay. The CI says the vessels will be back into San Fran on the twenty-third. There's also information he may go to Alaska, and we know he didn't go to Eureka," Davis said.

"Yes, so far no sightings. Coast Guard is sending up its P-3 again this afternoon to double-check Eureka."

"Good. Can I use your phone? I need to call IRS Agent Hagers," Davis said.

"Sure, go ahead."

Davis called Hagers's mobile phone and said, "Mike, the vessels left on Friday, and I heard from the CI they will be back on the twenty-third. We need to be ready with any search and arrest warrants you guys may need. Also, I just got my ass chewed by DEA Agent Banning."

"What did he say? He's a prick."

Laughing, Davis said, "I just heard the same thing from Taylor. He says this investigation is horseshit. I know you're working with DEA Agent Bud Hedge. He seems to be a good guy. Tell him if he hears any of this, that we're still good. The agents have no problem working together; it's when the bosses start running their mouths that we have problems."

"Will do, and we'll be ready with whatever warrants we need. Thanks, Tony."

"You're welcome, Mike. I'll let you know as soon as I hear something," Davis said and hung up.

"Here are your pictures that Dennis took off the Richmond–San Rafael Bridge," Taylor said, handing Davis a folder.

Pulling out the photos, he said, "Damn. Those are great. If you look closely, you can see inside the wheelhouse."

"Yes, he did a great job. Let's grab some lunch. Afterwards we can go to JTF-5," Taylor said.

"Sounds good," Davis said and followed Taylor to the cafeteria.

Eating his burger, Taylor said, "I told Case about us flying and taking pictures."

"What'd he say?"

"He said we were two crazy fuckers," Taylor said with a laugh.

Laughing, Davis said, "We get it done, brother; we get it done."

After lunch, Davis and Taylor got in Case's car with him and went to Coast Guard Island outside Alameda. At the gate, all three men showed their IDs and were allowed in.

Parking the car, Case said, "We'll meet the captain and then go to PacArea Intel where they're listening. You have your TSC?" Case asked Davis about his top-secret clearance.

"Yes, I'm cleared," Davis said.

Going inside Building 51-5, they were met by Coast Guard Captain Richard Wringer.

"Good morning, Dale, gentlemen," Wringer said shaking hands with Taylor and Davis, who gave their names. "Follow me, if you would please," he said, leading the trio into his office. "Have a seat, gentlemen. What can I do for you? As Dale knows, we are here to support federal, state, and local law enforcement in the interdiction of narcotics. We are a new organization, just enacted this past fall by Congress. So what do you need?"

"Tony, you want to fill him in?" Case said.

"Captain, we are working a case where we believe there will be multi-ton shipment of narcotics brought into San Francisco by a tugboat and barge," Davis said. "The owner is Carlin Rogers. He has an extensive criminal history dating back several years. We believe his organization brought in almost fifty tons of drugs this past fall, hidden in his barge. The tugboat he used last year was the *California Rose*. I have hidden a satellite tracking device on it. However, he recently purchased another tug, the *Valiant Venture*. And although I have a court order to plant another tracking device on that vessel, we were unable to do so. The *Valiant Venture* and barge left on Friday morning. We believe they are outbound to meet a mothership, receive the drugs, and return to San Francisco."

"How sure are you they are returning here?" Wringer asked.

"That's the problem. We have no way of tracking them. I give them a 75 percent chance. I have a CI that has provided good intel in the past. They feel sure the vessels are coming back to San Fran on or near the twenty-third of this month."

"Anything else to go on?"

"Yes. Last year they went to Hilo, Hawaii, before meeting the mothership. They may do that again this year."

"Hmm," Wringer said. "We could have a Navy sub sit off the coast of Hawaii and see if the vessels go there. If they do, we could then track them to the mothership."

"That would be great," Davis said. "But there's something about this case that's critically important. The Rogers vessels, including the mothership, must not be disturbed in any way until Rogers tries to re-enter the United States. We cannot interdict them until they return here or somewhere else in the US."

"And why is that?" Wringer asked as Case and Taylor looked at Davis.

"That's classified, sir," Davis said, looking at the men.

"I understand. However, I'll need confirmation of that from a higher source," the captain said.

"Yes, sir. I can make that happen," Davis said. "Who's the commander of JTF-5?"

"That is Rear Admiral William Leaf."

"Thank you, Captain. I'll make sure the proper authorities contact Admiral Leaf," Davis said as he looked at Case and Taylor who were looking intently at Davis. Taylor smiled and shook his head.

"Captain, what I really need from JTF-5 is for you to monitor any chatter that may come from the *Valiant Venture*," Davis said. " I need to know where they're at and when and where they are returning to."

"We can certainly do that."

"May I see that capability, please?" Davis asked.

"Yes. Follow me, gentlemen," the captain said, getting up from his desk.

Walking out of the room, Taylor nudged Davis with his elbow and chuckled. Davis shrugged his shoulders and smiled back.

The captain led the men to a stairwell and down to the bottom level. Walking up to an armed guard at the PacArea Intel entrance, Wringer received a salute from the guard, who asked to see the credentials of Case, Taylor, and Davis. Being Coast Guard Special Agents, Case and Taylor were admitted. However, Davis was not on the list of authorized visitors with a TSC.

"I'm sorry, sir, but you will not be allowed in. This is a very restricted area," the guard said.

Showing his ID, Davis said, "I'm the special agent in charge of this investigation. I only need to see how they intercept transmissions," as he stepped towards the door.

The guard placed his hand on his sidearm and said, "Sir, you're not going through that door."

CHAPTER 53

Call from Langley

"You guys go on in," Davis said to Captain Wringer, Case, and Taylor. I'll call the office and have them send over whatever paperwork we need here. May I use your phone, please?" Davis asked the guard, as the others entered the room and closed the door.

"Yes, sir. Go ahead."

Davis called the Customs office. "Louise, I need to speak to Sherman or Waskovic."

"Hold on, Tony. I'll get one of them."

"Tony, it's Harvey. You're on speaker with me and Sherman."

"Harvey, I'm at JTF-5, PacArea Intel, and they don't have a record of my TSC. The guard here . . . what's your name?" Davis asked the guard.

"Chief Petty Officer Mike Moore."

"Chief Petty Officer Moore is going to shoot me if I try to go through this door."

"Go ahead, Moore," Davis heard Sherman say.

Waskovic spoke up and said, "Tell the chief petty officer I'll contact JTF now and will send them whatever they need. You stand by there, and I'll have your clearance in a few minutes."

"Thanks, Harvey. Kiss my ass, Paul," Davis said as he hung up.

Waskovic laughed as he hung up, looking at the fuming Sherman.

"Fucking rookie," Sherman said.

Twenty minutes later the phone on Moore's desk rang. "Hello," he said. "Yes, sir. He's still here. . . . Yes, sir. Thank you, sir," Moore said hanging up the phone. "You're cleared to go in Agent Davis."

"Thank you, Mike. You do a good job, and I'll make sure Leaf hears about this. You keep it up," Davis said as he walked through the doorway.

"About time," Taylor said, laughing.

"Well, we got that taken care of," Davis said. "Sorry about that, Captain."

"No problem. Okay, as I was showing Case and Taylor, this is where we are able to listen to any vessel that uses KMI ship-to-shore service. So if they call land, we can monitor that call easily. If two vessels are communicating at sea via marine radio, it makes it harder to hear them with all the channels available. However, if we know what channels they use, we can still dial right into them."

"How do you locate a vessel?" Davis asked.

"When we hear them, we can get a straight-line direction from their signal. With additional listening posts in Hawaii and Alaska, if all three of us are listening to the same transmission, we can triangulate and get a fairly good fix on their location."

"Okay, how do I get you guys listening to any traffic from the *Valiant Venture*?"

"We started about ten minutes ago. Any received transmissions will be reported to Agent Case and Taylor as soon as possible."

"Damn. That's awesome. Thank you, Captain," Davis said.

"That's what we're here for. You get me that classified order to not interdict at sea, and we'll all be waiting for them when they return."

"I'll make that call this afternoon. You should have that information by tomorrow," Davis said.

The agents left PacArea Intel and returned to Taylor's office.

"What are you doing this afternoon?" Taylor asked Davis.

"I need to make a phone call. But I'll be available if anything comes in. I have a good feeling about PacArea Intel. They just may save our butts on this."

"Yes, they are good people and have the latest equipment."

"I'll talk to you later," Davis said as he left the Coast Guard office.

Taylor walked into Case's office and said, "What do you think?"

"I think we're going to bust these people. I'll find out who calls Admiral Leaf with the do-not-interdict order."

"Yes, I agree. I think we're going to pop the *Valiant Venture*."

"You keep supporting Tony. You guys make a good team, and you have an obvious friendship."

"Will do. Yes, he's fun to work with."

DAVIS DROVE BACK TO THE HAYWARD HOUSE and called Reynolds. "Jack, it's Tony."

"What's the latest?" Reynolds asked.

"Been a busy week. The vessels left on Friday. Been taking to the CI. She feels they're returning to San Francisco around the twenty-third."

"Yes, that makes sense."

"Yes, to me too. But I'm not counting that egg until it hatches."

"What do you need me to do?"

"I went to Joint Task Force FIVE today."

"What is that? I never heard of it."

"Military joint task force created to support law enforcement in the interdiction of drugs. It's run by the Coast Guard Pacific Intelligence Group on Coast Guard Island outside Alameda. I need you to call Buddy and have him contact Langley. Someone from there needs to contact Coast Guard Rear Admiral William Leaf at Coast Guard Island. He's their commander."

"What do you want him told?" Reynolds asked.

"He needs to be informed that no one is to interfere with the *Valiant Venture* or the Russian mothership while at sea. We cannot have them disturbed. The Rogers vessels must be allowed to return to San Francisco."

"Why are you telling me this?"

"JTF-5 is going to put a sub near Hilo to monitor if the *Valiant Venture* comes that way and then follow them to the mothership. I don't want a navy destroyer or Coast Guard Cutter swooping in on them and fucking everything up. They may get the drugs, but the KGB will still be in Afghanistan."

"I'll call Buddy as soon as we get off the phone. That shouldn't be a problem to have someone from Langley make that call. Anything else?"

"Yes, whoever calls JTF-5, make sure he tells them Chief Petty Officer Mike Moore is doing a great job."

"Who the fuck is Chief Petty Officer Moore?"

"The guard that was going to shoot me if I tried to enter the PacArea Intel room. He did a good job. Make sure they say that. An attaboy coming from the CIA just may get him a promotion someday."

"All right. That's probably a good thing to do for the kid. I'll call Buddy now. Keep me informed."

"I will, Jack. Thanks," Davis said and hung up.

AT 3:00 P.M., JTF-5 COMMANDER REAR ADMIRAL WILLIAM LEAF received a call from CIA Director William Weatherby.

"Yes, sir, Director. I'll make that crystal clear to Captain Wringer. He already advised me that I may be getting a call. But I didn't think it would be from you, sir. . . . Yes, sir. Go ahead. Let me write that name down. Chief Petty Officer Mike Moore. . . . Yes, sir. I know him. He's assigned to PacArea Intel." Laughing, RADM Leaf said, "I'm glad he didn't shoot your man, and yes, sir, this will go into his personnel file. Thank you, sir. . . . You too, have a good day."

After hanging up, Commander Leaf called Captain Wringer. "Captain, I need you to come to my office. . . . Yes, I did, and you are not going to believe who it was."

AT 4:00 P.M., TAYLOR CALLED DAVIS and advised the Coast Guard P-3 was not able to locate the *Valiant Venture* along the West Coast between San Francisco and Eureka.

"That doesn't surprise me," Davis said.

"No, me either. That makes two recon flights, and neither one could locate the vessels. I don't think they're up that way."

"No, I don't think they went north. They're going back to the same place they went last year. And if it were me, I'd be returning back to McAvoy or Sevenmile."

"Were you able to make the call on the classified info?"

"Yes. Commander Leaf will be notified soon, today or tomorrow, I would think."

Laughing, Taylor said, "You know how to get shit done, straight to the top."

"Sometimes, you have no choice," Davis said. His pager went off, and looking at it, Davis said, "Ray, I need to go. The CI just paged me."

"Okay. Talk later."

Davis hung up and called Irene. "You hear something?" he asked.

"Yes, I heard they're going to Alaska and then to Seattle. Carlin's brother, Harold Sr., is supposedly going to Seattle to meet them in a few days."

"I think all the Alaska and Seattle information we are getting is disinformation," Davis said. "But I can't ignore it. Thank you. Keep giving me whatever you hear."

"Yes, I think it's probably bullshit. But I'm going to pass it on anyway."

"Please do and thank you, Irene."

"You're welcome, and you make sure Willard is taken care of if anything happens to me."

"I will. You have my word."

Davis hung up and called the SAC Customs Office in Seattle. "Hello. This is Agent Davis from San Francisco. Can I speak to one of the agents, please?"

"Yes, just a minute, sir."

"Hello, this is Special Agent Duane Howard. How can I help you?"

"Duane, this is Special Agent Tony Davis, Customs San Francisco. I have a vessel we are watching, and they may be heading your way. We think they are to meet a mothership, take on a load of drugs, and return to the US. I heard from my CI a few minutes ago that they may be returning to Seattle."

"What's the vessel's name and description?"

"*Valiant Venture*, and it's pulling a barge. The *Valiant Venture* is a sixty-seven-foot tugboat, red and white in color. The skipper is Carlin Rogers from the Bay Area."

"What do you think they may be carrying?"

"Multi-tons of hashish and marijuana."

"Wow, okay. I'll brief the office and let you know if we hear or see anything."

"Thank you, Duane," Davis said and hung up.

12:30 p.m., Tuesday, May 10, 1988

TAYLOR CALLED DAVIS. "The *California Rose* notified VTS that it's taking a barge to Pittsburg."

"I'll meet you at McAvoy Harbor Café at two p.m.," Davis said and left the Hayward house. When he arrived at the café, Taylor was already in the parking lot.

"My turn to buy," Davis said.

"Knock yourself out," Taylor replied, walking into the restaurant.

Taking their usual stools off to the side, both men said hello to Joan when she brought them coffee.

"Well, hello to you guys too. Haven't see you in here for a while."

"We've been busy. Anything new?" Taylor asked.

"Not really. Rogers's vessel brought a barge into the harbor and then left. Other than that, not much is going on."

"When did they bring it?" Davis asked.

"Been here about an hour. You boys want the burgers or pancakes?"

"I'm going for the pancakes," Davis said.

"Yes, me too. I'm all burgered out for a while," Taylor said.

When Joan left, Davis said, "If you'll look over your left shoulder, that's where they may bring the drugs to if they don't go to Sevenmile."

Taylor slid on his stool and looked back across the Harbor. "The bait shop?"

Laughing, Davis said, "No, look past that."

"Looks like an old gravel plant."

"Yes, it is. If it's deep enough for a barge loaded with gravel, it's deep enough for a barge loaded with drugs."

"Ahhh yeah," Taylor said. "How do you know that?"

"I've been snooping around here now for over a year."

"Makes sense. Let's hope they don't get this far. If they do, we've fucked up," Taylor said.

"Absolutely. We stop the fuckers at the gate," Davis said.

Joan brought the men their meals and poured both more coffee. After finishing their meals, they walked back outside to their cars.

"Let's run up to Sevenmile and see if the *California Rose* returns there. You want to leave your car here and ride with me?" Davis asked.

"Sure," Taylor said, getting in.

At 4:00 p.m., Davis and Taylor watched the *California Rose* return to the Sevenmile Slough. As the vessel turned into the slough, there was a blue Chevy pickup truck parked at the worksite. Davis picked up his radio mic and called sector as he drove by. "Sector, this is Alpha 27141. I need a 10-28 on Oregon tag Papa, Alpha, Tango, zero-niner-two."

"Ten-four, Alpha 27141. Stand by." A minute later, the response came. "Alpha 27141, that is registered to Robert Aldrane, Haines, Oregon. No wants or warrants."

"Ten-four, Sector. Thanks," Davis said and hung up the mic that was kept hidden underneath the dash. "You know when I was a trooper, we had to have whip antennas that were ten feet long to reach to the next county. Now look at my antenna. It looks like a normal radio antenna, and I just talked to Los Angeles from bumfuck California. That has to be over three hundred miles."

"Technology keeps getting better and better," Taylor said.

"You ready to get the hell out of here?" Davis asked.

"Yeah, let's go."

CHAPTER 54

Storms and Briefings

2:00 p.m., Wednesday, May 11, 1988

The *Poliksena* had been making good time. It would've been able to rendezvous with the *Valiant Venture* the next day if it hadn't been for the Pacific storm that was beating the ship and men around like they were toys. Even some of the hardiest crewmembers were starting to get sick with the unusual movements the vessel was forced to make.

"How does the radar look?" Captain Babin asked Simeon at the helm.

"Not good. We're going to be in this bitch for next twenty-four hours."

Three hundred miles to the east, Carlin Rogers was calling on frequency 161.7. "*Western Star, Wester Star, Western Star,* this is *Ulu.* Over." Still there was no reply and with the new electronics on the *Valiant Venture,* Carlin knew he was sitting where he needed to be, smack dab in the middle of latitude 38°N, longitude 150°W.

Sitting at Davis's desk at the Customs office, he and Taylor had Irene on speaker. "Harold Rogers Sr. said Carlin, Harold Jr., Jim,

Bill, and Willard are on the *Valiant Venture* and they will be returning in twelve days. So the twenty-third is still the day. They're said to be delivering equipment to a survey company in Seattle."

"Thank you, Irene," Davis said. "Keep me updated as soon as you can." Hanging up, he said to Taylor, "Let's walk down the hall. I need to tell Harvey."

At Waskovic's office, Davis knocked on the door.

"Come in."

"I just got a call from the CI. It looks like the twenty-third is still in play. They supposedly are going to deliver equipment to a survey company in Seattle and then come back. I keep getting this Seattle information, and I'm starting to feel uncomfortable with it."

"You need to go to Seattle?" Waskovic asked.

"I think I should. Can you get me a flight for Friday?"

"Yes. Stop in tomorrow, and I'll have your paperwork. I'll get you a room at the Edgewater, nice place. Make sure you talk to Beckwith in Seattle. He's in charge of their Marine Group."

9:00 a.m., Thursday, May 12, 1988

Irene called Davis and said, "Harold Sr. flew to Seattle today. He may be going to meet his sons and bring them back by truck."

"Do you still think it's a ruse?" Davis asked.

"To tell you the truth, I don't know what to think now."

"Okay, keep letting me know whatever you get, and thanks." Davis hung up and called the Customs Office in Seattle. "Hello. This is Special Agent Davis. I need to speak to Agent Beckwith."

"Hold on, sir. I will transfer the call," the operator said.

"Dan Beckwith. How can I help you, Davis?"

"Dan, I had another call from my CI. They keep getting information that my target vessel, the *Valiant Venture*, may be returning to Seattle."

"Is that the same vessel that SA Howard briefed us on the other day?" Beckwith asked.

"Yes, it is."

"How about you flying up here and giving us, the Coast Guard, and the DEA a briefing?"

"I plan on doing that tomorrow."

"Great. Bring whatever pictures you may have."

Hanging up, Davis called US Customs, Astoria, Oregon.

"Hello. Customs Service," a man said.

"Hi, I'm Special Agent Tony Davis, Customs San Fran. Can I speak to the RAC?"

"Speaking. This is Ben Hawk. How can I help you?"

"Were you briefed on the *Valiant Venture* that we are looking for out of the Bay Area?"

"Yes, I was briefed out of the SAC's office in Seattle by SA Howard."

"Good, I keep getting information the vessel may be returning to the Seattle area, but I can't ignore everywhere else."

"Yes, matter of fact, I'm going on a Coast Guard Falcon flight this afternoon to search for it."

"I'm not familiar with the Falcon. What is it?

"It's like a small Lear jet. It's full of radars to search for surface vessels. Can you fax me pictures of the vessels?"

"I sure can. I have some great ones that were taken by the Coast Guard when the vessels were leaving. Give me your fax number. . . . I'll send these now. Thanks, Ben, and let me know what you find out."

"Will do."

1:00 p.m., Friday, May 13, 1988

DAVIS FLEW TO SEATTLE about the same time the *Western Star* and the *Ulu* made first radio contact.

"Affirmative, *Ulu*. I can see you now. Over," Captain Faucher said.

Carlin looked at his crew and said, "Okay, boys, you know the drill. Let's get with it. Willard, you take the helm. Let me know if you have any radar sightings or hear any radio traffic."

"Will do," Willard said as he watched Carlin, Jim, Harold Jr., and Bill climb onto the barge that was tied to the *Valiant Venture*. I'm going to make a bunch of money, he thought. The idea excited him so much he decided to call his mother. Picking up the mic, he called AT&T KMI ship-to-shore service and asked to have a call placed to the Spokane residence. He identified himself as being on the *Ulu*.

"Hi, Mom!"

DAVIS WAS PICKED UP BY SPECIAL AGENT HOWARD at SeaTac. That afternoon, Davis gave a briefing of the investigation from early 1987 to the present. Attending were agents from Customs, DEA, and the Coast Guard. All photographs were copied and disseminated among the agencies. During the briefing, an agent with the Coast Guard advised that in Seward, Alaska, Seattle Salvage had two blue containers sitting at a site run by the Kiewit Company. But so far, there was nothing to connect them to Rogers or the vessels.

At six that evening, Davis was sitting at the bar in the Edgewater Hotel, drinking a double Crown on the rocks when his pager went off. Looking at it, he recognized Irene's number. After paying Mark, the bartender, he walked back to his room and called Irene.

"What do you have?"

"Willard called me from the *Valiant Venture* earlier today. He said they would be back in San Francisco in fifteen days and that they are towing an empty barge."

"Thank you, Irene," Davis said, immediately calling Taylor.

"The CI got a call from the *Valiant Venture* today. Can you call PacArea and see if they have a location?"

"Yes, I'll call them now and call you right back," Taylor said.

Davis hung up and called Waskovic and Howard, advising them of the information.

Twenty minutes later, Taylor called. "They didn't hear it!"

"God damnit. Did you get on their ass?"

"Yes, I did. I spoke to the duty officer. I told him that was going in my official report and to do their fucking job."

"God damnit. Well, if they called once, they'll surely call again," Davis said. "Okay. Thanks, Ray. I'll let you know as soon as I hear anything."

PacArea Intel had indeed heard the call, but when the vessel identified itself as the *Ulu*, they punched it off. "I don't know how we could have missed it," the duty officer said after he got off the phone with Taylor. "Let's do our job, people," he yelled. "If the *Valiant Venture* comes up, we track that call." He grudgingly wrote in the Incident Log they might have missed a call from the *Valiant Venture*, but he didn't know how.

Saturday, May 14, 1988

THE NEXT MORNING JUST BEFORE DAYLIGHT, the blare from a foghorn coming from a vessel on the Puget Sound jolted Davis out of his sleep. He wasn't sure where he was until he looked at the Edgewater teddy bear lying on the other side of the king-size bed. That would be a cute gift for a girl, he thought as he drifted back to sleep.

At the same moment, on the *Poliksena*, Captain Faucher called Yukorov. "Vlad, it's Babin. . . . Yes, we met yesterday afternoon. We will begin offloading the drugs today. We'll be finished by tomorrow. . . . Yes, I'll follow them as instructed. . . . Thank you. Goodbye," Captain Faucher said and hung up.

Yukorov walked out of his Kabul office and told his driver to take him to General Vanerev's command center. Arriving there fifteen minutes later, he walked into building. At the general's office, he said to the secretary, "I need to see the general."

Picking up the phone, she spoke to the general briefly and said to Yukorov, "Go in, sir."

Yukorov walked to the general's desk and said, "General, the vessels have met, and they're transferring the shipment today and will be finished tomorrow."

The general picked up his phone and said to his secretary, "Get me my chief of staff on the phone." Holding the phone, Vanerev looked at Yukorov and waited. He then said, "Colonel, give the order. We begin our pullout tomorrow. We've been in Afghanistan long enough, and Colonel, make sure you notify Marshal Kavzo."

At 9:00 a.m., Agent Howard picked Davis up at the Edgewater and took him to the ferry terminal a half-mile down the road.

"Where we going?" Davis asked.

"You don't fly out until this afternoon. I'm taking you on a ferry ride to Bremerton and back."

"Cool. This place is so beautiful," Davis said.

After parking the G-ride on the ferry, Davis followed Howard up to a cafeteria where they both got a cup of coffee.

Sitting down at a table, Davis looked out the windows on all sides of the ferry and said, "I think this is the most beautiful place I've ever been."

"It is something. Perhaps someday you can live here. We need good agents."

"Thanks, but I doubt that. Would have to be a superstrong reason for me to move up here. I'll eventually get back East closer to family. But this is breathtaking."

"What do you think the odds are for the vessels to come here?" Howard asked.

"If I only went by CI information, I'd say fifty-fifty."

"But?" Howard asked.

"My gut tells me they're going right back to where they feel comfortable, and that's San Francisco."

After the ferry ride back to Seattle, Howard dropped Davis off at SeaTac to fly back to SFO.

"Thank you, Duane."

"Good luck, Tony."

6:00 p.m., Sunday, May 15, 1988

Davis was going through the Burger King drive-through in Hayward. As he headed back towards Newport Street, he began to slowly eat the fries. "I wonder where the fuck they are," he said. Returning to the safehouse, he turned on CNN and ate while watching the news. Suddenly he stopped and called Reynolds.

"Hello," Jack said.

"Turn on CNN."

"Why?"

"The Russians are pulling out of Afghanistan."

AT THAT VERY MOMENT ON THE *POLIKSENA*, 1,650 miles due west of Davis, Carlin Rogers and Captain Babin Faucher opened a bottle of French wine and did a toast for completing the offload.

The *Valiant Venture* and barge would begin heading due east in two hours. Carlin would wait two days before contacting Harold Sr. and telling him they were on their way back in. By Carlin's calculations, he should make San Francisco in eight days.

CHAPTER 55

38N, 145W

9:00 a.m., Tuesday, May 17, 1988

It was like the *Valiant Venture* had dropped off the face of the Earth. It had not been heard from for four days since Willard had called his mother. For the past three days, Davis called agents from Los Angeles to Seattle, and there was nothing. He even called the Royal Canadian Mounted Police (RCMP) in Vancouver, British Columbia. But no one had seen or heard from the *Valiant Venture* and barge.

Davis and Taylor had just returned from breakfast when Taylor's phone rang.

"Coast Guard, Agent Taylor speaking. . . . When? . . . Okay, we'll be right down."

"What?" Davis asked as he followed Taylor to his car.

"ET phone home."

"Fuck," Davis said, getting in the white Diplomat.

Arriving at PacArea Intel, both agents showed their IDs to Chief Petty Officer Moore, who opened the door.

"Thanks, Mike," Davis said.

"You're welcome, Agent Davis.

Going inside, they were met by Captain Wringer.

"Gentlemen, at 0800, the *Valiant Venture* made a ship-to-shore call to Harold Rogers Sr. Triangulation of the call placed them at latitude 38 north and longitude 145 west. The *Valiant Venture* confirmed this by stating to Harold they were at 38, 145."

"Show me, please, where that's at," Davis said.

Walking to the large table that was covered with a marine chart, Wringer pointed and said, "Right here, straight out from San Francisco thirteen hundred miles."

"How long will it take them to come back in if they're returning to San Fran?"

"A week," Wringer said.

"Awesome work, Captain," Davis said.

"Admiral Leaf got your phone call. We'll do whatever you need."

"Well, you tell Admiral Leaf that you made my day. Thank you. Can we get another P-3 flight tomorrow to get their course? I need to confirm they are coming back here."

"Yes, sir. I'll order that and report to Agent Taylor as soon as we know anything."

Davis turned and high-fived Taylor, saying, "I need to get back to my car."

Making it back to Yerba Buena Island, Davis said, "Ray, Coast Guard PacArea Intel just saved our asses."

"Goddamn, this is getting exciting," Taylor said.

"Yes, it is. Call me as soon as you know anything, and I'll do the same. I need to make some phone calls. Talk later," Davis said as he pulled out of the parking lot.

Taylor went inside to RAC Case's office.

"Have you heard?"

"Yes. Let's keep this thing very tight from here on out. I want you with Davis as much as he needs."

"Did you find out who called Admiral Leaf?"

"Yes, I did."

"Who was it?"

"I'm not allowed to say, but they have little stars on a wall in Langley, Virginia.

"Holy shit! I'm working with a spook."

"You keep that to yourself, and this comes from the top."

"Yes, sir."

Davis drove towards Vacaville and called Reynolds. "Jack, be there in five. Open the garage in four."

"Roger that."

Pulling into the garage at the Vacaville safe house, Davis got out of the Mustang and went upstairs, pushing the down button on the garage door and waiting there until it closed.

"What's going on?" Reynolds asked.

"They broke radio silence. They're thirteen hundred miles straight out from San Francisco, 38 north, 145 west. From Coast Guard calculations, they'll be back in one week."

"This shit is starting to get real," Reynolds said.

"Yes and quick," Davis said. Sitting down at the phone, he called Customs Agents Waskovic, Howard, Beckwith, and Hawk, relaying the latest information. He also notified IRS Agent Hagers and DEA Agent Bud Hedge.

Wednesday, May 18, 1988

ANOTHER COAST GUARD P-3 RECON FLIGHT was not able to locate the *Valiant Venture* at 38°N, 145°W. That afternoon, Davis had a meeting with USCG RAC Case, SA Taylor, and SSA Waskovic. They all agreed that a twenty-four-hour-a-day surveillance would begin on May 22 for Los Angeles, San Francisco, Eureka, Coos Bay, Portland, and Seattle until they knew exactly where the *Valiant Venture* was returning.

Thursday, May 19, 1988

PACAREA INTEL HEARD ANOTHER TRANSMISSION from the *Valiant Venture*. The triangulated location was 38°N, 138°W. It was starting to appear that the *Valiant Venture* and barge where heading straight back into San Francisco. And for the first time in two weeks, Davis and Taylor were able to take a deep breath. The phone call was placed to Carlin Roger's sister, Debra, telling her the vessel would be back in San Francisco by May 25.

Again, Davis called every agent that was involved with the investigation and gave them the update.

Friday, May 20, 1988

PACAREA INTEL MONITORED TWO MORE TRANSMISSION from the *Valiant Venture*, the first going to Carlin's sister, Sara, and the second going to his brother, Harold Sr. Both transmissions indicated the vessels would be in by May 25. The triangulated location was 38⁰N, 134⁰W, approximately seven hundred miles straight out from San Francisco.

That afternoon, Davis received a call from Customs Agent Brian Rocker of the Bellingham, Washington, office. He said the RCMP reported the British Columbia Chapter of the Hells Angels motorcycle gang was waiting on a load of hashish, coming to them in containers on a flatbed truck.

That evening at ten o'clock, Davis and Taylor watched the *California Rose* from Bruno's Yacht Harbor up the Sevenmile Slough.

"This place is dead," Taylor said.

"Yes, it is. Let's stay 'til midnight and then get the hell out of here," Davis said.

Early Saturday morning, May 21, 1988

WASKOVIC, DAVIS, CASE, AND TAYLOR MET and decided that daily P-3 flights were necessary until the *Valiant Venture* was located. They couldn't wait until the twenty-second to start looking. RAC Case would make sure the Coast Guard P-3 would change its search area. Up to that point, the P-3 had been doing routine SAR search patterns. flying 90 percent of the time north of the vessel's triangulated location. Case would recommend concentrating the search along latitude 38 until the *Valiant Venture* and barge were seen. So far, the

Valiant Venture had not been found by any flight. It was like they were invisible.

Sunday, May 22, 1988

THERE WERE NOW OVER TWO HUNDRED FEDERAL AGENTS involved in the hunt for the *Valiant Venture*. From Los Angeles to the Canadian border and beyond, agents were scouring every waterway that the vessels could hide in. Teams of agents from Customs, IRS, Coast Guard, and DEA were watching the homes of any person known or suspected of being involved with Rogers and Supply Masters, Inc.

Federal arrest and search warrants were obtained by the IRS for businesses, homes, and persons involved with the money-structuring case. They were just waiting for the *Valiant Venture* to be found and hopefully a load of drugs with it. When and if that happened, IRS Agents Rich Cain, Mike Hagers, and Bill Basler were ready to put handcuffs on the entire organization.

Davis and Taylor were on pins and needles at PacArea Intel. Davis arrived at 10:00 a.m., and Taylor was already there.

"Anything?" Davis asked.

"No, nothing. Not a damn thing," Taylor said, handing Davis a cup of coffee.

"I don't understand why we can't find them with the flights," Davis said.

"That's a lot of water to cover, and hopefully we can spot them today," Taylor said.

"Fuck."

"Yeah."

"Is there anything we're missing?" Davis asked.

"I don't think so. I've been wracking my brain, and I can't think of anything else to do. Agents Wayne Amos and Bruce Royal have driven by the *California Rose*, and nothing's going on there."

"Yes, and Robins and Landers are watching Harold Rogers Sr.'s place, and he's still at home. We need to find the fucking boat, maybe today," Davis said.

BY THE END OF THE DAY, no sighting of the *Valiant Venture* was made by the P-3, and no radio transmissions were heard by PacArea Intel.

"Where the fuck are they?" Davis asked Taylor,

"I don't know."

"Let's have a meeting at the SAC office in the morning. We need to decide how we're going to do the search if she comes in under the gate," Davis said.

"Yes. I say we take her to Yerba Buena Island. We have the manpower and equipment there to do what's going to be needed," Taylor said.

"I agree. Get Case and come to Montgomery Street at ten a.m. I'll contact IRS and DEA to be there too."

"Sounds like a plan. We'll be there."

"Thanks Ray," Davis said, leaving PacArea Intel and Coast Guard Island.

WHAT THE P-3 CREW DIDN'T REPORT to the agents was that at five that afternoon on their return to Alameda at 37°N, 127°W, approximately 250 miles offshore, they sighted the Russian stern trawler the *Poliksena* making erratic changes in course and speed.

"Do you see that?" the pilot asked the radar tech on the intercom.

"Yes, looks like evasive movements."

ON THE *POLIKSENA*, CAPTAIN FAUCHER told Simeon, "We're close enough. Make a couple of changes in course and speed. I don't want anyone knowing we were following the American. I don't like that damn airplane. Let's get out of here and head due west."

"Aye, aye, Captain," First Mate Simeon said.

IT WAS MONDAY, MAY 23, 5:00 A.M. in San Francisco and 4:30 p.m. in Kabul, when Captain Faucher called Yukorov. "We left the American. He'll be arriving in San Francisco this evening or tomorrow."

"Good, Captain. Thank you," Yukorov said and hung up.

Two hours later at 6:30 p.m. in Kabul and 10:00 a.m. in New York, Yukorov called Monarch National Bank and spoke with DePantera.

"Hello, Mr. Yuk."

"Hello, Mr. DePantera. I want to inform you that my vessel has left the American vessel. I've been told the American vessel will arrive in San Francisco this evening or tomorrow."

"Wonderful, Mr. Yuk. Would you like me to deposit the money in your account with the understanding that the money will not be released until I receive the shipment?"

"Yes, Mr. DePantera. Do that so I can advise my superiors the money is in the bank but not released, a sign of good faith, if you will."

"Yes, of course. To confirm, I'm paying for forty-three tons of product at 1.1 million per ton, total of 47.3 million dollars. Is that correct, Mr. Yuk?"

"Yes, Mr. DePantera. Then my fifty thousand per ton of Thai, which is thirteen tons, but that money will be delivered to me personally."

"Yes, Mr. Yuk. That is correct. I'll go ahead and deposit the 47.3 million in the account and will release those funds on delivery to my trucks."

"Very good, Mr. DePantera. It's nice doing business with you. Goodbye."

"Goodbye, Mr. Yuk."

CHAPTER 56

Golden Gate Bridge

10:00 a.m., Monday, May 23, 1988

ASAC Sherman, SSA Waskovic, SA Davis, RAC Case, SA Taylor, SA Hedge, and SA Hagers met in Sherman's office at Customs Headquarters, 1700 Montgomery Street.

"How do you want to do this, Tony?" Sherman asked.

"Ray and I were talking about this yesterday. We'll have to take the vessels somewhere to perform the Customs search. We can't do it underneath the Golden Gate Bridge. I agree with Ray; we need to take the vessels to Yerba Buena Island and tie them to the Coast Guard docks. We'll then have electricity for lights, equipment, and manpower to do a proper search."

"I agree with that," RAC Case said. "We have everything there we'll need, including the Naval Brig on Treasure Island. We can hold the crew there until the search is completed."

"I never thought of that," Sherman said. "That'll be needed to hold them for the amount of time it takes, as long as it is not over eight hours. We cannot hold them longer than that during a Customs search."

"I would think we should be able to do it in less time than that," Case said.

Davis looked at Taylor.

"Have you thought of a controlled delivery?" DEA Agent Hedge asked.

"Yes, I have," Davis said. "But where these people are operating, we'd be burnt. They'd discover us, and then they'd flee. We wouldn't have a controlled delivery, and then we'd have to hunt all these people down." Davis knew that was the truth; he also knew that as soon as the shipment of drugs made it to the offload site, the money would be released to the KGB by the drug syndicate out of New York and Toronto. He couldn't allow that to happen, no matter who took credit for seizing the drugs.

"I agree with Tony," Taylor said. "I've been out there for over six months, and there's nowhere to surveil from. We'd definitely get burnt, and then this investigation falls apart."

"All right," Sherman said. "I agree. We'll board the *Valiant Venture* underneath Golden Gate. We'll take her and the crew to the Coast Guard facility on YBI. The crew will be interviewed and placed in the Naval Brig until the search is completed."

After the meeting, Davis thanked everyone for coming and said to Taylor as he walked him down the hall, "I'll be over after a while. I need to talk to Sherman first." Walking back to Sherman's office, he closed the door behind him.

"What do you want?" Sherman asked.

"I want to say this is not over about the controlled delivery."

"What do you mean?

"This is a Customs, Coast Guard, and IRS case. The DEA has basically nothing to do with it, and that's no one's fault. That's just how this case happened."

"And?"

"The DEA wants to take over this case, and the only way to do that is a controlled delivery where it's out of our hands. Otherwise, they're going to have egg on their face after this goes down. Don't be surprised if you get a call after Hedge gets back to his office."

"Fuck the DEA. This is our case, and we're doing it our way," Sherman said.

"Thank you, Paul. I actually like your yellow fucking socks. They remind me of a florescent fishing bobber I used as a kid."

"Get the hell out of my office," Sherman said with a laugh.

"I'm going to YBI. Page me if you hear anything."

"Will do, you fucking rookie."

Davis smiled as he left the building.

1:30 p.m., May 23, 1988

AUSA EARL SWEDISH CALLED SHERMAN to request the interception of the *Valiant Venture* be delayed and a controlled delivery attempted. Sherman denied the request stating, "Earl, due to safety and logistical considerations, I feel it's best that we continue with the Customs search as the vessels try to enter the United States. A controlled delivery would be very doubtful, but thank you for your call." Hanging up, Sherman said, "Fuck the DEA."

3:00 p.m., May 23, 1988

CAPTAIN WRINGER, PACAREA INTEL, CALLED TAYLOR and said, "We have no additional sighting with the P-3 and no new transmissions heard."

"God damnit," Davis said as Taylor pushed the speaker button off on his phone.

"Where the fuck are they?" Taylor said.

"I don't know, but I can't drink anymore coffee. My heart is starting to do jumping jacks."

A torturous hour and fifteen minutes passed, and then Taylor's phone rang again. Pushing on the speaker button, he said, "Taylor."

"At 1615, the P-3 flew over the *Valiant Venture* and barge," Captain Wringer said. "They're fifty miles offshore, heading towards San Francisco. Hold on. They're talking to VTS now." After a pause, the captain continued, "They just advised they are inbound to Sevenmile Slough at five knots. At that rate of speed, they'll be at the gate at 2100."

"Thank you, Captain!" Taylor and Davis both yelled, jumping up out of their chairs. Taylor ran to Case's office and gave him the news.

"All right. I'll notify Captain Goodman on the *Cape Romain* and get an armed boarding party ready on *41403*."

"I need to go to my office. Ray, can you come over later?" Davis asked.

"Sure can," Taylor said as Davis left the office.

After getting in his Mustang, Davis called Reynolds. "They've been spotted fifty miles out and should be under the gate by nine p.m."

"Great. I'll notify Buddy. You having any problems?"

"None I can't handle. "I'm about ready to shit in everyone's punch bowl. Rogers will be stopped in five hours. I can almost guarantee the money won't be released. We'll see if our timing works or not. The Russians have already begun their pullout, I don't think they'll go back."

"All right. Call me as soon as you find the drugs."

"Will do, Jack."

"Fuck," Reynolds said, as he got off the phone and called Hayden.

WHEN DAVIS GOT TO THE CUSTOMS OFFICE, he ordered more agents from Coast Guard and Customs to watch the various possible offload sites and Sevenmile Slough. DEA agents were not made available for those assignments.

At 6:00 p.m., Taylor walked in Davis's office. "How's it going?"

"Like a one-legged man in an ass-kicking contest," Davis said. "I think we have everything covered. We have men everywhere, watching different locations. So far, no activity anywhere. Not at Sevenmile, not at McAvoy, nowhere."

"Okay, we've got an hour and fifteen minutes. Captain Goodman of the *Cape Romain* says we need to leave at eight p.m. to get to the gate by eight forty-five."

WHAT NO ONE KNEW WAS ROGERS DELIBERATELY had given a slow speed. He was traveling much faster at eight knots. He would pass into San Francisco Bay and under the Golden Gate Bridge long before anyone would be ready to stop him, even if someone were listening.

7:00 p.m., May 23, 1988

PACAREA INTEL MONITORED A TRANSMISSION from the *Valiant Venture* to Sara Lawson. Triangulation revealed the *Valiant Venture* was almost an hour ahead of schedule and would be arriving at the Golden Gate at 8:00 pm. Captain Wringer immediately called YBI to alert the *Cape Romain* and RAC Case.

Five minutes later, Taylor was paged by Special Agent Bruce Royal.

Taylor called YBI and immediately said, "Fuck!"

"What?" Davis yelled at Taylor, hearing his remark.

"The *Valiant Venture* is ahead of schedule. The *Cape Romain* must leave now if they're to intercept it at the Gate!" Taylor yelled back.

"You tell Commander Goodman he's not to leave that dock until we get there. If he does, I lose my nexus, and we'll not be able to cut open that barge. We leave now!" Davis yelled, running for the door and then to the parking garage across the street.

Taylor yelled into the receiver, "Bruce, you do not leave. I'm on my way!" Slamming it down, he ran for the door behind Davis.

Racing out of the building and across the street, Davis yelled at Taylor, "We don't stop for anything or anyone. Stay on my six!"

"Roger that!" Taylor yelled back.

Both men jumped into their cars and sped out of the parking garage. Normal driving would take forty-five minutes to get through San Francisco traffic and halfway across the Oakland Bay Bridge to Yerba Buena Island. When you're racing seventy miles per hour down the Embarcadero, running red lights and stop signs, it doesn't take near that long. Davis tried to use his red light, but it kept sliding off the dash. He finally threw it into the backseat so it wouldn't get under his brake.

"Stay with me, Ray," Davis yelled. He could hear a siren and see in his rearview mirror a San Francisco Police cruiser with its lights flashing right on Taylor's bumper.

Seeing another San Francisco Police cruiser coming from a side street, Davis swerved into the outside lane and punched the accelerator of the Mustang with Taylor staying right behind him.

"We're not stopping, Ray!" Davis yelled.

He could see Taylor trying to hold his badge up so the SFPD officers could see that he was a cop. But with the cars going so fast and darting in and out of traffic, it would be impossible to see what Taylor was holding. By the time the Mustang and Diplomat jumped up onto Interstate 80 and were flying across the Oakland Bay Bridge, there were three San Francisco Police cruisers chasing them. Seeing the SFPD cars stopping at the city limits, Davis and Taylor raced across the bridge and got off at the Coast Guard facility halfway to Oakland.

They slid their cars to a stop and ran for the vessels. USCG Cutter *Cape Romain* was away from the dock but standing by. The Coast Guard Patrol Vessel *41403* with an armed boarding party was still being held at the dock, waiting for the special agents. Jumping on board Taylor yelled at Commander Steve Moher, "Let's go!" Special Agent Bruce Royal was already on board and had threatened Moher if they left without Taylor and Davis. Both agents thanked Royal for making them stay.

Taylor looked at Davis and said, "I can't believe we made it!"

"You did good. I could see you holding up your badge," Davis said with a laugh.

"Yeah," Taylor laughed, "This is like a fucking movie."

Holding on to the railing of the speeding craft, the agents watched the vessels race towards the Golden Gate Bridge.

"Yes, just like a fucking movie," Davis said.

THE *CAPE ROMAIN* AND PATROL VESSEL *41403* made it to the Golden Gate Bridge at 8:10 p.m. Looking into the distance, Davis and Taylor could just make out the *Valiant Venture* coming towards them in the fading light. Davis looked up; they were directly underneath the Golden Gate Bridge.

"Look at that," Davis said to Taylor. "We'll remember this view for the rest of our lives."

"Yes, we will," Taylor said.

At 8:30 p.m., the *Cape Romain* and Patrol Vessel *41403* turned their flashing blue lights on to alert the *Valiant Venture* that they were being stopped. By bullhorn, Commander Moher advised the captain of the *Valiant Venture* to have his crew assemble on the fantail and prepare to be boarded.

At 8:49 p.m., Commander Moher, the armed boarding party, and Agents Davis and Taylor boarded the *Valiant Venture*.

Davis and Taylor went to the wheelhouse, where Davis asked the captain, "Sir, what's your name?"

"Carlin Rogers."

"Mr. Rogers, my name is Special Agent Tony Davis. I'm with the US Customs Service. Before I'll allow you to enter the United States, I'm taking you, your crew, and vessels to the Coast Guard facility on Yerba Buena Island. There, I'll interview each of you and inspect your vessels. If no contraband is found, you'll be on your way as quickly as I can release you. Do you understand what I'm doing, sir?"

"Yes, I do," Rogers said.

Davis noticed that Rogers had turned pale when he started talking. And he now would periodically take very deep breaths. Rogers asked permission to shorten up his towline that was 1,200 feet long. Davis gave permission, and Rogers ordered his crew to winch in the line. Bringing the barge in closer, the vessels passed underneath the Golden Gate Bridge. Conversation was minimal during the long, slow voyage to YBI.

CHAPTER 57

There Are No Fucking Drugs in That Barge

11:45 p.m., Monday, May 23, 1988

It was almost midnight at Yerba Buena Island near San Francisco and 11:15 a.m. on May 24, in Kabul, Afghanistan, when Yukorov called the Bank of Paris in Luxembourg. He confirmed that $47,300,000, had been deposited in his account that morning. The account total was now $91,450,000. He still had to pay drug lord Afridi and Rogers, but regardless, the general was going to have a lot of money.

At Yerba Buena Island, Rogers pushed the barge up against the dock at the Coast Guard facility with the *Valiant Venture*. The Rogers' crew with help from the Coast Guard, tied the barge securely to the dock and then the *Valiant Venture* to it.

Carlin Rogers and his crew—Bill Rogers, Jim Rogers, Harold Rogers Jr., and Willard Butler—were taken to different rooms inside the Coast Guard facility for interviewing.

Davis briefly spoke to Carlin in his room.

"Mr. Rogers, is there any illegal contraband on your vessels?"

"No, none that I know of, other than maybe the boys have a little pot somewhere in their bunk area."

"Okay, Mr. Rogers. There'll be some other agents coming in to talk to you. Afterwards, you'll be temporarily transported to Treasure Island Brig until I can get your vessels inspected and cleared."

"Am, I under arrest?"

"No, sir. You're just being detained until I clear your arrival."

"So you are aware," Rogers said, "the barge is full of fuel. Tell your crew not to be smoking around it; it may explode."

"Yes, sir. I will. Thank you. We should have you on your way shortly. I appreciate your patience," Davis said leaving the room.

Other agents would then talk to Rogers and crew to take their officials statements. Afterwards they would be transferred to the Treasure Island Brig while the search was conducted.

Search of the six containers on top of the barge was started as Davis and Taylor observed the Coast Guardsmen emptying the enclosures. Walking around, Case noticed a freshly painted weld between the rear and middle containers on the left side of the barge. The paint was still gummy. The weld was rectangular in shape and covered a two-by-four-foot area. Paint samples were taken.

By 1:00 a.m., Tuesday, May 24, the search of the containers was completed, and no contraband had been found. The deck hatches were opened with caution to prevent any accidental ignitions from the fuel fumes. The slow tedious search took hours longer than expected. By the time the containers were searched, Rogers and crew had been detained four hours, and they were now in jail cells at Treasure Island Brig.

ASAC Paul Sherman and SSA Harvey Waskovic were now both on scene. And both were experiencing concern over the time Rogers and crew were detained.

"We've got to move this along, Davis," Sherman said.

"Let me ask Case if we can get more men to help," Davis replied.

He found Case on the back section of the barge, watching a Coast Guard crew remove over fifty bolts from a four-foot square steel deck plate over compartment six.

"Could we get two crews going, one on each end of the barge?" Davis asked. "Harvey and Paul are getting antsy over the amount of time it's taking. We've already had the crew locked up for four hours."

"Yes. Let me speak to the lieutenant in charge of the work detail."

A short while later, two Coast Guard crews were working on both ends of the barge to access the six internal compartments. Compartment six was finally accessed after the large plate was removed off the deck. That compartment was empty, and it was discovered that to access compartment five, another fifty bolts had to be removed from a four-by-four-foot wall hatch separating compartment six and five.

Compartment one was accessed through a deck hatch and was found to contain eight feet of water. A large four-inch hose and pump were set up to drain the water out before anyone could go down inside. Compartment two was also accessed through its deck hatch. Coast Guardsmen, wearing breathing respirators to protect from the fumes, went down inside compartment two. They found another four-foot-square wall hatch that contained fifty bolts. But these bolts had been welded to prevent them from being removed and accessing compartment three.

The wall plate in compartment six was finally removed and the men entered compartment five finding two very large fuel tanks. Separating compartments five and four was another four-foot square steel wall hatch where the bolts had also been welded to prevent removal. The welded bolts could not be cut off with a torch, due to the explosion risk.

Having accessed the two forward and the two rear compartments, the two middle compartments had no deck hatch openings. However, there were fuel hatches on each side of the barge directly over these areas. Davis and Taylor were watching the Coast Guard personnel trying to break the half-inch bolts off of the wall plate in compartment two. It was tremendously difficult work. Each bolt was taking two to three minutes each to break, even with the powerful impact wrench and the cheater bar the guardsmen were using.

It was 5:00 a.m., and only about thirty of the fifty bolts had been removed from the compartment two wall hatch to access compartment three. Sherman and Waskovic were forced to make a decision.

"Tony, it's been eight hours. We can't hold those men any longer. We must turn them loose."

Paul, I need just one more hour, and we'll have that wall hatch open."

"I can't do that, Tony."

"If you turn those men loose, we'll never see them again," Davis warned.

"I have no choice," Sherman said.

Waskovic was standing nearby and said, "Tony, there are no fucking drugs in that barge."

Sherman turned and told Agents Aleo Bigettie and Paul Defano, "Drive to the brig and turn Rogers and his crew loose."

Davis walked over to Bigettie and Defano as they were getting in their car and said, "Drive slow, Aleo. Trust me, drive slow."

As the two agents drove away, Davis found Taylor standing on the barge. "Ray, where's the lieutenant?"

"He's in his office."

"Come with me. I need you to back me up on this." Walking into the lieutenant's office Davis said, "Can you cold drill?"

"What do you mean?" the lieutenant asked.

"Cold drill, half-inch drill bit and continuously spray WD-40 on it to keep the bit and metal cold."

"Yes, but if the barge is loaded with fuel, we have a chance of blowing up this end of San Francisco."

"Lieutenant, you need to trust me on this. There are fuel tanks in compartments three and four just like the two in compartment five."

"He's right, Lieutenant. I think you need to do listen to him," Taylor said, knowing Davis had been inside the barge and what Ron Carriage had told Davis the night at the bar.

"You're saying those two center compartments are void except for similar fuel tanks?" the lieutenant asked.

"No. I'm saying compartments three and four have fuel tanks in them, as well as fifty tons of drugs."

Looking at Davis and Taylor, the lieutenant said, "Okay," as he walked out his office. "Get a big drill with a good half-inch metal bit and a big can of WD-40," he instructed one of his men.

Looking at Davis, he asked, "Where?"

"Come with me," Davis said as he led the men to a spot over the top of compartment three. Tapping his foot he said, "Right here."

A minute later, two Coast Guardsmen were drilling two holes in the three-eighths-inch steel deck of the barge. One hole to look thorough, and the other to shine a light into. One guardsman was drilling while the other kept spraying the bit with WD-40, keeping it cool. It took almost five minutes for the first hole to be drilled. As they started on the second hole, the bit broke. Taking a new bit out of his pocket, the guardsman quickly used the chuck and replaced it in the drill. He started again, and after a few minutes, he finally drilled the second hole.

The lieutenant got down on his hands and knees. While shining his flashlight through the first hole, he looked through the second hole. Looking up at Davis, the lieutenant had a big smile on his face.

Davis looked through the hole next and could see hundreds of carboard boxes wrapped in plastic. He said, "I need one of those boxes out of there, Lieutenant."

Next to peer through the hole was Sherman. Looking up at Davis, he said, "I'll be God damned."

"Can I make the call, Paul?" Davis asked.

"Yes, and hurry!" Sherman said.

Davis raced into the Coast Guard office and instructed the secretary to call the brig, who did and then handed the phone to Davis.

"Have the crew members been released yet?"

"No, sir. The agents are just now arriving. They were having a little bit of trouble getting here."

"Let me speak to Agent Bigettie."

"Yes, sir. Just a moment."

"Hello," Bigettie said.

"Aleo, don't release them. Read them their rights," Davis instructed.

"No shit?"

"Yes, we found boxes. I'll be testing it shortly, but it's drugs."

"Holy shit! That's great."

"Thank you, Aleo, for taking your time."

"Damn. No problem, hillbilly."

Davis smiled and hung up and then walked back to where the Coast Guardsmen were working on the hole in the deck. After checking the air quality for explosive gases, they used a cutting torch to cut a two-foot-square hole in the deck. Reaching down in the hole, Davis brought up one box and laid it on the deck. Inside, there were several hermetically sealed packages of green leafy material. Taking a small piece of the material, he put it in a test kit for THC. The material turned a positive blue.

Walking over the top of compartment four, Davis motioned to the lieutenant. Tapping his foot, he said, "Here."

After those two holes were drilled, Davis looked into compartment four, got up, and walked into the lieutenant's empty office. Picking up the phone, he dialed Jack Reynolds's number. "We got the drugs, Jack."

"Goddamn, Tony. Goddamn. This is not over yet, but goddamn."

CHAPTER 58

YERBA BUENA ISLAND, SAN FRANCISCO

Tuesday, May 24, 1988

IN COMPARTMENT THREE OF THE BARGE were 1,249 twenty-one-pound boxes of Thai marijuana, totaling thirteen tons. In compartment four were 1,718 fifty-pound sacks of hashish, totaling forty-three tons. This was the largest recorded hashish seizure in the world, with a total of fifty-six tons of narcotics. There were enough narcotics to make every man, woman, and child in the United States high. Street value was over one billion dollars.

7:00 a.m., May 24, 1988

THE FIRST *SAN FRANCISCO CHRONICLE* REPORTER arrived at Yerba Buena Island. He wanted to know what all the scanner chatter was about in regard to an enormous drug seizure by the Coast Guard.

7:30 a.m., May 24, 1988

EARL, PHILLIP DEPANTERA'S TRUCK DRIVER, was in Pittsburg, California, when he called Monarch National Bank in New York. "Mr.

DePantera, they never showed. Word is the Coast Guard has seized the vessels."

"Leave the area, Earl. Get back into Canada today."

"Yes, sir. We'll leave now."

DePantera hung up and, with a few computer strokes, immediately withdrew $47,300,000 from the Bank of Paris, Luxembourg, account of Mr. Yuk. Picking up his phone, he called a wealthy politician in upstate New York. "Senator, we lost the shipment, but I've recovered the money."

By 9:00 a.m., the IRS had arrested everyone involved with the money structuring case, including Daniel Henderson, president of LendBest Bank, Sara and Doug Lawson, and others. A big IRS lock was put on LendBest's door by IRS Special Agent Rich Cain.

Billy Little received a phone call, telling him to run. He was also to call a foreign number and report what happened.

In Kabul, Afghanistan, KGB Station Chief Vladimir Yukorov was eating dinner when he received the call from Little. After terminating the call, he had his driver take him to the Russian officer's residence who was in charge of all Soviet Forces in Afghanistan, General Vadim Vanerev. The general was finishing his personal packing to leave Afghanistan forever.

"General, the shipment was taken by the US Coast Guard. The captain has been arrested. We will not receive that money."

General Vanerev sat down on a box. Looking at Yukorov, the general said, "Vlad, we can't stop now. I've had my entire corps moving towards Moscow for over a week. We'll have to postpone the operation for this year and regroup. But we'll not be doing it from Kabul. We need to get home. How'd this happen?"

Yukorov felt ashamed, embarrassed, and enraged for the failure and letting this very honorable man down. "I don't know, but I'm going to America to find out."

"What will you do?"

"I'm going to kill whoever's responsible."

It took until 3:00 p.m. to remove all the boxes of marijuana and sacks of hashish from the barge and onto the Coast Guard dock with the assistance of 125 members of the Coast Guard and Customs. All the narcotics where then loaded into two tractor trailer trucks and taken to the Customs warehouse in the city.

Rogers and crew were arrested and Mirandized. None gave up his right or spoke to law enforcement after their arrest. They were all, including Willard Butler, placed in jail, awaiting arraignment before the federal magistrate later that day.

According to the memorandum of understanding between the US Customs Service and the Drug Enforcement Administration, it was now DEA's responsibility to move forward with the handling of the arrested, while it was Customs' responsibility for the storage and security of the narcotics.

By 5:00 p.m., DEA agents and the US Marshals transported Carlin Rogers, Bill Rogers (Carlin's son), Harold Jr. and Jim Rogers (Carlin's nephews), and Willard Butler (Carlin's former stepson) to the federal magistrate where they were arraigned. Public defenders were assigned to each man. Carlin Rogers's public defender was Attorney Grey Thomas. After meeting with Mr. Thomas, Carlin knew he didn't care for the man.

It had been a grueling thirty-six hours for Davis and Taylor. They were exhausted, as were everyone involved in the all-night search and then the securing of the narcotics. At that moment, the CIA agents of Thorn weren't sure if this would save Mikhail Gorbachev. But against all odds, they'd stopped the drugs and the payment to the KGB and Russian military, thus giving the Russian friend of President Ronald Reagan at least a chance to continue his pro-democratic march and hopefully an end to the Cold War.

However, all this created a problem that Davis could not see any way around. How was he going to keep Willard Butler out of prison without exposing the deal with his mother? If word of this surfaced, it would paint a big target on her back.

And to make matters much worse, although unknown to Davis, a particularly ruthless KGB agent was now prepared to unleash hell on the people responsible for his embarrassing failure and rage, not to mention his personal loss of $650,000. Yukorov was coming to America, and it would be up to the agents of Thorn and an unsuspecting Customs agent to stop him from killing everyone involved.

Wednesday, May 25, 1988

Klass told Davis, "Get your hair cut and have a suit on tomorrow. You're going to be on TV when you seize the *California Rose*."

"Yeah, I'm going to be out in the open now," Davis replied.

"Yes, your undercover work is over after this. And remember when speaking to the press, you work for the Customs Service."

"Roger that."

Thursday, May 26, 1988

The next afternoon, KXTV10 news out of Sacramento shoved a microphone and TV camera in front of Davis when he stepped off a Coast Guard vessel and onto the *California Rose*.

The reporter, George Warren, previously started the live broadcast after being asked by the TV anchorwoman if he had any new information on the drug bust. Warren replied, "About all of it's new to us and today the fascinating story of how one man brought the Rogerses down."

After being asked by Warren why he was seizing the vessel, Davis said, "The *California Rose* was used by Carlin Rogers last year during August and September to bring about thirty tons of hashish into the San Francisco Bay Area. That's why we're seizing it today, as a result of the investigation into Rogers."

The video clip showed Davis climb onto the roof of the vessel as he gave a thumbs up back to Warren. No one knew he was checking to make sure the antenna cable was still there for the satellite tracking device. The video also showed Davis saying how much he enjoyed working for the US Customs Service. That video clip and interview were picked up by CNN and broadcast throughout the world.

"You son of a bitch!" Yukorov said as he watched the American news. He watched the Customs agent smile during the interview, and Yukorov's blood boiled.

George Warren closed the segment saying, "And by now, Tony Davis has some help in his investigation. Quite a story, Special Agent Tony Davis. Now back to you."

Vladimir Yukorov turned off the TV and again said, "You son of a bitch," as he left his Kabul apartment to fly to Moscow.

CHAPTER 59

Killer in America

8:00 p.m., Thursday, May 26, 1988

"Hello," Davis said answering his phone.

"Is this Agent Davis?" the man asked.

"Yes. Who's calling?"

"Tom Banning, DEA."

"Hi, Tom. What can I do for you?"

"I owe you an apology. You tried to tell me, and I wouldn't listen."

"It's all right, Tom. It worked out."

"Well, I wanted you to know that you proved all of us wrong."

"Tom, I very much appreciate the phone call. And I'll pass it on that you're not the prick everyone thinks you are."

With a laugh, Banning said, "I have that reputation. But I wanted you to know that I think you did one hell of a job and congratulations."

"Thank you, Tom. Again, I really do appreciate the call."

"You're welcome, Tony. Let me know if you need anything."

"Thank you. Good night," Davis said.

After hanging up, Davis called Reynolds. "I need a new house, Jack. I can't have anyone follow me to Hayward."

"Yes. Where are you going?"

"Opposite direction. I found a small house in Santa Rosa for rent,

3295 Newmark Drive. I'm signing for it tomorrow. I've been staying here at the Motel 6 in Rohnert Park the last couple of nights. Too risky to go to Hayward."

All right. I'll advise Buddy. Listen, your ass is hanging out now. You need to be supercareful. These fuckers will kill you in a heartbeat, and you know there're pissed. Grow a set of eyes in the back of your head."

"Yeah, I know."

"I'm sure Buddy is going to be adding profiles to the flight watchlist, but we can miss people too. So keep your head out of your ass."

"Roger that," Davis said.

9:00 a.m., Friday, May 27, 1988

Petroff knew something was wrong when Yukorov walked into his office without being announced, closing the door behind him.

"Vlad, what's going on?" Petroff asked.

"Have you been watching the American news?"

"No. Why?"

"The American captain has been arrested, and we lost the shipment."

"No money?"

"No, the buyer pulled it out of the account."

"What do we do now?"

"There's nothing we can do about the money. But I'm going to America."

"What are you going to do?"

"I'm going to kill a Customs agent."

Petroff looked at Yukorov and thought, That Customs agent is as good as dead.

Tuesday, May 31, 1988

General Secretary Gorbachev and President Reagan concluded their summit in Moscow. Afterwards, while the two men were walking through Red Square, Reagan made the statement to the press that the Cold War with the Soviet Union had ended. President Reagan briefly stopped to shake hands with a young boy who was accompanied by a slender blond-haired man with a camera around his neck.

The tourist never spoke to Gorbachev or Reagan. He stayed to the side and kept his gaze mostly downward. Some say the tourist was actually a young KGB agent by the name of Vladimir Putin, who was assigned to shadow the world leaders.

As Carlin sat in his cell during the past week, his heart ached over bringing his family into this. Those boys have their whole lives ahead of them, he thought. The guilt he now felt was horrendous, and the big man more than once got tears in his eyes over what he'd done.

If there was any way possible, he needed to take all the blame for what happened. But Carlin knew he had to get the trials separated. He'd been in the court system long enough to know if those boys were sitting in the same courtroom with him, they would all share the same verdict and fate. He couldn't, he wouldn't take that chance, not with his family and especially not with his son, Bill.

He hoped all the coaching he had given the boys in case they were arrested would pan out. They needed to continue saying they had no knowledge of what was in the barge. Carlin had coached them well, and the four young men stuck to their stories and refused to cooperate with the agents. Carlin Rogers didn't know it, but Special Agent Tony Davis hoped for all the same things.

"What's going to happen?" asked Irene Kasper.

"It's going to take several months before this goes to trial," Davis said. "Carlin and the boys' attorneys will need to see all the evidence during discovery. There will be many motions and continuances before we are ever before a jury."

"Who's the judge?"

"Judge Joe Kosic. From his reputation he's tough, but fair. The Assistant United States Attorney who's assigned to the case, Mike

Paul, will make him aware of our deal in regard to Willard. After that, we'll just have to wait and see how this turns out. Best case scenario is for the boys' attorneys to make a motion for severance of their trial from Carlin's. AUSA Paul and the judge may go along with that, knowing of our deal. If the boys keep to their stories that they knew nothing about the drugs in the barge, they may be all right. If they get the right jury, they could find reasonable doubt, that is, if they get a separate trial."

"What about Willard's arrest in Oregon with the four pounds of hashish last year? Wouldn't that mean he probably knew?" she asked.

"Yes, but nobody knows about that but AUSA Swenson and me. And I'm not bringing it up, unless I'm directly asked by the judge or while under oath."

"My God," Irene said.

"Yes, this is going to be walking a tightrope," Davis said. "But no matter what, Willard will not be in a prison. My main goal is to keep a target from being put on you. We are dealing with some very bad people."

Monday, June 6, 1988

A big blond-haired man with piercing blue eyes flew into SFO. Taking his small carryon suitcase, he walked into the US Customs terminal.

"What's the reason for your visit, Mr. Volkov?" the Customs inspector asked, looking at the government of Estonia passport.

"Work," the man said with the Russian accent.

"What kind of work do you do?"

"I'm assigned to the Russian consulate's office."

"Very well, Mr. Volkov. That's an interesting name," the inspector said as he entered it into the Customs data base and checked if the man was wanted or on a watchlist, making small talk to deflect Volkov's attention.

"It means *wolf*," the man said with a smile, his steely eyes peering at the officer, knowing exactly what the officer was doing.

Not seeing any hits on the computer screen, the inspector said, "Welcome to the United States. Hope you have a nice visit," stamping the passport and handing it back to Nicholai Volkov.

Walking out of SFO, the big man got into a cab and said, "Take me to Hotel Drisco Pacific Heights."

"Yes, sir," the cab driver replied, heading towards the Pacific Heights area, two blocks from the famed US military base, Presidio of San Francisco, and three blocks from the building used by the consulate general of Russia and the KGB agents who were assigned there.

9:00 a.m., Tuesday, June 7, 1988

PETROFF FINISHED CLEARING THE PAPERWORK from his desk and wondered if he should take another chance and warn Buddy about Yukorov going to America. The drugs had been seized and the money not paid. He'd done his part. But it kept gnawing at him. He read the news reports of Customs Special Agent Davis. He knew who Yukorov was going to America to kill. Picking up his phone, he called Yukorov's office.

"I'm sorry, sir. Mr. Yukorov is out of the country for a few weeks, maybe longer."

"Is he back in Kabul?"

"No, sir. He's in the United States."

Later that evening at ten o'clock, Colonel Petroff walked back into the Kremlin and went to his office, passing a roving pair of guards. I don't like that, he thought.

IT WAS 2:00 P.M., WHEN BUDDY HAYDEN was finishing his introductory speech to a Secret Service class. Feeling his pager buzz, he hoped it was Melinda who normally put in 696969, meaning she was horny and to hurry home.

Glancing down, he saw 1880. "Fuck," he said loud enough for the class to hear. "I apologize for that, but I need to go. Good luck, ladies and gentlemen," he said as he left the classroom. Walking the short distance to the DOD building, he felt apprehensive about this contact from the colonel. He didn't know why, but he knew he wasn't going to like this call.

At 3:00 p.m., Hayden's STU rang. Without having time to say the code words, Petroff interrupted and said, "Yukorov's in America. He's going to kill Davis," and hung up.

"Fuck!" Hayden said, hanging up the STU.

CHAPTER 60

Public Defenders

12:15 p.m., Tuesday, June 7, 1988

Davis was at the Customs office on Montgomery Street when his pager when off. Looking at 10330501 made him frown. What's the emergency with Jack? he thought.

"What's wrong?" Special Agent Kit Wallace asked, seeing the frown on Davis's face.

"I need to make a phone call. Be right back," Davis replied, getting up from the table where several agents were sitting, organizing phone tolls of Supply Masters, Inc. Going into his office, he shut the door and called Reynolds's bag phone number.

"Jack, what's going on?" Davis asked.

"Yukorov's in town. And he's here to kill you. Buddy got a call from the source."

"Do we have a picture?" Davis asked.

"Yes. We have an old file photo from ten years ago when he was working Bedford. What's your fax number?"

Davis walked to his fax machine, gave the number, and waited. Looking at the black-and-white photo as it started coming through, he said, "I've not seen him yet."

"Okay. He'll have several agents at his disposal from the Russian consulate there. Buddy checked the Customs entries, and a Nicolai Volkov arrived yesterday at SFO. He meets the description and works at the Russian consulate. He was traveling on an Estonian passport. We believe that was Yukorov."

"Thanks, Jack. I'll brief Klass now."

"You be fucking careful," Reynolds said and hung up.

KGB Agent Vladimir Yukorov was having his own meeting in the office of the consulate general of Russia on Green Street in San Francisco.

"Why are you here?" chief of consulate operations for the KGB, Adrian Lebedev asked.

"Most of those drugs came out of Afghanistan," the Kabul KGB station chief said. "I'm going to find out who was responsible for allowing that. This has been an embarrassment for me, and if some of my men are bad, I want to know who. We may have a mole."

"What do you need from us?"

"I need a team watching the Customs office every day. I want to know how Davis did this and who he was in contact with," Yukorov said.

"We already have sources watching that location daily. They are the smugglers, and we can get their information. I have contacts within their group."

"Good," Yukorov said. "I need every photo of him, who he's associated with, where he lives, who are his friends."

"I can get that. May cost a few thousand, but it's obtainable."

"Okay, get me that information, assign me an office and two good men with a car, and that's all I'll need. Oh, and one more thing, if he has a wife or girlfriend. That's important," Yukorov said. Because I'm going to kill that bitch, he thought.

At five o'clock, Special Agent Kit Wallace walked with Davis as they left the Customs office. As they were crossing the street to the parking garage, she stopped and said, "You want to grab a drink and something to eat?"

"Sure, as long as I can drive your beamer," Davis said, taking her arm. "Let's get out of the street."

THE SMUGGLERS' COUNTERSURVEILLANCE TEAM was in the corner apartment, fifth floor at Montgomery and Chestnut. The fifth floor got them high enough to be able to take pictures above the trees.

"Isn't that the guy that made the drug bust?" the man asked, snapping the shutter on the camera with the telephoto lens.

"Yes, that's Davis, and the hottie with him is Wallace," another man said. "Take as many pictures as you can. She drives the BMW. He has the tan mustang, I think. These may be important to someone."

DAVIS AND WALLACE PULLED OUT OF THE PARKING GARAGE as he gunned the engine of the 323i and raced to the red light on Bay Street.

"Has some torque," Davis said.

"Yes, it does. Where do you want to go?"

"Let's get out of the city. How does Spinnaker sound in Sausalito?"

"That would be great," Wallace said.

Davis ran the car a little faster than he normally would. He continually checked in his rearview mirror to make sure no one was following them. Although he was sure none were, he worried having Kit with him.

WHEN BILLY LITTLE HAD RECEIVED THE PHONE CALL from Carlin the morning of the bust, he had immediately left his home in Chico and driven to Carlin's rented home in Sonora to hide. He had been there since the morning of the twenty-fourth, having pulled his white Lincoln Town Car into the garage so it could not be seen. Still having the pager that Terrance George Valley had purchased for him two years before, it scared the shit out of him when it started to vibrate. Looking at the readout, it had a San Francisco number with area code 412, but he didn't recognize the number and hesitated to call it. "Hello," he said.

"Billy, it's Yukorov."

"Are you here?"

"Yes. I need you to get a message to Carlin. Tell him I'm here to take care of the Customs problem."

"What do you mean?"

"Tell him I'm here to kill Agent Davis."

"Listen man, I'm all for smuggling drugs and running whores, but I'm not getting anywhere near murdering someone. Carlin's attorney is Grey Thomas out of the public defender's office. You call him. He can pass any information you need to give to Carlin." Little was beginning to shake badly when he abruptly hung up the phone. "Fuck that," he said.

Yukorov hung up the phone in his room at the Hotel Drisco. It was 8:00 p.m., and he decided to call the public defender's office in the morning. Still feeling the jet lag from flying from Russia the day before, he turned off the lights and went to sleep.

Kit and Davis where finishing dinner and a couple of drinks at Spinnaker. The evening had been pleasant with their small talk about work and personal relationships. However, Davis felt like a coiled spring, waiting for something to happen at any moment. And he couldn't get rid of that feeling of dread.

"I need to tell you something," Davis said. "You can't repeat this."

"Okay. What?"

"It's not real safe to be with me. I've pissed off some very capable people."

"Who are they? Do you know specifics?"

"Yes, but . . ."

"I'm a big girl, and I can take care of myself. So, who is it?"

"I know that. But it may be best if we don't hang out too much in public. My picture has been splattered all over the place, and now they know who I am."

"What are you saying? It'd be all right if I sneak through your back window at night as long as I'm not seen coming through the front door in daylight?"

"No, of course not. You can walk through my front door anytime you like. But I'm saying that someone is now here from another country to kill me."

Kit sat back in her chair and said, "You're fucking serious, aren't you?"

"Yes, I am."

"Is that why you were driving that way coming here?"

"Yes. I needed to make sure we weren't being followed."

7:00 a.m., June 8, 1988

YUKOROV WOKE FROM A VERY SOUND SLEEP and pulled open the curtains to his room, facing the Golden Gate Bridge. Being in the fourth-floor suite, reserved for members of the Russian consulate, he had the view of the entire western end of San Francisco Bay. Thirty minutes later, there was a knock on his door. Opening it, he let in the bellboy who had brought him his scheduled breakfast, placing it on the coffee table.

It was after 9:00 a.m. when Yukorov picked up the phone and dialed a number at 555 Seventh Street.

"San Francisco Public Defenders Office. How may I direct your call? the operator said.

"I need to speak to Mr. Grey Thomas."

"Who may I say is calling, sir?"

"Tell him a very important friend of the tug captain."

"Hold the line, sir. It may be a few minutes. He's now finishing up a meeting."

Yukorov had been holding the line for over five minutes when it was answered.

"Hello. This is Grey Thomas."

"Mr. Thomas, I need you to speak to the tug captain for me."

"Who are you, sir?"

"I'm Mr. Yuk. I need you to tell the tug captain that I'm in town. And I'm here to solve some problems."

"I can do that. How may I contact you later?"

Yukorov gave Thomas his pager number and said, "I'll be expecting your call," and hung up.

At 1:00 p.m., the federal grand jury returned a six-count indictment against Carlin Rogers and crew for the drug smuggling operation. All attorneys for the defendants were notified. Later that afternoon, Grey Thomas was showing his ID and checking in to the Federal Correctional Institution at Dublin, California, just east of Hayward.

"I have an appointment with Mr. Carlin Rogers at three o'clock," he said to the front desk officer.

"Have a seat, sir. The staff will be with you shortly to escort you to the attorney-client room. I'll have Mr. Rogers taken there."

A few minutes later, an officer came through the locked door and said, "Mr. Thomas, follow me please." The officer led Thomas to the attorney-client room down the hall. "Buzz me when you're finished, sir," the officer said, locking the door behind Thomas as he entered the room where Carlin now sat at a desk.

"How are you holding up?" Thomas asked.

"I'm fine. How are my son and the other boys?"

"I don't have direct contact with them, but their attorneys say they're doing well under the circumstances. The grand jury indicted all of you just a couple hours ago. Six counts for basically the same thing."

Carlin took a deep breath and asked, "How do we split these trials up? If those boys are in that courtroom with me, they'll go to prison for most of their lives."

"That would be up to Judge Kosic, and he's not one to be too accommodating. He's as tough as they come. If you would be willing to agree to a plea deal, perhaps something could be worked out."

"I'm not pleading. I'm not cutting my own throat, but I'll do whatever I can short of that to get my trial separated from the boys'. They weren't involved with any of this; they never left the tug."

"Okay, we'll have to work on that, but it probably won't happen."

Rogers stared scornfully at the public defender for his dismissive attitude.

"I received a call from a Mr. Yuk this morning. He told me to tell you he's in town to solve some problems."

Rogers looked at Thomas and wondered what problem he could be referring to.

"He gave me his pager number, and I was instructed to call him back. Is there anything you want me to tell him?"

Rogers still remained quiet as he processed what Yukorov would be doing. "Yes. Tell him not to do a damn thing until he hears from me."

"That's it?" Thomas asked.

"Yes! Not a damn thing," Carlin said, glaring at his public defender. "We're done for today," Carlin said getting up from the desk.

CHAPTER 61

Make Him a Project

Thursday, June 9, 1988

The next morning, Grey Thomas paged Mr. Yuk to his office phone on Seventh Street. When it rang, he picked it up saying, "Grey Thomas."

"This is Mr. Yuk. Did you deliver my message?"

"Yes, I did."

"What did he say?"

"He said not to do a damn thing."

"I'll be in touch," Yukorov said, hanging up on the public defender. Getting off the phone, Yukorov thought, Why would Rogers say that? One thing was for certain: Rogers knew too much about him, and he needed to be careful not to piss him off. Rogers would also know he was there to kill someone, and he probably knew it would be Davis. So why not kill Davis? he thought. All right, he thought. I have time; I'll make Davis a project and be ready when the time comes. Leaving his room, he took the elevator to the first floor where two men in suits were waiting to take him the three blocks to the Russian consulate.

Monday, July 4, 1988

CARLIN WISHED HE HAD HIS INDEPENDENCE that day. Speaking to his attorney, Grey Thomas, did nothing to brighten his hopes that would ever happen again. The public defender's demeanor continued to sink as he was made aware of more and more of the prosecution's evidence. Carlin believed three things: (1) he was going to see a prison cell; (2) if he couldn't separate the boys' trial from his, they would be there with him; and (3) if the boys got a separate trial and Davis was murdered, a jury would have a hard time acquitting them due to a perceived connection. He was afraid that jury would want to send a message, and he would not take that chance with his son's life.

After receiving requested writing materials, Carlin sat in his cell and wrote a short letter he would give to Thomas and have him deliver to Yukorov. It said, "BRF, do not kill Davis. If you do, I will tell everything I know. I will tell how Gorbachev is the KGB's target. I may need you to kill someone soon, but not yet and not Davis. You do what I ask and I keep my mouth shut. PS the envelope should not have been opened and there is a C on the bottom right corner of the original envelope. If the envelope has been changed, kill Thomas. If not, tear off the corner of the envelope with the C and put the initials of the name you used for Valley. Give it to Thomas to return to me." Carlin wrapped the note in double paper and sealed it in an envelope.

Monday, July 11, 1988

THOMAS VISITED ROGERS AGAIN AT FCI DUBLIN. "They're going to move you to Lompoc," Thomas said. "The US Marshals don't feel it's secure enough here for you."

"When are they doing that?

"I don't know, in a few weeks at most."

"How about the boys? They can't make the $250,000 bond that's been set for each of them. Do they stay here?"

"Yes, your son and the others will stay here until the trial. They will transport you back and forth from LA."

Carlin took out the sealed envelope from his pocket. "I need you to contact Mr. Yuk and meet with him. You personally give him this," Carlin said handing the envelope to Thomas.

"Should I ask what it is?"

"No, this doesn't affect you. You do not read it. If that letter is opened when you give it to him, he'll know. He will give you something to bring back to me. Make sure you bring it back by the end of this week."

"All right, I'll do that. In a couple of weeks all the attorneys are to visit the barge with Agent Davis. Is there anything I need to look at, or is there anything you think I should do or know?"

"It's important to remember the boys were never on that barge once we left McAvoy Harbor," Carlin said. "And when we met up with the Seattle Salvage vessels, they were the ones on the barge getting supplies, and they were over one thousand feet away. We were under tow the entire time, and that cable is 1,200 feet long. That's almost four city blocks away. We couldn't see shit."

"That's good information to provide to the jury," Thomas said. "If we can give them anything at all to where they feel there's reasonable doubt, we have a good chance of acquittal."

There's no fucking way they will ever acquit me, Carlin thought.

AT EIGHT THAT EVENING, GREY THOMAS PAGED MR. YUK.

"Hello," Yukorov said after calling the number on his pager.

"I have a letter that I'm to give to you. Are you available to meet in my office at the public defender's building?"

"When?"

"Right now, if you can; 555 Seventh Street, second floor, room 202."

"Yes, I'll be there in fifteen minutes."

Getting out of the dark sedan, Yukorov told the two KGB agents to wait as he walked into the public defender's office, taking the stairs to the second floor.

Opening the door to room 202, he heard Grey Thomas say in an office to the right, "Back here."

Walking in the open door, Yukorov met the man with dark hair in the middle of the room and shook hands. "Mr. Yuk," Yukorov said.

"Grey Thomas. Please have a seat."

Yukorov sat down in a chair next to the desk where Thomas was now sorting through papers.

"Here, this is what Mr. Rogers told me to give to you," he said, handing Yukorov the envelope.

Opening it, Yukorov studied the BRF for a moment before he remembered Rogers calling him the big Russian fucker. He briefly smiled, but the smile evaporated when he read the rest of the letter. He didn't like being threatened by anyone. But knew he had no choice with what Rogers had written.

Taking a deep breath to control his temper, he put the letter in his jacket. Tearing off the corner of the envelope with the C on it, he took a pen out of his shirt pocket. Next to the C, he wrote GH for George Hannah, the name Valley had told him to use in Cali, Colombia, when he had first met Rogers two years earlier. Handing the torn piece of paper to Thomas he said, "Give this to the captain," as he stood up and walked out of the office.

Back at Hotel Drisco, Yukorov opened the file KGB Chief Lebedev had given him. It had cost twenty thousand dollars from the drug runners' counter surveillance group that was watching the Customs office. He studied Davis and Special Agent Wallace in the pictures. Glancing at the series of the two moving across the street at 1700 Montgomery Street, Yukorov said, "He cares for her, or he wouldn't have taken her arm." Next looking at Wallace's picture, he began to feel a rage build in him. "She's a fucking whore," he said. "I may not kill Davis, but I'll certainly kill his fucking girlfriend." He looked at pictures of her apartment building at 644 South Van Ness Avenue. First floor he read. That will make it easy, he thought.

Friday, July 15, 1988

Grey Thomas gave Rogers the piece of paper Yukorov had

handed to him, saying, "He said to give this to you."

Looking at the GH next to the C, Rogers said, "Thanks."

"Not much else has changed," Thomas said. "We're waiting to look at the vessels and drugs on September 1."

"When do you think the trial will start?" Carlin asked

"December maybe, more likely January."

"Have you thought of a way to have the trials separated?"

"No, I don't think that'll be possible. You need to prepare yourself for going to trial with the boys being there. It would take something very drastic for the judge to grant a severance."

Carlin Rogers looked at the man and thought, You motherfucker, I know what would be drastic as hell.

9:00 a.m., Thursday, September 1, 1988

Grey Thomas and the other four attorneys for the boys met Davis at the Richmond Marina Harbor where the *Valiant Venture*, *California Rose*, and barge were being kept as evidence. Davis explained the layout of the barge and showed where the drugs were eventually found. At 11:00 a.m., Davis took the group to the Customs office and showed the non-drug evidence to the group. At 1:00 p.m., Davis took the attorneys to the Customs warehouse and showed them the fifty-six tons of narcotics. The attorneys selected two bags of hashish and two boxes of Thai marijuana to be sent for their own analysis. Each attorney signed the chain of custody forms before removing the drugs from the security of the United States Customs Service.

Over the next three months, Davis did the everyday duties of an agent preparing for trial—attending meeting after meeting with the AUSA and other agents and traveling to wrap up any loose ends of information that seemed to continually come in. Davis and Taylor were able to have lunch a couple of times, but that friendship was placed on the back burner with all that was going on.

On November 3, Carlin Rogers stood in federal court and made motion to Judge Joe Kosic that there was a conflict of interest between him and his attorney. He asked for a mistrial to be granted and requested that his proceedings be severed from that of his crew. Judge Kosic denied his motion.

Still standing, Carlin then made motion that his counsel provided ineffective assistance, and again, he asked for a mistrial to be declared and his proceedings be severed from that of his crew. Again, Judge Kosic denied his motion and told Carlin to sit down or be removed from the court. Carlin was running out of options, and he knew it. Trial was set for January 23, 1989.

DAVIS HAD STAYED A FEW TIMES AT KIT'S apartment on Van Ness. The friendship he was pursuing with her was beginning to turn into love for the beautiful Customs agent.

On the morning of Thanksgiving, November 24, Kit was standing in front of the refrigerator when Davis got out of bed. The inside light of the refrigerator illuminated her body through her nightshirt, highlighting her large erect breast, slender waist, and gorgeous ass. Davis reached into the refrigerator, deliberately rubbing his elbow against Kit's breast. "Excuse me, just trying to get some OJ," Davis said, looking away.

Kit looked at Davis, smiled, and asked, "You sure it wasn't the milk?"

Davis stopped in his tracks and looked back at Kit. She was standing with her long dark hair over one shoulder, one arm on the fridge door, and the other on her hip. The refrigerator light still illuminated her body through the short nightshirt. It was more than he could take. Walking to her, he began to passionately kiss her lips while closing the refrigerator door and pushed her back to the bedroom, where they stayed until noon. Ordering chicken lo mein for dinner, it was the closest they were going to get to turkey. But neither cared as they curled up on the couch and watched college football games.

The next morning Davis was leaving Kit's apartment when she said, "Don't forget your key."

"What key?" he asked.

"I made an extra apartment key for you. It's on the dining table."

"Does this mean we're official?"

"No, but it does mean you may want to stop by every now and then."

Davis laughed and said, "You're still not getting a key to my house. I don't like it when women just show up."

"I know," Kit said. "You're a secretive asshole, but you can still have my key."

"Thank you, baby. I'll talk to you later," Davis said walking out the door, making sure it locked behind him. Heading down the steps, he looked both ways before getting in the Mustang parked on the street. Down on the next block, Davis could see a dark Volvo. Windows were darkly tinted, and he couldn't see if anyone was in the car.

Pulling out from the curb, Davis watched the Volvo pull out too. "Fuck," he said. Turning left on Lombard Street, Davis headed towards the Golden Gate and Santa Rosa. They are good, he thought, being able to see the vehicle only a couple of times driving the fifty miles to Newmark Street in Santa Rosa. But Davis was sure they now knew where he and Kit lived.

ALL RIGHT, TAKE ME BACK TO THE HOTEL," Yukorov said to the two men in the front seat of the Volvo. Glancing at 3295 Newmark Drive, Yukorov thought, I know where you and your bitch live.

DAVIS WAS PEERING THROUGH THE SIDE OF THE CURTAIN in the living room when the dark Volvo drove by. "I'll fucking kill you, if you touch a hair on her head," Davis said, placing the safety back on the 9mm and sliding it back in his waist belt.

CHAPTER 62

I Never Liked That Prick Anyway

Tuesday, January 16, 1989

Carlin Rogers cringed over not having a severance of his trial from the boys, and he was trying everything he could do to make that happen. But he was running out of options. January 23 was coming fast, and he was getting desperate. Carlin may have been a criminal, but he still loved his son, nephews, and stepson. And to Carlin, he was trying to save their young lives. Now sitting in his cell at Lompoc, he wrote another letter to the big Russian fucker. This is my last chance, he thought and then said, "I never liked that prick anyway." Sealing the letter in an envelope, he placed it deep in his pants pocket.

9:00 a.m., Monday, January 23, 1989

Carlin Rogers, Bill Rogers, Harold Rogers Jr., Jim Rogers, Willard Butler, and their appointed counsels were sitting in the federal courtroom before Federal Judge Joe Kosic. AUSA Mike Paul and Special Agent Tony Davis were sitting on the prosecution's side.

"Counsel, are there any last-minute issues we need to address before we begin jury selection?" Judge Kosic asked.

Carlin leaned over to Grey Thomas and said, "Do it."

"Yes, Your Honor," Thomas said, getting to his feet. "My client, Carlin Rogers, and I have failed to resolve our dispute, and I now wish to be removed from representing Mr. Rogers and make motion in that regard."

"Mr. Thomas, we have already visited this matter, and I have previously ruled. Motion is denied," Judge Kosic said.

Carlin then stood and said, "Your Honor, may I address the court?"

"Continue, Mr. Rogers," Kosic said, leaning back in his chair.

"Your Honor, I wish to fire my counsel, Mr. Thomas."

"Mr. Rogers, I have already ruled on this matter. You must have counsel."

"Your Honor, I wish to represent myself and proceed pro se."

"Mr. Rogers, I will not allow you to proceed pro se. Without representation by counsel, you are placing yourself in very grave jeopardy. That is something I will not allow in my court."

"Your Honor, this man doesn't know what the hell he's doing, and I'm pleading with the court to reconsider. I know what I'm asking, Your Honor. This is not my first rodeo," Carlin said, knowing if he didn't get rid of his attorney, he had zero chance the judge would grant a severance.

Judge Kosic looked at Carlin and said, "Mr. Rogers, do you understand that a man who represents himself has a fool for an attorney?"

"Your Honor, I can do a better job than this fool sitting beside me."

Judge Kosic looked at AUSA Mike Paul, who said, "Your Honor, I have no objections."

"All right, Mr. Rogers. I will remove Mr. Thomas from being your appointed counsel, but I will not allow you not to have counsel's advice if you wish to seek it. Therefore, I'm appointing Mr. Thomas as your standby counsel. Mr. Rogers, I will give you twenty-four hours to prepare. We will begin jury selection tomorrow morning at nine a.m., and Mr. Rogers, you can seek Mr. Thomas's advice if you desire. Court is adjourned."

The judge slammed the gavel down, got up, and walked out of the court.

The bailiff said, "All rise."

Carlin stood with the others and then pulled the letter out of his pocket. Giving it to Thomas, he whispered in his ear, "You give this to Yuk tonight. Make sure he's not seen with you, but do this tonight! You understand?"

"Yes," Thomas said, looking at Rogers.

"What the hell is Rogers doing?" Paul asked Davis.

"Saving his son," Davis replied. "Those boys are as good as gone if they go to trial with him, and he knows it." He watched Carlin give Thomas the letter and then was led out of the courtroom by the US marshals. I'm rooting for you, Carlin, Davis thought. That would make the problem with Willard and not exposing Irene a whole lot easier.

At five that afternoon, Thomas paged Yukorov and waited. When his phone rang, he said, "Grey Thomas."

"This is Mr. Yuk."

"I have another letter for you, but he said you are not to be seen with me."

"All right, where and when?" Yukorov asked.

"Ten thirty, my house. That should be late enough. I don't want you coming to the public defender's office."

"Where do you live?"

"I'm at 1944 Sweetwood Drive, Daly City. It's a little yellow house."

"I'll be there at ten thirty," Yukorov said.

At 10:30 p.m., Yukorov lightly tapped on Thomas's door with his knuckles.

Grey Thomas opened the door without turning on the porch light and said, "Come in."

Yukorov stepped into the living room as Thomas shut and locked his door. "Come with me. I made an office out of one of my bedrooms."

"Nobody else here?" Yukorov asked.

"No, been divorced now for a year, and I love it. Have a seat," Thomas said, pointing to a chair next to a desk in the converted bedroom. Handing the letter to Yukorov, he said, "This is the letter he gave me this morning in court."

"How's court going? Is there any chance he can get out of this?"

"I don't believe so. He and his crew are basically fucked. There is just too much evidence against them. I'll do the best I can, but I don't think it'll be good enough. I don't think anyone can help him or the boys now."

Yukorov opened the letter and starting reading as Thomas sat down behind his desk.

BRF, my son is going to prison with me if I can't stop this trial. My trial must be separated from the boys. The only way to do that, is if I represent myself. I can't do that while I still have other people involved. If you do this for me, I will never speak of knowing you or your involvement. You have my word. If you don't do this, I am telling the FBI tomorrow morning everything I know, and getting a plea deal in the process. For my silence, I never want to see the man who gave this to you again.

Yukorov folded the cryptic letter, placed it back in the envelope, and slid it into his jacket pocket.

"What did it say?" Thomas asked. "I don't think anyone can help him now."

Yukorov didn't reply and continued to think of what Carlin was asking. If he killed Thomas, he would have to leave the United States in a hurry. But he wanted to kill one more person before he left. He knew he would be pushed for time and would have to complete everything as quickly as possible. If he did nothing, the FBI would have him before he could get out of the country.

"I disagree," Yukorov said. "Someone may still be able to help him."

"Who?" Thomas asked.

"You."

"How am I going to do that?"

Yukorov stood up and said, “With your death,” as he pulled his Makarov pistol from his belt and fired one shot into the shocked face of Grey Thomas. The report of the blast was muffled inside the house as Thomas was knocked backwards out of his chair. The next-door neighbor would later tell the police he thought it was a car backfiring and he never looked out his window. Yukorov picked up the spent casing and put it in his pocket. He then unlocked the front door and opened it with his hand inside his jacket pocket so not to leave fingerprints. Walking out of the house, he left the front door open. In the car, he told the two men in the front seat, “We were never here,” as the sedan slowly pulled away from the home.

5:30 a.m., Tuesday, January 24, 1989

Across the street from 1944 Sweetwood Drive, Mrs. Mendoza was getting ready to go to work at Walmart. Walking out of her home, she could see the front door of Mr. Thomas's house open with a light on in the living room. Having a rash of burglaries in the area, she walked across the street to make sure everything was all right. He seems like a nice man, she thought. She knocked on the door frame, saying, “Hello,” several times, but no one came to the door. Not being able to see if his car was in the garage, she walked back to her place and called the police.

At 9:00 a.m., the bailiff said, “All rise. The United States District Court for the Northern District of California is now in session, the honorable Joseph P. Kosic presiding.”

“Be seated,” Kosic said as he sat down behind the bench. “I see we're missing a counsel. Does anyone know where Mr. Thomas is?”

“No, Your Honor,” AUSA Paul said.

“Bailiff, go see if Mr. Thomas is in the hall or bathroom,” Kosic said.

“Yes, Your Honor,” the bailiff said, leaving the room. Ten minutes later, the bailiff returned to the courtroom and whispered in the ear of Judge Kosic.

"What?" Kosic said as he spoke softly to the bailiff.

The bailiff returned to his chair near the side door as Kosic looked down at his desk.

"I have received disturbing news. Mr. Thomas has been found deceased. Mr. Rogers, I will need to appoint another standby counsel."

"Your Honor," Carlin said, standing, "I wish to proceed pro se, and I will not use any standby counsel if appointed. And if you appoint another counsel, I'll fire him as well."

"Mr. Rogers, I must make you fully aware that your course of action is placing you in a very precarious position. If I agree to allow you to represent yourself, you will first have to undergo stringent questioning by Mr. Paul. These questions and your replies will be on the record. If a verdict is rendered against you by the jury, your ability to appeal will be affected by you representing yourself. You will have total control, Mr. Rogers, and total responsibility for your future in these proceedings. Do you understand that, Mr. Rogers?"

"Yes, Your Honor, and I wish to undergo whatever we need to do to allow me to proceed pro se."

Judge Kosic said, "Very well, Mr. Rogers, we will begin questioning. Mr. Paul, are you able to voir dire Mr. Rogers, or do you need time to prepare?"

"No, Your Honor. I'm able to do that without any further preparations."

"Very well, Mr. Paul. You may proceed," the judge said.

For the next hour, AUSA Paul questioned Carlin on the various points of law and his ability to represent himself. As a man who had been in countless courtrooms over the previous twenty-five years, Carlin Rogers did surprisingly well in answering the questions, as well as any first-year attorney after passing the bar.

When Paul concluded his questioning, Judge Kosic said, "Mr. Carlin Rogers, before I rule, I want to again warn you of the gravity of these charges against you and the possibility of you receiving an exceedingly long sentence if found guilty by a jury. The penalty guidelines I must adhere to allow for very little discretion in sentencing. Do you understand that, Mr. Rogers?"

"Yes, sir. I do."

"Very well. Mr. Rogers, this court finds that you have knowingly and intelligently waived your right to counsel and you may represent yourself in these proceedings."

"Your Honor," Attorney Greg Summers said as he stood, "I move for a severance of the trial of my client, Bill Rogers, from Mr. Carlin Rogers's. I believe his representing himself poses inherit dangers for my client to receive a fair trial." The three other appointed counsels for Harold Jr., Jim Rogers, and Willard Butler joined Summers's motion. Judge Kosic had no choice but to grant the severance to the crew members of the *Valiant Venture.*

"Motion for severance is granted," Kosic said.

Carlin Rogers immediately stood, smiled, and said, "Your Honor, I move for a mistrial."

Judge Kosic looked at Rogers and said, "Motion for mistrial is granted. Mr. Rogers, we will reconvene at nine a.m., February 6 to begin your trial. At the conclusion of that trial, we will start the trial of the other defendants in this case. This court is adjourned," he said, striking with the gavel.

"All rise," the bailiff said as the judge left the room.

Paul and Davis walked over to the bailiff as Paul asked, "What happened to Thomas?"

"He was murdered last night in his house, shot in the head."

Davis looked back at Carlin as he was led out of the courtroom.

CHAPTER 63

Not in My Fucking Bedroom

2:00 p.m., Tuesday, January 24, 1989

Davis sat in his office at 1700, wondering who had pulled the trigger and why. Carlin's smile when he asked for the mistrial meant something. Davis only knew of one killer in town that would have the balls to do that in the man's house. He also knew that Yukorov wanted to kill him as well but hadn't even tried. Why? he thought. Davis then remembered something Buddy had said about Yukorov. "Fuck!" he said, picking up the phone and calling the Customs office at SFO.

6:00 p.m., January 24, 1989

Kit left SFO and drove to the West Coast Café in San Bruno. She was led to the table Davis had called and reserved for the couple and ordered the pitcher of strawberry daiquiris he had said to get. Sipping on her drink, she thought about the closeness she now felt towards the man. Even though he was not too willing to talk about his life, she still enjoyed being with him. Matter of fact, she was falling in love with Davis and refused to admit it.

Two hours later, she was reassessing her feelings when Davis failed to show up and she never received a page from him. By eight thirty, she was feeling pretty buzzed and decided to go home and not worry about someone she probably shouldn't be worrying about. I need to forget about these feelings, she thought. It wouldn't work anyway, and she was not going to set herself up for being hurt again. But after arriving home, undressing, and crawling into her bed, she couldn't help but want him there. As she got in bed, she slid the 380 PPK under her pillow.

Kit was sleeping soundly after the daiquiris and didn't hear Yukorov enter her bedroom. I'll make Davis's whore pay before I leave the US, he thought. He quietly moved to the far side of the bed where Kit's upper body was exposed with the sheet stopping at her rounded ass. As she lay on her stomach with one hand under her pillow, her right breast was exposed. Should be quick and easy, he thought, holding the piano wire with both hands.

Crouching for his final move, something made him freeze. Out of the corner of his eye, he saw something move into the doorway of the bedroom. Quickly turning and reaching for his pistol, he stopped as he stared at the 9mm being held by Davis. Neither man spoke nor moved, both professionals at the top of their game.

Not a sound was uttered until Davis finally said, "Drop it on the floor."

Yukorov straightened, dropped the Makarov, and said, "I have diplomatic immunity."

The voices startled Kit from her sleep. Pulling her hand out from under the pillow, holding the PPK, she pointed it first at the figure standing in the doorway of her bedroom and then at the man standing next to her bed. Pointing the pistol at both men back and forth, she screamed, "Freeze, you motherfuckers!"

Davis and Yukorov, in a world of their own, never acknowledge Kit's command.

"Diplomatic immunity doesn't work when you're standing in a woman's bedroom in the middle of the night, especially when you're holding a piano wire, you murdering piece of shit," Davis said.

"Tony?" Kit said, moving closer towards the door side of the bed while still covering the other figure in the dark with her pistol.

"Relax, Agent Davis," Yukorov said. "According to your American justice, I'm guilty of nothing more than trespassing, and my diplomatic status will more than cover that."

Kit moved out of the bed and turned the light switch on next to Davis and said, "Tony, who is this asshole, and what are you two doing in my bedroom?"

"This is Vladimir Yukorov of the KGB," West said. "He's the one who's been supplying Carlin Rogers with the hashish. He was Charles Bedford's handler, and he killed Grey Thomas last night. He's now here to kill you, Kit, to get at me."

Yukorov let the piano wire slip through his fingers and drop to the floor under Kit's gaze. Through his peripheral vision, Davis watched Kit's hand turn pale as she tightened her grip on the PPK.

"Not yet, Kit," Davis said. "There's plenty of time."

Kit had both hands on the PPK now, trying to keep it from shaking, as a sense of terror and then rage filled her as she realized she was to be murdered by this man. The only movement to West's 9mm was to the rhythm of his breathing, and the more pissed off he got, the calmer he became.

"You cost me an enormous amount of money and an incredible embarrassment," Yukorov said.

"This is a big game, asshole. Some of us can play it better than others," Davis said.

Yukorov stared at Davis.

"Tony, you need to leave now," Kit said in a voice Davis had never heard before. Glancing at Kit, he could see her jaw was tight, the look in her eyes had changed, and the PPK was perfectly still. He had known those same emotions: you're ready to kill when you reach that level. Her glare now burnt a hole through Yukorov.

"Your agency will have your badge if I'm harmed in any way," Yukorov said, looking at Kit.

"Get out, Tony," Kit demanded.

Lowering his pistol, Davis said, "You're fucked," as he walked out of the apartment and started down the stairs to the sidewalk.

"I demand that you allow me to walk out of here, Agent Wallace.

Remember I have diplomatic immunity."

"Not in my fucking bedroom," Kit yelled.

Yukorov was just hearing the word *bedroom* when the first of two slugs from the PPK tore through his chest. Davis welcomed hearing the sharp reports, followed by the heavy thud as the body of Vladimir Yukorov was slammed to the floor. There was a pause, and then another shot rang out. Davis got to the sidewalk and thought, Two center mass and one between the baby blues. Your ticket has just been punched, asshole. He turned and walked in the dark the two blocks to where the Mustang was parked.

Kit was standing over Yukorov's body when she picked up the phone from the nightstand. Her first call was to Robert Klass and then to San Francisco PD. Klass arrived five minutes after the first SFPD squad car. Kit was being interviewed by a SFPD detective when Klass walked in.

"You all right, Kit?" Klass asked.

"Yeah, Bob. A little shook, but I'm okay," Kit replied.

The detective looked up and recognized Bob Klass. Hell, everyone knew Big Bob Klass. "Mr. Klass, in the next day or so, I'll need to talk to you as well."

"That's fine. Just let me know when and where."

The detective continued questioning Kit as the body bag was being carried out. "Hey, Detective, you mind if I take a look at the perp?" Klass asked.

"No, go ahead," the detective said.

Klass unzipped the bag to where he could clearly see the face. Not saying a word or showing any emotion, he zipped the bag back up, and the coroner's office members continued carrying out the body bag, containing Vladimir Yukorov. Klass turned and saw Kit staring in his direction. He winked and turned to leave. "Kit, do you need someplace to stay tonight?" Klass asked.

"No, sir. I'm taken care of," she replied.

Turning towards the detective, Klass remarked, "This dirt bag should have picked a different house to rob. Nothing more dangerous than a scared women with a gun."

"I think you're right," the detective said. "No ID on the body, no weapons, just a lock pick. He's more than likely a drifter. The Bay Area's full of them. Probably will never know who he is."

Klass was opening the door as he paused and said over his shoulder, "Son, I think you're right on this one. Kit, if you need anything, you have my number. Try to get some sleep. I'll see you in the morning."

"Thanks, Bob. I'll be fine," Kit said.

The black sedan that had been circling the area finally drove back to Pacific Heights after the numerous police cars converged on the home.

After everyone left, Kit looked at the big blood stain on the carpet. Never liked this carpet anyway, she thought. Grabbing a few things and stuffing them in her overnight bag, she got in her BMW and started out of the Mission District. She stopped at the local 7-Eleven, filled up with gas, and placed a wiped off Makarov pistol and a rolled-up piano wire deep into the garbage can. She then headed across the Golden Gate Bridge towards Santa Rosa. There was someone she had to be with tonight.

Parking in front of West's house, she hurried to the front door and knocked. Davis, wearing only his jeans and holding his pistol, opened the door. They began to kiss passionately as Kit kicked the door shut with her foot.

A week later and authorities unable to match the fingerprints to anyone on file, the body of Vladimir Yukorov was cremated by the city of San Francisco and logged in as John Doe. His ashes were discarded by the director of the funeral home who had been hired to do the cremation. Two days after Yukorov's ashes were dumped in the county landfill, his fingerprints and hair samples mysteriously disappeared from the San Francisco Police Department's evidence room.

CHAPTER 64

The Aftermath

Monday, February 6, 1989

Carlin Rogers's trial began, and for two weeks, the prosecution presented its case to the jury, followed by Carlin's defense. Special Agent Davis was the government's star witness and was on the witness stand for most of both sides, having been questioned by Carlin for three days straight during his defense presentation. On February 22, AUSA Mike Paul and Carlin Rogers gave closing arguments. After Judge Kosic read the instructions to the jury, they were removed to the jury deliberation room. The jury was out less than two hours when they communicated to the judge that they had reached a verdict.

Returning to the courtroom, Judge Kosic asked, "Has the jury reached a verdict?"

The jury foreman stood and said, "Yes, Your Honor," handing a piece of paper to the bailiff, who took it to the judge. Glancing at the verdict, he handed it back to the bailiff, who returned it to the foreman.

"Will the defendant please rise?" Kosic said as Carlin Rogers stood facing the jury foreman.

"Mr. Foreman, will you read the jury's verdict?" the judge said.

"We, the jury, find the defendant, Carlin Rogers, guilty on all counts."

The judge dismissed the jury and then informed Carlin that sentencing would take place the following week. Carlin was then immediately removed from the courtroom.

Leaving the courthouse, the San Francisco television station reporter asked Davis how he felt, putting the camera and microphone in front of his face.

"Justice was served," Davis replied.

"How do you think the trial for the crew will go?" the reporter asked.

"We will see," Davis said, walking away from the camera and mic.

A WEEK LATER, CARLIN ROGERS WAS SENTENCED to life in prison without the possibility of parole. The harsh sentencing guidelines were a death sentence for the forty-one-year-old man. The guidelines had been enacted by Congress during the 1984 Sentencing Reform Act, and Judge Kosic was forced to abide by them. But even as difficult as that day was, Carlin still had hope his son and the other boys would be able to go free. He had done everything he could, including representing himself, to give them that chance. Having one fewer defense attorney in the world to him was worth it.

SHORTLY AFTER CARLIN'S SENTENCING, the trial began for the crew of the *Valiant Venture*.

Again, Davis was on the witness stand for days at a time, first for the new AUSA, Linda Greathouse, who was presenting the government's case and then for the four-crew members' appointed attorneys during the defense portion of the trial. During the defense presentation, Davis felt the attorneys were not bringing out many issues that would give the jury the opportunity to find reasonable doubt.

Finally, during the second week, Willard Butler's attorney, Guy Campshell, asked Special Agent Davis, "How far was the barge from the *Valiant Venture*?"

"I can only say what I was told by Carlin Rogers after we stopped them underneath the Golden Gate Bridge," Davis replied.

"Agent Davis, what did Carlin Rogers tell you?"

"He told me the cable to the barge was twelve hundred feet long and he needed to have the crew operate the winch to bring in the slack when we stopped the *Valiant Venture*."

"Did you allow the crew to wind in the cable?"

"Yes, I did."

"How long did that take, Agent Davis?"

"It took almost an hour."

"Twelve hundred feet is a long way. Would you agree with that, Agent Davis?"

"Yes, sir. I would."

"Can you give the jury some idea of how far twelve hundred feet is?"

Davis looked at the jury and said, "Four football fields."

"Now, Agent Davis, if you were on the *Valiant Venture* and you are twelve hundred feet, or four football fields, from the barge, would you have a clear view of what was happening on the barge in the daylight?"

"No, sir. It would be difficult."

"Okay, how about if you were only one football field away from the barge. Would you have a clear view of what was happening on the barge then?"

"No, sir. It would still be difficult."

"Why is that Agent Davis? Would your vision be obstructed?

"Yes, sir."

"What would be obstructing your vision of what was happening on the barge if you were even closer than twelve hundred feet?"

"The six containers on the top of the barge."

"Would you be able to see anything that was occurring between the containers or behind them, Special Agent Davis?

"No, sir. You would not."

"How about if it was nighttime out on the ocean and you were only one football field away. Would you be able to see what was happening on the barge then?"

"No, sir. It would be almost impossible."

"Your Honor, I have no further questions of this witness."

Davis smiled and thought, That's how you do it.

AFTER CLOSING ARGUMENTS, THE JURY RETIRED to the deliberation room. After two and a half days, the jury finally reached a verdict. Bill Rogers, Harold Rogers Jr., Jim Rogers, and Willard Butler were acquitted of all charges.

As soon as Davis got in his car, he called a Spokane telephone number.

"What happened?" Irene Kasper asked.

"They were acquitted of all charges. Willard's a free man."

"Thank you," she said as she began to sob.

EPILOGUE

Mikhail Gorbachev and Ronald Reagan

IN AUGUST 1991, AN ATTEMPTED MILITARY TAKEOVER of the Soviet government began. Mikhail Gorbachev was arrested and held in his dacha for three days in Crimea as the assault on the Russian White House was occurring. The coup d'état failed, and General Valin Varennikov, Minister of Defense Marshal Dmitry Yazov, KGB Head of the Foreign Intelligence Branch Vladimir Kryuchkov, and

Chairman of State Committee on Pricing Valentine Pavlov were all arrested. Secretary of Central Committee on Komsomol Boris Pugo shot his wife and then himself before being arrested.

The attempted Soviet coup in 1991 was not out of betrayal of the USSR but was of its perceived salvation. Although many placed their financial loss paramount over the liberal progressive policies of Gorbachev, others such as General Varennikov felt they were losing their country and whatever needed to be done to save it must be accomplished. To them, this was not treasonous but was as patriotic as any true patriot could be. To them, George Washington, Thomas Jefferson, and Samuel Adams were of the same cloth. They hoped history would be kind to their efforts.

All the conspirators who were arrested for the failed coup where eventually given amnesty by the Russian Supreme Court. But General Varennikov refused to accept the amnesty and demanded a trial. He also demanded that Mikhail Gorbachev be charged with treason and be tried as well, which he was not. On August 11, 1994, General Varennikov was acquitted by the Russian Supreme Court. The court concluded the general had merely been following orders from Marshal Yazov and had acted in the best interest of preserving and strengthening the country.

During the coup, former President Ronald Reagan said, "I can't believe that the Soviet people will allow a reversal in the progress that they have recently made toward economic and political freedom. Based on my extensive meetings and conversations with him, I am convinced that President Gorbachev had the best interest of the Soviet people in mind. I have always felt that his opposition came from the communist bureaucracy, and I can only hope that enough progress was made that a movement toward democracy will be unstoppable."

The US president at the time, George H. W. Bush, decried the coup as a "misguided and illegitimate effort" that "bypasses both Soviet law and the will of the Soviet peoples." Calling the attempted coup "very disturbing," President Bush put a hold on US aid to the Soviet Union until the coup was ended.

AS A RESULT OF THE FAILED COUP, Gorbachev resigned on December 25, 1991. The following day, on December 26, Declaration 142-H of the Supreme Soviet's upper chamber recognized the independent self-governments of the Soviet republics. This declaration formally dissolved the Soviet Union and ended the Cold War.

ON SUNDAY, MARCH 15, 1992, US Customs Special Agent Tony Davis and Customs Inspector Ralph Delpre were sitting in the little St. Monica's Catholic Church in Coos Bay, Oregon. Both felt the spiritual need to pray to God and be thankful for all their blessing.

During this particular Mass, Davis leaned over to Delpre and said, "I'm leaving."

"But the service isn't over," Delpre replied.

"No, Ralph. I'm leaving the government," Davis answered.

"What are you going to do?"

"I'm going home to West Virginia."

"And do what?"

"I'm going to medical school," he answered, nodding his head.

Delpre didn't answer for several minutes and then asked, "What made you want to leave?"

"I'm tired of lying to everyone every day about everything," he answered, looking at Delpre. "My name is not Tony Davis; it's Nathan West."

Delpre was quiet again for a few moments, looked at his friend, and said, "God bless you."

With a shaking of hands, West stood up and left Davis and Delpre in the church in Coos Bay.

July 11, 2019, Fish Creek, West Virginia

DR. NATHANIEL WEST HAD RECEIVED CARLIN ROGERS's medical records and studied them intently for several days. He felt compassion for the big man who had spent so many years behind bars. Thirty-one years, West thought. He thought of all he'd been able to do in those thirty-one years, the children and grandchildren that were born.

West opened up his computer and began to type a letter to Senior Federal Judge Charles Breyer, United States District Court, San Francisco, California. This is the actual letter the doctor from West Virginia sent after receiving the phone call from Cait Boyce, ex-wife of convicted Russian spy, Christopher Boyce, the Falcon.

Support for Calvin L. Robinson Compassionate Release
July 11, 2019

Dear Judge Breyer,

My name is Dr. Norman Wood. In 1988, I was a Special Agent for the US Customs Service and assigned to the Organized Crime Drug Enforcement Task Force, San Francisco CA. I was the undercover operative as well as the Special Agent in charge of the Dredge Master Case where we interdicted fifty-six tons of hashish and marijuana from vessels operated by Calvin L. Robinson. I am the Special Agent that put Calvin Robinson in prison.

Your Honor, I spent almost twenty years in law enforcement and now over twenty years in medicine. I must admit that my attitude has changed considerably from lock them up and throw away the keys, to a more experienced, fair, empathetic, and compassionate line of thought. In the past, in my medical practice as a family practitioner, I usually had to tell at least one of my patients monthly that they were going to die. It is a heartbreaking part of my job, and it has never gotten any easier.

I have learned these absolute truths over the past twenty years of providing care for terminally ill patients. When you are at the end of your life, the big house, the fancy car, your bank account, mean nothing. All you want to do is spend time with your family and loved ones. Not to be able to do so, is a cruelty that few of us can fathom.

I have reviewed Calvin's medical records and it appears in a very strong sense, from the diagnosis and reports that have been relayed to me, that Mr. Robinson is gravely ill, and his continued current health could very quickly deteriorate to death in a matter of months.

I know Calvin Robinson in a way that most people, even relatives would never see. I followed him for over a year, and that is all I did. I was in his back pocket, and he never knew it. I knew where he slept, what he ate, who he called, who he met. I knew the delicate and secret life that he was living. I spoke to him while undercover. I was that close to him. I know the nature of this man and violence was never a part of what he did. Calvin did commit crimes, but I have known many of much worse character.

Before I became a Special Agent, I was a West Virginia State Trooper. I have arrested men for murder, rape, robbery, and everything else you can think of. I have known truly evil men and Calvin Robinson is not one of them. I have known murders who have served less of a sentence than Calvin has for operating a tugboat and smuggling. I understand what the sentencing guidelines were at that time and we had to abide by them. But, Your Honor, this man has paid his debt to society, and then some.

If I thought for one moment, Calvin was a danger to others or he would try to continue his criminal past, I would never write this letter in his support. I have not spoken to Calvin in person yet, but we have communicated with emails and I can tell you that he is remorseful and repentant. He holds no ill will towards me, and speaks of religion and God that he has come to know since being incarcerated. I know a con job when one is presented to me and I believe Calvin is sincere in what he says and believes. I can also say that I have communicated with members of his family and friends, and they continue to provide support and stand by his side.

In closing Your Honor, I sincerely hope that this letter has given you information to where you can find this 77-year-old nonviolent man, who is terminally ill and who has paid his debt to society, can be free to spend his last few months with his family and loved ones. I sincerely feel, granting a few months to a man who has paid

31 years for this crime is appropriate and right. I will make myself available during the August 16th hearing for a phone conversation with you, if desired.

Sincerely and with respect,
Dr. Norman Wood
Physician Director
WV Division of Corrections and Rehabilitation

After receiving the letter from Dr. Wood, Judge Breyer canceled Calvin Robinson's hearing scheduled for August 16. The judge signed the Compassionate Release, and Calvin Robinson was freed from federal prison. Calvin is now living with his family in northern California.

Special Agent Ray Tipton USCG and Special Agent Norman Wood USCS, US Coast Guard Headquarters, Yerba Buena Island, San Francisco, California. Bags of hashish and boxes of marijuana in background. May 24, 1988.

Forty-three tons of hashish in bags and thirteen tons of marijuana in boxes taken from the barge pulled by the tugboat Intrepid Venture, *Coast Guard dock, Yerba Buena Island, San Francisco, May 24, 1988.*

Intrepid Venture *and barge leaving San Francisco, May 6, 1988. Picture taken by Special Agent Dennis Robinson USCG from the Richmond–San Rafael Bridge.*

Coast Guard personnel cutting hole in deck of barge to remove hashish. May 24, 1988.

Coast Guard personnel removing bolts from wall hatch in barge.

Forty-three tons of hashish inside barge. Fuel tank on left. May 24, 1988.

ASAC Pat Sheridan USCS and SA Harry Washiewicz USCS after the drugs were found.

SA Norman Wood

Photo taken by SA Ray Tipton USCG while SA Norman Wood USCS flew the plane. Intrepid Venture *(*Valiant Venture*) in upper left of photo with* Ruby R *(*California Rose*) tied to barge on Sevenmile Slough. May 4, 1988.*

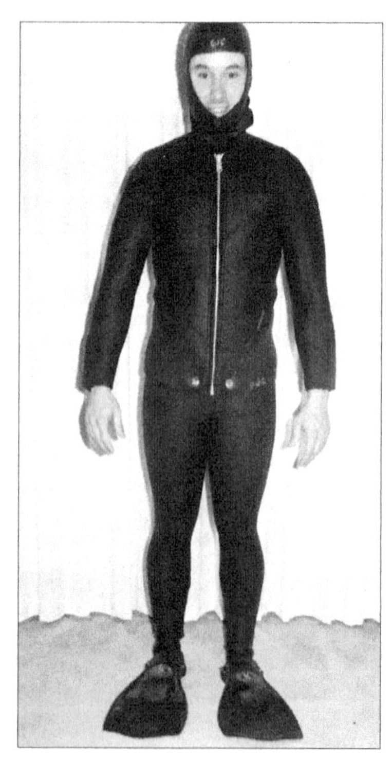

SA Norman Wood

SA Norman Wood and Mustang.

DRIVER LICENSE

NUMBER	DATE OF BIRTH	CLASS
4172363	11-05-54	4

EXPIRES	CODES	ORIGINAL DATE
11-05-92		05-18-89

ISSUE DATE	HEIGHT	WEIGHT	SEX
05-18-89	5 11	185	M

DAVIS, TONY LEE
1313 N BAYSHORE DR
COOS BAY OR 97420
OREGON

Special Agent Norman Wood, USCS

Trooper Norman Wood West Virginia State Police 1978

ABOUT THE AUTHOR

NORMAN WOOD, DO, is a native West Virginian. He is the physician director of the West Virginia Division of Corrections and Rehabilitations. He is a former West Virginia State Trooper and Special Agent for the US Customs Service. As undercover Special Agent Tony Davis, he is credited with making the largest drug seizure in US history while assigned to the Organized Crime Drug Enforcement Task Force San Francisco in 1988. The following link is a video of Special Agent Wood being interviewed by reporter George Warren: www.youtube.com/watch?v=viOlYqGgAGo&t=59s.

Dr. Wood is now an inventor with four awarded US patents for safety harness designs. His company is Elevated Safety Systems, at Elevatedsafetysystems.com.

Wood lives in a log home in Marshal County, West Virginia. He enjoys his morning runs, horseback riding, fishing, and his new passion, writing.

Norm and Calvin Robinson still talk.

Made in the USA
Middletown, DE
10 August 2023

NOON

1324 LEXINGTON AVENUE
PMB 298
NEW YORK, NEW YORK 10128

GENIEVE FIGGIS, GENTLEMAN WITH A HAT (DETAIL), 2015

NOON

NAME ______________________________

ADDRESS ______________________________

CITY ____________________ STATE ____ ZIP ________

___2017 ___2016 ___2015 ___2014 ______OTHER

TO SEND A GIFT

NAME ______________________________

ADDRESS ______________________________

CITY ____________________ STATE ____ ZIP ________

___2017 ___2016 ___2015 ___2014 ______OTHER

PLEASE INDICATE QUANTITIES AND INCLUDE PAYMENT — $12.00 AND $17.00 FOREIGN.